Children of Sinai

By

Clarke Nixon

Paperback Edition August 2021
First Edition April 2019
ISBN: 979-8-4574731-7-1
Copyright © Clarke Nixon 2019

Authors' Note

This story is entirely a work of fiction based on Biblical events, theories, historical finds, and Clarke's imagination. It is an interpretation only, and not intended to cause any offence. Great care has been taken with the research, and much has been learned, especially regarding the Israeli/ Palestinian people. Should there be any inaccuracies we can only apologise; history is very complicated. We wish peace for the people living there, as we do for all people suffering conflict.

If you would like to read more about Children of Sinai please visit www.childrenofsinai.com

This book is dedicated to my late mum, Jeanne.
She was a beautiful lady,
and my first and longest best friend.

Shelley Clarke

Contents

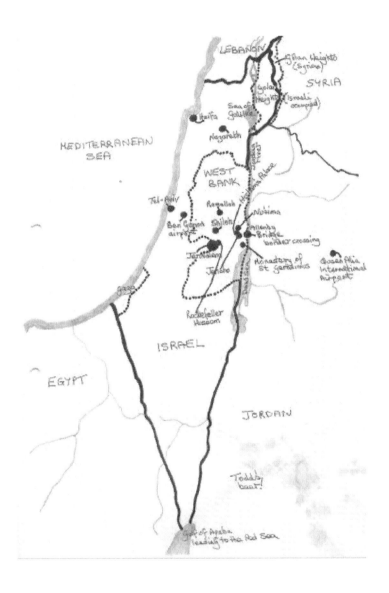

Children of Sinai

By

Clarke Nixon

Part One
Haverhill, Suffolk 2002

'I, Amnon, son of Nahum and Shoshannah, born in the Land of Goschen, descendant of Abraham, Isaac, Jacob and Joseph, was born into the Levi tribe. Before me, my mother's older sister, Jochebed and her husband Amram had four children, Aaron, Miriam, and twin boys. Amram denounced Jochebed as he did not believe the twins were his. After seeking council he took back this accusation. The twins were believed to have been conceived and born in a holy manner, as Jacob before them. There was hope of a prophecy being fulfilled.

The Pharaoh heard of the prophecy and feared that he would lose his slaves and power, so ordered the slaughter of any twin boys up to the age of three. There was much anguish and outrage. Jochebed wrapped her babes, placed them each in their own basket and tasked her younger sister Miriam to hide them in the reeds of the river.

The baskets floated away. One boy was found by Princess Beketaten, who raised him as her son, and named the Prince Munius. The other boy, feared drowned, was found by a Nubian trader, who raised him as his son and named him Nour.'

Excerpt from the writings of Amnon
2nd millennium BC

'And the spirit shall come unto the tribe of Levi in the Land of Goschen. Twins shall be born to the sons of God, under the ring of light. Drawn from the water their paths shall diverge. They shall meet as strangers to free their people and lead them home.'

Prophecy 2nd millennium BC

Chapter One
The Dream

John blinked awake sometime in the early hours of Friday morning. He lay for a moment, letting his heartbeat settle, aware of a light sweat coating his skin. The same dream, haunting him on and off for weeks now, was starting to affect more than his sleep; his waking hours were suffering too, from the worry about what it meant for his mind. And he'd disturbed Jen more than once, which wasn't fair either.

He eased carefully out of bed, and padded softly downstairs; a cup of warm Horlicks and a comfortable sofa might settle him back to sleep. But the dream played endlessly in his mind, like a video on a loop. So much detail could be lost in that place between sleep and wakefulness, and the frantic scribbling in the notebook he'd kept beside the bed hadn't lasted long. Apart from the illegible handwriting he'd tried to decipher the next day, it had been one of the things that had woken Jen last time.

If the sleeping mind was supposed to create dreams to sort out information that hadn't been resolved, or organised, during waking hours, why was he dreaming of climbing? And not just any mountain, but that *same one*? The same details, same strange words echoing in his head? Neither mountain nor words meant anything at all.

John turned blearily to look at the clock: 3am. *Christ!* Instead of heading to the sofa, he grabbed his drink, went into the study and switched on his PC. A Google image search for mountains provided page after distracting page of towering, majestic beauty, but no help. The one in his dream was quite distinctly shaped, wide and sprawling but with a smaller one on top. After an hour, with his eyes burning and his frustration mounting, he called it a night and curled up on the sofa. It seemed barely a minute later when he felt a hand on his shoulder, and the glare of the morning sunlight through his closed eyelids.

'You okay?' Jen's voice was quiet, but it broke through the fuzz in his mind and he forced his eyes open, to see her standing above him, already dressed.

He licked his lips and tried on a smile. 'Yeah.'

'That dream again?' The hand on his shoulder was less urgent now, and more sympathetic.

He nodded, and yawned. 'It's driving me crazy.'

'I know.' She pushed his legs aside and sat down. 'Look, I know you're tired, but it's eight o'clock. You'll be late if you don't start getting ready now.'

'Happy anniversary to you, too.'

She smiled. 'I hadn't forgotten. I just didn't want to throw it at you before you've even opened your eyes. Happy anniversary.' She smoothed his hair back and kissed his forehead. 'Still taking me to dinner tonight?'

'You betcha.'

Both of them jumped as Holly and Hannah exploded into the lounge, dressed for school. The exuberant twins were almost eight years old now, yet they still couldn't resist such an opportunity, and immediately clambered onto the sofa, where John made them shriek by tickling them while Jen went into the kitchen to finish packing lunch boxes. After a moment she called them through for breakfast, and soon John could hear them, still giggling, as they tried to out-do each other with the popping of their Rice Krispies in open mouths. He smiled at the sound. They were bundles of fizzing energy that often left him bemused and exhausted, but they were good kids for all that.

Jen came in with coffee. 'We'll talk this evening over dinner,' she promised, already hunting around for her flip flops. She slipped her feet into them, picked up her bag and car keys and called for the girls.

At last John reluctantly got up to get ready for work. Passing through the kitchen, coffee in hand, he dropped a kiss on each of his daughters' heads.

'Behave at school,' he told them. 'And if you're very good I'll let Auntie May babysit you tonight.' They exchanged looks of delight, and made solemn promises that made him smile as he went upstairs, wondering how he'd managed to get so lucky.

In the shower, coffee still gently steaming on the side of the bath, he pursued that vaguely grateful thought and felt it solidify. He really *was* lucky. Always interested in linguistics, he'd found himself at Cambridge, doing his MPhil at the same time as Jen, who'd been chasing a career as a speech therapist. She had been genuinely fascinated in the direction in which his own ambition lay; developing speech recognition and translation software, and, as their relationship had deepened they'd found their studies actually complimented one another's.

Moving in together had only helped; they'd pushed each other on, and eventually both been accepted onto the PhD programme... and then Jen had fallen pregnant. It wasn't as if they hadn't taken precautions, and Jen's initial dismay had been tempered by philosophical acceptance; her career would still be there later, but she was clearly destined to become a mum first.

That acceptance had evolved naturally into genuine happiness, and the twins were born in the May of 1994, while Blur were singing about Parklife, and PJ and Duncan were getting Ready to Rhumble; when the Rolling Stones had set off on tour, and the last British troops left Hong Kong.

As the hot water splashed over John's face now, he shook his head in quiet awe at the way Jen had moved so smoothly and naturally into her new role, and taken everything in her stride. It couldn't have been easy. Nor could it have been easy to watch him complete the studies she herself had worked so hard towards, but she'd swallowed any resentment she might have felt. Even when he'd secured his place as a Research Fellow she had never displayed the slightest hint of regret, or of bitterness. Yeah, he was lucky. He just hoped Jen still felt the same.

At the end of a day that had seemed to go on forever, John drove the half hour from Cambridge to their home in Haverhill. A lot of his thinking happened either in the car or in the shower, and it strayed once again to the twins; in particular how Jen had noticed the odd little language that had developed as the girls had begun to talk, and how their vocabulary had grown over the years.

Neither she nor John had been able to understand it, but it had sparked Jen's latent interest in speech and she'd begun carrying out her own investigations into what she called *Hally*.

Holly and Hannah were already in their pyjamas after their bath, and settled on the sofa in front of Blue's Clues. He waved at them, called out a 'Hi' to Jen wherever she was, and headed upstairs to get ready for their evening out. The bedroom smelled of perfume, and the clothes piled high on the chair, were evidence she had been undecided on what to wear. Not that it mattered to him; she looked beautiful in anything. Although there were some outfits that definitely had an effect on him, they were not for public... He shook off the distracting thought, and concentrated on making himself presentable.

'Wow,' was all he could think of saying as he entered the study twenty minutes later. Jen was at the desk, classically gorgeous in a simple black shift dress, her long streaky blonde hair was clipped high on her head with little wispy bits at the side – he'd always found that both cute and alluring; part elegant, part reckless. Like her. He gave a low whistle, and Jen smiled.

'You don't look so shabby yourself.'

'Nice of you to say, but next to you I feel like that bloke in Die Hard.'

'Before or after the ventilation system?'

'Put it this way, the Nakatomi Plaza is burning.'

She smiled slowly, letting her eyes rove over him. 'You know, Willis looked pretty good then, too. You'll do.'

He grinned back. 'If it wasn't for that knockout little black number you're wearing, I'd swear you were the teacher, not me.'

'It's the glasses,' she said wryly, drawing them back down from where they had sat on her forehead. 'Make anyone look clever.'

He could sense any response along the lines of *you are clever*, would come across as patronising, so instead he asked, 'And how are the studies going today?'

There was a cautious excitement in her eyes as she stood up. 'I've been thinking about you and the twins all day.'

'I like the sound of that.' He moved closer and drew her to him, feeling her hands stealing around to the small of his back. 'Go on?'

'I was wondering... I thought maybe that's what you're hearing, in your dreams. Hally.'

'What, you think I understand it better when I'm asleep?'

'It might be your brain *trying* to understand it,' she persisted. 'It's something in your subconscious, and your brain wants you to rest as much as you do, so perhaps it's trying to help you understand, so you can sleep.'

'And the mountain would symbolise what?'

'The struggle. Something you're trying to overcome.'

'You might be right,' he mused. 'Taxi'll be here in about quarter of an hour, but show me—'

'Mummy! Daddy! Auntie May is here!'

'Later,' she promised him. Then she gave him a sly look, and to his amusement he felt her squeeze his behind.

'And since it's our anniversary, I might even show you a lot more than that.'

Downstairs in the hall, all was happy greeting and chatter. The twins adored their great-aunt, and she them, and there already seemed to be high competition for her attention, even as she took off her coat and tried to hang it up.

'Alright, alright, let the dog see the rabbit,' she huffed, and took advantage of their temporary confused looks by darting away from them, and throwing her coat in the general direction of the newel post. 'Now, I forget: which one of you's best at everything in the whole world, ever?'

'Me!' The girls yelled in unison.

'Good. Then you'll be best in the world at clearing my favourite spot on the sofa, and finding me the fluffiest cushion. Go!'

They scampered off, as John reached the hall and picked up her coat from the floor. Hanging it more carefully, he smiled at his aunt. 'You've got them well trained.'

'Worked well enough with you,' she observed, and smiled. 'My, don't you scrub up well!'

'It's a special night.'

'Indeed, and where is your lovely wife?'

'Just finishing up, she'll be here in a sec.'

Holly returned, having beaten Hannah to the door and pushed her out of the way. 'Ready, Auntie May.'

'Then lead on, what are you waiting for?' She winked at John, and allowed herself to be escorted into the front room. John followed, ruffling the thwarted Hannah's hair as he went.

In her mid-sixties, May Taylor was a handsome woman and had attracted more than her share of hopeful suitors, but she had never married; following the death of her sister, the raising of her now-orphaned, two-year-old nephew had become her sole focus, and she had given herself over to it gladly. The reward for both of them was a relationship as close as any mother and son, and the girls looked on their great aunt as a kind of grandmother.

They were seating themselves either side of her as Jen made her entrance, and John smiled to see the flush of pleasure on his wife's cheeks as she accepted her due compliments; she didn't often have chance to get dressed up, and to see her now, looking more like the girl he had first met at university, gave him a little pang of guilt; he should take her out more. It was no more than she deserved, and they didn't spend enough time just talking. Conversation always dissolved into a discussion about school, or shopping lists, or gas bills, or any of the hundreds of things that swallow up a family. Yes, school and bills mattered, but so did the exchange of ideas, news, thoughts... even the arguments that went with them were important—

'Where are you eating tonight?' Aunt May was asking.

'The Midsummer House,' Jen said. 'I'll leave the brochure by the phone, it's got the number on it.'

'You want to get yourself a mobile telephone,' May said. 'For emergencies.'

'We've talked about it,' John said, putting a plate of Jaffa Cakes on the coffee table. 'One each,' he cautioned the girls.

'Well, two for me, of course,' May said.

'Of course.'

'Midsummer,' May mused. 'Oh dear, isn't that the place that kept flooding last year, when the Cam burst its banks?'

'Only twice,' Jen said. She was fiddling with the new earrings John had given her. 'The water got into the wine cellar one time, I think. Still,' she smiled fondly at John, 'It has great memories for us, doesn't it? We had our first dinner date there,' she added to May.

'It's got a Michelin star now too,' John pointed out, 'so things can't have been too bad that evening.'

'Oh thanks!' Jen said. 'I won't take that personally.'

May shook her head at John, who wondered what was wrong, until he replayed the sentence in his head and realised how it had sounded. He coloured, but before he could apologise Jen and May started laughing, and of course the girls joined in although they probably didn't know why. A horn pipped lightly outside.

'Saved by the cab,' John muttered, and Jen laughed harder as she tugged him towards the door.

'Have a wonderful time,' May said over her shoulder. 'Don't hurry back, I need time to steal all your biscuits.'

'Watch her,' John said to the twins. 'If there are no biscuits left when we come home I'm holding you responsible.'

To a chorus of protest, he grabbed Jen's hand and they made their escape.

Midsummer House sat on the banks of the River Cam, a modestly sized but beautifully-kept building, so obviously a normal residence that, the first time they had come, they had been sure they were in the wrong place; only the number of cars parked nearby had convinced them otherwise.

Tonight, boasting its newly-gained Michelin star, the restaurant was busier than ever. John and Jen were shown to their table and chose their wine, and as John handed the wine list back to the waiter he wondered how long to leave it before he brought up Jen's findings regarding Hally again. This was supposed to be a romantic anniversary dinner, after all, and for a good five minutes he carefully stepped around the subject, gradually becoming aware of a widening smile on Jen's face.

'I know what you really want to talk about,' she said at length, when his bland comments about the décor in the restaurant had run down. 'So, pin back your ears and stop waffling.'

'Fire away,' he grinned. Anything that might give his brain a good night's rest was just fine with him, romantic or otherwise.

'Okay. With cryptophasia, what I've found out, is that – as far as I can tell – no two sets of twins have the same "language." Every set seems to be unique. It develops at the same rate in both, and I assume the same goes for triplets.'

'Cryptophasia.' He tried it out. 'I like your word better.'

'Because it doesn't sound so much like a disorder?' She nodded. 'Same here. Anyway, I've been recording the girls, and then playing it back to them. They've been able to tell me enough, to translate enough, so that I've started to build a dictionary.'

'Wow!'

She stopped talking as the waiter served their wine, then took a deep drink and sighed. 'That's hit the spot.'

'A dictionary,' he prompted, forgetting his resolution not to press. 'How many words does it have?'

'Not loads, but they seem to be enjoying my puzzlement as much as I'm enjoying learning their language.'

'Must make them feel pretty good, to fox a parent! Why don't I take what you have, and enter it into my translation software? Imagine the looks on their faces!'

'That'd be too funny for words!' Jen took another drink. 'This started out as something to help you, but to be truthful I think it might make a really interesting study…'

She fell silent, and John looked at her shrewdly. Now it was her turn to stare around the restaurant, looking for something to comment on. He let her, for a few minutes, and then reached across the table and took her hand.

'Are you thinking about your doctorate?' She held his eyes with hers, and he saw a glisten of tears there that alarmed him. 'Jen, I didn't mean to—'

'No, it's alright. I'm happy. This…' she waved her fingers at her brimming eyes, 'is happy stuff.' She sighed. 'You can read me like the girls can read each other. That's pretty special, you know that?' She wiped at her smudged mascara. 'Now, have you chosen what you want? They'll be over to take our order in about ten seconds flat.'

'So you are thinking about it?' he persisted. 'And you're changing it to this cryptophasia thing?'

'Thinking of pitching it at least. It'll take a hell of a lot of time to work it up, but,' she shrugged, 'the girls are that bit older now. When better?'

'Good.' He squeezed her fingers, then let go and picked up his menu, adopting an impatient tone. 'Now for crying out loud, haven't you decided yet? They'll be over any minute now.'

Jen blew a genteel raspberry, but her smile stayed in place as she turned her attention to the menu.

Over dinner, talk moved more naturally, from Jen's change of direction to their university days, friends they had made and lost touch with, and those they had kept. They toasted their years together, on the champagne John had pre-ordered, and Jen was just starting to get giggly when the waiter approached their table again.

'Mr and Mrs Milburn? There's a telephone call for you.'

John rose. 'I'll take it. It'll be nothing,' he assured a worried-looking Jen. 'She's probably just asking where we keep the emergency custard creams.'

Jen didn't look soothed, and as he followed the waiter out to reception John felt his own apprehension creeping through him; Aunt May wouldn't have disturbed them unless it was important.

But it wasn't Aunt May on the other end. It was Hannah, sobbing so hard he could barely hear her. Holly yelling in the background wasn't making it any easier, and his panic only increased.

'Stop, sweetheart! Take a deep breath. Tell me again.'

'It's Auntie May,' she hiccupped. 'She's fainted and I can't wake her up!'

His blood froze. 'Fainted? Are you sure?'

'I don't know!' She started to cry again. 'We did what you said, and called for an ambulance. It's coming. They wanted me to stay on the phone with them but I told them I had to call you and Mummy.'

'You did exactly right,' John said, hearing his own words sounding thankfully calm through the rushing in his ears. He felt distant and helpless. 'We're on our way home right now. Go back to Auntie May and sit by her. Call the ambulance people again if you have to, they'll talk to you.' He replaced the phone, and turned to see the concierge nodding, and already dialling for a taxi on the other line.

'We have a contract,' the concierge said, covering the mouthpiece, 'they'll be here in five minutes.'

As the cab drew up outside the house the paramedic was already closing the back doors of the ambulance. John drew Jen into a quick, trembling embrace. 'I'll go with them to the hospital.'

She nodded, her tear-streaked face white in the reflection of the street lights, and brushed across with eerie blue streaks from the flashing ambulance light. 'I hope... I hope she's—'

'I know,' he said, and kissed her quickly. 'Go on in, the girls will be terrified.'

He identified himself to the paramedics, and they opened the ambulance again so he could climb inside with Aunt May. With an oxygen mask taped to her face, she looked tiny, and somehow insignificant on the stretcher … Just a nobody.

Except she wasn't.

The hours crawled by. The hospital was predictably busy at this hour on a Friday night; mostly drunks, but not exclusively. Aunt May was admitted to A&E, but soon transferred, leaving John wandering the corridors, increasingly frustrated and frightened, looking for the various X-ray areas and MRI scanners. Eventually he found her room, and sat in the crowded corridor staring at the door behind which his family's future was being decided.

When the consultant emerged he stood looking around until he caught John's eye. He looked tired, as all doctors seemed to these days, but when he saw John he didn't flinch, or look as if he wished he were elsewhere. John took that as a good sign.

'What happened? Was it a heart attack?'

'It was a brain haemorrhage, Mr Taylor—'

'Milburn,' he corrected automatically, his mind turning over as he tried to take in what the consultant had said. 'Sorry, it doesn't matter. Haemorrhage?'

'The result of a ruptured aneurysm. Were you aware she'd been diagnosed?'

'No.' John's voice was hoarse. 'She never said.' *Typical of Aunt May.* 'Is she… will she be alright?'

'There's no way of telling at the moment, I'm sorry. She's being monitored now. She's stable, and sleeping, so there's really nothing you can do here.'

'Can I see her?'

'Just for a minute or two. Then I suggest you go home and get some rest, and tomorrow we might have a better idea of how the land lies.'

John nodded, still trying to straighten his thoughts. Just a short time ago he had been under tastefully-lowered lighting, drinking champagne, toasting his happy life… and now here he was, in a corridor so brightly-lit it hurt his eyes, the smells and noise of sickness and sadness all around, and larger-than-life Aunt May lying silent and helpless a few feet away.

He pushed open the door and took a deep breath, then crossed to the bed and sat down. Her hand was fitted with a cannula, and lay limp on the cover, but he took it and held it gently, searching for something to say and finding nothing. Something was stopping him, an odd superstition, as if to speak of anything profound now would simply close the door on her life, and give her permission to go. To leave them.

Finally he just whispered, 'See you tomorrow. I love you,' and left. He walked on weary feet to the taxi rank by the hospital entrance, and all the way home he tried to think of a way to explain to the girls what an aneurysm was, without frightening them to death.

'Holly says they'd been playing a game when it happened,' Jen said, when he'd taken off his coat and told her what the doctor had said. She'd changed into nightclothes, and sat with her feet tucked under her on the sofa, and her eyes, when she looked up at John, were still red-rimmed and a little swollen.

16

'What sort of game? Not Twister, I hope, I've told them—'

'Nothing physical,' Jen said. 'Some gambling thing, just with sweets, though. It sounds as if she had some kind of seizure, from what they said.'

'Poor kids. I'll go up and see them if they're still awake.'

'They will be. They've been waiting for you, but I told them not to come down when they heard you come in.' She looked away. 'I didn't know if… you know.'

'I know.' He stooped to kiss her on his way to the door. 'Pour me a drink?'

He knocked gently at the girls' bedroom door, and immediately the low murmuring on the other side of it stopped.

'Daddy?'

He went in, and they both sat up in their beds and stared at him, with identical expressions of hope and fear. 'She's asleep, and they're taking good care of her,' he said quietly. He moved into the gap between their beds and took one hand each. 'Mummy and I are so proud of you both, for doing what you did.'

'I was too scared to speak properly,' Hannah reminded him, but he smiled and lifted her hand to his lips.

'Of course you were scared, anyone would be. But between you,' he looked at them both in turn, then kissed Holly's hand too, 'You probably saved Auntie May's life. Remember that, next time you're scared.' The girls looked at one another with awe.

'Can we visit her?' Holly wanted to know.

'As soon as the doctor says it's okay.' John climbed stiffly to his feet. 'Now snuggle down, it's late.'

'It's Saturday tomorrow,' Holly protested, but half-heartedly.

'Today,' John pointed out. 'And Auntie May won't want the two of you falling asleep on her bed tomorrow, will she?'

He kissed them goodnight and pulled their duvets up around their ears, pretending not to notice he was covering their heads. 'Now get some beauty sleep, you both need it.'

'Daddy! That's mean!' The chorus followed him out onto the landing, and, with a smile, he reached back in and snapped the bedroom light off.

Downstairs he took the glass of wine Jen had poured him, and they sat talking quietly of Aunt May, of the girls, and finally of Jen's decision to re-apply for her PhD. Eventually, as the clock's hands reached two o'clock, the talk slowed and they rose from the sofa and put out the lights. John's eyes were grainy and hot as he trailed after Jen up the stairs; surely after a night like this, even with the worry for Aunt May keeping his mind active, he would finally get a dreamless night's sleep.

Jen watched her exhausted husband slide into bed and close his eyes, but she herself was too wide awake to ready herself for sleep just yet. She angled the bedside light off him and onto her book, and after only a couple of paragraphs she heard a gentle snoring coming from his side of the bed. She watched him for a moment, seeing the lines of tension smooth out, leaving his brow clear

18

once more, and she resisted the urge to lean over and kiss him there; if he woke now he might never get back to sleep.

Her own worry for Aunt May prevented her from concentrating on her book, and the thought of two highly-strung, over-tired girls to contend with tomorrow persuaded her to replace her bookmark and turn out the light. She had drifted into a light doze when John's voice jerked her awake again.

She turned onto her side. 'What did you say?'

But he slept on. She lay still, struggling to understand his mumbling, but none of it made any sense, and after a minute she climbed out of bed and groped for the dressing gown on the back of the door. In the pocket was the small dictaphone she'd been using to capture Holly and Hannah's language, and she held it close to John's head and pressed the record button.

The dreams had not stopped after all.

Chapter Two
Karen's Legacy

May was in a room of eight beds but at least hers was by the window, which was struggling to let in some of the mid-afternoon daylight. Jen tried not to grimace at the clinical smells and noises, and instead thanked goodness her girls had had the good sense to dial for an ambulance at all. She put a bright smile on her face as they crossed the room, never sure whether to acknowledge the other patients or not, and settling for a little nod whenever she caught an eye.

'She looks different in hospital,' Holly confided to Hannah in a loud whisper. 'She looks smaller.'

'That's because her nightie's too big for her,' Hannah whispered back, and that made Jen's smile feel more genuine, and glad they'd brought some of May's things; at least she'd be able to get out of that awful square hospital gown.

John leaned over and kissed his aunt, and Jen did the same, and the two of them settled into seats on the window side of the bed. May, sitting up against her pillows, gave a furtive look around the room, then gestured to the girls to climb onto the bed.

John frowned. 'I don't think—'

'Hush,' May said. 'These two saved my life, I think we all deserve a little hug, don't you?'

John and Jen exchanged glances and Jen shrugged. John subsided, and the girls lay happily in the crook of each of May's elbows, while Jen kept an eye out for returning medical staff, and May gave them a brief update on her morning.

'Anyway,' she finished, after skimming across the surface of what must have been a much deeper subject than it seemed, 'what about you two monsters, eh? You'd started to tell me about some museum trip last night, before things got sticky.'

'It's the Museum of London,' Holly said importantly. 'Somewhere you can go to find out about the old days.'

'And ark... arkilogists,' Hannah put in, not to be out-done. 'They're the ones who find out stuff about *people* of the old days.'

May smiled and kissed each earnestly-furrowed forehead in turn. 'Your grandparents were archaeologists,' she said, pronouncing the word carefully. 'They travelled the world finding amazing and beautiful things, just so people like you could learn about things like that. Lots of people were very interested in what they found.'

Hannah nodded. 'Daddy told us.' She sobered. 'It's so sad they both died.'

'But at least that meant you could be Daddy's mummy,' Holly added. Jen couldn't look at John for fear her smile would be returned, and that it would hurt the girls' feelings; how easy it was to find a silver lining, when you were a child. Long may it continue.

'Was Grandma Karen very pretty?' Holly wanted to know.

'She was. She had the biggest blue eyes, and lots of blonde hair, in waves all down her back.' She winked. 'She was just as beautiful as me, in fact.'

The girls giggled. 'What about Granddad George?' Holly asked.

'Granddad George was very handsome, too. He had darker hair, and brown eyes. He and Grandma Karen loved each other very much, just like your own mummy and daddy.'

Holly pulled a face at Hannah: *ick, mushy grown-up stuff!* This time Jen did look at John, who was biting his lip to keep from laughing. There was relief in there, too; May was so much brighter than they'd feared.

'We're going to be arky-wotsits when we grow up,' Hannah said with conviction.

'You'll have to work hard then,' Jen said. 'Right, that's enough twaddle to be going on with. Go and get yourselves something from the snack machine down the hall.' She handed them a pound coin each. 'Daddy and I want a little chat with Auntie May.'

The door swung shut behind the girls, and Jen turned back ready to speak, but stopped as she noticed a marked change in May. The older woman had sagged against her pillows, and her face lost its impish sparkle; she had clearly been putting on a stellar show for the girls, and Jen's heart sank.

John had noticed it to, and moved closer to his aunt. 'How are you really feeling?'

'Oh, not too bad, poppet,' May said. 'I'm just tired, and I have a doozy of a headache.' She gave them a faint smile. 'Like a hangover, but without the fun.'

'What did the doctor say?'

'They're going to put in a stent to seal the leaking artery.'

'Then what?'

'Then I'll be my daft old self again.' May took each of their hands. 'Look, I'm lucky I got here when I did, you make sure those girls know that. At my age, any longer and I'd have been a goner.'

'Don't,' John said, and Jen rubbed his arm.

'It has to be said,' May insisted. She cleared her throat. 'And on that note, should anything go wrong – it won't,' she added quickly, 'but just in case, there are some things I want you to know.'

'What things?'

'You already know your parent's home in Godalming came to me through your mother's bequest.'

'The one you sold.'

'It wasn't an easy decision. I didn't want the circumstances surrounding your mother's death to overshadow you as you were growing up; you know how people talk. A fresh start seemed the best way. There's plenty of money left over, even after paying your university fees.'

'And the fact that you gave us the deposit on our own house,' Jen said. 'We could never have got a foot on the ladder without your help.'

May patted her hand. 'Now then. My will, and some of my more personal effects, are in a biscuit tin, in the locked drawer of my bureau.'

John flinched. 'Aunt May, why are you telling us—'

'You'll be financially secure.'

Jen forced a firm tone into her voice. 'Look, I won't hear any more of this talk. The doctors say you're going to be alright.'

'You've got years of mad behaviour in you,' John added. 'Besides, you haven't taught the girls all they need to know about gambling yet.'

May laughed. 'Well alright, maybe I'll stay around until they've graduated from sweets to pennies.' She fixed John with a look. 'There's something else. In the attic of my house there's a little hole in the wall. If you look there you'll find another box, and another biscuit tin.'

'What's in that one?'

'I don't know, it's your mother's private stuff. Very precious, I understand, but she asked me not to look. Just to store it safely. This is very important...' May boosted herself upright, with a huge effort, and her eyes seemed to burn across the space between them as she looked first at John, then at Jen. 'If I do die without going home... and I have to be realistic; there's a very good chance I might, you *must* take that box away before the house is sold on. Don't forget it, whatever you do.'

'We won't.' John looked troubled. 'I promise. But what is it with all these biscuit tins?'

May gave him a ghost of her old grin. 'Well since you're so snippy about me stealing your biscuits, I have to buy my own.' Her voice took on a faintly nostalgic note. 'The tins're too pretty to throw away. Remind me of my childhood.'

The sombre silence was broken by the welcome return of Holly and Hannah, who offered their crisps around before settling into the seats beside May's bed. Neither seemed to notice anything amiss among the adults, and May once more made a sterling effort to appear her usual brisk self, until she grew too tired.

'Right, let's leave Auntie May to rest for a while,' Jen said, surreptitiously brushing crisp crumbs off the bed onto the floor. 'We'll come back tomorrow.'

'Bring me biscuits next time,' Aunt May said, and her smile followed the young family down the corridor as they returned to their own lives.

It was the last time any of them ever saw it.

May's house had sold quickly. John signed the papers with a heavy hand, and a heavier heart, and another piece of his childhood slipped away into memory. It had taken several weeks to first gather the strength, and then to actually pack up May's things; her personal belongings were taken to John and Jen's home, to be sorted later. The bureau would have pride of place in their study, alongside their own modern desk, and all else would be donated to the various charities May had favoured.

Closing the hatchback on the last few bits and pieces, John stood staring awhile at the home where he'd grown up. No longer anything to do with him; he had no right to sit on the back patio now, drinking Aunt May's tea; no need to wander through the rooms and think about painting the walls; no reason to climb the ladder to the attic and sit in the dusty silence, just enjoying the light slanting through the tiny window onto the knotted wooden floor. His world had shrunk a little more. May and Karen had had no other relatives, and now they were both gone he was the only one left related to her by blood. Would he be able to do her life justice?

He felt Jen's arm slide around his waist, and he drew her closer and kissed her, and they stood a while, wordless. After a moment they released one another by unspoken agreement, and drove home. They talked, tentatively, at first, of the funeral; it had felt too raw before. Now they brought out the memories and smiled over them, marvelling over how many people had turned out to pay their respects, and how many of them had outrageous stories to tell. The things May had said, both out of turn and strikingly apt, though not always the most tactful, were a recurring theme among the mourners, and there had been much laughter in May's sitting room during her wake. She had been a singular woman, and John was going to miss her, they all would. But she had given them that gift of laughter, and that was something to treasure, not throw away in a wash of regret and tears.

Later, when the girls were in bed, and Jen was working in the study, John realised he'd been putting something off. Filing Aunt May's death certificate had seemed the final door, closing on a life that had been the driving force behind his own. But it was time. And while he was at it he could find homes for the ring binders filled with his old school reports, inoculation records and the mountain of Aunt May's correspondence that had remained unsorted since her death.

He sat on the floor in the sitting room surrounded by it all, and opened his mother's death certificate. *Death by drowning and acute overdose of paracetamol and dextropropoxyphene.* He sighed, as Jen's arms came around his neck from behind and she read it aloud over his shoulder. He hadn't even heard her come in.

'Aunt May told me about this,' he said. 'But not until I was in my early twenties.'

'Overdose? You mean she took her own life? I thought it was an accident.'

'It could have been. No way of knowing, but like Aunt May said, people talk.'

'And that's why she sold up.'

He nodded. 'I was only two when it happened. Mum used to get bad headaches, so she took a lot of medication, that wasn't unusual. One day she left me with Aunt May and went for a picnic in Phillips Memorial Park. They found her blanket and stuff on the grass, and her body on the riverbank.'

'God, the poor woman,' Jen said quietly. 'To have gone through all that, and losing her husband. It can't have been easy for her.' She hugged him from behind. 'It was probably the dextroproxyphene. They stopped prescribing it because of the effect it was having on some patients.'

'Effect?' He half-twisted to look at her.

'Weird side-effects. Like hallucinations, confusion. The drug contained an opioid, and became addictive, apparently. If your mother grew confused, forgot she'd taken her medication, and accidentally mis-dosed, then compounded it by taking more…'

John spoke slowly. 'It could explain the accident.'

'That's what I was thinking, yes.'

27

'That does make sense.' He lifted the hand that lay on his shoulder, and kissed it. 'Thank you, that helps. It really does.'

'Will you be okay going through the rest of that stuff?' She nodded at the pile on the floor.

'Yeah. Thanks.' He smiled around at her, and she dropped a kiss on his forehead.

'Shout if you need help. Or just someone to talk to.'

'I will.' He watched her go back into the study, then picked up a bundle of letters, secured with the pink ribbon that usually came tied around title deeds. They were all addressed to the old house at Godalming, and the post marks ranged from 1965 to 1966; the stamps depicting butterflies and town emblems. Israeli stamps. Seeing his mother's handwriting on the envelopes awoke a hunger in John that he hadn't even realised had been there until now. A hunger to learn more about her. It was probably a direct result of losing the woman who had replaced her in his life with such love, but whatever the reason, here was his chance.

The letters seemed largely concerned with the dig in Jericho, where she and his father had worked alongside old friends Mark and Denise Elliott, along with an Israeli couple they'd befriended, Uri and Maya Malik. There was much affection there, it seemed, and they were a close group.

Here, in Karen's own words, was the joy she'd found in the surprise pregnancy that had resulted in John himself. He lowered the letter, and smiled; something was happening right here, on these scraps of paper, these – probably hurried – lines from one sister to another;

holding them in his hand he could feel the pull of distance and time that connected him to his mother.

He blinked and read on, moving on to later letters. Among the descriptions of the life she still loved: the fun, the excitement and the laughter; the jokes George had loved to play – John skimmed quickly past any hint of discussion of their sex life – there was a recurring theme: the heat was unbearable; her headaches were becoming worse. John swallowed past a lump in his throat. Would it have helped anyone to know what was coming? Probably not.

Jen came back in, and this time she sat down on the floor beside him. He squeezed her hand and opened a smaller tin, which turned out to be full of photos his mother had sent to her sister. Smiling pictures of his parents and their friends, some of him as a baby, in the arms of various proud-looking members of the group, as if he belonged to them all, but there were no photos of the dig itself. He rifled through the letters he'd just read, then found the one he was looking for:

'I'd send a photo, but the authorities won't allow archaeological information, or even the boringest, blandest photos of any of the digs to leave the country! I was all for sending one anyway, after all, who would have known? But George said it wasn't worth being thrown off the dig. Bloody bureaucrats!'

John smiled. He had no recollection of his mother's voice, but it seemed she and May had had a fiery personality in common at least, and he could hear the words echoing in his head anyway.

'What's in here?' Jen picked up an envelope and peered inside. 'Photos of you!' She pulled them out, some of them cut down, some full-sized, dog-eared and clearly much-looked at. 'You were quite cute,' she mused.

John huffed. 'What do you mean, I *was*?'

'Oh go on then,' Jen said with an exaggerated sigh. 'You're still a bit of a hottie.'

'I should think so too.' He dropped the fake haughtiness and picked up a pile of drawings, fastened together with a bulldog clip. 'Look at these, I can't believe she kept them!'

'What are they?' She took them from him, and laughed. 'Cute, and a mega-talented artist!'

The drawings were ones he'd made at play school and nursery; simple stick-drawings evolving through the years, no real artistic merit, but Aunt May must have loved them nevertheless. They reminded him of the ones he and Jen had kept of Holly's and Hannah's, and he felt a sudden pang as he imagined the girls going through those at some hazy time in the future, smiling and crying over them. He shivered.

Jen had found something else, and he turned his attention to it, eager to dismiss the melancholy that was creeping over him again. 'What have you got there?'

'Hospital bands, and…' she turned the card over, 'your blood type. What were these for, d'you think?'

'I had to have an emergency appendectomy when I was a kid,' he said, looking more closely. 'Hmm. The date would fit. I suppose that's what those were about.' He gave a soft laugh. 'I'm amazed Aunt May didn't keep my appendix while she was at it.'

'Don't speak too soon,' Jen pointed out, 'We don't know there isn't a hidden drawer in her bureau.'

John grinned. 'Come on, let's put all this back, I don't know what to do with it just now. I'll find somewhere for it later.'

'What about your mother's things?' Jen sounded hesitant as she helped him put the letters and envelopes back in the tin. 'Why do you think they were hidden in the attic, instead of with the rest of her stuff?'

'No idea. I think Aunt May would have told us if she'd known, though.'

'Well she knew how important they were. I wonder why she never spoke up sooner.'

John shrugged. 'You know how it is. You just don't think about it, never imagine you're going to go out babysitting one night, and never...' he broke off as his voice turned hoarse. 'Well, you know.'

'Come on.' Jen stood up and tugged him to his feet. 'Let's go into the dining room, and spread all this out on the table.'

'Good idea. I think a glass of wine would go down well, too.'

'We'll raise a toast,' Jen said gently, and stretched up to kiss him. 'You bring the tin, I'll fetch the wine.'

They sat side-by-side, sifting through the paperwork that John had taken from his mother's biscuit tin. A couple of the envelopes were sealed, but others were just tucked closed, including one containing his father's birth certificate and Karen and George's wedding certificate, and one with a few Valentine's cards and romantic birthday cards, from George to Karen. John didn't feel right opening them to read them, but just seeing them gave him a deep-down warmth.

'Look, there're some of those old film containers, for 35mm film. We used to have to send these off to Truprint, remember? Took ages to come back.'

'At least two weeks.' John popped the lid off one, and Jen did another. Both did, indeed, contain the familiar black cartridges, and when they checked they found none of the three others had their foil wrappings on either. 'All used. I wonder what's on them?'

'Drop them in to that Photo Express place tomorrow,' Jen suggested. 'They might be able to salvage something.'

'Good idea.' John put the containers to one side, and returned to the tin, where there was one more layer to look at. 'My old passport. And Mum's and Dad's.' He opened his mother's, and some cards slipped out. 'National Health number, blood type, some weird thing that looks like…' he shrugged, 'health documents, probably. Israeli ones.' He went to put them back in the tin, along with the passports, then stopped.

Jen looked up from her wine glass. 'What's wrong?'

'Not sure. Hold on.' He went into the sitting room again and returned with Aunt May's tin. He found his blood type card, then opened his parents' passports, in turn. His stomach did a slow roll, while he tried to think, and he began to feel a bit sick. 'Jen, look at this.'

Jen took the passports, then looked at the cards in John's hand. 'I don't get it,' she said at last. 'They're both O positive, but yours says A positive… there must be a mistake here, there never any question about who your parents were!'

32

'But we both know two O positive parents can't produce an A positive child,' John pointed out, his voice tight. 'Christ, Jen…'

'It must be a mistake,' Jen repeated firmly. She picked John's childhood passport out of the tin and opened it. A mixture of items fell out, and she picked up the hospital baby bracelet stating his name, date of birth and blood group. 'There! See?' she showed him. 'I told you!'

John's eyes focused on the bracelet, and he let out a shaky breath. 'O positive.'

'Right. Same as both your parents. The hospital must have got it wrong when you went in to have your appendix out.' She finished her wine, and stood up. 'I think this has been enough delving into the past for one day, don't you? We can finish another time. Why don't you go and find a decent film we can snuggle up together and watch.'

John picked up his glass, and the wine bottle, and followed Jen back into the sitting room. She sat in her favourite corner of the settee, and waggled her empty glass for a re-fill.

'I get that that must have been a shock,' she said, as he obliged, 'But it's all cleared up now.'

'Yeah.' He sat down and put his feet on the coffee table. 'All cleared up.'

He wished everything could be clarified that easily, and although he tried to relax, he knew, without the slightest shadow of doubt, that tonight he would dream about that mountain again.

Chapter Three
The Photos

Charlotte's Tea Rooms in Cambridge wasn't the most modern café in town, but it was quiet, elegantly-decorated, and had a wonderful, traditional atmosphere. Jen was glad there was no piano here today, either, and she reflected that Aunt May would have approved of that, too; although this had been her favourite place to eat out, her keen musical ear meant she had never been able to hide a wince whenever a wrong note jarred her.

As the waitress showed them to their chosen table by the window, Jen smothered a little grin, but it did not go unnoticed by John, who raised an eyebrow.

'Just reminded me of something,' Jen said. She pointed over to another table, now occupied by a family of four. 'Do you remember when we were sitting over there, and you pulled Aunt May's chair out for her?'

John groaned. 'How could I forget? She didn't even notice!'

'She just sat there on the floor, laughing,' Jen said, still smiling. 'Never saw the waiting staff move so fast!'

'She blamed me, too,' John said, looking mildly aggrieved, then laughed. 'Cheek of it! Said she'd never brought me up to be a gentleman, so what on Earth possessed me to start behaving like one now!'

They gave their order to the waitress, and as the girl took the menus away John gave a small exclamation. 'Talking of Aunt May,' he reached down and picked up the small-ish bag beside his chair. 'I took her advice. Ta-da!'

'What's that?'

Jen took the box John proffered, and saw an identical one still nestling in the bottom of the bag. 'One each?'

'We are now the proud owners of the new Nokia 7650.'

'Mobile phones?'

'With built-in cameras, no less.' John looked almost boyishly pleased. 'I've just picked them up so haven't had a chance to look at them yet. We'll have a play later, after the girls have gone to bed.'

'I can't wait! These must have cost a fortune.'

John smiled. 'The world moves on, got to keep up with it.'

Jen pushed the box back across the table to him, and couldn't help a smile as she watched him give it another once-over before he put it back into the bag. He seemed more relaxed than he had of late, although still more tired than she liked. She decided against questioning him about the dreams; he was looking so cheerful it would be a shame to spoil the moment.

'Oh,' he said, nudging the bag under the table again, 'I took those films to Photo Express.'

'What'd they say?'

'Apparently it's possible to develop films from as long as thirty years ago, provided they've been stored in the right conditions.'

'Thirty?' Jen whistled. 'And were these stored in the right conditions?'

'I told them where we found them, and they said they couldn't guarantee perfect pictures but they'll do their best. There might be discoloration. Either way, they'll call when they've got the results.'

'It's quite exciting, really, isn't it? I can't wait to see what's on them, but can't help wondering why your mother didn't develop them herself.'

John shrugged. 'Who knows? Maybe it's memories she didn't want brought up.'

'But then why keep the films?'

John gave her a small smile. 'You've done enough research, would you be able to bring yourself to throw something like that away? Just in case?'

'Point taken.' Jen looked up as the waitress arrived with her tray. 'Ah, can't beat a good cheese and ham toastie.'

As she'd known he would, John rolled his eyes. 'Croque monsieur.'

'Crock of something,' she agreed, and smiled her thanks at the waitress, who pretended not to notice the exchange. When the girl had gone, she leaned conspiratorially across the table. 'Is it me, or are these waitresses getting younger? Feels like we're being waited on by twelve-year-old girls.' She took a bite. 'Wow, whatever you want to call this, it's lovely.'

'Nothing but the best, for my girl,' John said, and grinned. 'Especially after a not so bad first date.'

'That'll teach you,' Jen began, but broke off as John stood up and knocked on the window. 'What—?'

'Hang on.' He jogged to the door, and Jen raised a hand to the startled waiter nearby, to show him it was okay; John wasn't doing a runner to avoid paying for his meal. Instead he returned quickly, with his friend Todd Hampton in tow.

'Jen, good to see you!' Todd leaned down and kissed Jen's cheek. 'I haven't seen you since May's funeral. How are you? How are those girls of yours?'

Vastly popular, both with his theology students, and with the academic staff, Todd Hampton drew eyes everywhere he went; initially for his height and his good looks, but then for his infectious humour, and the sense of accessible intelligence he projected into most situations.

John went to order an extra latte, while Todd took a spare chair from a nearby table and sat down. He flashed a look over at John, who was leaning on the counter waiting to be served.

'Is he okay?'

Relieved to see Todd had noticed, Jen shook her head. 'You know John. Puts up a good front, but to be honest I'm worried about him.'

'Is he still having those dreams?'

She nodded. 'He doesn't talk about them, I think he wants me to forget about them. But he talks in his sleep, and it's not always—'

'What are you two looking so serious about?' John slid back into his seat. 'They're bringing coffee over.'

'Todd was asking me if I thought you'd notice if he stole half your toastie.'

'Croque monsieur, surely?' Todd said, sounding pained, and as John shot Jen a "told-you-so," look, the atmosphere lightened again. But Jen took comfort from seeing Todd's concern, only thinly disguised behind the jocular manner.

After they'd eaten they wandered back through the town centre, and as they made small talk it became clear that both John and Todd had a free period immediately after lunch. Jen caught Todd's eye, and tried to send a silent plea.

He gave a faint nod. 'Well then, why don't I come back with you to the common room for a catch-up,' he suggested. 'It's been a while.'

'Yes, go,' Jen said. 'I've got stuff to do anyway. I'll see you later.' She kissed John, then leaned in to kiss Todd as well, and, keeping her face turned she whispered, 'thank you.'

She watched them go, heading back to the university, and crossed her fingers in the hope that Todd would be able to reach where she couldn't seem to.

Passing beneath the huge archway that was the entrance to Kings College, John noted the number of young women who smiled at Todd and turned to follow his progress across the grounds.

He gave a good-natured sigh, and shook his head. 'How do you do that?'

Todd grinned. 'Animal magnetism. Besides, *I* don't look as if I've not slept for a month.' He grew more serious then. 'You're not looking great, John, as your oldest friend I think I can say that. It can't still be that dream, surely?'

John hesitated for a moment, but Todd was right, he was his oldest friend, and if he couldn't trust him, who could he trust? 'Yeah, it's partly that, disturbing my sleep, but there's more.'

'What else?'

John tried to find the right words; old friends or not, there was a sort of fantastical element to the turn his mind had been taking. 'Jen assures me there are rational explanations for it all, and I know I should believe her. But it's really getting to me.'

Inside the building they fell into an easy silence as they made their way to the senior common room. The elaborate oak door led into a high-ceilinged room with oak beams and panelling, and such an air of quiet study that it usually urged John into a calmer frame of mind. Today though, he remained agitated as he dropped his briefcase onto one of the large sofas that flanked the fireplace.

'Sit down, I'll get the coffees.'

When he returned, blowing steam off the mugs, Todd had settled into the opposite sofa, and now sat forward, his expression intense. 'Right. Start at the beginning.'

John took a deep breath. 'Well, you know about the dream, obviously, and I told you about the strange words I hear.'

'Unsettling,' Todd said, sipping his coffee

'It wouldn't be so bad, maybe I could handle it, if it wasn't so... *vivid*, and didn't happen so often. It's like...' he shook his head, 'like I'm living two lives and never getting sleep in either.'

'Christ.' Todd put down his cup and linked his hands on his knees. 'I had no idea it had got so bad. Has something happened to make it worse?'

'When Aunt May died she passed on some of my mother's things. Secret things, hidden away in the attic.' He explained about the box, and the rolls of film. 'Jen said last week that it's time to stop it all. To stop obsessing.'

'Is it putting a strain on the two of you?'

'We rowed.' John shrugged. 'I'd thought she was on my side, but she's really had enough now. Says it's affecting the girls.'

'Affecting them how?'

'Both of them had a dream too, about climbing a mountain together.' John picked up his cup again and stared into the murky brown depths, as if the answers lay in the swirls of coffee and milk. 'Their description of it fitted mine exactly.'

'Well it's pretty obvious they must have heard you then,' Todd said reasonably. 'Kids listen in all the time, and twins often have the same dreams.'

John shook his head again. 'Jen would agree with you, but we've never discussed it in front of them.'

Todd frowned. 'Hmm. There's nothing outright weird in anything you've said, and Jen's right; it could all be explained away as coincidence, or overheard conversation.' He saw the way John was looking at him, and pursed his lips. Then he rummaged in his case and pulled out an A4 pad. 'Draw the mountain.' He threw the pad to John, who unclipped a pen from his breast pocket.

After a few minutes he passed the pad back, wordlessly. Even seeing his own drawing made him feel slightly queasy.

Todd studied it for a moment. 'Believe it or not, I do know of a mountain like this. It's very distinctive.' He grinned at John. 'Most men dream about stockings and suspenders. Not you, you have to dream about this old thing!' He tilted the pad and squinted. 'Actually, come to think of it, it does look a bit like a boob with a massive nipple. Are you sure you're not dreaming about boobs?'

John managed a laugh. 'Even if I was, I'd hardly dream about climbing them!'

'Well, each to their own,' Todd chuckled. 'I wouldn't say no.'

John gave him a scathing look, then sobered. 'Even if the mountain's real, it still makes no sense. Does it?'

Todd thought for a moment. 'Look, maybe you're making too much of it. Seriously, mate, you know how it goes; you worry about something you just make it worse. It plays on your mind.'

'So what do you suggest?'

'Do something to take your mind off it. Anything. It'll soon bugger off.'

John was less convinced. Hadn't he been trying that? He sighed. 'Okay, out of curiosity then, what's this mountain that looks like this?'

'It's called Mount Hira.' Todd frowned, calling the details to mind. 'It's proper name is Jabal al-Noor, the Mountain of Light. The Islamic prophet, Muhammed, climbed it, and he found a little cave where he had his first Heavenly revelation and received the verses of the Quran.'

John looked at him, suddenly dry-mouthed. 'Where is it?'

'In Saudi. Quite the place for pilgrimages. We covered it with one of our year groups last year.' He raised an eyebrow and gave John a faint smile. 'Muhammed actually had several dreams before this revelation. Maybe you're on the brink of one, too.'

But John couldn't return the humour. Not now. 'Mount Hira has a cave?'

'Yes, but only a—'

'The girls' dream had a cave at the top of their mountain. It had rugs, and pictures on the walls. They had a picnic, sang songs… Todd, their cave is identical to mine. And get this,' John's voice turned hoarse, barely audible. 'I have never told a single soul about the cave in my dream. Not even Jen.'

The following Friday John picked up the photos, a film for the girls, and, on a whim, some fish and chips. Jen went into raptures over the smell of supper, and the fact that she needn't cook after all, then she asked about the milk.

'Milk?'

'I sent you a text message.'

John cleared his throat. 'Oh, I didn't see it.' He had, but in truth he had been so excited at picking up the photos it had completely slipped his mind. How could he tell her that though, when she already believed his obsession was getting in the way of daily life. 'You know me and gadgets,' he added blithely, 'not quite got to grips with it yet. Sorry.'

'Hmm.' Jen clearly didn't believe him, but the fact that she didn't pursue it gave him the confidence to show her the packets he'd collected.

'Look, Photo Express has done a great job. There're about 160 of the things that actually developed! The rest of them were blank. I flipped through them in the car and they seem to be mostly journal pages. My father's, I think, plus some pictures of the dig itself.'

Jen was suitably impressed. 'Bloody hell. How on Earth did your mum get those out of the country?'

Before John could answer, Holly and Hannah bounced up, gleeful that it was Friday at last, which meant a later bedtime.

'Do you want to watch something while we eat?' John asked, and was almost deafened by the enthusiasm of their response. 'Great. We'll watch Teletubbies. I thought you'd like it, since they have their own language, just as you do. I picked a copy up from Blockbuster on the way home.'

The girls exchanged martyred looks, and Holly's chin dropped dramatically into her hand. 'Daddy! That's for babies.'

Hannah copied her sister. 'It'll be so *boring*!'

'Hmm.' John frowned, and met Jen's eyes; she was arching an eyebrow in warning, and he relented. 'Well in that case it's a good thing I picked up Shrek instead, isn't it?'

The girls whooped their delight, and John took them through to the living room to put the tape in the machine, and set it up at the start of the film. Jen came in with supper on a tray, and they settled down to watch.

As funny as the film was, John found himself eating faster and faster, his mind kept straying to the packets of photographs that sat on the kitchen table, and the journal entries they held. As soon as he could, without raising any protests, he excused himself, picked up the photos and went through to the study.

He sat at the desk, shuffling through the photos and making sure they were in some kind of order. There were images of crumbling walls; holes in the ground; steps that appeared to lead nowhere, or into walls; a few photos of broken pottery. Those pictures gave way to ones that made John's heart beat faster: photographs of some stone tablets, some ancient-looking script. The rest were parts of hand-written records in three distinctively different styles.

He presumed the two journals were his father's and his partner Mark's. The sheets of notes were definitely in his mother's handwriting, he recognised it from her letters to May. This would explain why the films had been sent out of Israel undeveloped, but it had still been risky; the penalties for letting this kind of thing leave the country would have been extremely severe. What could be worth that risk?

He settled down to read, distracted briefly by the sound of the twins and Jen breaking into laughter in the lounge, and he smiled at the wall behind which he could picture them all so clearly; nibbling on the crispy bits, eyes on the screen, enraptured faces bathed in its light. Part of him wished he could put all this to one side and join them, but a much bigger part kept him in his seat, his hand reaching for his keyboard.

By the time the film had finished, and Jen had sent the girls to ready themselves for bed, John's fingers were sore from typing.

'How's it going?' Jen asked, poking her head around the door.

'Hard work,' he confessed. 'The writing's distorted, probably because the film itself is so old. But I'm getting there.'

'You're transcribing?'

'As far as I can.' He flexed his aching fingers. 'I think just a little bit each evening's a good idea, though.'

'Did you talk to Todd about it last week?'

He nodded. 'He says he thinks he's seen the mountain before.' He told her about the conversation, the drawing, and Todd's explanation about Muhammed. 'But apart from that he seems to think I'm stressing about nothing,' he finished. 'It doesn't explain the odd words, after all.'

'Not much help, then. Oh!' Jen tapped the door jamb and backed out of the room. 'I recorded you,' she called back, heading for the stairs. 'I'll get the machine.'

She returned a moment later with her dictaphone. 'Let me just rewind it, to get back to the start of when you began speaking in your sleep.'

John's scalp tightened at the thought that he would soon hear his own voice speaking words he could not now recall, and as the tape hissed to a halt and Jen pressed the 'play' button, the door opened and the twins came in. Jen held her finger to her lips, and they all listened in silence. Holly and Hannah's voices were first on the tape, telling their mother their own words for things.

Holly giggled. 'That's us!'

'We sound funny,' Hannah said. 'Do we really sound like that?'

'You do,' John said with a faint smile. 'You sound like Teletubbies.'

Their protests were halted as John's own voice sounded. Sleepy mutterings that John had to strain to hear. His disappointment was reflected on Jen's face as he shrugged.

'Means absolutely nothing to me. Just gibberish, like the dreams.'

'What's gibberish?' Holly wanted to know.

'Nonsense,' Jen said.

'But it's not though, it's our words!'

John looked at Jen, then his daughter. 'Are you sure?'

She nodded. 'You said: "Where are you?" and then something beginning with "D." Didn't he?' She looked to Hannah for confirmation, and Hannah nodded.

John swallowed hard. 'Wow. Thanks, girls.' He could see them revving up for more questions, but he couldn't face that just now; he was still in some kind of mild shock at the way things were turning. 'You're pretty amazing sometimes, you know. Now,' he said briskly, 'it's time for bed. Give us a kiss, I'll come up and see you before it's time to go to sleep.'

John sat back down at the desk to think. He was frowning at the photos when Jen returned from settling the girls, and he reached for her hand. 'Well. That was weird.'

'Not really,' Jen said. 'I've said it before; you'll have heard the girls using those words. You were probably trying to make sense of them in your sleep.'

'I haven't heard them.'

'You must have heard the tape?'

John gave her an apologetic look. 'Sorry, but no. I meant to, but what with one thing and another I just didn't get around to it. I haven't even looked at the dictionary you're making. I'm really sorry, Jen.'

She shrugged, but he could see she was hurt. 'Let's listen to the tape again.'

Jen rewound it and they listened twice more, but as hard as they tried they couldn't decipher the "D" word.

'Sounds like dahvee,' Jen said, frowning.

'That's all I can make of it,' he agreed. He put his hand on Jen's cheek and stroked it with his thumb, trying to ease the worried look. 'I'm sorry, Jen,' he said softly. 'This has got me totally baffled. I hate how it's taken over my life, I just want things back the way they were. The only way I can do that is to understand it.'

Relenting, Jen reached up to put her arms around his neck. She kissed him. 'Maybe you need to see someone. A doctor.' John drew back and frowned down at her, but she shook her head. 'Not like that. I mean someone who can give you something to help you sleep. You're making yourself ill.' She stepped away and tugged at his hand. 'Come on up to bed.'

John was sorely tempted, and looking at Jen's faintly flushed cheeks, he could see sleep wasn't on her mind, either. But the stacks of photographs on the table behind were exerting a pull he could not ignore. He let go of her hand, after giving it a conciliatory squeeze.

'I'm going to stay up just a little bit longer,' he said. 'This journal's really interesting.' It was an understatement, but it made no difference; Jen's face closed down again.

'Will you see someone?'

'I will,' he promised. 'First thing Monday if I can get in.'

She regarded him for a moment, then nodded. As she turned away he thought he saw the faint gleam of tears in her eyes, but her voice was bright enough as she called, 'Don't be long,' over her shoulder.

Much later, when John eventually climbed the stairs to bed, the upper landing was all in darkness. He'd forgotten to say goodnight to the twins, and Jen had long since given up waiting and turned out the light. As he undressed in the bathroom he found himself thinking back over all the times he'd said he just wanted things back the way they were, and by the time he slid into bed beside his sleeping wife he'd realised that, as much as he wanted to be able to promise her he'd leave it all alone, he couldn't.

Part Two
Jericho, Israel 1965

'And Moses went into God's mountain with only bread and water. I placed damp clay in a sheep's bladder, to stop it from drying out, sharpened my reed pen and waited. As I watched, it seemed he was not climbing alone, when I knew that he was! Day became night and we were all afraid. We bowed our heads to the heavenly ring of fire. Those without reverence were blinded. As night became day, my friend returned with God's words. I was proud to be tasked to write them in the clay. The holy tablet was placed in an oven to harden. We then set off to join the rest of our people who should be camped at the edge of the Promised Land.'

'The people waited no more and, believing Moses to be dead, reinstated the old gods. Having no faith in Maor and believing him to be cursed, he was banished from the land. When Moses returned he was angry. The false gods were destroyed and the people were denied entry to the Promised Land. God gave his people a new prophecy and the spirit was laid to sleep.'

Excerpts from the writings of Amnon
2nd millennium BC

'When Ishmael and Isaac war over water, twins shall be born to the sons of God, under the ring of light. The spirit shall awaken and they shall be born unto Levites in the Holy Land. Strangers unto each other, they shall meet to protect my children and guide them to the truth.'

Prophecy 2nd millennium BC

Chapter Four
Friends Reunite

Queen Alia International Airport, Amman, Jordan. May 1965
'Nine hours.' George threw an incredulous look at his wife, who returned it and sat down on her upturned suitcase, fanning her face. 'Nine *hours!*' He followed her example, and then wiped sweat from his forehead with his sleeve.

'How far to the first checkpoint on the bridge?' Karen asked.

'Mark didn't say. Hopefully the taxi won't take too long getting there. I'm done in.'

Three hours later they were crossing the Allenby bridge on the shuttle bus between Jordan and Israel, on their way to the final checkpoint. To make matters worse, whether it was the heat or the general way of things, everyone seemed to be barging them, pushing to get ahead, and trying to elbow them out of the way.

At last they reached the end of the queue, but there was more misery to come in the form of endless questions fired at them by fierce border control officials. The questions were not only professional, pertaining to their previous visit to Egypt, as well as this one, they were often deeply personal.

George squeezed Karen's arm; he could sense her building up to a refusal to answer. 'Remember what Mark said', he murmured, 'play the game.' She did, albeit reluctantly, and eventually they emerged into the West Bank, papers stamped, both feeling as if they'd been through the wringer while the impassive border staff moved on to their next victims.

George stopped at a pay phone and called their friends to let them know they were on their way to the car park. As they arrived a battered jeep pulled up, windows down to allow two sunburnt, smiling faces to hang out.

'Kar! George!' Denise shouted, waving. 'Get in!'

George heaved their suitcases into the boot, and he and Karen collapsed onto the back seat, sighing in relief at the faint breeze that stirred their hair once they got going.

Denise twisted in the front seat, and reached back to grasp Karen's hand. 'Flippin' eck, it's good to see you! We've missed you!'

'And we've missed you! I can't believe we're actually here.'

'You took your time,' Mark observed, negotiating a tight corner with practiced ease.

George snorted. 'Trust me, if it hadn't taken so bloody long to get our visas sorted we'd have been here the day after you called.'

'Tell me about it,' Mark said. 'You wouldn't believe the paperwork and politics here, it's off the scale.'

'We've just had to go through that whole rigmarole again,' Denise added. 'Just to get ours extended. How was the journey?'

'Went smoothly enough,' George said. 'Bit of a delay at Istanbul, and Karen was a bit iffy on the second flight, but you've perked up a bit now, haven't you, love? We're both exhausted now, though.'

Karen nodded. 'It was probably just tiredness. And you know I hate flying, so the stress won't have helped.'

'We remembered,' Mark said, 'that's why we suggested you travel overland to Jericho. Plus it's a lot cheaper.'

'Is it a long way?'

'Not from here. And it'll be quicker getting back; the delays can be horrendous at customs and immigration. Did you remember to ask for an entry card?'

'Yeah, thanks for that,' George said. 'Your advice has really helped. I mean, I never would have thought twice about an Israeli stamp on my passport making life difficult. Egypt was a lot easier.'

'Ah, Egypt!' Denise let out one of her irrepressible barks of laughter. 'Kar, d'you remember when George nearly gave you a heart attack jumping out of that tomb?'

'I could've killed him,' Karen said, grinning. 'And Mark, for egging him on.'

'And wrapping him in loo roll!'

'Yes! Deni, do you realise that that was *four years* ago? Where's the time gone?'

'God knows. I keep wondering if that trader ever found a wife to swap his camels for after you turned him down.'

Karen laughed. 'I'd forgotten about that! I remember I wrote and told my sister, and, typical May, she wrote back that if he was good looking I should take the bloody camels, and she'd be on the next flight out!'

Denise chuckled, and turned back to face the front. 'So, what have you been up to?'

'Dig-wise? Not much. We've been busy with research and stuff for the past year. How about you? I seem to remember something about you guys digging up dead bodies in France, the last time you wrote.'

'Oh, God,' Denise groaned. 'That was an awful job. It took us a whole year to get them out of the crypt. They were making way for a café, would you believe?'

'Blimey. As if they need any more of those.'

George shifted against the hot vinyl of the seat. 'Why Israel this time, then?'

Mark shrugged. 'Why anywhere? You never know what you'll find, or where you'll find it. It can get a bit soul-destroying picking over cleaned-out digs, hoping to stumble on something someone else has left behind. But…' he threw a grin over his shoulder, 'it so happens that this time we didn't have to apply. We were requested, specifically.'

George exchanged a surprised look with Karen. 'Why all the secrecy though? When you called it was pretty obvious you'd found something and want it kept quiet.'

Mark met George's eyes in the rear view mirror for a moment, before shifting his gaze back to the road. 'Tomorrow, my friend. Let's just get there, and then get some food and rest.'

Jericho, Palestinian Territories, Israel

It was just after midnight when they arrived at the two-bedroomed apartment Mark and Denise had rented in Al Nahkheel Street.

'Here we are,' Denise said, pushing open the door. 'Not much to see, and we'll probably be a bit cramped

53

with four of us, but it's clean, private, and close to work. I hope it's okay.'

'It'll be fun,' Karen assured her. 'We all know each other well enough, after all.'

'We'd have liked to have arranged separate lodgings, but the budget's pretty tight, and it's privately funded.'

'It's okay, Deni, honestly.' Karen kicked off her sandals, and her expression melted into relief as her feet touched the cool, tiled floor. 'Oh, that's lovely.'

'It's hot, but not as hot as we'd expected,' George said, dropping his suitcase and rolling his shoulders.

'Give it another month,' Denise assured him. 'It'll be in the 90s during the day.'

'Can't wait,' George said with a wry smile.

They sat down to a meal of shawarma with hummus, salad, and pitta bread, and Karen noted how both Mark and Denise easily deflected any talk of the new dig. It must be more complicated than any of them were ready to deal with so late at night, after a day's travel, and despite the curiosity she was more than happy to leave it until tomorrow.

Conversation naturally became reminiscences, and particularly the end of the contract in Egypt, when they had been credited with the finds of a few artefacts that had made everything worthwhile.

'It would have been great to have found a new chamber in Tutankhamun's tomb, wouldn't it?' Denise said, scooping up some stray hummus with her bread. 'Or Queen Nefertiti's. We weren't greedy, after all!'

They all laughed, and, watching them, Karen reflected how different Mark and Denise were in comparison to herself and George; Denise, petite and blonde, with her never-ending supply of energy was the perfect foil for Mark, who was tall, dark and quiet. He sat now, calmly enjoying his wife's ebullience, and shooting Karen and George the occasional grin as he ate. It was clear to see who held the dominant hand in their relationship, whereas with Karen and George the line was more blurred... George was the boss when Karen allowed it. She swallowed a smile at the thought, and patted his hand. He looked at her, surprised, and she shook her head and continued her meal.

When they finally went to their room their bed looked utter bliss, even shrouded in the mosquito net as it was, and buried under two large suitcases. They pulled the cases onto the floor but didn't bother to unpack anything, just undressed, barely mumbled 'goodnight,' and fell asleep at once.

The following morning they saw exactly what Denise had meant when she'd said there wasn't much room. Walking sideways around the bed, Karen put her book on the single bedside table, while George took over half the chest of drawers with his clothes and then went for a shower.

Karen followed in her turn, and when she went into the kitchen, a towel around her head, he was leaning against the counter, drinking coffee.

'They've nipped out,' he said, and gestured at a note on the counter:

"Gone shopping, back with breakfast shortly."

Even as she read it, the door opened and her friends came in, laden with bags.

'Morning,' Mark said, dropping one of the bags on top of the note. 'Hope you're both feeling nicely rested.'

Karen rubbed at her damp hair with the towel. 'Very well, thanks. I think it was a case of: zonked as soon as our heads touched the pillow.'

'Well make yourselves at home. Somewhere!' Denise laughed and gestured through the archway at the room beyond. It was a small and neat lounge diner, with a single settee, a table –covered in paperwork and books – with four chairs, and a small TV on another table. In the corner a portable air conditioner purred, and the morning sun bathed everything as it streamed in through French windows, beyond which they could see lemon trees surrounding a small patio.

'Heavenly view,' Karen said, giving a little sigh of pleasure. It was such a relief to be here, with the nightmare of travel firmly behind them.

'Breakfast this morning will be a typically Israeli one,' Denise said. 'Totally kosher, so don't go looking for bacon.'

'Service with a smile,' George grinned. 'I like it.'

'Yes, well, after this it's every man for themselves,' Denise flung a cushion at him. 'I'm not your servant. Speaking of which, Mark? Will you *please* clear your crap off the table so we can pretend to be civilised?'

As delicious as the breakfast looked, and smelled, Karen did little more than push hers around on the plate and drink some of the fresh fruit juice. She managed a few mouthfuls and wished she felt like eating more, but George was making up for it; she watched him devouring omelette and salad, cheeses and breads, and rolled her

56

eyes at him. He grinned back at her, unabashed, and forked up another mouthful of omelette.

'Help me clear the plates,' Denise said to her, 'and we'll get some coffee on the go while the guys sort out the paperwork.' They went through the kitchen, and Denise raised an eyebrow at the food still on Karen's plate. 'Too much food last night?'

'I just feel a bit… off, this morning,' Karen said. 'Probably all that travelling. Don't worry, I'll eat you out of house and home later!'

'Are you coming?' Mark called. 'We want to get started.'

They carried coffee through, and sat back down at the table, now elbow-deep in paper and books once more. Mark waited until they'd settled, then took a deep breath.

'Right then, we studied all the results of the excavations of Warren, Garstang, Kenyon and Wood. Decided to set up a fresh site, to dig deeper into the retaining wall and remaining north wall sections of the old Jericho city.'

'Were you looking for something specific?' George asked.

'Well, we were asked to focus on the first Israelite settlement. We know that more than twenty different time periods of habitation in Jericho have been analysed already, one of which linked in with the time of the Exodus. So of course it was worth a closer look.'

'Definitely,' George agreed, sitting forward.

'Before we got started we rummaged around in the space between the inner and outer walls, which was used

57

as a storage area. And some houses were built into the walls.'

'What kind of finds had been picked up before?' Karen wanted to know.

'Pottery jars full of grain, mostly, but we found a few small pieces of broken jars inscribed with…' He paused for effect, and looked directly at Karen, 'cuneiform!'

Karen's eyes widened. She was about to ask for details, but Denise nudged Mark.

'Oi! What's this we?' She looked at Karen and George. 'I found those pieces, while he was having words with the helpers.'

'Oh, and that's another thing,' Mark said, taking the interruption in his stride. 'We don't trust our helpers. They don't follow orders, and they're nosy.'

'Nosy?'

'Deni found Shay rootling through my paperwork last month.'

Karen was appalled. 'What did you do?'

Denise winked. 'Told him to fuck off. What else?'

'That's my little wild cat for ya,' Mark laughed.

'We had no choice in the help we were given for this dig,' Denise went on. 'It's dead strict; any photographs, and all paperwork, have to remain on site. We're just there to find, assess and pass on our findings to our boss. But…' she gave a sly smile, 'You know me. I might have accidentally taken a photo or two of those pieces before they left the site.'

'Oh, I'm so glad to hear you say that!' Karen said. 'When you said you'd found cuneiform… I mean, it's normally only found in Iraq.' She sat back, excitement growing as she thought more about it. 'There *was* that find in Hazor though, and the biggest of all were those tablets found in Egypt.'

George frowned. 'Which?'

'The clay tablets from Mesopotamia. The diplomatic correspondence.'

'Ah yes, I remember. The Amarna letters. What was the pharaoh called? Akhenaten?'

She nodded. 'They found hundreds of them.'

'This is why we need your expertise, Kar,' Mark said. 'You must be one of only about fifty people worldwide who'd be able to decipher it. Give me hieroglyphs, any day!'

'There wasn't much,' Denise put in, 'but our boss was pretty excited anyway, and wanted us to crack on and look for more. So we did.'

'As exciting for me as this is,' Karen said, 'surely you didn't call us both all the way out here to decipher a few bits of pottery? Or to help you look for more. So what's going on?'

'Told you she was shrewd.' Denise nudged Mark, who grinned back.

'Before we tell you,' he said, 'I need to tell you there are some... odd things going on at this dig.'

George raised an eyebrow. 'Odd?'

'Okay. All evidence from earlier digs disappeared years ago; we only have records, drawings and photos. If anything significant was found there's no physical proof of it. Any findings here have to be reported privately, so we don't know what happens to them, but I'm betting they'll never be made public either. Even if they were, there are authorities and organisations that wouldn't recognise certain findings, particularly any that might challenge the sanctioned scriptures.' He shook his head. 'It's odd for us not to have control.'

Karen and George agreed. Something was definitely off.

Denise took up the story. 'We started on the north wall, since it's the only place to have survived so many traumas. Long story short though, after weeks of fruitless poking around, we finally found a small hole in the ground, under the lower wall stones. We didn't get too excited to begin with, because it's solid bedrock. But…' she took her time draining her coffee cup, and Karen resisted the urge to throw something at her; her own excitement was rising again.

'I poked a two-foot rod in,' Denise went on, wiping her mouth on her sleeve. 'It went down the full length and didn't hit anything. Then Mark made the hole a bit bigger, and when we shone the torch down it… well, we were somewhat amazed.'

'Deni!' Karen spluttered, trying not to laugh. 'You're doing this on purpose, stop it!'

'I put the camera in,' Mark said, 'took a few shots, took the film to a friend of ours, Uri, and he developed them.' He reached beneath a pile of papers, and drew out two photographs. 'Ta-da!'

Karen seized them before George had the chance, but they pored over them together. The photos showed two stacks of clay tablets, covered in script.

'Wow,' George breathed. 'I don't believe this... it's amazing! I'm assuming you sealed the hole again, until you knew what you'd found?'

'Yeah.' Mark rubbed his hands together. 'So if Karen reckons what we have so far is just some archaic shopping list, we'll open it up again and carry on as normal. But,' he lowered his voice a little, 'If it's more than that, we're going to need to keep this hush-hush. We don't want anything happening to *this* find.'

'God, no!'

'George, you can help me with the excavation of the tablets, once Karen's done her bit. The wall will need to be supported and I don't want the crew getting wind of this.'

Denise grabbed at Karen's hand across the table, her excitement getting the better of her at last. 'Do you have any idea what it's been like, waiting for you two for two whole months? Now you can put us out of our misery! We've managed to get a timeline analysis done on one of the pieces, and the date fits.'

'How on earth did you manage...ah.' Karen nodded. 'Your friend Uri?'

'Of course.'

'He's in on rather a lot, isn't he?'

'We couldn't have managed without him, to be honest,' Denise confessed. 'His name's Uri Malik, you'll meet him and his wife tomorrow evening at dinner.'

'What are they like?'

'Lovely. Well,' Denise gave Karen a mock-scowl, 'Maya is drop dead gorgeous, so of course I hate her.'

Karen laughed. 'What do they do?

'Uri – he's half English but I don't know which half – studied in Haifa and London. He's a doctor at the second largest hospital in the West Bank. Maya's a midwife there. They're great fun.'

A few weeks later, George eyed his wife across the table, and decided she had never looked so quietly thrilled. She looked as if she was bursting to tell them what she'd found, and after the weeks of hard work she'd put in, she deserved her moment. It was infectious, and he could see Denise and Mark looking at one another in rising excitement.

'Out with it,' Denise said, 'you're just getting your own back, aren't you?'

Karen laughed. 'Well, the script on the pottery is nothing to write home about, but the writing on the tablets reads: two loaves of bread, a sack of flour—'

'Stop it!' Denise said, flicking a peanut across the table.

'Okay. It's definitely *not* a shopping list.' Karen picked up the photos, her smile widening. 'In fact, even based on what little I could read, this could actually be one of the biggest finds ever.' The others exchanged looks of delight. 'We need to get those tablets out and photographed so I can get the full story,' Karen went on, 'but what we have so far appears to be…' her voice went a bit husky and she cleared her throat, 'part of an eye-witness account of the Hebrew exodus from Egypt.'

There was a stunned silence, and finally Mark broke it with a harsh whisper. 'What?'

'Bloody hell,' George muttered. No wonder Karen had been so secretive and excited these past few days, while she checked and re-checked the wedge shaped script.

'The thing is,' Karen said, 'I need the rest, to work out how this was recorded in the first place. The Hebrews had no written language then.'

'No, that's right,' Mark said. 'They passed it all on by word of mouth.'

'There's more,' Karen said.

'More?'

'The story is of Munius and Nour, twin brothers who led the Hebrews out of Egypt.'

'Oh, my God!' Denise stood up and began to pace, and Mark and George stared at one another, and then at Karen, whose smile was like a shaft of sunlight cutting across the table.

'Wait for it,' she murmured. 'Munius is an Egyptian name, right? And Nour is a Nubian one. Which is a bit odd. But… in Hebrew they translate as Moses and Maor.'

This time the silence went on for longer, and then so did the exclamations and the questions but when they finally died away, George caught sight of his wife's face. She still hadn't finished, he was sure of it.

'Karen?' he prompted quietly.

Karen looked down at the table, then raised her eyes to his, and after the revelations and surprises, and after the shouts and the excited laughter, and the buzz of discovery, her next words were all for him.

'I'm pregnant.'

Chapter Five
The Invitation

Monastery of St Gerasimus, Palestinian Territories, Israel. September 1965

Karen felt the insistent push of a foot, or a hand, under her ribs, and pushed back with a little grunt. It had been good to take this time to look around the monastery, but the extra weight she was carrying was making her back twinge, and she longed to sit down, just for a few minutes. She adjusted the scarf she wore over her head and shoulders, flapping it to raise a breeze; despite the cooler autumn weather it was still uncomfortably warm in the full glare of the sun.

'We're going off to have a look at the crypt,' Mark said, irrepressible as always. 'Coming?'

Denise shook her head. 'I had enough of crypts and old bones in France to last me a lifetime, thanks.'

'I'll pass too,' Karen said, relieved. 'You boys go off and have fun, I fancy putting my feet up for a bit in that lovely little courtyard.'

'Sounds good to me,' Maya put in. 'We'll wait for you there.'

The three of them walked slowly back through the beautiful, cool cloisters, to the courtyard where the central well beckoned like a desert mirage, and Denise looked critically at Karen's feet.

'Your ankles are swelling up.'

'Sit down then,' Karen joked, 'and let me put my feet in your lap.'

To her amusement Denise obeyed, straightened her long, patterned skirt, and patted her knees. 'Come on then.'

Laughing, Karen accepted, and then sighed with pleasure as she looked at the floral displays around them. The monastery had been a surprising oasis in the Judaean Desert; only a quarter of an hour from Jericho, and so when Uri had suggested a day out there, following them in the jeep had been easy, and worth every minute.

'I've got a stiff neck from staring up at that dome,' Denise said. 'What amazing artwork.'

Maya nodded. 'Beautiful. But I prefer the mosaics. Especially the Gerasimus lion.'

'That's quite a story,' Denise said.

'It is. There are several similar though, come to think of it. Androcles and the lion, and St Jerome.'

'And Daniel in the lion's den,' Karen supplied. 'Always wondered what it would be like to earn the gratitude of a wild beast by yanking a thorn out of its paw.'

Denise snorted. 'Mark got a splinter in his toe once; he was hopping around like a lunatic. I pulled it out, but I can assure you I didn't get any gratitude from *that* wild beast!'

They laughed, and Denise began to massage Karen's sore feet. 'It's a good point though, Maya. I do believe there's a certain amount of truth in the scriptures. Although I'm also sure some were manufactured. It'd be a way to explain what couldn't be fully understood, or to make a moral point.'

'Many stories of holy people have striking parallels too,' Maya agreed. 'Look at Jesus, Buddha, Krishna, Horus—'

'And not to mention virgin births,' Karen said, smoothing her own bump. 'Not just Jesus, either. If you believe Amnon, Moses and Maor's parents nearly separated because Amram thought Jochebad had been unfaithful. She swore she hadn't been.'

'What about Romulus and Remus?' Maya added. '*Their* father didn't believe a word of it either.'

Denise gave her a sidelong look. 'So, do you think these ladies were trying to get away with having a bit on the side?'

Maya smiled. 'I'm sure there were some who were. But Uri, myself, and our ancestors do believe some conceptions were genuinely divine.'

'Ooh, sounds interesting,' Denise said. 'Do tell.'

'Later, when we're all together,' Maya promised. 'Oh yes, I'm cooking and you're invited.'

'Of course, we'd love to come.' Karen swung her legs off Denise's lap. 'What are we having?'

'I'm doing brisket with tahdig and salad.'

'I love all your cooking,' Karen said, 'but I especially love tahdig. Thank—Oh!'

'You alright, Kar? Another headache?' Denise asked, frowning.

'No. I'm fine. The brat just gave me a massive kick.' Karen rubbed at her belly, and the tenderness and pride in her voice belied her words. 'He's going to be a feisty one.'

'He?' Maya raised her eyebrows. 'You're certain it's a boy?'

'George won't have it any other way.' Karen rolled her eyes, but smiled. 'He says he clearly remembers the night of conception, and he'd willed all the boy sperms to win the race!'

Denise grinned. 'Men are so funny about having boys. Must be in their genes to want to carry on the family name.'

Maya smiled too, but there was a hint of melancholy in her eyes. 'I'm so happy for you. But also a little envious, I confess. Uri and I can't have children.'

'Oh,' Karen felt a wave of compassion, and guilt. 'I'm so sorry—'

'Don't be.' Maya squeezed her hand. 'We are reconciled to it now. His brothers will carry on the family name, and his sister Rena is expecting a child soon. I shall enjoy being an aunt.'

'It's funny how things work sometimes,' Denise mused. 'You,' she nodded at Karen, 'tried for years to get pregnant, didn't you? Then… poof! Out of the blue, just when you'd given up hope. You,' she looked at Maya, 'want children but can't, whereas presumably I can, but don't want them.' She sighed, and patted Maya's knee. 'Life can be very unfair.'

Karen stretched her aching back. 'Seems like being mentioned in a prophecy can be the kiss of doom. Remember that plaque we saw inside? The one about Mary and Joseph fleeing here, and hiding in a cave to escape Herod?'

'Indeed,' Maya said. 'The monastery was built here to commemorate that very event. And those *lovely*, wise men, also drawn by a prophecy, were the ones who betrayed them.'

'Hmm,' Karen said. 'Ring any bells? A similar prophecy came to Pharaoh Akhenaten too, which is why Moses and Maor were set adrift to begin with.'

'But these prophecies mention twin boys,' Denise pointed out. 'Jesus wasn't a twin.'

'Ah,' Maya said, 'actually Uri and I have heard reports, though unsubstantiated, that Jesus might have had a twin called Thomas.'

'No way!' Denise stared at her. 'If that's true, what happened to him? And why is he never mentioned?'

'He has been,' Maya said. 'In some scriptures at least, but I've not read them. Perhaps his parents left him with family, to keep him safe?'

'But Herod was out to kill all boy babies. How would it keep him safe?'

'We think Herod only ordered the killing of twins, because of the prophecy, so if Mary and Joseph fled with just one of them, the single child left behind in Bethlehem would have been safe.'

Karen's arms went instinctively, protectively, around her belly. 'I can't imagine what it would be like to have to give up a child, even to keep it safe.

The crypt

'So many bones,' George exclaimed. 'I'm surprised they weren't buried after the Persian invasion though.' He peered closer at the cabinets. 'They look so small, don't they?'

'Those poor monks would have been, when they were alive,' Mark said. 'Living in caves, feeding on bread and water. Meeting here once a week for a decent meal and a cup of wine wouldn't have undone all that damage. And they wouldn't even have had that, if Gerasimus hadn't changed their routine.'

George moved on. 'I get their piety and all that, completely understand, but what I don't get is why anyone needs to suffer to be devout. Solitude, bad diet, and no women!' He shook his head. 'I couldn't do it.'

Mark chuckled. 'I'm with you on that one. Although knowing you I suspect it'd be the bad diet that put you off, more than anything else.'

George flung him a look of mock indignation. 'What are you trying to say?'

'Nothing. Nothing at all.' Mark stuck his hands in his pockets and looked away, whistling, and George punched him in the shoulder.

Uri joined them, his mind clearly still on the bones. 'The monks devoted themselves to prayer,' he mused. 'Possessions, and worldly cravings are a distraction to concentration.'

'I can see that,' Mark agreed, winking at George. 'Particularly worldly cravings in a womanly direction.'

'I visited the Shah Jahan mosque once,' Uri went on. 'In Woking, when I was a student in London. I was quite shocked at the way men and women were segregated during prayer. I asked the imam about it, and he said most Europeans do find it odd, but it's not to demean women.

Far from it, in fact. It was so the congregation could concentrate on prayer.'

'How so?' Mark asked.

'Well, just imagine you're kneeling behind an attractive young lady,' Uri said. 'Prayers begin; she bows her head to the floor—'

'And you're looking straight at her bum!'

Uri smiled back, and nodded. 'Tell me you'd be able to concentrate on prayers then!'

'And it's not just bottoms that are a distraction,' Mark added. 'I don't think I've ever been able to get through an episode of Grandstand without Deni interrupting.'

'And what about at uni?' George asked him. 'Going from an all-boys' grammar into that environment... you probably fared as badly as I did, concentration-wise.'

'Oh yeah! We met the girls there,' Mark explained to Uri, seeing his puzzled look. 'Those were the days; slogging hard through the week, getting blitzed at weekends... And girls wore stockings, not tights.'

'Ah, stockings!' George sighed. 'Must have been a woman who invented tights, bloody things. So inaccessible!'

Uri grinned. 'Yep, see? Easily distracted. We're all doomed!'

When the laughter had faded George turned to Uri again. 'Where did you meet Maya?'

'National service. We were both assigned to the medical corps, then went to university afterwards. Didn't you have to do that?'

'No,' Mark said. 'By the time we came of age it had almost been phased out; they weren't so strict with students in the UK. Thank God.' He shuddered. 'I heard it could be hellish. I don't think there are many countries now that still have National Service.'

A little later they walked back through the church, and George found his attention once more caught by the frescos of the saints. He stopped to look, and the others almost cannoned into him.

'What is it?' Uri asked. 'That's the second time you've done that with these paintings.'

'Something's…' George shook his head. 'I don't know, something's niggling. Look, all these figures are depicted as holy, just because of the halo. But what if it's not a halo? It looks like each figure is standing in front of the sun. So, in effect, the sun is the halo. It's nothing more than a ring of light when something's in front of it.'

'Ah,' Uri said. 'You're thinking of Karen's translation, yes? Moses and Maor being born under such a ring. It is puzzling. Amnon doesn't write in the plural here. If the twins had been born with halos, he'd have said so. But he writes in the singular, and not only that, but that they were born *under* it, not *with* it.'

Mark frowned. 'So then… what could possibly have been in front of the sun, to make it a ring instead of a ball?'

'Oh, good grief!' George rolled his eyes. 'It's the moon, guys! It's a bloody eclipse! Not the full one though. I can't remember the name for it, off-hand, but it doesn't block out the whole sun.'

Mark raised an eyebrow. 'And the significance of this is…?'

'It's just something that's been bugging me.' George shrugged. 'No big deal really, I suppose.'

But Uri was grinning again. He slapped George on the back. 'Bigger than you think, my friend! Extremely important, in fact.' George and Mark looked at him questioningly, but he shook his head. 'It's relevant to something I want to talk to you about tonight. You're coming to eat?'

'Try and stop us.' George felt a flutter of excitement at the thought of more revelations to come, and he couldn't suppress a smile of anticipation as he followed the others out into the fragrant, sunny courtyard.

The three women were sipping iced lemon tea from flasks, and fanning themselves as they chatted quietly. The men joined them, and Mark put a hand on Denise's shoulder.

'What are those types of eclipse called again?'

She blinked at the seemingly off-the-wall question, but immediately supplied, 'Full, partial, and annular.'

'That's the one.' He dropped a kiss on her head. 'Thanks, doll. Uri, it's the annular eclipse I was thinking of.'

'Great. I'll go to the library this afternoon, while Maya's preparing dinner.'

'Are we having that crispy rice thing again?' George wanted to know.

'It's called tahdig,' Maya said.

'Well I'll say ta, and I definitely dig it!' George rubbed his hands. 'I call dibs on any leftovers.'

Karen prodded him. 'Always the stomach first, with you! Anyway, what's all this about eclipses?'

'I'll explain it all tonight,' Uri promised. 'For now, I suggest a late lunch and a freshen-up. You'll come over at seven, for eight?'

Maya sat on the patio, under the canopy, sipping at a glass of Adom Atik and enjoying a cooling evening breeze. She never tired of this view from the hilltops of Nu'eima, looking down onto Jericho city and the Jordan valley, beautifully framed by palm trees. The patio was looking particularly good too, with banana, orange, lemon and grapefruit trees on either side, and Maya's own potted herbs dotted around.

She heard footsteps behind her, and Uri's voice drifted out from the spacious villa.

'Something smells delicious.' He put his hands on her shoulders, and she covered one of them with her own.

'I haven't cooked brisket in a while, and I know it's one of your favourites.'

'You're amazing. The perfect wife and friend, and beautiful too.' He bent and kissed her neck, and his voice took on a teasing note. 'I chose well with you.'

Maya turned, seeing the impish grin on his face. 'You forget I was the one who allowed you to choose me!' She felt his lips curve in a smile as he kissed her again.

After a moment she pulled back reluctantly. 'Do you think they'll understand?'

'Understand?'

'What we're going to tell them tonight.'

'Don't worry, mami. They might not believe, but they'll understand. They're smart people. I put forward a good case to Eegool, and they're happy for us to invite the others to join us.'

'I hope so,' Maya said, turning back to look out over the vista before her. 'I would dearly love for them to work with us properly, but I'd hate for anything to spoil our friendship. They're good friends, I care deeply for them all.'

'And so saying,' Uri gestured towards the road. 'Here they come.'

The Jeep CJ might be battered, it might be old, and it might give the impression it would never complete the journey on which it had embarked, but so far it had never let them down. Mark braked in the dusty driveway and the jeep rattled into silence. They all climbed out, stopping to look down across the valley before going into the house; since Jericho was the lowest city on Earth, anywhere they went they looked down on it. An amazing sight.

Karen gave George a grateful smile as he hung back to walk with her up the steps. 'You can go ahead, I don't mind.'

'I know you don't. But I want to walk with you.' He gave her waist a squeeze, and her smile widened. His solicitousness hadn't come as a surprise, exactly, but it still touched her. By the time they reached the patio Mark and Denise were already sitting down with Maya, and Uri emerged from the villa with drinks for them all: a tumbler of iced lemon tea for Karen, and four more glasses and a bottle of wine for the others. He'd even draped a white napkin over his arm.

'Who's the new waiter then, Maya?' Mark asked with a grin.

Uri put the tray on the table, and handed out drinks to Karen, Denise and George.

Mark pulled a face. 'Oi, waiter, what about me?'

'I beg your pardon, sir?' Uri deadpanned.

'My wine.'

'Your... *wine*, sir?'

Mark scowled at the empty glass, and looked around at everyone else sipping their drinks and grinning. 'The waiting staff's shit here, I don't know why we keep coming back!'

'Because the chef's amazing, that's why,' George supplied, predictably enough and to everyone's amusement, and Karen coughed as her tea went down the wrong way.

'Yes, she is! But do try to only eat what's on your own plate this time, or we'll never get asked back!'

Denise held her glass up to catch the evening sunlight. 'Nice wine this, going down a treat.'

'I don't know how you do it, Maya,' Karen said. 'Honestly. You work like mad all week, and we've been out for hours in the baking heat today, but your place is spotless, the food smells amazing, and you sit there looking as if you've spent the day at a beauty salon.'

Maya flushed with shy pleasure. 'I would be a bad hostess if it were any other way,' she said, then added with a little grin, 'plus, the wine helps.'

Denise chuckled. 'Wouldn't help me, I'm a shit hostess! I'd be happy to cook for you all again, but my kitchen would still look like a bomb's hit it, my hair would be all over the place, and I'd be three sheets to the wind.'

'Three… what?'

'Sheets to the wind. It's an English sea-faring phrase, means crazy drunk.'

'Ah! We say fershnikit.'

'I like that better,' Karen laughed. 'I might have to start using it… George, why are you fidgeting?'

'I'm trying to sit still,' George said, 'but my stomach is edging towards that lovely smell.'

'Then let's take your stomach to the table,' Maya said, standing up. 'Come on, everyone, zazim! Oh, and Deni, you were a *fun* hostess! We really enjoyed that evening, it was wonderful. We just had backache from sitting on the floor to eat.'

'Sadly the only way we could all eat together in our poky little villa,' Denise said, looking around in admiration as they followed Uri indoors. 'Still, I thought, if it's good enough for the Japanese, and the Indians, it was good enough for us!'

'True enough,' Mark said, 'but I'll bet the Japanese and the Indians don't have to lug drunken, snoring wives from the garden shrubbery to the bedroom!'

The good humour continued throughout the meal, and when they'd finished eating Karen put her spoon down with a sigh. 'That was a fabulous meal, thanks, Maya. The sprog and I are stuffed.'

The others sounded their agreement, and followed George in raising their glasses to Maya.

'My pleasure.' She looked at Uri, silently urging him to broach the main subject of the evening, eager to get it out of the way.

Uri cleared his throat. 'So, what's new on site?'

'Nothing much.' George grimaced. 'And our patron is getting impatient. Shay told us that if nothing of importance is found by the end of the month, he's pulling the funding.'

'Understandable, I suppose,' Uri said. 'But I know how you must feel. He knows nothing of the tablets, of course. I suppose that means you'll all be going back to England? Inevitable, but a shame.'

George nodded. 'We don't want to leave just yet, although naturally I'd prefer our son to be born at home.' He picked at the crispy rice leftovers, caught Karen's little grin, and crossed his eyes at her to make her laugh.

'I'd love to see the Beatles,' Deni put in, 'and wear my mini-skirt again, and get a colour TV. But saying that, I don't want to leave yet, either. Israel's such a beautiful country, and we'd miss you.'

Maya spoke slowly. 'We'd miss you too. But...' she hesitated, 'there is a way you could stay a while longer, at least until your visas expire.'

The four guests sat up a little straighter and exchanged glances. 'How?' Mark asked.

Maya turned to Uri, who took up the narrative. 'We belong to an organisation called Eegool. Have you heard of it?' None had. 'It's built up over many years, and we have several patrons within it. The funding is granted for the finding and safekeeping of archaeological artefacts relevant to our own beliefs.' He looked at each of them in

77

turn. 'We would welcome your expertise, and we would fund any future digs.'

'Ah,' Mark said. 'That explains your interest in archaeology.'

There was a low buzz of excitement at the table now, and Maya relaxed a little. Uri nodded.

'Yes. However, before you consider this offer, I must warn you – there is a larger organisation. Very powerful people. It's called Veritas, and they put all their resources into stopping us.'

'Badly named then,' Denise said bluntly. 'Call yourself *truth*, and then try to stop it coming out? Goes against the grain a bit.'

'Why *are* they trying to stop you though?' Mark wanted to know.

'Partly because some of the evidence we've found has the potential to end the fighting between Jews and Arabs, which they don't want.'

Karen was puzzled. 'Why would anyone want to stop that from happening?'

'Because peace isn't profitable,' George said, his expression unusually grim.

'Exactly.'

'How can the discovery of this evidence help?' Karen asked.

'Well, for instance Amnon gives a clear description of the location of the biblical Mount Sinai. It's Mount Hira, which is on Arab soil, and only Muslims are allowed to visit. Now, if we could prove this to be true, we might be allowed to visit too, and share a sacred place. It could be one step closer to peace. Veritas don't know of this, but that's just to give you an example.

Maya twirled her wine glass thoughtfully. 'Amongst the artefacts we protect, we have some small sections of tablets that record part of Maor's life. Including his experience in the desert.' She held up a hand to stay the tide of questions she could sense coming from their English guests. 'It's not complete, and until you discovered Amnon's tablets we had no idea who Maor even was.' She took a sip of wine, gathering her thoughts. 'The other important find is a stone tablet that was found on a Shiloh dig, also written in cuneiform. A prophecy. From your translation, Karen, we now believe this to be the prophecy Amnon recorded for Moses.'

She watched Uri pick up a folder from the sideboard, and when she looked back, Karen was staring at her with wide eyes. 'Why didn't you tell us about this before? It's amazing! Can we see it?'

Maya shook her head regretfully. 'We really wanted to tell you, but our work is classified. We had to wait for approval from Eegool before we could discuss it with you.'

Uri gestured to Denise and Mark to move their plates aside, and then opened the folder. He took out two photos and laid them side-by-side, where they looked incongruous among the modern paraphernalia of a hearty meal. 'This is the tablet.' He pointed. 'And this is the translation. We've not been able to work out a time frame for the prophecy. It tells of another twin birth, but we think it must refer to sometime in the future.'

'Why?'

'Because it's supposed to happen when Muslims and Jews fight overseas, and that has not happened. Yet.'

Karen went around the table to look at the photos, and read the translation out loud. 'When Ishmael and Isaac fight overseas, twins shall be born to the sons of God, under a halo. The spirit shall awaken and they shall be born unto Levites in the Holy Land. As foreigners they shall meet to protect my children and guide them to the truth.' She looked up, her eyes shining at this new discovery. 'I believe this was written by the same person, yes. It's very similar to the one prophesising Moses and Maor's births. Where's the tablet?'

Uri's face darkened. 'It was another item stolen from a site. We're lucky the professor who discovered it had the foresight to photograph it, and to keep the photos safe. It would be prudent of us to do the same, including notes and journals, since you won't be able to take any of them home with you. These, amongst other finds, are stored at our Mevo Shiloh base, an abandoned IDF base converted for our use. I'll take you there soon.'

While the others talked among themselves, Karen picked up the photo of the tablet and studied it. Maya saw her eyes pass slowly over it, as if absorbing the very ink with which it was printed.

'We do not expect you to believe in this the way we do,' she said earnestly, 'but we hope you will join us in our search for more evidence.'

'We're archaeologists, Maya,' Mark assured her. 'Our job is to find evidence to prove such things, whether we believe or not is irrelevant. I think I speak for us all when

I say we would love to help you. It's got my curiosity going like Billy-o!'

Denise agreed. 'I'm definitely up for joining Eagle.'

'It's Eegool,' Maya corrected with a smile. 'It's the Hebrew word for circle, the symbol of eternity. But Eagle's good too, since it's the symbol for immortality.'

'I'd like to talk it over with Karen first,' George said. 'We're honoured, of course, by your invitation Uri, and it's such an exciting prospect. But we have other responsibilities to consider before we decide.'

'Of course.' Mark subsided. 'Got a bit carried away there, mate, sorry.'

George shook his head. 'I agree with what you said, though. Facts are our business. However, who's to say what's true and what isn't? There's not much that can be proven one hundred per cent either way. And even when we find evidence it's still open to different interpretations.'

Karen put the photo down. 'You're right that Ishmael and Isaac signify Arabs and Jews. The Holy Land would be here, in Israel. The translation of the word 'halo' isn't entirely accurate, but not incorrect either.'

'No?'

'It should be "ring of light," not "halo." Although both mean the same thing, we've just become used to a halo being associated with something holy rather than a natural occurrence. Amnon used this terminology.'

'Ah!' George looked at Uri. 'Now I see why you got all excited when I mentioned an annular eclipse.'

Uri nodded. 'I spent a lot of time at the library this afternoon, and discovered that this eclipse occurs once a year. It's only visible in certain parts of the world at certain times, and always falls on a new moon.'

'New moon, new beginning,' Deni said. 'A new birth! It's all starting to make sense now. But if this thing *is* going to happen, how will you know who the twins are? Supposing the prophecy is real, of course.'

Maya began clearing the table, ordering her thoughts as she did so. The others helped, listening with increasing interest as she told them that, according to statistics, Israel had the highest instances of multiple births in the world. 'And yet,' she added, 'no twin births have been recorded in thousands of years in our ancestral line, the Levites, descendants of Levi. Not that we can find.'

'So you're from Moses's line?' Karen asked. She sat down and pulled the photos towards her.

'Like many thousands, perhaps millions.' Maya sat down opposite her. 'And no twins? That's a strange phenomenon in itself. But the prophecy says twins *will* be born to this line again. At a particular time. According to our beliefs it will be a time of immense wonder... how could it be otherwise?'

'Of course.' But Karen's attention seemed to have been pulled back towards the photos again, and she sounded distracted.

'The twins will be protectors,' Maya went on. 'They will do good things. *Great* things.'

'But they will need their own protection,' Uri added. 'The protection of Eegool.'

'If history were to repeat itself, our enemies will also be aware of these details, and the twins' lives will be endangered.' Maya fiddled with her wine glass, in which a small amount still remained, staring at it as if it held the solution to their problem. 'We think the danger will come from Veritas, and that they are the ones who stole the Shiloh tablet. Which means they have also been able to translate the prophecy.'

Uri nodded. 'And going back to the part about the fighting overseas; I've written down the dates of all upcoming annulars covering the next ten years. I suppose that's all we can do for now. As I said before, Arabs and Jews haven't fought overseas, not yet anyway. So it's something we must look out for in the future. At least we have a focus, a warning.'

Maya was about to speak to Karen, to ask her if she'd been listening to what was being said, but before she could do so her friend looked up from the photograph.

'That part of the professor's translation is wrong.'

'Wrong?'

'Definitely. It's an understandable mistake, but the part that mentions "fighting overseas" should actually read, "war over water." Does that mean anything?'

Maya and Uri's eyes locked, and Maya's heart began to beat hard. She lifted a hand to her mouth, her mind working almost too fast, her thoughts tripping over themselves. Uri ran from the room, leaving the others looking at each other in bemusement, and returned in a moment with a handful of notes.

'Karen,' he muttered, 'you're a genius!' She looked at him blankly, and he tapped the papers with a shaking finger. 'It changes everything. *Everything!*' In answer to her continued questioning look, he said, 'This year there have been serious border clashes between Israel, Syria and

83

Jordan. They're fighting for control of water from the River Jordan! Not *fighting overseas*, but a war, over water! It's this year. The annular eclipse this year is due to fall on 23 November, between 1:24 am and 07:04 am…' He blew out a harsh breath and his voice dropped. 'That's in two months' time.'

Chapter Six
The Fathers

George looked from Maya to Uri and back again, unease gnawing at him now, and suppressing his earlier sense of discovery. 'Why's all this happening now?'

'Now?'

'All these coincidences: us all being here to work on the Jericho site, meeting you two, the discovery of Amnon's tablets, not to mention Karen being able to decipher them… And now, if the Shiloh prophecy is to be believed, it's all going to come true while we're still here!'

'Maybe it's fate,' Uri said. 'You're right, it's a lot to take in, and in such a short time.'

'I don't believe in fate.' George's voice was tight. 'The idea that someone or something has any control over me, and my actions. *My* choices.' He caught Karen's troubled look, and moderated his tone. 'Sorry. I just don't like it.'

Maya spoke up again, and she sounded eager to soothe. 'Maybe destiny is a better word for all this. We might have all been destined to be together here, now, so everything could come together just like this. I mean, we've all made our own choices, and acted independently, yet here we all are.'

Denise nodded. 'Then maybe the best word to describe it is simply… *luck*.'

George shot her a grateful look. 'That's more like it.'

'Okay.' Mark sat forward, moving his glass so he could link his fingers as he frowned. 'So, if you already have artefacts in storage at Shiloh, why did we move Amnon's tablets here to your basement, to be stored?'

'Basements are quite rare in Israel,' Uri said. 'We thought the tablets would be safer here until the site closes down. Eventually they will be transferred to the Mevoh Shiloh base too.' He put the photos back together and shuffled them into his folder. 'Tonight though, I have other things I'd like to discuss with you.'

'Other things?' George's head was already spinning, but he noticed Karen didn't look surprised.

'Of course,' she said. 'Maya mentioned something about alternative forms of conception.'

Uri picked up the open wine bottle and offered if around. 'Amnon mentions the sons of God. We, at Eegool that is, believe we know what this means.'

'I seem to recall the expression *sons of God*,' George said. 'We're the sons of man, so do I assume we're talking about divine intervention?'

'Shall we go outside?' Uri gestured towards the open patio doors, where a fragrant breeze lifted the curtain as if the evening beckoned them once again into its cool twilight. 'We can talk properly out there.'

'Good idea.' Denise shot Maya a grin. 'I can see you itching to get these dishes washed. Come on, out of sight, out of mind.'

Between them they carried glasses, jugs of iced juice, and a large wooden bowl of fruit, out to the patio, where they settled into the comfortable furniture ready to continue talking.

Uri sat back in his seat and crossed his legs; he looked ready to talk all night. 'The sons of God are angels that visited us from time to time and impregnated the daughters of Man. Genesis describes the offspring as Heroes.'

'The Nephilim?' Mark asked. 'Is that what you're talking about?'

'Yes.' Uri selected a pomegranate from the bowl and patted his pocket for his knife. 'The angel's spirit entered the male body prior to intercourse, and part of their genetic coding was added later, during fertilisation.'

'And no-one realised?' George knew he sounded sceptical, but he was aware of Karen's hand smoothing the bump of their child, and this talk was making him uncomfortable.

Uri shrugged and sliced the fruit in two. 'Sometimes, because of the possession, the man was unaware he had had intercourse. Of course this left some women in a spot, being pregnant by a man who denied having lain with her.'

'Well no wonder Mary claimed she was a virgin, if Joseph was denying having been anywhere near her.' Karen arched her back and grimaced. George was about to ask if she wanted to go home, but Denise was sitting forward eagerly now, and he knew it would be pointless.

'So,' Denise pressed, 'did these angels keep coming back because they had such a great time with us, or was there another reason?'

'They were trying to help us,' Maya said. 'Help us spread out from where mankind was all grouped together.

The angels did something, something that helped us adapt and survive.'

George was unable to suppress a mild snort. 'The *angels* did that?'

'George!' Karen hissed. She turned back to Maya, leaving him feeling reprimanded and foolish. 'Go on, Maya.'

Maya bit her lip and avoided George's gaze. He felt bad, but… *angels*? They were scientists! They'd witnessed evolution first-hand, through countless digs and discoveries!

'They also gave some of us part of their spirit,' Maya went on, 'but over the generations it kept dying out. However—'

'If your theory is correct,' George interrupted, 'after all these attempts to ensure a part of their… spirit survived, the angels just concentrated on Levi's tribe. Why's that?'

'*George!*'

'Actually that's a good question,' Uri said. He seemed to sense the tension, and smiled at everyone, reminding them they were all friends. 'We don't know the answer, but the question would be asked no matter which tribe or race of people.'

'I'm a bit confused,' Denise confessed. 'If the thing itself died out, why didn't the human race revert to the way they were, just sticking to one place?'

'Two separate issues,' Uri said. 'One was the catalyst for a new mutation in our evolution, the other was the selective donation of part of its spirit, or genetic coding if you prefer. That's the part that's mentioned in the prophecies, and because of the laws of genetics, that part can die out.'

'But why's it always twins?' Karen asked.

'It might be that the spirit was too strong for one person, so it had to be divided.' Maya smoothed her skirt over her knees and seemed to be gathering her thoughts. 'There have been many great men in Levi's line of descent; we have kept genealogical records going back thousands of years.'

Karen frowned. 'Weren't the records destroyed when the Romans burned down the temple in Jerusalem?'

'Many people believe so, but the records were taken to safety before the fire broke out.'

Mark spoke up. 'How can this spirit be laid to sleep, then re-awoken at will? Are you saying it's controllable?'

'We don't know,' Uri said. 'There are so many questions that can't be answered. At least, not yet. We simply trust that one day they will be.'

'So going back to your association with Eegool,' George remembered the honour that was being extended and shook off his sceptical tone with an effort. 'Since we've been invited to join you, we can assume it's not Jewish-based?'

'Not at all,' Uri assured him. 'Our membership covers every race and belief-system, it's what was intended at the start of it all. Eegool members agree on every point we've discussed here, except for one.'

'Which is?'

'Some believe it's all God's intervention,' Maya said, 'sending his angels to save us. Others hold it to be the plan of a higher being or beings, and maybe they were the original creators, the Fathers.' Her face took on a hopeful look that was almost fierce. 'But despite this division we are *all* united in the hope that the artefacts, along with the discovery of Mount Sinai, can be used as negotiation in peace talks.'

Denise looked less convinced. 'It's a wonderful idea, Maya, and I'm sure we all hope that one day the world will be at peace. But I'm a bit sceptical. I mean, no matter what you do there will always be shitty people out to ruin things. I don't want to offend anyone, and obviously I respect your beliefs, but I'm not a believer, and neither is Mark.' She smiled to take the edge off her words, and George silently thanked her for saying exactly what he was thinking, but in a far nicer way than he'd so far managed.

'That said,' Denise went on, her smile turning into a grin, 'this has got to be one of the most bloody interesting things I've ever heard, I'm definitely up for discovering more.' She looked at Mark, who nodded.

'Hear, hear! We'd love to join you.'

Maya visibly sagged with relief. 'Thank you! You've no idea how much that means to us. And as for what you say, you absolutely do not need to believe in a god of any kind to believe in all this. Indeed it's often helpful to have another viewpoint, and some of our current members are atheist.'

Karen looked across at George. 'I'm certainly interested too, but George and I need to discuss it together first.'

'Of course,' Maya said. 'I want to thank all of you for your respect, and your consideration.'

George felt a flush of remorse, but Maya's smile was for him too, and he acknowledged it with a nod. 'Regarding the prophecy,' he said, 'I assume, in your professional capacities, you'll have access to the details of any multiple births that occur during the annular eclipse?'

'We will,' Uri said. 'Or we hope so, as long as the births take place in a hospital. We hope that'll be enough, and it'll be the duty of all Eegool members to ensure the safety of these children.'

'Well,' George said, looking around at the others, 'you've given us a lot to consider, and I think I speak for us all when I say we're honoured to have been taken into your confidence. I have a feeling we'll be talking about this a lot over the next few—'

'Ooh!' Denise broke in, 'I've just had a thought. Your brat's due around the time of the next annular eclipse, isn't he?'

'Roughly,' Karen said. 'But he's just one brat, not two.'

'Well, stranger things have happened,' Denise grinned. 'Tell you what, Kar, if you give birth to the next prophets and think I'm calling you Holy Mother Karen, you've got another think coming.'

Amid the laughter that followed, Karen shifted in her seat to ease an ache in the small of her back. George saw it, and rubbed her arm gently,

'Time to go?'

She shot him a grateful look, and the four guests began to gather their belongings together in readiness for leaving. George disappeared into the house to find his jacket, and Karen fished the jeep keys out of her bag and was already jingling them with mild impatience when he re-joined them outside. Mark and Denise were snuggled up on the back seat of the jeep, and Maya and Uri stood with their arms about each other, watching Karen wriggle behind the steering wheel, with little smiles and winces of sympathy.

Driving away from the hilltop house, back towards Jericho, the Mount of Temptation stood to their right, silhouetted against the evening sky and towering over them all. For once no-one exclaimed at the beauty of the night; the evening had left them all with a lot to think about. Eventually Denise broke the silence.

'Wow, that was… heavy.'

Karen nodded, her eyes on the road. 'And talking of heavy, that's probably going to be the last time I run you lot anywhere in this. I'm going to be waddling like a duck soon, and my belly-button's going to turn inside out.'

'Yuck, gross.' Denise belched and Karen laughed.

'Hark who's talking!'

George sighed. 'So, do we go along with this Nephilim theory then? It doesn't sit well with me, I'm afraid… I mean, *angels*? I prefer to keep my feet well and truly embedded in reality, you all know me,'

'We do, darling,' Karen said, 'but who are we to say what's real and what isn't? Science and technology are moving so fast nowadays, maybe in our child's lifetime these things can be properly investig… George!' From the corner of her eye she had seen him reach into a paper bag that lay between his knees, and pull out a piece of crispy rice. 'You didn't steal the leftovers, did you?'

He popped it into his mouth, keeping his eyes facing front. 'Nope. Maya gave them to me when I went back in for my jacket. She understands my stomach.'

'We all understand your stomach, mate,' Mark put in. 'it's you we don't always understand!' He grinned as George twisted in his seat and pulled a face. 'You told us yesterday that you and Karen had been working on some parts of Amnon's story,' he went on, 'and you said you were looking into Maor's journey, right?'

George nodded. 'Moses travelled through the land of Sinai, around the Red Sea to Midian where his wife and children lived; it was Maor who led their people to the Promised Land, via the wildernesses of Shur and Zin.'

'And you were looking at what?'

'The geography of that whole area, really. It's near the Med, and in that area the parting of the waves could actually have been a tsunami.'

Mark nodded thoughtfully. 'That makes sense, more so than it happening at the Red Sea. I could give you a hand if you like, check out the wind factors around the delta.'

'That'd be great, thanks.'

'What interests me,' Karen said, negotiating the narrow street towards the villa, 'is the part where Amnon writes how everyone was frightened when they saw Moses wasn't alone, even though they knew he was.'

'And the eclipses,' Denise put in 'They seem to play an important part in this whole thing, don't they? But if you remember, Amnon didn't describe that one on the mount as a ring of light, but a ring of fire in the heavens.'

'Meaning?'

'I'm thinking what we're talking about here is a total eclipse, and the ring was the sun's corona. If there was anyone watching it they could have ended up with serious retinal damage.'

Karen smiled. '*You'll* end up with serious retinal damage if you don't cut down on the vino, Deni!'

'Well I reckon if anyone's in danger of going blind, it's the boys… if you get my drift!'

'Everyone always gets your drift,' Mark pointed out, and the pair of them dissolved into tipsy laughter on the back seat as she poked him in the ribs.

Karen frowned as they neared the villa, peering through the windscreen; everything was pitch black. 'That's odd…'

Denise leaned forward between the front seats. 'I thought you were going to leave the lights on? I can't see a bloody thing.'

'I thought I did,' Karen muttered. 'Sorry, folks.'

George took her arm as they made their way up the dark path, and although Mark did the same for Denise, Karen couldn't help reflecting that she would have done better alone; after all that excellent wine Uri and Maya had provided, she was steadier on her feet than anyone. When they finally reached the front door George let go of her and began patting his pockets for the keys, and through the heavy shadows she could see Mark was doing the same.

'You must have got them,' George said.

'No, you have,' Mark argued.

Karen took them from her bag and jangled them in front of the men's faces. 'Both wrong. Come on.' She led the way indoors and switched on the light, and while Denise went to make coffee and Mark turned on the air conditioner, Karen and George settled on the sofa with identical sighs of relief and then chuckled at one another.

'That was an evening I'll never forget,' Karen said. 'My head's spinning, I'll need to jot down some notes or I'll never sleep.'

'I'll get your notebook for you,' George offered. 'You stay put.'

It took him three attempts to stand up, and Karen eventually gave him a helping hand by pinching his behind. He leapt to his feet with a yelp, and turned a baleful eye on her, but she just smiled sweetly and saw his lips twitch in response.

'Thank you,' she said, and closed her eyes in the bliss of relaxing in familiar comfort. She heard George rummaging on the messy table that held all their notes, folders, books and other paperwork. They really should tidy up. Sometime.

'I can't find it,' he said at length. 'Did you leave it on the table?'

'Yeah, on top of the photo folder.'

'Photo folder…' there was a pause, and more rustling of papers. 'Nope, can't find that either. You must have left them somewhere else. The bedroom maybe?'

'I don't remember seeing them there when I got changed,' Karen levered herself off the sofa with a groan and joined him. 'Might have put them in the bedside table drawer, though, with the journal we were looking at the other evening.'

'Okay.'

He went off to look, and Denise brought the coffees through. Karen shoved aside some books to make a space and just as Denise put the tray down they heard a shout of alarm from the bedroom.

'Come here, you lot, you need to see this!'

They squeezed themselves into the tiny bedroom, and Karen immediately saw what George had found; the window frame was damaged, and the window wouldn't close properly. Denise drew a sharp breath, and Mark swore.

'Someone broke in while we were out,' George said grimly. 'Now we have to find out if they've taken anything.'

'Oh no…' Karen went back out to the lounge, to look again amongst the organised chaos on the table.

Denise rushed off to her own room and reported nothing missing from there, and Mark soon decided nothing had been taken from anywhere else in the villa, but Karen's heart was sinking further the more she searched.

'They've gone. The photos, and my notebook.'

'Shit,' Mark breathed. 'Look, before we panic let's all check everywhere.'

'There's nowhere else to look, Mark,' Denise pointed out. 'Everything was on this table, you know that. We need to call the police.' She lifted the telephone receiver and began to dial.

'Wait!' George pressed the cut-off button. 'What are you going to say? That someone's broken in, and stolen pictures and notes of one of the most significant and valuable finds in history? A find we're not supposed to know about and that hasn't been reported to the authorities?' He shook his head. 'We'd be arrested and charged with antiquity theft before you could blink.'

'Well shouldn't we at least call Uri?' Karen felt sick at the loss, but the thought that someone had crawled through her bedroom window and then had their dirty, thieving fingers all over their precious paperwork was just as bad.

George took her hand and squeezed it. Everyone had sobered up very quickly, it seemed, and his voice was gentle. 'No, love. It's late, there's nothing he could do now. We'll tell him in the morning.' He sighed, and his expression darkened again. 'Damn, someone must have suspected we've found something. I bet this was Shay's work.'

Mark's brow lowered and his jaw was jumping. 'The bastard. Coming in here and taking our stuff. All our work... I'll kill him.'

'Not if I get to him first,' George said. 'This'll get back to Veritas... I'll bet they were the ones who made sure we were hired in the first place. Now they'll know everything we know.' He shook his head. 'I don't know why I didn't suspect something before. How could a private dig obtain excavation permits? Digs are normally conducted by Israeli military archaeologists... These people must have powerful connections.'

Denise put the phone down reluctantly. 'I can't believe the audacity of the sod. He's taken everything!'

'Maybe not quite...' Karen went back into the bedroom and checked the bedside table. With an exclamation of relief, she seized what she was looking for and returned to the others. 'They still don't know the location of Mount Sinai.' She showed them the photos and pieces of paper. 'George and I were working on these. They might have some of our notes, and most of the photos, but not these, or the full translation.'

'Maybe not,' Mark said tightly, 'but they've got enough. I'm guessing we'll be out of jobs by tomorrow.'

'These people might be dangerous,' Karen said, troubled. 'Are you two sure you want to get involved?'

'This is why I want us to think carefully before we join,' George told her. He turned away, his hand curled into a fist, and a moment later he had driven it into the wall. 'Damn!'

Karen flinched and put her hand on his rigid forearm, drawing him back to her.

Denise looked from him to Mark. 'You said it yourself, George, there's nothing that can be done now, so you two might as well calm down. You can fix the window in the morning.'

George nodded. 'And tomorrow we'll get more film, and take pictures of every bit of paperwork we have, as Uri suggested. This won't happen again!' He looked at his reddened knuckles, and Karen gave him a sympathetic smile.

'Well,' Denise said, sounding calmer herself now, 'It's bloody lucky you two were working on that stuff – at least we have something Veritas doesn't, which puts us ahead if only by a narrow margin.'

Karen went back to the sofa and George sat down beside her. She could feel the tension in his frame as she leaned against his shoulder, and covered his swollen hand with hers where it lay along his thigh.

'So,' he said, 'if we *are* out of jobs tomorrow, I assume you two will join this organisation with Uri and Maya.'

'Mark and I have decided Eagle's a good fit for us… yeah, I know it's *Eegoooool,* but you have to admit Eagle sounds better.'

'It does when you add about fifty extra 'o's to the proper word,' Karen pointed out, but she couldn't help smiling.

'We'd carry on our work, albeit on a different site,' Denise went on, 'and research something truly fascinating at the same time. We want to be part of this amazing discovery.' Her eyes were shining now. 'See it through to the end. It's so exciting! And we have no responsibilities but each other, so what the hell!'

'Yeah.' Karen couldn't deny a little twinge of envy, but a timely push from the baby banished it. How could she want anything else? 'I do see the attraction, but everything's changed for us now, we'll soon have this little one to think of.' She squeezed George's hand. 'I think you might join up, but I know you'd put your foot down on me doing the same – not that I'd blame you. Maybe I could help out unofficially, in a research capacity? I wouldn't have to set foot on a dig that way, and I'd still be useful.'

George put an arm around her shoulders and kissed her temple. 'We'll see.'

Monday 22nd November. 11:40pm

Karen blinked awake, her heart racing for no particular reason… she hadn't been dreaming, so what had woken her so suddenly? She realised she had curled into a ball during sleep, and as she moved to straighten she felt a wetness along her thighs. A thrill of excitement and fear rippled through her, and she reached out to wake George – he looked so peaceful, snoring away there, but this was it, he couldn't sleep away this one!

'George! Wake up! My waters have broken!'

'Hmm?'

'We have to go to the hospital. Now!'

'Hosp…' He sat bolt upright and rubbed his eyes. 'Hospital? Okay, it's okay, sweetheart. I'll, um, I'll get dressed, you grab your bag.' He switched on the bedside light, and Karen moved to rise, but at the same moment as George flung back the covers, she felt the stickiness on her legs and knew it wasn't amniotic fluid at all…

'Oh God,' George breathed.

Karen looked down and her heart clenched in terror. The blood had matted her thin nightie to her legs, and the bed covers were drenched in it. The sheets glistened, and through the cramping pain that gripped her she could feel more warmth soaking into the sheet beneath her.

'No,' she whispered, 'something's wrong, don't let anything be wrong… George!' Tears burned on her cheeks, and her throat was tight, and by the time George had eased her to the side of the bed she could barely speak for the pain and the terror.

The door burst open and Denise came in, her expression cautiously excited at hearing voices and movement from the guest bedroom so late at night, but as her gaze fell on Karen she went white. She sat down, heedless of the blood that soaked her own nightclothes, and put her arm around Karen's shaking shoulders.

'It's going to be alright,' she said in a low, comforting voice. 'Really, Kar, it will be.'

Karen hitched a breath and tried to reply, but fear and pain had the upper hand and her voice wouldn't work. She gripped Denise's hand, knowing she was hurting her friend, but also knowing Denise wouldn't care. They sat in dread-filled silence as George stumbled around the room dragging on his clothes.

Mark came in, bleary eyed, wondering at the commotion, and George told him to call the hospital and tell them they were on their way in. Wordless and pale, Mark withdrew and did so, while George seized his keys and wallet and shoved them into the pockets of his shorts.

Then he came around the bed and Denise moved aside. Looking up, Karen could see tears standing out in her husband's eyes as he tried to look calm. For her. Despite the fear, she felt such a surge of love for him in that moment she could almost have smiled. He bent and slid a hand beneath her knees, then carried her as he'd once done a proud bridegroom carrying his bride across the threshold, but this time it was out into the night.

As George laid her gently on the back seat of the jeep, Karen looked back at the house and saw Denise standing in the doorway, her hands to her mouth, openly weeping for the first time Karen could remember.

George splashed water on his face, wishing it was cold enough to numb the rest of him. He raised his dripping face to stare into the men's room mirror, saw the haunted look in his own eyes, and blinked away yet more tears. He couldn't remember ever crying as much as he had once Karen had been taken out of his arms and into the operating theatre; he'd held it together for her as long as he could, but watching her disappear through those doors it was as if she'd taken his heart with her. Her and the brat, as she affectionately referred to it.

Mechanically, his mind on what might be happening in there, he washed as much of her blood off his hands and out of his shirt as he could. Emergency caesarean. They'd be cutting her open… he shook his head and braced his hands on the porcelain sink, lowering his head and waiting for the shuddering to pass. When he felt steadier he left the men's room, and found a pay phone to call Mark and tell him what was happening.

'We can't get hold of Maya or Uri,' Mark told him. 'But that's good, right? It means they must be working late at the hospital.'

'Keep trying them,' George said. 'They could be anywhere. On their way home, even.'

'Will do. We've ordered a taxi, but we'll keep calling Uri until it gets here. We'll be with you as soon as we can.'

George replaced the receiver and went to reception to ask if they could get a message to Doctor Malik, and then there was nothing left to do but wait. He sat in the waiting room, his hands clasped between his knees, and his eyes fixed with a kind of horrid fascination on the bits of dried blood he'd missed. Karen's blood. So, so much of it…

'George!' Uri hurried over to him, and he realised he'd been staring, with burning eyes, for around twenty minutes. His mind must have been going over and over what had happened, what might be happening now, but he couldn't remember a single thing.

He stood up. 'She's in—'

'I know, they told me. Listen, I know the surgeon well, and Karen's in the best possible hands, trust me.'

'How long will she be in there?'

'These procedures typically take about an hour.'

'Oh, God, Uri, you should have seen her. The blood…'

Uri put a comforting hand on his arm. 'I know, it's terrifying to see. The cause of it was the placenta separating prematurely, which is uncommon and not without risk, but I've spoken to the surgical team, and they assure me she's going to be fine.'

'If only I'd got her here sooner.'

'You couldn't have. Listen, you did everything you possibly could.'

'And the baby,' George muttered, as if he hadn't heard. 'Karen's waited so long for this, if anything goes wrong I don't know what she'll do. Or me. The baby will be fine, won't it?'

Was it his imagination, or did Uri avoid his gaze?

'They're doing all they can, George. We just have to wait now.'

It must have been half an hour longer, or thereabouts. George was hunched over on the waiting room chair, his arms folded, his gaze mindlessly following the pattern on the tiled floor. The inactivity became too much, and he stood up, arching his back and hearing the bones crack, and began pacing. Like every expectant father, he thought bleakly. Pacing the waiting room, only this time—

A movement from the adjacent corridor caught his eye, and he turned to see Uri coming towards him.

'How is she?' George blurted.

'Come with me.' Uri led him over to a secluded area. 'Karen's fine. They've given her a transfusion and she's being taken to recovery. You'll be able to see her very soon, I promise.'

George thought his legs might buckle under him, and absurdly he felt tears start into his eyes again. This time of relief and gratitude. 'And the baby?'

Uri fixed him with a long look, then guided him to a seat. 'Sit down, George. We need to talk about the baby.'

Part Three
Haverhill, Suffolk 2002/3

The dream of a mountain returned and it called to Moses. He left Zipporah and their two sons to trek along the shores of Al Bad. Turning inland, he eventually found the mountain on top of a mountain and knew it was the one in his dreams. He thought he saw a fire at its base but it was a stranger wearing the bright clothing of the Nubians. As they approached each other they knew they were brothers and had shared the same dream.

Climbing the mountain together, they came upon a cave and took rest there. They were awakened in the night by a bright light and that is when God told them both they had to return to Egypt to lead their people, and His children, out of slavery to safety and to a new land. This was his covenant with Abraham.'

'Maor had another dream in which he climbed the same mountain with his brother and heard the words of God. When he awoke, he was not in the place he had laid to sleep but walking around the land talking in a strange language.'

Excerpts from the writings of Amnon
2nd millennium BC

Chapter Seven
The Journals

Jen closed down the PC with an impatient little sigh; repeated Googling of dream websites had been useless, John's dreams didn't seem to fit into any of the categories she found; if they'd begun after his beloved aunt's death it might have been put down to grief, but that wasn't the case. It was an unsettling thought; May's death from the ruptured aneurysm was too close for comfort to her sister's susceptibility to violent headaches, and Jen didn't like where her thoughts were leading… a bit of fresh air might blow them away. Maybe John would return from his doctor's appointment today with good news.

She was just reaching her coat down from the hall peg when she heard a key sliding into the lock of the front door. John came in, looking tired and pale, and Jen put on her brightest smile.

'What are you doing home this early?' She kissed him, and he hung up his jacket.

'I've been signed off work for a week. Doctor Marsh has prescribed temazepam, which should help me sleep at least.' He took the bottle from his pocket and shook it.

'Have they said what they think's causing it?'

'Possibly stress. He wants me to go back in a week.'

'Is that it, then?'

John shrugged. 'Blood pressure was fine. I had a blood test to check sugar levels, and they're going to call with the result of that on Friday.' He belatedly realised she had her coat in her hand. 'Going out?'

'Just a bit of shopping,' she said, replacing it. 'It can wait. I'll make you a cuppa. It all sounds hopeful,' she added as they went through to the sitting room. 'I love you very much,' she added, squeezing his shoulder, 'you know that. We'll work this out.'

John sank into the sofa with a sigh of relief; exhaustion was written all over his face. As Jen passed him to go to the kitchen he put out a hand and caught hers.

'I love you too,' he said quietly. 'More than you know.'

She bent her head and kissed him again, this time more lingeringly. 'I'll make that cuppa,' she said at length, breaking away, 'and then leave you to enjoy some quiet time.'

John tugged her back to him. 'I know this has been hard on you too,' he said. 'I know you'd like it all to go away, and so would I. But I have to finish transcribing from those old photos. I need to.'

Jen nodded. 'I know.'

'I reckon it'll just take a couple more days, then it'll be done. It's really interesting, and I can't wait to go through it all with you.'

'John, it's—'

'Then I want to go through all your research with you. It might not seem like it, but I am interested. Honestly. I just have to do this first. Is that okay?'

'Of course it is,' she assured him. She smiled and brought his hand to her lips before releasing it. 'I'm actually looking forward to hearing all about it.'

It was late that evening when John finished transcribing his father's journal… more like a diary, really. Some of the photos hadn't developed, so there were pages missing here and there, but he was able to get most of it. His father's friend Mark's journal was more technical, and John read it, but didn't transcribe it. He put the photos of the completed pages, and any relevant pictures, into envelopes which he carefully labelled and put in the desk drawer.

The following day he worked on his mother's notes; the translations from the clay tablets they had found. He couldn't wait to find out what they had discovered, judging from his father's journal they had become involved in something odd, but amazing – in rising excitement he worked from the notes long into the evening, and finally e-mailed a copy of everything to Todd before shutting down the computer.

He found Jen in the sitting room, flicking through the TV guide, a newly-opened tin of Roses on the arm of the settee next to her. Unseen, John watched her for a moment, and the words building behind his lips died. She looked tiny against the big cushions. Cute, yes, in her comfies, but… lonely. Remorse overtook the need to blurt out what he'd learned, and instead he sat down next to her and put one arm around her while the other reached for a chocolate.

'You slept well last night,' Jen said, slapping his hand away. 'Oi, they're mine!'

'Yeah, I feel so much better for it too,' he said with a little grin. He nodded at the magazine. 'What are you looking for?'

'Just something to watch, but nothing's grabbing my fancy.' She tossed it aside.

'Well I know something that's taken mine.'

'Really?' Jen opened a coffee cream and wafted it under his nose. 'One of these perhaps? Or a caramel?' With a sly smile she whipped it away and popped it into her own mouth. 'Mmm!'

John snorted laughter and pulled her to him, lowering his mouth to hers and feeling her lips part; he tasted coffee as the kiss deepened, and she responded with enthusiasm and muffled laughter.

'If I'd have known it was my chocolates you're after I'd have dressed for the occasion!'

'Comfies work for me too,' John murmured, moving away and grabbing the waistband of her pyjama bottoms. 'And they're easier to take off.' He proved it, and moved to kneel over her, feeling her fingers twist into the front of his T shirt. She drew him down to her, and slid her free hand around the back of his neck; he could feel her breathing quicken as they kissed, and backed away just long enough to remove his own jogging bottoms before covering her body once again with his.

It had been a while since either of them had been so eager; John could feel the urgency building between them, and the temptation to lose himself in the moment was strong, but he tried to curb it for Jen's sake. When he looked down into her delicately flushed face he could see she knew what he was doing, and that she loved him for it. Wordlessly she raised her hips, pushing them against him, her eyes on his, telling him that all she wanted was to be with him, and that outweighed anything else. She urged him on silently, and with a deep sigh he went with her.

Later, lying in a breathless heap together, John tugged at Jen's Minnie Mouse pyjama top and grinned. She looked pointedly at his T shirt, and even more so at his socks, and rolled her eyes as they both laughed.

'We haven't done it like that for a while,' John said, realising neither of them had even considered the possibility one or both of the girls might come in. 'I'll take it slower next time,' he added, nuzzling her ear by way of apology.

'We haven't done it at all for a while,' she pointed out. 'Slow or fast, I don't care. That was amazing.' Her voice softened. 'I've missed you.'

'Me too.'

'Should we go up?'

'Probably a good idea, before we have company.' John kissed her again, tossed her pyjama bottoms to her, and followed her up to bed.

He awoke the next morning and glanced at the clock. 8am; he'd slept well again. His gaze slid from the clock face to the mug of lukewarm coffee beside it and he smiled at Jen's thoughtful gesture. He hadn't even heard her come in. A minute later he was padding downstairs in his dressing gown and slippers, remembering last night with a smile, and when he arrived at the kitchen door, the radio, and Jen's singing along to it, masked his already quiet footsteps.

The girls were finishing breakfast, scraping egg yolk up with the crusts of their toast, and they looked up as their father came in. He put a finger to his lips and pointed to where Jen stood at the sink, engrossed in scrubbing a stubborn stain from the frying pan. John crept across and snaked his arms around her waist, making her shriek and drop the pan, sending a wave of frothy water over them both.

'John!' she spluttered, wiping soap from her chin, and turned to face him. Her smile was even wider than his. 'Now look what you made me do!'

'Oops.' He grinned and drew her close, heedless of the drenched shirt that soaked his own. 'Someone's looking happy, and *very* pretty, this morning. Cat get the cream, then?'

Jen winked. 'Mmm, coffee cream…'

'What cat?' Holly broke in.

'What cream?' Hannah added. 'Are we getting a cat?'

'No,' Jen said, laughing.

'Then why did Daddy ask if it got the cream?' Hannah persisted.

Jen exchanged a look with John. 'It's just… an expression,' she said finally. 'A thing grown-ups say when we mean someone looks happy.' She slipped out of John's embrace but reached up to kiss him on the way. 'Now hurry up and get your coats, it's time for school.'

As the girls trailed off through the sitting room with their mother, John heard Holly's voice again. 'Mummy, why are there chocolates all over the floor?'

By the time Jen returned from the school run John had finished printing and arranging all his paperwork on the table. Everything he had learned, about Moses's twin brother Maor, the confusion over who had led the Israelites to the Promised Land, all left his head spinning. And then to learn about Veritas and Eegool, and his parents' and their friends' involvement…it was so much to take in.

'Are you ready for this?' he asked Jen.

'That good then?' She sat down opposite him. 'Let's hear it.'

As he talked he watched her eyes widen. The confusion over which Miriam had put the babies in the reed baskets, and which story had made it into the bible as truth, was particularly interesting to her. 'I thought it was Moses's sister?'

'Me too, but there was some question over whether she'd have been old enough. This was their aunt, who the sister was named for. The twins were found in separate places, and didn't meet up again until they were grown. The whole story is incredible!'

'How did they know it wasn't some kind of hoax?'

'Dad's friend Uri, the doctor, knew some people who were able to get the tablets dated and authenticated. He's also the one who got the first photographs of the tablets secretly developed so Mum could work on them.'

'But why all the secrecy? Surely archaeological finds are supposed to be made public for the benefit of everyone or am I being naive here?'

'I thought so too, but apparently not. Dad mentioned that every scrap of physical evidence from previous digs, at Jericho in particular, had either gone missing or been stolen. He was sure there were people trying to either sabotage, or hide, any significant finds. Hang on a minute.' He shuffled through the paperwork and found the part he was looking for.

'Listen to this. *They say that religion is man-made. I agree. And it's been used to exert control over the population; it's a business, that uses people's beliefs as an excuse to invade other countries for its own purposes and profit.*' He watched Jen's expression; she seemed as surprised as he'd been, by the vehemence in the words. 'It goes on to say, *"Countless acts of horrifying wickedness have been executed under the pretence of divine mandate. In our field, we constantly come up against religious organisations that fear any new evidence that may challenge long-held belief systems. There is a group of global elitists dedicated to keeping races apart, and I believe they are amongst us. It is for this reason that we have unanimously decided not to admit the existence of the artefacts at this time. They will be kept under the protection of our friends."*

'Wow,' Jen shook her head. 'Mind you, we've said a lot of the same things, that not all religions can be right. One of them can't have all the answers.' She looked uncomfortable. 'I didn't like that bit about the powerful organisation though. Is there any more about it in the notes, or who those other friends are?'

'Not much. Just those two groups, Eegool, the good guys, and Veritas, who are trying to stop them. It makes me wonder if that's what's behind Mum hiding those films in the attic.'

'Could be.'

'In which case, what we have here could be of immense value, and I haven't got a clue what to do with it.' John put down his notes and rubbed his eyes. 'I still can't work out why Mum would go to such lengths to get all of this out of the country secretly, only to hide it and never use it.'

'Maybe she intended to, but died before she could?' Jen glanced around, as if she expected the goons from Veritas to be looming behind her chair. 'I think, until we know more, we should keep this to ourselves.'

John nodded. 'Although I did email a copy to Todd. As a theologian I'd be interested to hear his views on it all.'

'That's different.'

'It's not just revelations about Moses and his twin,' John went on, 'it would be an amazing find anyway, purely because it's a written record, and the Hebrews of that time didn't have a written language. This Amnon was a special scribe, taught by the Egyptians.'

'And he's described the actual route of the *Exodus*, you said?'

'Yeah. The only problem is, the discoloration is so bad on some of these photos I can't read Mum's notes properly.

'I wonder where the actual tablets are now,' Jen mused.

'We might never know. To be honest I'm not sure I'd want to get involved in that side of things. I would've liked to have been able to read the full story though.'

'I know. It's fascinating.'

'It ends with Maor being banished back to Nubia, Moses losing it with his people, and Amnon recording a new prophecy. He was the one who recorded the commandments, in cuneiform—'

His phone pinged with a text message, and he picked it up. 'Todd. He says, "I read what you sent me. Is it a wind-up?" I'd better answer.' He tapped out the brief message: *Nope, 'fraid not!*

The reply came quickly. 'He wants to meet tonight, at the Rose and Crown. 8pm. Is that okay with you?'

'Of course. But alcohol doesn't mix well with sleeping tablets, just remember that.'

'Good point,' John said, gathering up his papers again. 'I'm driving anyway, I'll stick to Kaliber.'

The Rose and Crown was a sixteenth century coaching inn, with the generously-sized car park that went with its history. John parked up, and as he pushed open the pub door he heard cheering coming from the back of the room: quiz night. Typical. There were groups huddled around their tables, alternately whooping and groaning as the quiz master read out the correct answers, and the flashing, whistling and beeping of the fruit machines cut across the comfortable din. At the far end of the bar, Todd sat engaged in conversation with the barmaid, Sinead Gallagher, and John crossed the tatty floral carpet to greet them both.

Sinead smiled at him. 'Haven't see you for a while, John. Are you all okay?' Her voice, gentle as it was with its soft Irish brogue, lifted with practiced ease above the shouts of the quiz teams.

'All good thanks,' John said. 'I've missed your carveries, we must come again soon. You okay?'

'You must. I'm not too bad, my love. What can I get you?'

John ordered the non-alcoholic beer, and Todd raised an eyebrow as he picked up his own half-finished drink. 'Sinead, if it's not too busy could you keep the beers coming please? Put them on my tab.'

'No problem.' Sinead took John's money to the till. 'We've live music tomorrow night, if you fancy popping in.'

Todd moved away. 'Might just do that,' he called back.

John followed him to the back of the room, where there was a quieter spot and they could talk more freely. 'She likes you, you know,' he said, jerking his head back towards Sinead.

'What's not to like?' Todd threw him a grin. 'I like her too, she's a good girl. Pretty, smart, and a wicked sense of humour.'

'And?'

'We see each other now and again. It's fun, but I'm not ready for anything serious. Not yet, anyway.' He changed the subject. 'Why the Kaliber?'

'Sleeping tablets.'

'Ah. That explains why you're looking less deathly than you were last week. So, apart from catching up on your Zs, you've finished sorting out that stuff of your mum's.'

116

He shook his head. 'I'm totally gobsmacked if I'm honest. Really thought you were having me on.'

'Nope.' John told him what he and Jen had discussed. 'What do you think?' he finished, watching Todd's face carefully.

Todd didn't answer for a moment, then he pursed his lips. 'Okay. I agree with all the points you two have made, but there are even more that I don't think you've realised.'

'Such as?'

'For starters, with Biblical timelines being so confusing, no-one has ever been able to pinpoint the dynasty in which Moses was born. This Amnon clearly mentions the Pharaoh Akhenaten, who ruled during the eighteenth Dynasty, and stemming from that, other biblical texts could possibly be analysed more accurately. On the downside, I may have to relearn everything I teach.' He gave a rueful laugh. 'Not even kidding!'

John smiled. 'So what does this mean?'

'If we could only read the rest of your mother's notes, we could even confirm the location of Mount Sinai.' Todd gave a low whistle. 'John, mate, this work is as big a find as the Rosetta Stone, maybe bigger. There's just so much to this, it's mind-blowing!' He took a gulp of his beer, and John drank his, waiting.

'I read somewhere that a smaller tablet had been found on a dig in Shiloh,' Todd went on eventually, 'by Stefan Jakobsen, I think, a Danish professor. It would've been discovered before your parents' friend's found their tablets. Your mum might not have known about that one. It was a prophecy and also written in cuneiform.' He stared at the whitewashed ceiling and dark oak beams for a moment, though clearly not seeing them. Instead he was recalling the information.

'Amnon stated he wrote the commandments down for Moses, and they were transported to Shiloh for safety. He also wrote down a new prophecy, and that too was taken to Shiloh. These holy works were eventually to be taken to Jerusalem. The commandments have never been found, but…do you see what this could mean?'

John lowered his drink, his heart speeding up. 'The piece found by the professor was written by Amnon…it all ties in! Bloody hell! No wonder they were all trying to keep this find secret.'

Todd nodded. 'Reading between the lines, I'd say they put themselves in danger by not giving up the artefacts. Although I can't work out how.'

'I think someone on site was spying on them. Denise caught one of the workers going through Mark's paperwork, and he thought they were being too inquisitive. Perhaps someone found out what they'd discovered.'

'Makes sense.'

They both jumped as two fresh beers appeared at their elbows, and Sinead grinned.

'I don't think I've ever seen the two of you so serious!'

Todd doffed an imaginary cap. 'Much obliged, fair maiden. Do not be afeared, it is but a temporary phase, frivolity will resume shortly.'

Sinead forsook her own accent for a cockney one. 'An' thank gawd for it, sir.'

They laughed with her, and waited until she had retreated behind the bar, to continue their conversation.

Impatient, John leaned forward. 'So, what's the prophecy then?'

'I don't know.' Todd blew some of the froth away from the rim of his glass. 'I read about the find somewhere, saw a photo of the tablet and its translation, but I've searched all over the 'net and I can't find a damned thing. So frustrating.'

'It is odd,' John agreed, frowning. 'So many unanswered questions.' He brightened. 'But I'll bet this Doctor Malik would be able to answer some of them. I'll call the hospital where I was born, tomorrow. See if he still works there.'

'Good idea.' Todd took a long drink. 'My spidey senses are telling me not to breathe a word of any of this, not until we have a clearer picture of what we're dealing with.'

'That's what Jen and I think.'

'I even think we ought to go and pay a visit to this Doctor Malik, if you can get hold of him that is.'

'In Israel?' John stared.

'Would you be up for it?'

'I don't know. I'd never considered actually going there. Don't get me wrong, it would be good to see where Mum and Dad worked, and to hear about them from someone who knew them so well. But it's a long way to go, and there's no denying it's a troubled country.' He picked up the cardboard beer mat and idly began peeling the edges. 'Having said that, the more I learn about my parents, the closer I feel to them, if that makes sense. I'd have liked to have gone to Mount Hira.'

Todd shrugged. 'Well that wouldn't have happened anyway, unless you convert to Islam. Non-Muslims aren't allowed anywhere within the Mecca boundary line.'

'Really?' John sighed. 'I'd have liked to have seen the mountain in my dreams for real, it might have put an end to them. Still, I'll have to think about it. It bothers Jen and me that they might have got involved in something dangerous, and what if we stir it all up again?'

Todd downed his pint and slammed the glass down, his eyes shining. 'What if? Where's your sense of adventure, man? Come on, let's do it!'

John relayed the conversation to Jen when he got home. She frowned when he got to the part about Todd's suggestion that they travel to Israel, and muted the television.

'You've seen the news. That suicide bombing on a bus in Tel Aviv was only this month.'

'True, but Jericho's a tourist-orientated city. The Palestinian Authority goes to great lengths to make sure it's safe to visit. Besides,' he shrugged, 'I haven't decided I'm going yet.'

Jen gave him a sidelong look and got up to go to the kitchen. He followed her, sensing he hadn't yet appeased her, and he was right.

'Look,' she said at length, dropping tea bags into two mugs, 'the Israeli-Palestinian conflict has been going on all this time with *no* trust on either side. Maybe your father's right,' she added, 'those in power have done what they can to scupper the very idea of peace. It's just not profitable.'

She flicked on the kettle, and leaned against the counter top, facing him. 'I've been busy too, while you were out.'

'Oh?'

'Well, your story of Moses and Maor piqued my own interest in twins again. I Googled "twins in the Bible," and you won't believe what came up. Look.' She disappeared into the office and returned with some notes of her own. 'Right. Abraham was the patriarch of the Jews through his son Isaac, and the patriarch of Islam through his son Ishmael. Isaac had twin boys Esau and Jacob. Jacob's sons became the 12 tribes of Israel.' She looked at him to make sure he was following.

He nodded. 'Go on.'

'Okay. One of those tribes was Levi, into which Moses and Maor were born, and later Jesus, although on his mother's side which didn't count then.' She pulled a face. 'With Muslims, Jews and Christians all coming from the same ancestor, you would've thought they'd have more religious views in common, wouldn't you?' She sighed, and put the papers down as the kettle switched off. 'Anyway, there are some theories that Cain and Abel were twins, and from the translation of the Gnostic Gospels it's possible that Jesus might even have had a twin, called Thomas.'

John frowned, wondering if he was remembering correctly 'I'm pretty sure that name derives from the Aramaic for twin actually.'

'There you are, then! I know this may have no bearing on what was found at Jericho but how interesting is that? And did you know Vin Diesel and Keifer Sutherland are twins?'

121

John passed her the milk, and gave a snort of laughter. 'They're nothing alike!'

'Ha ha,' Jen said darkly, and dug him in the ribs as she passed his tea. 'They each have a twin sibling.'

He grinned. 'Well I don't know what Gnostic Gospels are, I've never heard of them.'

'Some Arab peasant found them in Egypt. Secret gospel texts, recording speeches from Jesus that no-one had known of before.'

'Such as?'

'He spoke of spiritualism, and enlightenment, more like the teachings of Buddhism than what we know of Christianity. So how come we know nothing about them?'

John cupped his hands around his tea mug, and gave her a bleak look. 'We're back to Dad's theory,' he said. 'The largest religions in the world, controlling everything; believing hand-picked stories from centuries ago, and denouncing anything that contradicts them. It seems nothing is allowed to change what certain people have decided fits their own religion.'

The next day was Friday. John checked the clock; Israel was two hours ahead, it was a perfectly acceptable time to ring, and he double-checked the number for the Ramallah Government Hospital. The receptionist unfortunately spoke little English, so she passed him over to someone else, with a brief word of explanation.

The voice was brisk. 'Mr Milburn? I understand you're trying to locate one of our doctors?'

'Please. His name's Uri Malik, he worked there in the mid-1960s, when I was born in your hospital.'

122

There was a long pause, and he could hear clicking in the background as the hospital records were interrogated.

Finally the voice came back. 'I'm very sorry, we have no doctor by that name currently working here. Since it was over 30 years ago it's likely he's retired. I couldn't give you any contact information in any case, naturally.'

'Of course.' John fought down the disappointment. 'I did hope you might be able to pass on my own details though.'

'If we could. Do you know anything else about him that might help?'

'Just that he lived near Jericho, and that his wife's name is Maya. She might've been my mother's midwife.'

Jen appeared in the doorway, her eyebrows raised. He shook his head, and returned to his conversation; the voice on the other end had brightened. 'Maya? Maya Malik? Indeed, I know of this lady, she was a well-respected midwife, and delivered my sister's children! Please, give me your email address and phone number, and I will see she gets the message. That's all I can do, I'm afraid.'

John flashed Jen a grin, and gave his details. 'Thank you so much, that's a great help. Please explain that I'm the son of George and Karen Milburn. They were all friends.'

'I will. Good luck, Mr Milburn.'

The connection was broken, and John was about to relay the latter part of the conversation to Jen when his mobile sounded. 'It's the surgery,' he said. 'Blood test results. Hang on.'

The surgery gave him the news he wanted; that his blood tests had all been returned normal. He gave a worried-looking Jen the thumbs up, then, guiltily aware he'd not told Jen he was asking for the additional test, he said, 'And the… other test?' From the corner of his eye he saw Jen frown, but he didn't meet her gaze.

'Yes, we have that result too. You are A positive.'

A cold, sick feeling crept up from John's stomach, into his throat, and he felt his jaw go tight. 'That's not possible… are you sure?' His voice came out hoarse.

'Quite sure, Mr Milburn, I did the test myself. You are definitely A positive.'

Chapter Eight
Christmas

Boxing Day 2002

'Who wants a snowball?'

Jen carried the jug into the lounge, and put it on the dining room table, brought in earlier by John and Todd, and extended to accommodate their guests. The pale yellow Advocaat was whipped to a froth with lime and lemonade, and dribbling down the side of the jug, and Jen caught the drip with her little finger and licked it; perfect. With the dishes out of sight in the dishwasher, and the plates and tubs of leftovers balanced precariously on one another in the fridge, it was time for the fun stuff: drinks and games.

The lounge looked especially pretty this year, with lights twinkling at the windows, cards on strings above the fireplace, and the Christmas tree draped in tinsel and overflowing with decorations; the girls had certainly outdone themselves on that.

The girls in question had spotted the snowball arriving on the table, and exchanged wide-eyed glances.

'Are we allowed some this year, Mummy?' Hannah asked.

Jen hesitated, but Holly put on her best smile. 'Pleeeeease?'

Jen gave in. 'If it's okay with your dad.' She looked at him, and he nodded. 'Go on then, get two extra glasses.'

In a flash they had returned, with their glasses held ready, and Jen laughed. 'Funny how fast you can move, when you want something!' She lifted the jug and poured, watching each twin's face grow bright with anticipation, and feeling a little pang for her own vanished childhood, when such a treat would be remembered for months to come and relayed with relish in the playground.

Her parents, Sue and Tony, were here as always, for Christmas, but this year the Milburns had also invited Todd, and he had brought a welcome surprise in the form of Sinead as his guest. The eight of them had just fitted snugly around the extended table for the traditional Boxing Day cold turkey, bubble and squeak, and an array of pickles, and now the eating was finished Sue rose and took hold of the edge of the festive table cloth. 'Put the jug on the sideboard, Jen or it'll stain your table.'

'You can leave the cloth, Mum,' Jen said, 'we'll need it for Left, Right and Centre. It cuts down the noise of the dice.'

'Ah, we remembered to bring our penny pots,' her father said. 'Is it still five 2ps each?'

Jen saw the twins mentally working out how much they could earn, and smiled. 'Yep. Everyone get your money ready, I'll just fetch some nibbles. Help yourselves to snowballs.'

'Can I have a glass of bubbly, dear?' her mother asked. 'You know I don't like Advocaat. Too slimy for me.'

'Can I give you a hand, Jen?' Sinead asked, filling her own glass.

'No thanks, I'm fine. John, could you come and open the Cava for Mum? It's got one of those stoppers that breaks windows.'

'He's looking for the dice,' Todd said. 'I'll do it.' He followed Jen to the kitchen, and she took a bottle from the fridge.

'So how's it going then?' She nodded towards the sitting room, where Sinead could be heard laughing with the girls. 'We're so glad you brought her, she's great.' She rummaged for some clean bowls for the snacks while Todd grasped the Cava bottle between his knees and began wrestling with the stopper.

'Yeah, she is. Thanks for inviting me, and being so welcoming to her.'

'I wanted to thank *you*, actually, for pulling John out of the gloom he'd sunk into. Finding out George wasn't his father—'

'Understandable.' Todd pulled the stopper out with a loud 'pop' and quickly set the bottle on the counter. 'I just gave him the "ungrateful git" speech, and reminded him how lucky he is. Blood means nothing, it's how you're loved that matters.' An expression of rare seriousness crossed his features, and Jen remembered his own childhood had not been a happy one. He cleared his throat and changed the subject before she could speak. 'So, are you sure you're fine with John and me going to Israel next year?'

Jen poured crisps into the waiting bowls, and nodded. 'I am now. I was worried at first, I won't deny it, but he needs to do it and I'm glad he's not going by himself.' She tore open another packet of crisps with her teeth. 'I know

127

he's going to find out about his parents, but it'll do him good to have some fun, too. He's become a bit—'

'Boring!' Todd gave an exaggerated yawn, patting his mouth.

'No!' Jen looked at him, exasperated. 'I was *going* to say, withdrawn. He's had a lot on his plate lately, and a lot of responsibility too. Something you seem to know nothing about,' she added.

'Touché, Madam.' Todd grinned. 'Look, you know I love that man like a brother, but… he has got boring, and that's not like him. So we need to get him out of whatever he's mired himself in.' He leaned in to kiss Jen's cheek, to take the sting from his words, and reverted to his former, light-hearted mood. He flung one arm dramatically ceiling-ward. 'And, without further ado, the bold Knights of Haverhill will begin their quest to the Holy Land, do battle with evil… uh, things, and bring back the sacred paraphernalia and… other stuff—'

'Oi!' John's voice cut through both the performance and Jen's laughter. 'We're ready! Todd, you're not doing the Knights of Haverhill again, are you?' He appeared in the doorway, rattling the dice in his hand. 'Come on, we've done a practice run for Sinead, since she's a newbie.'

For the next hour the house was filled with the sounds of excitement and laughter as they played, and alternate groans as Sue predictably won the first kitty, and cheers as Sinead won the second.

Todd put on a whiny voice to make the girls laugh. 'Beginner's luck,' he moaned. 'Not fair!'

128

'Ah, you're just a sore loser,' Sinead grinned, scooping the money into her pot. 'I must say, this is a great game.'

'We've played it for years,' John said, 'but only at Christmas.' He turned to the twins. 'Right, you two scallywags, time for bed so the grown-ups can do boring grown-up stuff.'

'Bet it's not really boring,' Holly said, with a faintly sulky tone. but they dutifully kissed everyone goodnight, and bade them a "tov noct" as they left the room.

'It means goodnight,' John explained, as the adults scraped back their chairs to go into the lounge. 'Right, who's for a real drink?'

They all settled in the comfier chairs, with a glass of their chosen spirit, and John went around turning off the main lights until all that remained was the twinkling from the tree lights, and the warm glow of a low-watt bulb from the lamp in the corner.

For a while no-one said anything, and the silence was comfortable and peaceful, each lost in their own thoughts, then eventually Tony spoke, somewhat hesitantly.

'I was thinking, is it wise to encourage that strange language the girls use? I don't want to sound negative, but… they're the only ones who can understand it. What's the point?'

'Nothing wrong with encouragement,' Jen said. 'They've been using their own language since they were toddlers, and it hasn't held them back. They're top of their class, and popular as well.' She heard the pride in her own voice, and saw it reflected on John's face. 'My interest was in why twins develop a language of their own at all,' she went on, 'it doesn't happen if they're split up at birth.

129

What makes Holly and Hannah unique is that, while the language of most twins is mainly babble and has no structure, theirs does. And the vocabulary has grown with them.'

'I went through Jen's research last month,' John put in. 'It's fascinating. She's worked really hard on this, checking other sets of gifted twins. It seems that in all cases only one twin achieves real renown, the other remains in the background. But they need each other, and the need is greater for the one in the foreground.'

'I compiled a dictionary, of sorts,' Jen told them. 'John's putting it through his translation programme, and we're now able to translate simple Hally sentences into English.'

'Hally?' her mother asked, blinking.

'Our name for their language, taken from both their names.'

'Well it all sounds very complicated, but well done both of you. That's immensely clever!'

Sinead reached for her glass. 'I'm impressed! Are you going to do anything with all this?'

'I hope to submit it as the research proposal for my doctorate.' Jen waved away the murmurs of congratulation. 'Anyway, that's enough shop talk for now.'

'I'm glad the girls are happy at Perse, it's a good school,' her mother said.

'Yes it is. That's where John and Todd met. They didn't allow girls back then.'

'More's the pity.' Todd winked at John. 'Dad was going to ship me off to boarding school, but changed his mind at the last minute, thank goodness.'

'And you boys are off to Israel?' Tony asked, leaning forward to take a handful of crisps.

John nodded. 'In March, yes. I've managed to locate some friends of my parents, and they've invited us to stay with them. I'm really looking forward to it.'

'And why are you going?' Tony asked Todd.

'To explore. I teach kids about these places, it'll be good to learn more about them, see them first hand. Besides,' he grinned, 'John here needs a chaperone.'

The laughter swelled, and Jen raised a finger to her lips and pointed at the ceiling; they didn't want to bring the girls back down in fear of missing something.

'I'd say it was the other way around,' Sinead chuckled, flicking Todd's leg. 'You're the one needing a chaperone.' She turned to Sue. 'I'd heard you weren't well, but you're looking fantastic.'

'It's these new HIV tablets,' Jen's mother said solemnly. 'They're wonderful.'

Sinead looked at Jen, startled, and Jen grinned. 'She means HRT.'

Tony rolled his eyes. 'If that doesn't say it's time for charades, I don't know what does; the less talking the better! Who's up for it?'

Later, after Jen's parents had retired for the night, the remaining four decided on a nightcap. While Jen and Sinead settled down on the sofa with their hot chocolate, John took Todd into the study.

'Wow.' Todd ran his fingers over the polished wood of the desk. 'Love this.'

'It was my Aunt May's,' John said. 'We got rid of our old one, since we didn't need two. There was no choice to be made, we love this one.'

'Nineteenth century?' Todd asked, stroking the slatted wood of the tambour. 'Oak?'

'I'm impressed.'

Todd grinned. 'Don't be, I'd like to go on, but that's all I know, and that's only because my dad's got the same one in his office.'

'It's got a secret compartment too,' John said, feeling a little bit like a child showing off a toy. 'You need a key for the lid, and then there's a lever inside one of the drawers that opens a panel on the side. Quite clever, really.'

Todd sat down and rolled back the tambour, and he nodded in appreciation at the smoothness of the action, then his face took on a distant look.

'We don't bother keeping it locked,' John began, then frowned. 'Are you okay, mate?

'Hmm?' Todd swam back. 'Yeah, sorry. I was just remembering a time a few years back, when I sat at Dad's desk just like this, and… Hah! *That's* where I read about that Professor Jakobsen's discovery. You know, the tablet with the prophecy I told you about.'

'I didn't know your dad was into that kind of stuff, he doesn't seem the type, somehow.'

'I didn't think so either. The ruckus it caused was… well, not good.'

'Ruckus?'

'I went into his study to ask him something, but he wasn't there. He'd left his papers out though, and you know me; I just glanced at it out of curiosity, but got so

132

engrossed I sat down and had a good old read of it. Needless to say I didn't hear him come back in, and he went apeshit!' He sighed. 'We've never got on that well, sometimes I think he'd prefer it if I didn't exist.'

John didn't think it was entirely the drink talking, and he felt the flush of remorse and sympathy. 'Sorry, I should have realised when you had that go at me about my own father.'

Todd shrugged. 'Yeah, well. That's done now.' He picked up his Irish coffee and drained the glass. 'The man's an arsehole, but I don't really care anymore if I'm honest. He's hardly ever home, he goes all over the world on business. It's better when it's just mum and me, and I'm pretty sure she feels the same way.'

'How is she?'

'Fine. We had a nice day yesterday, just the two of us.'

'Good.' John waited a moment, then went on, 'Do you think you'd be able to get hold of a copy of that paperwork?'

'No idea, but I'll have a damned good try while he's away.' Todd's jaw cracked in a massive yawn. 'Mate, it's been a great day, thanks. You have a wonderful family, I just wish I could say the same about mine.'

'I've called a cab for you,' John said. 'Shouldn't be long.'

'Better go and rouse the guest of honour, then.'

When they returned to the lounge they found Jen and Sinead in fits of laughter. 'She's been telling me about her family,' Jen explained. 'She's the eldest of nine children. Nine!' She shook her head. 'And I was frazzled after two.'

Sinead twisted on the sofa and grinned lopsidedly. 'Hey, handsome,' she sang out to Todd, waving her hand in the air, reaching back for his.

He took it. 'Hey, gorgeous,' he said with a little laugh. 'I think it's time to leave these good folk in peace. John's booked a taxi.'

'Okay, but can we come again? It's been good craic, so it has.'

'She gets more Irish with every tipple,' Todd said in an aside to John, then turned back to Sinead. 'Yes, but only if you're a good girl.'

'Ah, you know how good I can be.' Sinead said, and Jen stifled a laugh behind her hand.

Sinead pulled herself up with Todd's help, and slipped into the coat he held for her.

After they'd made their farewells, the guests wobbled off down the path towards the waiting taxi, and John heard Sinead's voice drifting clearly back. 'I think I might be a wee bit sl…schl… sloshed. Are you going to take advantage of me, sir?'

'Certainly not, young lady,' Todd said firmly.

'Ah, go on!'

Jen's giggles burst free at last, and John put an arm around her, his own smile widening as Todd turned and winked before he bundled Sinead into the back seat of the taxi.

Sweat trickled down his back and stung his eyes, and John blinked it away, his feet slipping and sliding over the rocks and pebbles. It was late evening, and he could see his way clearly enough from the lights emanating from the town below, but it was hard work. Punishing. Part of the path was worn smooth by the feet of millions of the pilgrims who flocked here every year, but for the most part it was difficult and dangerous.

He judged he'd been climbing for around an hour when he sat on a rock to catch his breath. His mind turned to all the times he'd done this before… but why had he? What compelled him to keep climbing up to this particular cave? He knew the toughest part was to come; he'd have to hold his breath to squeeze through the small crevices by the entrance, the bigger rocks forming a protective wall. When he reached the cave he knew he'd be exhausted, but that a calm would fall over him. A peace. And that was what he sought now.

He stood, reluctantly, feeling his muscles stretch and ache, and began the second half of the climb. A moment later he stopped, his heart beating fast. Voices. Not the usual male voice he was accustomed to hearing up here, but higher. Children. As he turned his face towards the sound the voices became clearer, and he recognised them: Holly and Hannah.

'Daddy! We're up here!'

'Where?' he called back, his voice hoarse with exertion and dust. 'I can hear you, but I can't see you!' He began to climb faster, slipping in the loose dirt, a new urgency pushing him on.

'Stop rushing, Daddy! Stop fighting the dream.'

'Relax, *please* relax!'

John slowed, straining through the gloom to see his daughters, but there was nothing except the summit of the mountain, and the darkening sky. But he did as they asked, and sat down again. He took deep, slow breaths, and when he looked up again he saw flickering shapes, which gradually solidified into the familiar shapes of Holly and Hannah.

A blink in time, and then he was there with them at the entrance to the cave. He was still sitting down, but he reached out and drew them to him, embracing them.

'What happened back there? Why are you two here?'

Holly shrugged. 'We come here a lot. It feels… like we belong.'

'A bit like being at home,' Hannah added, 'but not quite the same. It's hard to explain.'

'But how did I get here?'

'You're dreaming,' Holly said. 'Like we are.'

'No, I mean… how did I get to the top like that? I usually have to climb the whole way.'

Hannah giggled. 'Easy. You relaxed.'

'We go straight to the cave when we come here,' Holly said. 'We used to climb too, like you, but each time we did it, it got easier and then we realised we didn't need to climb after all. We just… get here.'

'And you're both okay?'

'Of course,' Holly said.

'Are we all having the same dream, at the same time?'

'I think so,' Hannah said. 'We don't understand it all yet.'

Holly looked down the steep mountainside. 'Sometimes when we come here there are others climbing too.'

'Others?'

'Children, like us. They climb, but they never get to the cave.'

'Really? How many do you see?'

'It's different each time,' Hannah said, 'but we're starting to recognise some of them now.'

John fell silent, all out of questions for now, and just enjoying this time with his girls. He put an arm around each of them and stared out at the night sky, and he wondered if he, or they, would remember any of this in the morning. He was about to ask, when he was jolted by another voice calling him. After a moment he heard his name cried out in urgent tones, and recognised the caller: Jen.

She had awoken into darkness, still faintly buzzing from the good company and a little too much wine, and immediately aware of the emptiness in the bed beside her. John must have got up to use the bathroom; she was glad she would be awake when he returned, she was just in the mood to snuggle up, secure in the knowledge that no alarm clock would wake them at seven o'clock the next morning.

When she felt herself drifting off again and realised he still hadn't come back, she pulled on her dressing gown and went out onto the landing. There were voices coming from the girls' room, John's included – perhaps one of them had called out in the night from a bad dream, and John was calming them. She pushed the door open and saw John sitting on the floor between the two beds with his back to her, maybe reading to the girls as he'd used to do when they were little, but something felt... off. The

137

light spilling in from the landing showed her the girls flat out, sleeping, and when Jen put a gentle hand on John's shoulder he didn't move.

Jen's heart began to flutter and her skin prickled. Hardly able to bring herself to move, she managed to walk around in front of John, and crouched down, and a moment later she had fallen back in shock, her hand to her mouth to stifle the scream that rose in her throat. Her head hit the bedside table but she barely registered it, and when she looked properly at the girls she saw the same thing: eyes wide open, and pure white.

'Jen?' John's voice cut through her terror, and when she turned back to him he looked quite normal, if a little bemused. He looked around him, as if surprised to find himself here at all.

'Are you alright?' she asked in a shaky voice.

'I'm fine,' he assured her, still seemingly disorientated, but at least with her again.

'Mummy?' Both girls had sat up, and Holly's voice was small, but they too appeared normal again.

'Oh my God, are you two alright?'

'We're okay. What's up?'

'What am I doing in here?' John climbed to his feet. He looked pale, but composed now, and concerned at Jen's evident upset.

'That's what I'd like to know,' Jen said. 'The three of you had me worried sick. I heard you all talking, and when I came in all of you looked as if you were in some kind of trance or something. Your eyes were all rolled back in your heads…' she was fighting tears now. 'What were you *doing*?'

John pulled her to him, and she could feel him shaking as much as she was. She buried her face in his shoulder, and gradually she became aware of smaller hands clutching at her. The girls had scrambled from their beds and the four of them clung together for a while, until Jen felt herself growing calmer. She eased herself out of John's embrace and sat on Holly's bed. Holly sat next to her, and John and Hannah sat opposite while John told her about the dream. She listened, in growing disbelief, and yet... they were all telling the same tale.

'How is that possible?' she managed at last.

'I don't know, love,' John said quietly. 'Neither do the girls, but it seems they've been having the dream as often as I have. We just never knew about it.'

'Why didn't you tell me?' Jen asked them, in her gentlest voice.

The girls looked at one another, and she saw Hannah giving Holly a little nod. You tell her...

'We were going to,' Holly began, then bit her lip. 'But when Daddy had the dream, it upset you so much when you thought it was affecting us.'

'We thought you'd be cross with us, too,' Hannah finished.

Jen tightened up with remorse. 'Oh, girls! No. I'm so sorry. Please, don't ever feel you have to keep anything secret from me again. I'm not going to be cross, though you're right, it did upset me. But only because I love you, and I worry, and I don't understand what's happening.'

'Nor do we,' Holly said, 'but we know it's nothing to worry about. The dreams can't hurt us, they're lovely dreams. We always feel happy the next day after we've had one.'

'Then why does your dad get so tired?'

Hannah looked at her as if she was simple. 'Because he's been fighting them. We don't, do we, Holly?'

'Nope. Daddy's had to climb the mountain every time, but we just go straight to the top.'

'But...' Jen looked at John hopelessly. 'It's just a *dream*! You're not supposed to get tired from what you do in a dream.'

The girls thought for a moment, but in the end they just shrugged. 'Have we done something wrong?'

'No.' Jen sighed, and ruffled Holly's hair. 'Of course not. What am I going to do with you, eh? You're supposed to be dreaming about being pop stars or other stuff, aren't you?' She hoped the lightness in her voice would banish any fears. 'Come on, let's get you back into bed so you can get some proper sleep. We can talk about this in the morning. Don't worry about telling me, okay?' She kissed them goodnight. 'Everything will be fine.'

She and John went back out onto the landing, and as John pulled the twins' door to behind them, they heard another opening down the landing. Jen's mother stood, wrapping her dressing gown around her and blinking at them owlishly.

'I heard voices. Is everything alright?'

'All's fine, Sue. Thanks.' John clicked the door shut as quietly as he could. 'They just had odd dreams, that's all. Probably all the excitement of Christmas, and that snowball they had. They're back off to sleep now.'

'Ah. Good.'

''Night, Mum,' Jen said. 'Don't worry if you hear any more voices, John and I are going to have a Horlicks and then go back to sleep. See you in the morning. Love you.'

In the kitchen Jen, moving on autopilot, took down their two mugs and opened the jar of Horlicks. She wordlessly filled the kettle and flicked it on, then braced her hands on the counter top and burst into tears. A moment later John had turned her towards him and pulled her close, rubbing her back and kissing the top of her head, as helpless and lost as she was.

When her tears subsided she drew back, and he sat her down at the small kitchen table, before finishing making the drinks. He brought two steaming cups over, and said nothing, but sat down beside her and waited for her to speak. Eventually she found some words to get started.

'I can't tell you how scared I was up there. To see you and the girls like…' She shook her head, struggling to find an accurate description. 'Like zombies,' she finished. 'It was the worst thing ever. It was like your bodies were there, but you were somewhere else, and I didn't know what to do.'

John gripped his mug in both hands and lowered his head. 'I can't explain it, Jen. I'm sorry. I don't remember walking into their room at all. I just went to bed, perfectly happy and content, and the next thing I know I'm sitting on the floor, and you're there asking me if I'm alright.'

'Do you remember much about the dream?'

He nodded. 'Most of it. It's like they said, they showed me how to relax, and how to get to the top of the mountain without climbing and exhausting myself.'

141

'Things are so simple when you're a child,' Jen said. 'I wish I could look at it with a child's eyes. Accept it unconditionally. But it's not normal, and it's happening to the people I love! God, John, why don't we understand it?'

'Let's try.' John's calm voice worked to some small degree, and so did the hand that covered hers, still warm from clutching his hot drink. 'We can both agree that this is more than just some… ordinary dream.'

'Definitely.'

'Could it be hereditary memories then? I read something about that in the paper, although it doesn't really fit, as we're not dreaming about the lives of other people.' He shook his head. 'This was certainly a synchronised dream, but it felt so real.'

'How though?' Jen asked. 'No-one has synchronised dreams.'

John considered. 'Dream telepathy then? Is that a thing?'

'I don't know.' Jen pulled her hand from under his, and wrapped it around her own cup. She was starting to feel very cold, and not just from the chill December night. 'They're starting to sound more like out of body experiences, to be honest. Have you shared them with the girls before?'

'No, and that's got me wondering why. My previous dreams I've been alone, or I've heard a male voice calling to me.'

Jen took a deep breath, struggling to process everything that had happened this long, strange night.

'Taking the girls' advice then,' she said slowly, 'let's pretend all this is normal, and try to work it out.'

'Okay.'

'We know that we only dream during REM sleep. That's a given. So maybe that's the first time you and the girls have been in REM at the same time? But then what about this other person, the male voice. Who could he be, and how could he be sharing his dream with yours?'

'It's not just him,' John said. 'The girls told me there are other children sometimes, and they talk to one another.'

Jen sat back in surprise. 'So… this thing, whatever is is, could be happening to others? People we don't know?'

'Yeah, I think so.'

'All this has happened just this year. Why? Why now? We had all that to deal with, losing poor May, and then all this stuff about Jericho and Amnon. Now this.'

John's head snapped up, and he grabbed her hand again. 'Jen! Amnon… you remember his story? I think this might all be connected somehow!' His eyes were wide and stunned, and she could see the puzzle falling into place. 'Remember that when Moses climbed Mount Sinai… or Mount Hira as we now know, Amnon wrote that it seemed as though there was someone with him, even though there wasn't?'

'Yes, but what—'

'He also described Maor as wandering around in his sleep, talking in a strange tongue.'

'Okay…'

'I know we can't be sure of the timing here,' John gripped her fingers tight, 'but what if Maor climbed the mountain at the same time as Moses, only in a dream state? And *that's* who the people saw on Mount Hira. He might have been just as unaware of what he was doing as I was, when I walked into the girls' room tonight.'

'But how could the people "see" him? *They* were all awake!'

John shook his head. 'I have no idea. But when I was climbing tonight I heard the girls' voices but I couldn't see them. It wasn't until they told me to relax, and I was able to, that I saw their outlines properly. I don't understand it, but I really feel this has something to do with the past. It's like a… a jigsaw puzzle at the moment, but I'm certain things will start to become clearer the more we find out.'

'I hope so.' Jen looked at him steadily, remembering the other thing that had struck her when she'd walked into the twins' room. 'There's something else I can add to what you've just said: when Maor was wandering around he was speaking a strange language.'

'Yes.'

'When I came into the room tonight you were talking to the girls, but it wasn't in English. John, you were *all* speaking Hally.'

Chapter Nine
The List

February 2003

Todd sat down and ran his hands over the desk, his mind turned inward for a moment as he thought about the man who owned it and what he would do if he caught his son sitting—

'What are you doing in here?'

Todd stumbled to his feet, his heart in his mouth, only registering that the voice was female as it spoke again.

'Well?'

'Mum, you made me jump!'

'Serves you right, you know you're not allowed in here. So, I ask again, why are you?'

Todd drew out his prepared excuse, thinking how lame it sounded even as he spoke. 'Well a while ago I saw something here that I thought would be of interest to some of my students. But the desk's locked, and I assume Dad keeps the key, so,' he shrugged and gave her a bright, forced smile, 'that's that.'

He stepped away from the desk and began to cross the floor, but his mother held up a hand. 'Is it that important to you?'

'It is, yes.'

'Wait here.' His mother vanished, leaving Todd standing in the middle of the office, still trying to get his guilty heartbeat under control. She returned a few minutes later holding out a key, and smiled at Todd's puzzled look. 'I had this cut years ago.' The smile slipped a little. 'Your father can be very secretive, and I thought perhaps it had something to do with why he's away from home so much, and doesn't always come home at night.'

Todd took the key. 'And did you find anything?'

She shook her head. 'After a while I stopped looking, and I almost forgot I had the key, too. Find what you're looking for then give it back to me. Your dad won't be back until later this evening.' At the door she stopped and gave him a worried look. 'Make sure you leave everything as it is.'

'Thanks, Mum. I will.'

The moment the door clicked shut, Todd hurried back to the desk and sat down in the luxurious leather swivel chair. He fitted the key, which turned easily in the lock, and rolled up the tambour, keeping half his attention on the door. Just in case. There was nothing inside but an empty writing pad, some pens, and some other stationery.

Todd clicked his tongue and began pulling out the small drawers, but found only stamps, a calculator, and a few receipts. Nothing of importance. But the second-to-last drawer looked different to the others. Shallower. He pulled it right out, and bent to peer into the recess, but it was too dark to see so he slipped his hand in instead, and felt around. Just as John had described, he found a small lever, and with a leap of curiosity he pulled it. A compartment popped open on the side of the desk.

He withdrew an A4 manila envelope, and slid the contents out, his scholar's mind noting the order of them, and as he pushed them apart on the desk he found what he was looking for; a copy of the photo of the tablet, with the inscription and, underneath, the translation and some additional notes. As he was about to replace the documents he noticed a third sheet, and he slid it out and began to read.

What the hell...?

Later he parked in the driveway and, leaving the copies he'd made on the front seat of the car he double-checked the order of the originals and tucked the envelope inside his jacket. Inside he made straight for the office, but was halted as his mother came out of the lounge.

'Did you find what you were looking for?'

'Yes I did, thanks.' He slipped off his coat and showed her the envelope. I made copies, so I need to get these originals back where I found them before anyone's the wiser.'

His mother had clearly noted the nervous tremble in his voice that he was trying to hide, and she looked at him with a faintly suspicious frown. 'What's going on, Todd? Is everything okay?'

'Everything's fine, Mum. Don't worry. Hey,' he changed the subject quickly, 'once I've finished here, d'you fancy—'

'Your father's back!' His mother's head turned sharply towards the door, and now Todd could hear the idling of his father's car engine. 'He's early. Hurry and get that envelope back where you found it. Now! I'll keep him talking.'

Todd shot into the office, and flung his coat onto the back of the chair. He reached into his front jeans pockets for the key, but it wasn't there. His heart staggered in his chest as he checked his coat pockets, telling himself the key was tiny and could easily be caught in a seam. His breath came shallow and sharp as he found a hole in the material… *Christ, no…!*

Outside he heard the car door slam shut, and his fingers turned into useless, unfeeling lumps as he dug around once more in his jeans pockets. Finally, and with a surge of relief, he dragged the key from his back pocket and somehow fitted it into the desk's lock. The front door opened and Todd rolled up the tambour of his father's desk with agonising slowness, fearful of making any sound, but the slamming of the door masked the slight clunk as the slatted wood came to rest against the stays. Keys rattled into the bowl on the hall table, and Todd heard his father's bellow:

'Clare!'

Clare Hampton walked back into the hall, adopting a surprised expression. 'Richard? I wasn't expecting you back this early.'

'Neither was I. Some damn fool didn't tell me the meeting itinerary had changed, and I need to collect some extra notes. Bring me a coffee, I'll be in the office.' He started for the door, muttering, 'I'm constantly amazed at the ineptitude and incompetence of others.'

'Let me take your coat,' Clare said quickly. 'Come and have a drink with me in the lounge, I want to talk to you about Todd.'

'I don't have time,' Richard said, though mercifully his hand dropped away from the office door's handle. 'I saw his car's in the drive, so I assume your son is hiding upstairs.'

'*Our* son, Richard,' Clare said, her voice brittle. 'He's *our* son, and no, he's not hiding. He's marking essays.' She dropped the tone in favour of a more pleading one. 'You're hardly ever here, so surely you can do me the courtesy of sparing a few minutes?'

Richard eyed her for a moment, then gave an exaggerated sigh and put his briefcase down before shrugging out of his coat. Clare hung it up, and led the way into the lounge, still terrified her husband was going to change his mind, and his direction, and go to the office after all. But he followed her, clearly still reluctant, and poured himself a whisky instead. She sat down, hoping he'd join her, but he remained standing and looked at her with an impatient frown.

'So? What do you want to talk about?'

'Well, Todd's going to Israel soon—'

'Yes? And?' He gulped at his whisky and raised his eyebrows.

'Since you've been there a few times yourself I thought you might take some time out to give him some travel advice, or—'

'You interrupted my day for *that*?'

Clare rose to her feet, her blood thrumming now. 'There's never a good time, is there? I don't know what it is you dislike so much about your own son! He's a good man, hardworking and well-respected. It must hurt him that you constantly push him away.'

149

Richard lowered his glass and sighed. 'I had hoped that, as an adult, Todd would help me with my work and grow a bigger backbone.' His voice hardened. 'But no. He's too soft, and that's your fault, Clare, no-one else's. He's a mummy's boy, always was and always will be. You've ruined him.' He finished his drink with a small grimace, and banged the glass down on the mantelpiece. 'I've no time for either of you.'

Clare saw he was about to revert to his original intention of going to the office, and with a final, desperate attempt to stop him she stepped forward and put a conciliatory hand on his arm. It remained rigid beneath her fingers.

'What happened to us, Richard?' she asked softly. 'We were happy once.'

'Not us, *you*. You were the one who changed, not me.'

'I couldn't keep up with your impossible, unrealistic expectations.' Clare shook her head. 'You expected too much of me. Of everyone. And when you do that you live your life constantly disappointed.'

'Don't lecture me!' He flung her hand off his arm, and when he looked at her his expression was unmoved. 'My father brought me up that way, and I never disappointed him. I expect nothing less from my own son, but thanks to you he's just a constant source of embarrassment.' He gave a short laugh. 'I sometimes wonder if I'm his real father at all! Why couldn't he have been more like me?'

Her words fell out before she had time to bite them back. 'I think two narcissistic sociopaths in this house would have been a bit too much to—' Her head rocked back under the force of the slap, but although the pain was bright and hot, and brought tears to her eyes, it didn't travel beyond the physical. She had become numbed to the other kind of pain long ago.

Richard was breathing hard as he stared at her, silently awaiting her reaction, and she was reasonably sure he hadn't heard the office door click quietly shut, and Todd's footsteps going towards the stairs. She stepped aside to let her husband pass.

***

Jen finished folding the laundry, and checked her phone once again. She'd been doing it every few minutes, but there was still no reply to the text she'd sent earlier. From the lounge came the sound of the twins singing along to Christina Aguilera's *Beautiful*, each doing their best to emulate the singer – to the extent of borrowing their father's hats and dragging two of the kitchen stools in front of Top of the Pops.

John, tidying the kitchen after their evening meal, caught Jen's eye and pulled a face. 'D'you think they'd be upset if I closed the door?' he pleaded in a low voice. 'I can't stick that song at the best of times, but I don't think I can take much more of that squeaking.'

'Ssh!' Jen smiled. 'Let them be, the song'll be over soon.' She raised an eyebrow as she picked up the washing basket. 'Besides, your impression of Elvis is much worse. It's clear where they get their singing talent from!'

John assumed a mock hurt expression. 'Well, we can't all be brilliant at everything now, can we?' He nodded at

Jen's phone. 'Any word from Mandy about babysitting yet?'

'Not yet.' Jen sighed. 'She must be on nights, and sleeping.'

'Well we can't leave the girls on their own.'

'No.' She went into the utility room to hang up the basket. 'It was nice of Sinead to ask us round to hers, but if we can't get hold of Mandy…'

'I'll text them to come over here instead,' John said, taking out his own phone. 'This is too important.'

'I'm glad we agreed to bring Sinead into all this,' Jen said, coming back in. 'It'll be good to have her on board, and another female perspective would be useful too.'

'Especially now Todd's found that picture of the Shiloh tablet. Makes sense for all of us to be on the same page. Right, sent.' He put his phone back in his pocket as the girls came dancing into the kitchen to put away the wooden spoons they'd been using as microphones.

'Did you hear us?'

'We did.' John shot Jen a glance but she avoided catching his eye. 'You were very… entertaining.'

'We'd be even better if we had some sparkly eyeshadow,' Holly said hopefully.

'Yeah, and if we had our hair done like Christina too,' Hannah added.

'Woah,' Jen said, 'you're too young for eyeshadow, unless it's just for indoors.' As their faces fell she went on, 'Tell you what, tomorrow I'll do your hair in little plaits all over your heads. It'll be nearly the same as hers.'

The girls exchanged delighted glances, and John's phone pinged. He read the message and nodded to Jen, and she clapped her hands once, sharply. 'Right, stools back where they belong, and the same with Dad's hats. Then get off upstairs to get ready for bed, Todd and Sinead are coming over to see us.'

'But it's Friday,' Hannah protested. 'Can we stay up with you all, just for a bit? Please?'

'Not tonight, we've got important things to talk about. Boring things,' she added quickly, noting the perk of interest. 'You can pop back down to say hello, then Dad's got you some popcorn and a film. You can watch it in our room. Go!'

An hour later the doorbell rang, and Holly and Hannah, who'd clearly been on tenterhooks waiting, bounded down the stairs and beat Jen to the front door.

Hannah reached it first, and flipped up the letter box cover. 'Who goes there? And what's the password?'

Todd's voice floated in. 'It's us.'

'You can't just say that!' Sinead had evidently nudged him out of the way and taken his place, and the next moment she blew a raspberry through the letter box.

'Ew!' Hannah giggled and pretended to wipe her face. 'Okay, password accepted!'

They pulled open the door and Sinead handed them a big bag. 'I've been having a bit of a clear-out. No fighting over anything though!'

To Jen's relief, the girls' excitement was enough to stop them pleading once more to be allowed to stay downstairs, and they disappeared back up to their room, dragging the bag between them.

'Come through,' Jen said. 'We're in the kitchen.' She led them in, and began putting out plates and trivets next to the cheesecake on the counter.

'Something smells nice,' Todd said. 'Ooh, cheesecake! My favourite.'

'Everything's your favourite,' Sinead observed with a grin. 'Something does smell good though.'

'I found some Christmas leftovers in the freezer,' Jen said. 'Sausage rolls, and a pizza I'd forgotten about. Sound okay?'

'I'll say,' Todd said.

'How are you both? And sorry for dragging you out—'

'We're fine,' Todd assured her. 'It's no problem for us to come to you. John's text arrived just as we'd got back from shopping.'

'I hope you didn't go to any trouble for us, thinking we were coming over.'

'Did you miss the part where Todd'll eat anything?' Sinead laughed. 'No, honestly. We had to go anyway.' She sniffed the air again. 'I think the food's done.' While Jen took hot food from the oven and spread it on the trivets to cool, Sinead took hers and Todd's coats to hang up in the hall. John and Todd began putting plates on the table, and the sounds of raised voices from upstairs put Jen on edge for a moment, until one of the shrieks turned to laughter and she relaxed.

'I wanted to thank you both,' Sinead said when she came back. 'It's good of you to bring me in on all this, I'm honoured. Todd's filled me in on what he knows so far, and it's a strange one alright. But I'd be glad to help where I can.'

'Oh, we're glad to have you,' Jen said. 'It'll be good to hear your views. We're discovering more as we go along of course, but we just can't make any real sense of it. It's... well, unbelievable!'

'Well you say that,' Sinead help brush away pastry crumbs from the counter top, 'but in Ireland we believe in all sorts. I mean you can't be Catholic and not open to the supernatural.' She threw the crumbs in the bin and dusted off her hands. 'My mam used to say, "Just because you've never seen something doesn't mean it doesn't exist. If something unbelievable happens, you *have* to believe it.'

'She sounds like a wise woman,' Jen said.

'She is that. Mad as a box of frogs mind, but very wise!'

John took some wine and beer out of the fridge, and handed a can to Todd. 'So, how did you manage to find the paperwork?'

Todd pulled the ring from his can. 'Cheers. You remember at Christmas, you showed me your Aunt May's desk, that's the same as my Dad's, and told me about the secret compartment?' John nodded, and Todd took a pull on his can. 'Well, after a bit of a search I found the lever at the back of Dad's desk, too. They were in there. I got copies made before Dad got back.'

John put down his beer and picked up the wine. 'I thought your dad kept the desk locked.'

'He does, but – ow!' Todd withdrew his questing hand from the plate of sausage rolls, and gave Jen a hurt look. 'No need for that, Jen! Long story short, it turns out Mum had a copy of the key cut years ago, when she was digging up evidence of Dad's extra-marital shenanigans.'

'And did she find any?'

155

Todd shrugged. 'Not that she told me. Though I don't know whether she would, even now. Anyway she doesn't bother looking anymore. Doubt if she cares, to be honest.'

Sinead sighed. 'Why she stays with that man I'll never fathom.'

Jen sensed a dip in the mood, and kept her voice light as she took a glass of wine from John. 'Let's go and sit in the other room.'

Once they were settled around the coffee table, Todd took a folder out of his satchel and handed out copies of the photos. 'This is the tablet, and this is the translation. You'll notice the translation is hand-written, with lots of handy scribbled notes.'

John was frowning at the copy he held. 'This handwriting is my mum's.' He looked up. 'How did *your* father get hold of *my* mother's work?'

'Wow.' Todd's eyes were wide. 'I had no idea that was your mum's work. Not a clue, seriously. So,' he mused, 'she must have known about the other tablet after all.'

'It might have been photographed along with the others,' John said, 'But quite a few of the pictures Mum took didn't come out so it must have been one of them. The first line of the prophecy reads, "When Ishmael and Isaac war over water, twins shall be born to the sons of God, under a ring of light." Mum's noted that Ishmael and Isaac is really a way of describing Muslims and Jews.'

'Right. Though the two haven't actually fought over religious concerns. Both religions, and Christianity too, incorporate so many similarities they're bunched under the umbrella of Abrahamic Religions.'

Jen and John looked at one another. 'Jen was reading something about that the other week,' John said. 'How Ishmael and Isaac were both sons of Abraham, but went their own way religion wise. Isaac had twins too,' he added.

'Yes, but the reason for the conflict in recent history is down to government interfering over their rights to lands.' Todd sat back and laced his hands behind his head. 'The war over the river Jordan was one of the things that led to the six-day war. That wasn't until 1967, but it all kicked off in 1965.'

'The year my parents and their friends were in Jericho,' John said quietly.

Todd nodded. 'Your mum also wrote that this ring of light in the prophecy was actually an annular eclipse. When the moon comes between the Earth and the sun.' He sat forward again, hitting his stride. 'Because the moon is smaller, you can still see the sun's light around the edges, making it look like a ring. Apparently these things happen every year, I looked it up. Your mum reckons several of the prophets might have been born during one, hence them being depicted with a halo. Or a ring of light.' He gave John an odd look. 'Weirdly, the one in November happened on the twenty-third.'

John blinked. 'The day I was born.'

'I know. Coincidence eh?'

'It's not the only one either,' Sinead piped up. 'I spent ages looking up the dates of other annulars, trying to match them to well known people, or religious icons, and came up with nothing. But I did find something you'll find interesting.' She glanced at the ceiling, and for a

157

moment Jen wondered why, then it became clear. 'There was an annular eclipse on the tenth of May 1994.'

Jen felt a chill. She saw John staring at her. 'Holly and Hannah's date of birth.' Now they were all looking up, as if they could see the twins through the ceiling that separated them.

Sinead nodded. 'So Todd said. John, I think you and they have a gift, but what the purpose of it is we have yet to find out.'

John stood up and began to pace. He looked agitated, as he'd done when the dreams had become too much for him last year. 'Why me?' he said at last. 'I mean, if we do have a gift, and it has to do with all this,' he gestured at the papers strewn on the coffee table. 'I'm an only child, so I don't fit into the equation.'

'Can't you get any information from Malik or his wife?' Todd asked.

John shook his head. 'I tried, but they've not got internet, and they won't talk about any of this on the phone.'

Jen picked up one of the photos. 'Look, what about this bit: *born to the sons of God*. Karen's written "Nephilim." What are they? Does she mean the sons of God are Nephilim, or that the twins being born under the prophecy would be?'

'The twins,' Todd said. 'The Bible says that angels, the sons of God, mated with human women, and their offspring became part human, part spirit. Aka Nephilim. They would live long and healthy lives and do great things.' He pointed to the translation. 'Look, Karen's drawn a line from that word, down to some names with

158

the heading *twins*. Isaac's sons, Esau and Jacob; Moses and Maor; Jesus & Thomas; Mohammed... and then *1965*, with a question mark.'

Jen made a small sound of recognition. 'I hadn't heard of Mohammed having a twin, but I read about Jesus and Thomas, didn't I, John?' He nodded. 'This all seems to be about twins, eclipses and Levites.'

'At Christmas,' John said, 'when we had that episode with the girls and me sharing a dream, they told me they've had it before, and seen and spoken to other twins on the mountain.'

'Ah,' Todd said, sounding a little hesitant for the first time. 'I have some information that might be relevant to that.'

'Like what?'

'I'll get to it in a bit.'

'I've heard of Nephilim,' Sinead said. 'Some people seem to think there's something demonic about them, but if they're part angel how could they be demons? I think they must have been amazing.'

'Maybe because it was only the fallen angels that did the dirty deeds, and gave them all a bad rap,' Todd suggested.

'Look though,' Jen said. 'Karen's written, "not *cast out*, or *fell*, but *descended*." So, these angels weren't expelled for evil deeds, they came down to mingle with us.'

'And to fornicate,' Sinead added.

'Yes.' Todd sent her a loaded look. 'And that.'

'Israelis and Palestinians have been fighting over land since long before you were born, John. It's been, what, fifty years? And still no sign of a peaceful resolution.' Jen shook her head. 'I can't begin to imagine what it must be like to live that way.'

'It's not just Israel,' Sinead said quietly. 'I think every country in the world has fought over something, at some point. Look at Ireland. Split itself in a war over being ruled by your own government. Thirty years of bombs and bloodshed, and for what?'

Jen flushed with a strange kind of hot shame, as if she were personally responsible. Well, she'd certainly brought the subject up, and she felt badly enough about that. She put a hand over Sinead's.

'It's been dreadful. Shocking. I'm so glad it's over now.'

Sinead's rare, solemn expression faded into a smile. 'So am I.'

'Right,' Todd said briskly, shattering the last of the melancholy mood. 'Shall we have a break before I show you what else I've found? I could use another beer, and the smell of sausage rolls is beginning to do my head in.'

'Oh, hell!' Jen leapt to her feet. 'Forgot all about them, they'll be stone cold by now! I'll bring them in.

For a few minutes all was activity as they brought food and fresh drinks into the living room, and Sinead popped upstairs to the bathroom. When she came back down she grinned at Jen.

'I just looked in on the girls, they're decked out in about three different outfits each, all at once, and glued to the telly.'

Jen laughed. 'Thanks for bringing them that stuff, I think it'd have been hard to keep them upstairs knowing you two were here.' She put the cheesecake on the sideboard, and joined the others gathered once more around the coffee table. They all looked expectantly at Todd, who was looking more uneasy by the minute. Jen frowned at John, and he gave a minute shrug.

Todd took a deep breath. 'Okay. When I found the envelope in Dad's desk there were three pieces of paper in it, not two.' His hand was shaking a little as he withdrew the third sheet. 'The handwriting is my father's. You…you won't like this, I'm afraid.'

The paper had a grid drawn on it, filled in with handwritten information. For a moment Jen stared at it, nonplussed, then John snatched it off the table, his face white. 'What the hell are *our* daughters' names doing on this list?' He stood up, striking the paper with the back of his hand, and staring furiously down at Todd. 'Why's your father interested in our girls? And who are these other children?'

'Whoah,' Todd said, 'Don't shoot the messenger. I have no idea, I swear. I'm as confused as you are.'

'John, the girls…' Jen gestured to the ceiling, and John lowered his voice, but began to pace, becoming more agitated.

'I don't get it. I just don't! He's even written down the area where these children live! Is he… God, is he *watching* them?'

'Sit down, mate, come on.' Todd stood too, and gestured to John's seat on the sofa. 'Okay, let's look at the information we have, and work through it.' When John continued to pace, he sighed and sat down again. 'Right. At the top of the page there, you have David and Doron

Malik, born 23 November 1965. Israel. Two things leap out here.'

'Yeah. The name Malik, and the birth date.' John glared down at the piece of paper in his hand as if he thought it might turn into a serpent and bite him.

'The rest is a list of twenty-three sets of twins around the world. Including yours. All born on the same day.'

Jen drew a sudden, sharp and painful breath, her hand rising to her mouth. 'Oh, my God…'

John's pacing brought him to the coffee table, and he waved the paper at Todd. 'So basically an ancient prophecy predicted a date when these Nephilim would be born, and,' he pointed to the other sheet of paper, visibly struggling to sound calm, 'presumably your father believes them to be these Malik twins.'

Todd nodded. 'Seems so.'

'But all those other children, those other twins… I just don't know where to start thinking.'

'Mate—'

'Don't you bloody tell me to calm down!' John's temper had clearly reached its limit. 'Those are *our* children's names! *Our* girls, on a secret fucking list that belongs to a sociopathic arsehole! What am I supposed to think?' He screwed the paper into a ball and threw it onto the table, then left the room with long, angry strides. Jen heard the back door slam, and flinched at the sound.

Todd broke the excruciating silence, his voice low and as unlike him as Jen had ever heard him. 'Um, would it be better if we left, d'you think?'

'No.' Jen stood up. 'I think it'll be okay, he's just gone into the garden. I'll go out and talk to him. Help

162

yourselves.' She waved vaguely at the food, but as she left the room she suspected even Todd's appetite would have been blunted now.

John breathed in the chilly night air. It hurt his lungs, and each angry exhale plumed white in front of his face. Hands rammed deep into his pockets, his thoughts were in turmoil; guilt at the way he'd leapt on Todd, fury and confusion at the thought that his girls were pawns in some... what? Experiment? Research? He barely heard the back door open and click quietly closed again, but a moment later he felt Jen's small, warm hand slide into his pocket, easing his curled fingers open and linking them with hers.

Neither spoke for a few minutes, but gradually her presence calmed him. After a while he felt a shiver run through her, and he took his hands from his pockets to draw her closer, putting an arm about her shoulder and feeling her sink gratefully against him.

'I'm sorry,' he said at last. 'I didn't mean to lose it with everyone, but I'm so worried.'

'I know. Me too. But we have to stay focused, and work out what's going on.' She slid an arm around his waist. 'I don't like this any more than you do, but freezing your nuts off isn't going to help, is it?'

He gave a short huff of laughter, and she twisted in his arms to take his face gently between her hands. ''Those two have worked really hard trying to help us. Let's go back in and see what else they have to say, eh?' She stretched up to press her warm lips to his chilly ones.

'Okay,' he said when she moved away. 'But on Monday we tell the school we suspect someone's watching the girls. We have to make damned sure all the staff know no-one's to pick them up except us.'

'I was thinking the same. I even thought about going to the police, but—'

'What would we tell them?' He shook his head. 'No, it's down to us to sort this out. From here on in, though, we don't let those girls out of our sight.'

'Agreed. Now let's go in before we both die of hypothermia.'

Back inside they were greeted with trepidation, and Todd rose, his expression sheepish. 'I'm sorry, John. I didn't mean to upset you, but you had to know. Believe me, I find this situation embarrassing enough.'

'I know, mate. It's not your fault.' They all sat back down. 'It was a shock,' John confessed, 'but that was no excuse for being rude. Especially after all you've done.'

The tension thawed, and Todd found his smile again. 'So we're okay? Good. Listen, Sinead went off on a tangent earlier, before we came over – she's like that, has a suspicious nature. She'd make a great detective. Anyway, she did come up with something interesting.'

Sinead picked up the story, at a nod from him. 'While I was researching all this, I looked to see if there was any meaning to the number twenty-three. Twenty-three sets of twins,' she clarified, at their blank looks. 'Or forty-six of course. Turns out forty-six is the number of life, which an annular eclipse is thought to represent.' She acknowledged their murmurs of interest with a little nod. 'Also, in Jewish gematria, where they assign numerical value to a word, forty-six is the number of the tribe of Levi. Everything we've read so far is about Levites, so that could be important.'

'Hmm.' John frowned. 'Not sure where Levites fit in though, since we're obviously involved, but we're not Jewish.'

Jen picked up the crumpled list, and smoothed it out on her knee. She studied it for a moment. 'There are no actual addresses on here,' she pointed out, 'just areas. Most of these twins were born in Israel and the USA. A couple in France and the UK, and only one in Germany and Spain. The other UK twins live in Brighton.' She looked up, and John could see the idea brewing even as she spoke. 'That's only a few hours away. I need to contact their parents if I can, and go and see them.'

'How?' Sinead asked.

'I'll contact all the junior schools in the area.'

Todd shook his head. 'There must be over fifty schools, and even if you struck lucky they're not going to just give out a child's personal details.'

Jen subsided, but typically not for long. 'Okay, I'll write a letter, get it photocopied and send one to each school and ask them to pass on a message to the parents of those twins. I'd be surprised if there were more than one set of twins with the surname Nasir.' John noted her determination with an inward smile. 'I'll put my contact details on and hope that they get in touch with me,' she finished, and her expression said she was absolutely certain they would. She was probably right.

'Sounds like a good plan,' Sinead said. 'I'll give you a hand with that if you like.'

John took the paper from Jen, smoothing out more creases. 'What's this "C2" at the top of the grid?'

'No idea,' Todd said. 'The only references we could find were to cervical vertebra, and diatomic carbon. Nothing relevant to any of this that we could see.'

John peered more closely. 'Did you see this small mark at the bottom of the paper?' He put the sheet on the table and pointed. 'Looks like a gothic "V".'

'I did notice that,' Todd said. 'I thought maybe a logo? It's not my dad's personal headed paper, he owns the Meridian Medical Research Centre, so it can't be that either.'

John noticed Jen looking at him, an odd expression on her face; half excited, half nervous. 'What were those organisations your father mentioned?' she asked. 'One was Eegool? And the other one... I think it began with a "v" didn't it?'

'Veritas!' John understood her expression now, but he blurted it out anyway. 'Todd, your father could be working for the enemy!'

Todd's face clouded, and Jen spoke up again. 'Well, we don't know that, it's not proof—'

'No, it's not,' Sinead put in, 'but John might have a point. Hear me out, a minute. You're all very wrapped up in discovering the complicated, weird stuff, it's possible you might have missed some of the simpler points. When Todd and I were chatting about our childhoods a while back he told me his family moved here around the same time as you, John. After we read all this, it got me thinking. Can I ask you both some questions?'

'Go on,' Todd said.

'John, your mother and aunt lived in Godalming up until your mum died, right? Then you and your aunt moved to Haverhill in 1968?' He nodded, and she turned back to Todd. 'When did you and your parents move to Cambridge? And from where?'

'I think it was '69. Before that we lived in Guildford.'

'Okay, and how did you and John become best friends?'

'We both went to Perse,' Todd said. 'We were in the same class, and we got on really well.'

'Yes, but how did you become *best* friends?'

Todd frowned. 'Well, for my thirteenth birthday I asked Dad if I could have a bunch of friends over from school. I'd planned horror videos and takeaway. Dad refused; he didn't want a load of sweaty, boisterous teenaged boys messing up his house. He said I could have one friend only, and asked to look at the list I'd made. He pointed to John's name, and said, "him." That was it. You don't disobey Richard Hampton, even if you're his son.'

'So you didn't pick me yourself?' John was surprised at the squirm of embarrassment that thought gave him, even now so many years later.

'Sorry I never told you that. But you have to admit it ended up a good thing. We got on like a house on fire, and have done ever since.'

John waved it away. 'It's okay, no worries. Besides, you're right.'

'Todd,' Sinead said, 'you told me your dad had been dead set on sending you off to boarding school, but then changed his mind last minute and got you into Perse.'

'Well, yeah. But what has—'

'Hush. Don't interrupt now. Right, if Richard *is* a member of Veritas, and knew of John's mother's work in Jericho, wouldn't he want to keep an eye on her when she returned to England? To make sure she didn't talk to anyone about it?'

John and Todd looked uneasily at one another, but didn't speak. Sinead went on, 'Guildford is next door to Godalming, just as Cambridge is to Haverhill. And he moved his family very soon after May and John moved. What if he'd lived in Guildford to keep an eye on your mother, John? What if,' she said, her voice rising, 'he orchestrated your friendship, so he could keep an eye on *you*?'

'And now he's—'

'Yes! Now he's doing the same thing to your girls.' She blew out a harsh-sounding breath. 'Veritas might know more about what's going on here, and they certainly knew of the discovery in Jericho, but didn't know if Karen would ever speak of it. It could account for why she never developed the photos, nor did she ever disclose any of the evidence. Not even to your aunt. Maybe she knew she was being watched.'

A silence descended on the room, and all John could hear was the low hum of traffic outside, and the muted sound of the TV upstairs. He cleared his throat, feeling more than a little sick. 'Are you saying Mum kept quiet all this time to protect me?'

'I'd say so.' Sinead's voice turned gentler. 'Don't forget, her husband and two best friends had died out there. Coming home alone with you she'd have felt very vulnerable; it must have been hard keeping all that knowledge to herself.'

The next question was harder, but John managed it through tight lips. 'Do you think she might have thought those deaths weren't accidents?'

Sinead shook her head. 'I don't know. But there are a lot of coincidences here, wouldn't you say?'

A creak from the stairs cut through the silence that followed, and Jen got up to open the sitting room door a crack. She looked back and pulled a face at John, then called out. 'I can see you, disappearing around that corner! Come on down, then!' John heard her laugh. 'What on Earth have you got on? Come and show your dad.'

The girls came in, and the others couldn't help grinning too. Holly was wearing a scarf wrapped about her waist, a feather boa around her neck, and huge dangly earrings; Hannah had chosen stripey tights, and still wore her own pyjama top but with numerous beaded necklaces dangling over it.

'You look like gypsy princesses,' Sinead approved.

'Why did you come downstairs?' Jen asked.

'We wanted to show you our outfits,' Hannah said.

'And we heard shouting,' Holly added. 'We wondered what was going on.'

Jen's voice was deliberately bright. 'Oh, that was nothing to be worried about. We were just playing a game.'

The girls seemed relieved to see everyone smiling, and twirled for their audience. Todd whistled in appreciation, and they came over to John for a hug. He didn't want to laugh at them, so he pulled them close and kissed each clear forehead, ruffling their hair.

'I'm glad you came down actually,' he said, in confidential tones. 'But don't tell your mum I said that. I wanted to ask you something.'

'What?'

'Do you remember any of the names of the children in your dreams?'

Holly tipped her head on one side. 'Yeah, there's Sofia and Rosa. Rosa's always giggling.'

'And I remember Leon and Luca,' Hannah added.

John glanced across at Todd, who scanned the list on the table and nodded.

'Well done, you two!' John let a moment pass, then asked casually, 'Do you remember any Indian children?'

'What, American Indians, in teepees?'

'No, people who come from India.

'Like Mr and Mrs Chakrabarti, at the shop?'

John nodded, and the girls thought for a moment. 'I think so,' Hannah ventured at length. 'There's Alima and Ruhi. I think they might be Indian.'

Todd checked the list again and gave a brief nod, and Jen came over to where the girls were perched on the arms of their father's chair.

'How would you like to meet them properly?'

The look that flew between the twins was one of delight. 'Yes please!'

'They're really nice!'

170

'Well,' Jen said, 'as soon as I can talk to their mum and arrange it, we'll go and visit. Okay? Now, say goodnight to everyone and go back up. It's time for bed now, so take off all that lovely stuff and clean your teeth. Do a good job, after all that popcorn!'

When the girls had done their round of kissing goodnight, and were just about to leave, John called them back. 'Just out of curiosity, how do you all understand one another? You all have different languages.'

Holly smiled. 'Not when we're on the mountain, Dad. On the mountain, everyone speaks Hally.'

Chapter Ten
Brighton

Jen pulled her bathrobe around her and was about to call in on the girls when she noticed their bedroom door was already open. A peek inside confirmed they'd dressed already; pyjamas strewn across two beds, and at least three different T shirts lying abandoned on the floor in front of the dresser, not to mention hairbrushes and clips all over the place. She'd known they were excited for their trip, but hadn't appreciated quite how much.

She went down to the kitchen to find them finishing breakfast. 'Well well, looks like you *can* get up early after all,' she teased, picking up the kettle to fill it. 'I'll remember this on your schooldays, young ladies.'

'Told you she'd say that, didn't I?' Hannah said to Holly, who was scraping around the bottom of her cereal bowl for the last dribble of milk.

Holly nodded, then dropped her spoon into her bowl and checked her watch. 'Forty seconds!'

'To eat a whole bowl of cornflakes?' Jen wasn't sure whether to be impressed or concerned, but Holly's pride in her time-telling abilities made her smile. She and Hannah had received identical pink watches for Christmas, from Jen's parents, and missed no opportunity to show off their new skills.

'It's now ten minutes 'til eight o'clock, so we've got half an hour until we go.'

'That gives us ten minutes to get to Sinead's, so we'll be ready to set off by half past eight,' Hannah added, not to be outdone.

'With you two as my time-keepers, I'll never be late for anything, will I?' Jen dropped a teabag into her cup. 'Just as long as Sinead's as on time as you are, of course. Put your bowls in the sink, and while you're waiting for me to get ready you can go and make your beds. Then get your brushes and bobbles ready for me to put your hair into tails. It's gone a bit wild since those plaits.'

The girls vanished upstairs, and Jen sat in peace for a few minutes, sipping her tea. Today's trip was making her feel a little anxious, but it would be more fun in the car than by train. Not to mention cheaper, for the four of them. And they could break the journey at a motorway services and eat pancakes as a treat.

She'd been surprised at how fast the response had come from Mrs Nasir; just four days after she and Sinead had posted their pile of letters to all the primary schools in Brighton, Jen had received a text.

Hello, Jen. My name is Farrah Nasir, mother of Alima and Ruhi, and yes, my girls have that same dream! I very much look forward to meeting you. A visit was arranged for the same week.

Jen glanced at the clock, and realised she'd been musing for too long. She poured a cup of coffee for the still-sleeping John, and left it beside him before going into the bathroom to wash and dress. Passing back through the bedroom to pick up her bag, she paused for a moment,

173

and smiled. John was looking peaceful and snoring lightly, and she bent and kissed him goodbye. He stirred and muttered, 'Have fun. Love you,' before falling back into his slumber.

They pulled into the car park at the back of the Rose and Crown, and Jen glanced up to see the curtain of the flat twitch, and then Sinead's waving hands. Minutes later she had joined them, her open coat flapping in the stiff breeze. When she got into the passenger seat she was met with a chorus of disappointment.

'Don't you want to sit in the back with us?'

'Of course I do, but you must learn to share me, even with your mum.' Jen couldn't help smiling at that, and Sinead went on, 'Tell you what, after we've stopped for our pancakes I'll sit in the back with you scallywags for the whole second half of the trip. How does that sound?'

'Squashy, but good,' Holly grinned.

Sinead twisted to fasten her seat belt, and saw the girls properly. 'Oh my, look at your crinkle hair! Very cool.'

'We undid our plaits, and our hair went whoosh! All over the place,' Hannah told her.

'And we got bored with being Christina,' Holly added, 'so now we're Cher.'

Sinead raised an eyebrow at Jen. 'They've watched Mermaids,' Jen explained, 'and switched their allegiance.'

'Ah. Well I love it,' Sinead said. 'Right, what are we waiting for? Let's roll!'

Suburbia fell behind them as Jen battled the traffic around Cambridge. Soon they were heading for the motorway, and it was a relief to finally shift into top gear and relax, after the start-stop of town driving, and seemingly endless sets of traffic lights.

'Put some music on,' she said to Sinead, and Sinead rummaged in the glove box and came up with some mix CDs. With the steady thrum of cars and lorries accompanying them, the four of them passed the time singing along to a selection of current songs and old rock music, and after around an hour Jen checked the rear view mirror and saw Holly wriggling in her seat.

'I need the loo,' Holly said.

'Won't be long now, then we can stop for a wee.'

'I don't want a wee, I want… the other!'

'Pew!' Hannah sang out with glee, holding her nose.

Jen tried not to laugh. 'I can't stop here, poppet. Just… squeeze your cheeks together.'

She looked in the mirror again, and saw Holly's face, and this time she couldn't stop the laughter.

Sinead looked into the back seat, and erupted in giggles. 'Not *those* cheeks!'

Hannah was only too happy to join in, pointing and laughing, while Holly folded her arms, her face thunderous. 'What!'

No-one felt able to reply, but soon Jen pulled in to the services on the M20 and even Holly forgot her embarrassment in the excitement of choosing the syrup flavour for her pancakes.

Sinead wedged herself between the twins on the back seat for the rest of the drive, bringing a definite air of holiday to the journey. 'So, has John's passport arrived?' she asked.

175

Jen turned the music down a little. 'No, it's been a right pain. He didn't have six months left on his passport, and you need that to get into Israel, so he had to renew it.'

'Damn.'

'He sent it all off in November, and he's been chasing it ever since. The latest is, they say it was sent in January, recorded delivery. We never got it, we must have been out and it got taken to the sorting office, but John went to check. They've got no record of it.'

'But it's only a couple of weeks before they go. What will he do?'

'Nothing else they can do, they'll have to postpone the trip. He's not happy, but the passport office is all about the buck-passing. Less than helpful. His old passport is to be cancelled, and he's had to reapply. But he's not taking any chances with this one, he'll drive to London and pick it up himself when it's ready. He's going to talk to Todd about it while we're away, but I doubt if he'll go until after the girls birthday.'

Hannah had clearly become bored with the grown-ups' conversation. 'Sinead?'

'Hmm?'

'Are you and Todd going to get married?'

'Um—'

'Cos if you are,' Holly piped up, 'can we be bridesmaids?'

'Girls!' Jen spared a quick glare into the back seat. 'That's rude! You don't ask questions like that!'

'It's okay,' Sinead said, and addressed her eager companions. '*If* we get married, then yes, of course you can. Along with my four sisters. But I think you girls will probably be married before me, so can I be *your* bridesmaid?'

The girls chorused their assent, and Jen squinted at the looming road sign. 'Ooh, look! First sign for Brighton, won't be long now. You have to look for signs to Woodingdean, okay? We'll go straight there to see Mrs Nasir and the girls, then after we've had a chat we'll go down to the pier for a bit before we have to head home.'

They drove up the hill towards Cowley Drive, with the girls vying to be the first to spot it, but Jen pulled over before they got there; partly because the view was beautiful, and partly because she wanted to relax and gather her thoughts before meeting Farrah. The village of Woodingdean was set between the downs, and Brighton Racecourse, and there were green hills along the way. Looking back down the hill Jen was startled to see how high above the sea they'd climbed; it was breathtaking.

Holly was the first to spot the street, and before long they were standing outside Farrah Nasir's front door, listening to the Big Ben chime echoing through the hallway beyond. The door opened and the lady who greeted them did so with a wide smile. She was small, and dark-haired, and her voice was low and pleasant.

'You must be Mrs Milburn.'

'Jen, please. And this is Sinead, Holly, and Hannah.'

'I'm Farrah. Welcome, please do come in.' She led them to a large room, tastefully decorated in terracotta and pastel shades. Half of it was tidy, the other half a mess of bolts of material, an industrial-sized sewing machine,

177

and what looked like hundreds of different shades of cottons stacked on a bookcase.

'I'm sorry about the mess down that end,' Farrah said. 'It's my workshop. Would you like a drink? Something warm? I've baked some cakes if you're hungry; I expect the girls would like that. Did you find us without too much trouble? It's so nice to meet you! Goodness, listen to me, I'm rambling! Sorry.' She gestured to the settee. 'Please let me take your coats, and make yourselves comfortable.'

Jen took off her coat and smiled. 'Don't worry, you're probably feeling as anxious as I am.' Farrah smiled back, and visibly relaxed, and Jen sat down. 'Sinead and I would love some coffee, thank you.'

'And the girls? Juice?' They nodded, suddenly shy, and looked around for the Nasir twins. Farrah dropped her voice. 'I haven't told my girls about your visit yet. I wanted to see their reaction to meeting Holly and Hannah.'

'That's a good idea,' Jen said.

When Farrah had put a tray of drinks and cakes on the coffee table, and invited everyone to help themselves, she went out into the hall and called up the stairs.

'Alima! Ruhi! We have some visitors I'd like you to meet.'

She came back into the room, twisting her hands together and looking nervous once more. Jen knew how she felt; she was feeling a squirming sensation in her own stomach. Presently two sets of feet thudded down the stairs, and the Nasir twins came in; pretty girls, their dark hair neatly plaited and hanging down their backs, straight and glossy. They opened their mouths to greet Jen and Sinead, and then stopped, mouths open and eyes wide, as they saw Holly and Hannah.

'It's… you!' one of them said.

'You're real!'

Holly and Hannah blinked in surprise. 'Of course we are,' Holly said.

'I'm Ruhi,' the first twin said. She came over and touched Holly's arm gently, brushing her sleeve and pressing gently to make sure. 'This is Alima.' There was a pause, then she gave the visitors a bright smile. 'D'you want to come up and see our room? We've got dressing up stuff.'

'We love dressing up,' Hannah said eagerly. And just like that the bond was forged and the four girls disappeared upstairs, already chattering.

Sinead smiled. 'Ah, if only everything in life was that simple!'

'So,' Farrah said, lifting the cafetiere with a hand that shook slightly. 'As I suspected, the dreams are more than dreams, then.'

'Yes, they are.' Jen took the proffered cup. 'Thank you so much for getting back to me. It's lovely to meet you, and so good to know we're not alone in this.'

'My girls told me they had dream friends, and mentioned Holly and Hannah's names. So when you got in touch I had to meet you.' Farrah blinked rapidly, evidently close to tears, but Jen couldn't tell whether it was relief or fear. 'It's been difficult, I've been so worried. I thought there might be something wrong with them, but the doctor made me feel silly for checking. He took blood tests, probably to shut me up. They came back normal. The girls have always been in perfect health, physically.' She shrugged. 'That's strange in itself, don't you think?'

'I know what you mean. Neither Holly nor Hannah suffers from colds. Holly broke her arm a few years ago, but that's it. My husband had appendicitis as a child, but he's never had any of the usual illnesses either. I assumed they'd inherited his immunities, but maybe that's not the case after all.'

'There might be more similarities,' Sinead suggested.

'If you don't mind my asking,' Jen said to Farrah, 'how are the girls doing at school?'

'Not at all. They're both top of their class, and they excel at sciences.'

'Holly and Hannah are the same, although they're whizzes at maths. What about languages?'

'They both speak fluent English and Hindi. And their own, made-up language too.'

Jen glanced at Sinead. 'I'm betting their language is the same as Holly and Hannah's.'

'But that's not possible, is it?' Farrah said.

Sinead looked at the ceiling through which the sound of giggling reached them. 'We thought that, too, but we can check when they come down. We don't have any answers yet, I'm afraid, but we hope the more we discover, the closer we'll be to understanding it all. We do think all the children involved are gifted though, and have a special purpose.'

'*All* the children?' Farrah looked from her to Jen. 'How many are we talking about?'

'Twenty-three sets of twins,' Jen said, and saw Farrah's face go slack with astonishment.

'How… how many of these others have you contacted?'

'You're the first,' Sinead said.

Jen sat forward, her hands clasped in her lap. 'Farrah, is there anything else the girls have mentioned about their dream that you can remember?'

'Only that they climb a mountain, and talk to other children. Are these the other twins you talked about?'

Jen nodded. 'Anything else?'

Farrah frowned, and her eyes took on a distant look as she searched her memory. 'Oh! They've seen a man on this mountain, too.'

'That's probably my husband.' Jen saw the disbelief on Farrah's face, and quickly explained about the episode at Christmas. 'Have you or your husband had the same dream?'

'No, and nor has Sunil, our son. He's older than the twins.' Farrah looked distracted and unsettled, and her gaze fell on their empty cups. 'Can I get you another drink?' It seemed she was seizing on anything familiar that might anchor her to the world she knew, and although Jen privately thought she oughtn't to drink any more, facing a long drive home, she nodded.

'Could I use your bathroom?' Sinead said, her thoughts clearly following the same path.

'Of course. There's one in the hall.'

Sinead made herself comfortable and walked more slowly back through the hall, hearing Farrah still in the kitchen.

She glanced around her, admiring the deep gloss of the skirting boards and the dust-free corners, and then noticed the pile of magazines on a carved occasional table. The top magazine drew her eye with its colourful saris and jewelled hair pieces, and she picked it up for a closer look. Near the bottom she read, *Hajj News – Incidents at Mecca and Jabal al-Nour.* The Arab name for Mount Hira… she read on:

More devotees die after being crushed in crowds. Influenza outbreak follows pilgrims home. Angels reported ascending Jabal al-Nour, see inside cover.

Sinead turned the page and continued reading, only stopping when the kitchen door opened and Farrah came out. Startled, and feeling a little guilty, she closed the magazine.

'I'm so sorry. I didn't mean to be nosy, but the cover caught my eye.'

'Don't worry,' Farrah said, still looking a little distant. 'It's absolutely fine. My husband likes to keep up with the news from Mecca, but he has another copy at the restaurant so please do take it, if it interests you.'

Sinead smiled. 'That's very kind, thank you.' She followed Farrah into the lounge and slipped the magazine into her bag.

'My husband has worked out that the mountain the girls dream of is Jabal al-Nour,' Farrah said. 'We are a good Muslim family, and he has taken it as a sign that he should do the Hajj.'

'Hajj?' Jen looked uncertain.

'The pilgrimage to Mecca,' Sinead said. 'All Muslims must make this pilgrimage at least once in their lifetime.'

182

'That's correct. The magazine you have there has a report on the one that happened a couple of weeks ago. Ravi has been putting off going, due to finances. He's been saving like mad to go with Sunil. He owns the Aloo Moon here in town, and has been trying to arrange help with it while they're away next year.'

Jen nodded, and they all turned towards the door as they heard the girls coming down. Quickly, Jen asked, 'would you mind if I show them a photo of my husband? Just to see if they recognise him?'

Farrah shook her head. 'Of course not.'

The girls came in, and after a few minutes of listening to them all talking about the Nasir girls' brilliant dressing-up box, Jen steered the conversation back to the matter in hand.

'I've heard you have your own language,' she said. 'Would you say something to Holly and Hannah in it?'

There followed a brisk, faultless exchange between all four girls, and Sinead saw Farrah blink, and stare in shock as what would have been something only she and those closest knew about, was shared so effortlessly with these strangers.

Jen called Alima and Ruhi over, and began looking through the photos in her wallet until she found one that showed John's face clearly. 'Have you ever seen this man in your dreams of the mountain?'

Alima peered at the picture. 'Hmm, we might have. We didn't see him up close, and it was only once, so I'm not really sure.'

Ruhi looked over her sister's shoulder. 'It does look a bit like him, but I think the man in our dream has longer hair.'

'He was looking for someone called Dahveed,' Alima said helpfully.

'Oh yeah!' Ruhi brightened. 'I forgot that. He kept saying, "Where are you, Dahveed?"'

'And did he find him?'

'No.'

Sinead saw Jen frown suddenly, as if she were trying to remember where she'd heard that phrase before, but it was clearly evading her at the moment. Jen thanked the Nasir girls, in Hally, for their help. They looked at her in astonishment, as did their mother.

'How can you speak this language too?' Farrah asked.

'I've been learning for years. Since the girls were little. We call it Hally. The fact that it's clearly not peculiar to Holly and Hannah means it had to have originated somewhere, and I want to be prepared in case I need it at some point.'

It was time to go, and although Jen's twins clearly didn't want to, they were soon placated with the promise of ice cream on the pier. They took their leave, with promises to stay in touch, and drove back down to the waterside. Jen managed to find a parking space not too far from the pier.

'In a few months, that'll be pretty much impossible,' she said, sticking the car park ticket on her window. 'Come on, let's have a wander.'

They walked through the famous warren of narrow lanes, peering through shop windows and exclaiming over the unusual and beautiful items for sale. Then they headed towards the pier, and the girls marvelled at the shops and cafés, painted in outlandish colours and styles, but stopping short of garish; it was a little like walking through an art gallery. Everyone seemed to have their own style of dress, and their friendliness made the visitors feel welcome in the diverse and charming city.

'Everyone's so *smiley!*' Jen said, and Sinead nodded.

'So much more laid back than Cambridge.'

They found a small, family-run café opposite the pier, where the girls could sit outside with their milkshakes, while Jen and Sinead sat at a window table so they could keep an eye on them.

Jen played with the tablecloth fringe, waiting for her drink to cool. 'You remember what Farrah's girls said,' she began, 'about the man looking for someone called Dahveed?'

'I knew that had got to you,' Sinead said. 'You got a real faraway look on your face. Did it remind you of something?'

'I couldn't remember at the time,' Jen said, 'but now I think back, there was a time when I recorded John dreaming. When I played the tape back, the girls told us he'd been speaking in Hally, and was saying, "where are you?" but we couldn't make out the next word. It was Dahveed! The Jewish pronunciation of David, which doesn't make a lot of sense. But I'm not convinced it was John they saw, in which case John was simply repeating what he'd heard the man saying.'

'The twins on that list Todd copied were David and Doron Malik, weren't they?'

'Exactly!' Jen pushed her cup aside, and Sinead was pretty sure she'd only ordered from habit. 'I think the man in the dream is Doron Malik, and he's looking for his brother!'

Sinead bent to her bag. 'I think our trip has been even more fruitful than we realised.' She took out the magazine, opened it, and put it on the table in front of Jen. 'Read that.' She tapped the part about Jabal al-Nour.

'This bit?' Jen read aloud. ' "Some eye witnesses have also reported seeing what they believe to be angels ascending Jabal al-Nour. One pilgrim, 42 year old Omar Farooqi, described the phenomenon as shimmering shapes climbing upwards. He took a photo whilst climbing the mountain to reach the Cave of Hira. Experts have dismissed the claim as religious fervour following the Hajj, and say that the shimmers are merely heat haze or mirages. Look at the photo and see what you think, readers." Wow. ' Jen stared at the accompanying photo.

'You don't think that's—'

'Damned right I do!'

***

Office of Richard Hampton.
'Put Romm on the job, I'll let you know when. I want this stopped. Now! The idiots are still trying to get to Israel, I don't know what they think they're going to accomplish! I should've put a stop to this years ago… Don't tell me what to do, you imbecile! Just remember who you're talking to. I saved your miserable arse from jail, and I can just as easily put it back there.'

186

Hampton cut off the squawking voice of his caller, and stopped pacing the floor. He took a deep breath and stared at the ceiling, feeling his rage bubble and spit; an imminent volcanic eruption. He was surrounded by incompetents! Did he have to sort *everything* out himself? Christ, everyone let him down eventually: his colleagues, his wife, his parents... not to mention his son, the *great* theologian. A theologian! He was a fucking embarrassment, and one Richard had long since given up trying to bring into the family business. He had washed his hands of the weak-minded little shit long ago.

Richard put his phone away and sat down. He pulled the metal waste bin closer, and then opened his briefcase on the desk, studying its contents thoughtfully. After a minute he reached into his pocket and found his lighter, flicked it once, twice, and the flame caught. With the light and heat of it dancing before his eyes he stared at it for a moment, hypnotised, then took a passport from his case.

It didn't take long to turn into ashes.

Part Four
New York, Cambridge & Israel 2003

'… and Nour led his brother's people through the Wildernesses to the land that was shown to him. His trials were many but with the strength of his spirit, delivered them to safety. And within the thousands he led The Father's children, two by two, and the forty-six were delivered also to safety. Whilst awaiting his brother's return, the people cast him out and he returned to Nubia.'
Unknown author 2nd millennium BC

'Let Us make man in Our image, after Our likeness …'
From the Borean Study Bible, Genesis 1:26

Didn't God make them one and give them a portion of spirit? What is the one seeking? Godly offspring.'
From the Christian Standard Bible, Malachi 2:15

'When I have completed shaping him and have breathed into him of My Spirit …'
From the Qur'an, 15:29

'Let us make a human in our image, after our likeness …'
From the Torah, Bereshith 1:26

Chapter Eleven
The Arrivals

Tel Aviv, Israel. Saturday evening, 24 May 2003

After a full day's travelling they were in Israel at last, and a soft hotel bed was only a hopeful hour away. John's eyes stung with a mixture of tiredness and heat, but he grinned at Todd. 'We finally made it! A couple of months late, but we're here.'

'Give me a shower, and a few beers in the hotel bar, and I'll be a happy man.' Todd dug his passport out of his pocket. 'What about you?'

'Sounds good,' John conceded. The bed wasn't going anywhere, after all. He found his own passport, and the two of them exchanged glances of weary resignation as they joined the snaking queue at passport control.

It took almost an hour of alternately pushing their cases ahead of them with their feet, and then sitting on them, but they finally reached the desk. Todd was first through, shoving his passport back into his jacket with a Heaven-ward look of relief, and John handed his own over, impatient to join him on the other side. He kept his hand outstretched for its return, but his smile faltered as he saw the immigration officer peering at the page closely. Now what?

'Would you step to the side, sir?'

'What? Why?'

The official merely gestured, and John obeyed, mystified. Todd raised his eyebrows, and John shrugged, his unease deepening as the official called a colleague across. The man also checked the passport, and then studied John carefully.

'I'd like you to come with me,' he said at length.

'Why?' John asked again. 'Aren't you at least going to—'

'Now, please.'

'What's going on?' Todd's voice cut across the airport din.

'No idea! Look, you go on, I'll catch up with you at the hotel.'

'I'll wait here until I know what's happening.'

John nodded, secretly relieved. 'Okay, thanks, mate. Shouldn't take too long, it must be a routine security check.'

Inside the small, box-like interrogation room was a table and two chairs, and hardly anything else. John took the chair indicated and sat down. Although it was a relief to take the weight off his feet, the sudden sense of isolation made him wish for the noisy airport again, and some sense of normality. Despite what he'd told Todd, this didn't feel like some random check; that guard had been scrutinising him pretty carefully.

'Wait here,' his escort said. 'A security agent will be with you shortly.'

Left alone, John's unease turned to frustration. Why him? Why now? He was knackered, and he'd been *so* close to that hotel… He tried to pass the time by wondering what Jen and the girls were doing now, but it only brought a wave of envy that, whatever it was, he wasn't doing it with them. This stark little room only made the contrast with the home comforts of a cosy evening that much more acute.

It must have been around half an hour later when the door clicked open again, and John stood, automatically holding out his hand to introduce himself. The newcomer merely glanced at it, making him feel stupid, then turned to thank the guard who'd shown him in.

'You don't need to stay,' he added, taking some paperwork off him.

'Just a moment, Romm, I need to—'

'Later.' He put the papers, including John's passport, on the table in front of him, and waited until they were alone once more.

'Sit.'

John did, biting back an irritated retort. Instead he searched for a more polite tone. 'Can you please tell me why I've been detained like this?'

Romm sat opposite him. 'You are John Milburn, yes?'

'Yes.'

'I am in charge of security here at Ben Gurion. Why are you here?'

John blinked. 'Here in this room? I have no idea. If you mean here in Israel, I'm on holiday with a friend.'

Romm gave him a disbelieving look, and sighed. 'But you came to Ben Gurion Airport.'

'Well, it's the most direct route. We're booked into a hotel at Tel Aviv.'

'Why?'

'We plan to do some sightseeing, then travel on to Jericho.'

'I see.' Romm paused and shuffled his papers. 'Why do you want to go there?'

'Some old friends of my parents live there, I'd like to meet them while I'm here.'

'So you have Palestinian friends?'

John kept his patience, with an effort. 'No, friends of my *parents*. I've never met them. My parents worked here in the sixties, when I was born. My mother returned to the UK when I was three months old.'

'And your father remained in Israel?'

'No, he... he died here.'

Romm didn't show the slightest flicker of sympathy. 'Your passport,' he tapped it, 'states you were born in Ramallah, in the Palestinian Authorities.'

'Yes, but I don't see the prob—'

'You should not have come to this airport, Mr Milburn. You are Palestinian.'

'I'm not! I'm a UK citizen, of UK parents. I was just born here.'

Romm's eyebrow went up, his calm voice contrasting with John's rising agitation. 'Why do you question my authority? Why do you deny you are Palestinian?'

'I just—'

'You should have travelled by the Allenby Bridge, not this airport. Palestinians cannot enter Israel.'

'What? This makes no sense! I have a UK passport,' he gestured to it, 'and I should be granted entry as a tourist. Like my friend was!'

'I ask again, why are you questioning my authority? Do you think you know more of our laws than I?' He gave John a thin smile. 'It is at our discretion whether we allow someone into our country. Or not,' he added pointedly.

John couldn't think of a response, so when Romm asked for his phone he gave it almost gratefully; there was nothing on it that looked the slightest bit suspicious, so perhaps this would be the thing that convinced the security chief of his innocence.

Romm opened the text messages and, while reading, began to fire questions about John's parents, their occupations, John's own occupation... then about Uri and Maya. The interrogation seemed to go on for hours, but finally Romm finished with the phone. John reached to take it back, but the guard placed it face-down on the table in front of himself instead.

'We've established your passport states you were born in Ramallah. So I ask again, why are you here?'

John barely stifled a groan. 'This is going nowhere. I want to contact my embassy.'

'You're perfectly within your rights to do so, of course. But they will not interfere with our immigration rules.'

'Rules? I thought you said it was at your discretion?' But John was too tired for point-scoring, and sighed. 'They can help clear up what is obviously a mistake here.'

'I'm insulted at your implication that I've made a mistake, in my professional capacity.'

I don't care if you're insulted! John swallowed his fury and tried a conciliatory tone. 'I don't mean to insult you, Mr Romm, I'm just frustrated that you insist I'm Palestinian when I'm clearly not.'

'Now it's my judgement you're questioning?' Romm's voice was hard. 'I'm not happy with the responses you've given, Mr Milburn, nor am I convinced of your reasons for wanting to enter my country. I will arrange an escort to take you to a cell, where you will remain until we can organise your deportation papers.' He began gathering up the phone and paperwork on the table. 'You will be returned to the UK, at your own expense of course. Your passport will remain confiscated until you board your connecting flight home from Istanbul. I suggest you do not try to return. By any route.'

'Wait… deported?' John stared. 'This is a joke, right?'

'I do not make jokes about such important things, Mr Milburn.'

As the door swung shut, and silence fell once more on the little room, John wondered if anyone had told Todd what was going on, and if his friend would still be waiting for him. The time seemed to tick by agonisingly slowly, and without a watch or phone it was hard to tell how long he'd been sitting there alone, but he'd have bet it was hours rather than minutes.

Eventually two guards came to escort him to his cell. One of them returned his watch, which he snapped onto his wrist… he'd been right: a little over two hours since that Romm bloke had left him to his thoughts.

Emerging into the busy airport once more he saw Todd, who struggled to his feet, from where he'd been sitting on the floor. 'What's the deal?'

'Can I have just a minute?' John asked the guards. After a brief glance at one another, and a shrug, they allowed him to outline what had happened. Todd's face

194

went through what would, under normal circumstances, have been an amusing and varied set of expressions: curiosity; worry; disgust; and finally anger on John's behalf. 'What can I do?'

'Tell Jen I'm coming home,' John said on a sigh. 'And get her to call Uri and Maya too. They're not expecting us for another week anyway, but we might as well let them know what's happened, and why I'm not coming.'

'Right. I'm coming back with you.'

'No, you're not!' John gave him a grateful look. 'It's good of you to offer, but why should you miss out because of me? No. You carry on with the plans as we've made them.'

'Come.' One of the guards gripped John's arm, clearly bored by the conversation now. 'A van is waiting.'

The detention centre was no more welcoming than the interrogation block; after an escorted toilet break John was taken to a grubby little room, in which two other men sat in surly silence, sparing him little more than a mildly curious glance. At least he hadn't been subjected to a body search, which was something to be thankful for... Still, without food, and after the indignity of being taken out of line and locked away, it was hard to find even that silver lining as a good sign; they didn't suspect him of anything but being born in the wrong place. And what could he do about that?

With both hard benches occupied, he sank down on his heels in the farthest corner, and rested his arms on his raised knees. His stomach growled, reminding him he'd not eaten since the rather insipid, plastic-tasting meal on the plane, but it would be pointless to ask for anything; he was as much a criminal here as a tourist. For a while he actually managed to drift in and out of a troubled sleep, but his dreams now were not of a mountain and a strange language, they were of mundane, everyday things that drove his predicament home harder each time he opened his eyes.

A voice calling his name filtered down into one such dream, and he blinked awake to realise it wasn't a colleague yelling at him at all, but that someone had let down the metal flap on the door to the cell. He glanced at his watch: two o'clock in the morning. Jesus! He climbed stiffly to his feet in response to the irritated rattling of the flap, and went to the door.

'What's happening?'

'You're to be taken to a hotel for the remainder of the night.' The door opened, allowing him to step outside. 'Your phone and luggage will be waiting for you. In the morning you will be deported.'

'Yeah. Well as soon as I get back to the UK I'm going to—'

'Not the UK. Jordan.'

John frowned. 'Jordan?'

'Your flight leaves at eight. Be outside the hotel by six-thirty at the latest, and you will be brought back to the airport.' The guard walked quickly, and John winced as he forced his aching legs to keep up.

'Once you board the flight to Queen Alia airport,' the guard threw back over his shoulder, 'you will have your passport returned to you. You will then be escorted across the Allenby Bridge into the Palestinian Authorities. Your passport will be stamped *Palestinian Authorities only…* ' he broke off and shot a disapproving look at a still bemused John. 'You are lucky they are not being stamped *entry denied.*'

'But I'll still be interrogated by Israeli officials there, won't I?'

'No.' The guard studied him with curiosity now, as well as distaste. 'You must have friends in high places, Mr Milburn. I've never known such leniency.'

Stepping into his hotel room was like walking into Paradise. John spotted the mini bar at the same moment the light flickered on, and a moment later he had twisted the cap off a whiskey miniature and downed the bottle's fiery contents. He seized another, hesitating briefly as he remembered he had to be awake and functioning in less than four hours, then shrugged and drank it anyway. If he hadn't earned it, who had?

Sitting on the edge of his bed he sent a text to Todd, asking him to cancel his Tel Aviv hotel room and re-book in Ramallah, and then one to Jen to reassure her he was okay. It was gone midnight at home, but of course she rang him back immediately.

'I couldn't sleep anyway,' she said. 'Are you sure you're alright?'

'I'm fine, love. I'll call you as soon as I get to Ramallah, okay?' He asked after the girls, and after a few minutes he remembered what time it was in England, and reluctantly said goodbye. He was already feeling the warmth of the whiskey creeping through him, bringing a tiredness that was actually welcome now he finally had that soft bed

197

he'd been yearning for since teatime. For a moment he dithered between showering now or later, but a single whiff of his shirt sent him into the bathroom, before he collapsed into bed and fell into a thankfully dreamless sleep.

The next day's journey was long and tiring, but not unpleasant. From the Allenby Bridge he travelled up through the West Bank; apart from the new sections of the Israeli separation wall, standing gloomily over the terrain, and a few bleak areas that bore evidence of conflict, the scenery was beautiful. Dusty and old, but with so much to see in such a small part of the country that the time passed quickly despite everything.

The Royal Court Hotel turned out to be the perfect choice, too; situated on Jaffa Street in central West Bank, to cut down on travelling. Todd had done well, and John smiled his approval. He looked up at the impressive façade and could see all the front-facing rooms at least had balconies, perfect for looking out over the city. After a more leisurely shower this time, he went down to dinner, and then into the bar. A couple of beers would settle his mind for a much-needed early night and a chance to catch up on all the sleep he'd missed.

Whilst passing pleasantries with the barman he noticed a rather attractive map of Israel hanging behind the bar. He mentioned he'd like a copy of it, and the barman was only too happy to help, but not in the way John expected. He took the map off the wall and placed it in front of John, then he tore a sheet from a large notepad, and rummaged around for a pen.

John stared at this little collection for a minute, then gave his thanks with a smile and began to draw. It was more therapeutic than he'd thought it would be, and as the pen skimmed over the paper, yesterday's troubles drifted to the back of his mind.

He was halfway down his second beer, and starting to yawn, when a tap on the shoulder almost made him drop his glass. His mind already on the worst case scenario he turned, and relaxed.

'Todd! What are you doing here?'

'Well that's a nice welcome, I must say!' Todd slid onto the stool next to him. 'Couldn't let you stay here all alone could I?' he gestured to the barman and indicated he'd like two more pints. 'The bold knights of Haverhill have to stick together.'

'I'll drink to that.'

'Besides, I didn't fancy the hassle of stressing my way through the checkpoints every day, just to see your ugly mug. The Tel Aviv hotel was great, gave us a partial refund. What are you doing?' He nodded at John's drawing.

'Just passing the time. I thought I'd draw a map of the area, and fill in the places we visit. Something to show the girls when we get home.'

'Good idea.' Todd peered closer. 'Hey, that's not bad at all.'

The barman brought the drinks, and Todd raised his. 'Cheers!'

'Cheers.' John tilted his own glass, and Todd leaned in to clink his against it. Beer foamed up and spilled, soaking his wrist as well as the corner of John's map. 'Oops, sorry.'

'Don't worry about it, mate' John picked up the map and shook it, then moved it out of the way. 'It's only a sketch, and we're not heading into that area anyway.'

Todd squinted at the stain. 'Maybe we could pass it off as low-flying cloud or something?'

'You're an idiot.'

'Talking of idiots, d'you remember that time we…'

The early night didn't materialise after all, but John didn't care.

***

New York, New York

Richard Hampton paid the cab driver and stood squinting up at the massive tower block in Times Square, already feeling the afternoon heat baking through his clothes. Thank God this meeting had been called in May; another couple of months and his shoes would melt to the pavement –*sidewalk*, he corrected himself, with an inward shudder – not to mention the worsening smells; petrol and oil mingling with the smell from pretzel stands on every corner, with their bright yellow, salty cheese… how could anyone bring themselves to walk these streets? Or use the subway? Taking a cab was the only bearable way to get from A to B in this revolting city. It reminded him of Hong Kong, with the endlessly flashing lights, and billboards, and the oblivious crowds surging across the choked streets with no thought for traffic. Not that it could move very fast. Hampton had only arrived yesterday, and already he was ready to leave.

He sighed and went up the shallow steps, then took the lift to the fourth floor, and the offices of Whyte and Gleed, Architects…which just happened to also be the covert centralised head office, where Veritas co-ordinated its global management. He let his eyes drift appreciatively over Louise Miller, Charles Whyte's PA, who rose to show him into the office; damned good looking woman, she was, and, well, he might be sixty but he could still play the game… The bigger the challenge, the greater the prize.

Ms Miller kept her eyes averted as she knocked on Charles's door, and pushed it open to allow him to enter; Hampton took that as a good sign. He let his hand slide along her arm as it held the door open, and then she was gone. He was surprised to see he was the only delegate in the office, and only Charles seated at the conference table.

'Rich.' Charles rose and came over to shake hands. 'Good to see you. How are you?'

'Good to see you too, Charles.' Hampton swallowed his irritation at the shortening of his name, but only just. 'I'm well. You?'

'I'm great!' *Bloody New York voice, definitely put on.* 'Anyway, shall we dispense with the pleasantries? Neither of us enjoys it.' Whyte's eyes turned shrewd. 'Let's get down to business.'

'Fine with me. Why have you called me here?'

'I wanted to speak with you privately.'

'About what?'

'I want to discuss current developments.' Whyte broke off as Ms Miller came in with a tray of refreshments, and

201

smiled. 'Thanks, honey.' But when she moved to pour the drinks he waved her away. 'We'll pour our own, Lou. Thanks.'

Hampton watched her withdraw from the office, and heard her high heels clacking away on the melamine floor beyond the plush carpet. He did enjoy a challenge.

Louise pulled the door closed behind her, and breathed a sigh of relief that she wouldn't be expected to take notes from that particular meeting. Aside from anything else, that Hampton guy was the creepiest. Charles Whyte she'd always thought was okay; he'd been a courteous boss for the six years she'd worked for him, and, knowing where his affiliations lay, she felt safe. She'd been happy working here… until recently.

With a glance at the office door, just to make sure, she took up a small key and unlocked the stationery cupboard. She reached inside, and her blindly searching fingers found the button right away and pressed it. The hidden machine's lights blinked on and it whirred into life, recording everything.

Back at her desk Louise put her ear-phones in, and began typing. For a while she mechanically hit the keys, her mind half on other things, then she began to slow, and eventually she stopped typing altogether. Her fingers were shaking, and as the conversation unfolded she felt hot tears spring to her eyes. *Babies? Christ…* It was one thing to know that the two men to whom she was listening were the kind of evil who started wars – wars like the one in Vietnam, which had killed her much-missed older brother thirty years ago – but this… How many more had died for their greed? And how many to come?

The sickening conversation wound down, and Louise ripped out her ear-phones just as the door opened and Hampton came out. She could see Charles through the gap, leaning back in his seat, a satisfied look on his face that was mirrored on Hampton's. The departing delegate found some reason to come close to the desk before leaving, and Louise felt the hairs on the nape of her neck prickle in disgust. Some flirtatious banter—offered by him, convincingly reciprocated by her—and an offer of drinks, which she turned down with a 'perhaps next time,' and he was gone. Thank God.

She crossed to the stationery cupboard again and switched off the recording, wondering how she was capable of such breezy behaviour when her insides were churning like this. She held on tightly to the promise of protection for herself and her mother, and slipped the tape into her bag. Before she picked up her coat she scanned her desk for the few personal items she kept there, and put them in beside the tape. Today would be her final day at Whyte and Gleed.

***

Ramallah, Palestinian Territories, Israel
Todd and John had spent the week sightseeing, exploring, and getting relaxing massages from a hammam in Nablus. The stress of their arrival in Israel had quickly melted away, and before they realised it, Saturday had crept up on

203

them and it was time for John's visit to Uri and Maya in Jericho. Todd waved him off into his cab from the balcony, already looking forward to exploring the other side of Israel, which would have been in breach of John's visa restrictions. He'd join John later in the week.

The cab pulled away and Todd sat down, enjoying the cooler evening air as it brushed over the city. What a view! He'd never tire of it. He finished the last of his beer, and picked up his phone to call Sinead before he went out.

'Hi, babe. How's it going?'

'Fine!' She sounded delighted to hear from him. 'What've you two been up to?'

'This and that, you know. Been here and there.'

'You paint *such* a wonderful picture.'

He grinned. 'Seriously, it's been great. Exhausting, but great. I'll have some amazing photos to show you when I get back. It's good to see the old John back, too. He's been ribbing me something chronic.'

'How d'you mean?'

Todd chose his words carefully. 'Well there are some, uh, gorgeous women here in Israel, and I've had one or two looks of course. But I've not been interested,' he hurried on.

'Really?' Her tone was arch but he could hear the smile in her voice. 'Glad to hear it. It makes a change for John to be the one taking the piss though.'

'Yeah. Like I said, the old John. It's great. So what have you been doing while your Prince Charming has been away?'

'Not a lot. Studying, working, you know. I popped in to see Jen and the girls. Oh, and yesterday I visited your mum.'

'*My* mum? Really?'

Sinead sounded hesitant now. 'Do you mind?'

'No, of course not. I was just a bit surprised. Actually it's really nice of you. Is she okay?'

'She's fine. I like her, and we got on like a house on fire.'

'So I imagine.'

'We talked about my family, and then she got out your baby pictures.' She laughed as Todd groaned. 'We had fun, but she's going to give you hell when you get back, for not bringing me around to meet her before.'

'Shit.'

'Ah, don't worry,' Sinead chuckled. 'She loves you.'

'Of course, what's not to—'

'I know! What's not to love?' When the comfortable laughter had died down, she went on, 'Did you know your father had been in Israel at the same time as John's parents?'

'No, I didn't. Huh, any other father might have given his son a few pointers before visiting a country he's been to himself, don't you think?'

'That's what I thought. Your poor mum was all on her own when she had you, your dad got back a few days afterwards. He went to visit you both in hospital, and in the photo Clare showed me he had a large dressing on his neck.'

Todd frowned. 'Yeah, I think I remember something she told me about that, he'd gashed it slipping down a rocky hill, I think she said. Not that I can imagine my father slipping down anything.'

'Clare said she caught sight of it a few days later at home, when he was coming out of the shower. She said it looked more like claw marks. Then she clammed up. I had the feeling she wanted to talk more though.'

'Strange. Not really sure what to say, but I'm glad the two of you got on; she does get a bit lonely sometimes, though she'll never admit it. Anyway, I'm dead chuffed you took the time to go and see her, we'll both go together next time, okay?'

'I'd like that.' Sinead's voice turned brisk. 'Now get on and enjoy the rest of your exploring. I'm back off to work now, the pub's getting busy. Give my love to John whenever you next see him.'

'Wednesday,' he said. 'I will.' He hesitated, and then said, in a quieter voice, 'Sinead… I'm having a great time, but I do miss you, you know.'

After a pause, in which he heard all the unspoken words that warmed him, she said, 'What's not to miss?'

John's journey to the Maliks' villa in Nu'eima was carefully planned around Shabbat; with no public transport available he hired a private taxi, and as Maya had promised to cook him an evening meal he timed it to arrive after sundown; it didn't seem fair to rush her on the day of rest.

The taxi delivered him to their home just after nine, and as he walked up the steps with his luggage his attention was caught by the two waving figures above him on the patio.

'John! Up here!'

Uri was the first to greet him when he reached the top of the steps and put down his suitcase. He held out a hand, and when John took it he was pulled into an unexpected but warm embrace. 'Welcome, John.'

When it was Maya's turn she put a hand either side of John's face and studied him for a moment, then she too hugged him tight. When she broke away John was both mystified and touched to see tears standing in her dark eyes.

'It's so wonderful to meet you at last,' she said softly. 'Thank you for finding us, I can't tell you how much that means.'

'My thanks to you, for inviting me,' John said. He smiled. 'I'm looking forward to hearing about the old days, and what you all got up to.'

'Please,' Maya said. 'Come and sit. You must be thirsty. I'll make tea for now, then Uri will open a bottle of wine; we'll celebrate while we eat.'

In their seventies, both Uri and Maya were still a handsome couple; John decided they must have been quite something in their youth, but above all they were kind and welcoming, and although at first their joy at seeing him had been a little overwhelming, he had to admit it felt good.

'How have you enjoyed your visit so far?' Maya put a cup of tea at his elbow, and sat down opposite.

'It's been wonderful. We've only been able to visit places in the West Bank, due to my visa restrictions, but what we have seen has been amazing.'

'Where have you been?'

'Well for a start we visited the hospital where I was born. I took flowers and chocolates to the receptionist who helped me find you.'

'That was very kind of you,' Maya nodded, and Uri added his approval.

'The local people have been so friendly and welcoming, a wonderful contrast to the attitude of the Israeli airport officials. Oh, and the food!' John grinned. 'The restaurants! I could just sit all day and eat!' He patted his stomach appreciatively.

'Perhaps, but I guarantee you will have found nothing to compare to Maya's cooking.' Pride shone from Uri's eyes as he looked at his wife. 'And what will your friend Todd be doing for the next few days?'

'He'll be exploring Tel Aviv,' John said. 'Either wandering through the museums, or lying on Golden Beach I should think. He'll join us on Wednesday.' John put down his cup. 'Uri, I believe the only reason I've been able to visit at all is down to you. I'm so grateful. Whatever strings you managed to pull, I'd have been back in England now, without your intervention.'

'It was my pleasure,' Uri assured him. 'I still have some authority although I'm retired.'

'Ah, you mean with Eegool?'

His hosts exchanged a quick, pleased glance. 'You know of Eagle?' Maya asked. 'We call it that now, it sounds more… International. It was Denise's idea, and we thought it a good one. But if you know of Eagle then you must also know of Veritas? We think they've been trying to prevent you visiting us.'

208

'Yes, I know of them both,' John said. 'And more. I found my mother's hidden films, which I had developed, and I've learned so much from them. But I still have so many questions, and I hope you'll be able to help me with them.'

Uri nodded. 'Of course, my boy, we'll answer what we can. But tomorrow. This evening is for relaxing, and for getting to know one another.'

'Of course.' John tried not to show his disappointment; there would be time for questions later, after all.

'Maya is cooking tahdig,' Uri said, rubbing his hands. 'It was your fa… George's favourite.'

John met his embarrassed gaze and shook his head slightly, absolving him; no matter what, George would always be his father, although John was still deeply conflicted about his feelings towards Karen.

'If you've read your mother's notes,' Uri said, 'you'll know it was George who discovered a link between certain events, and eclipses?' John nodded, and Uri went on, 'We decided long ago that each year, on the event of an annular eclipse, we would honour our lost friends. So, we eat tahdig, drink Adom Atik, and we remember.' He reached out and patted John's forearm. 'You have arrived on such an evening.'

'Really?' John smiled. 'I recently discovered that I, and my daughters actually, were all born on an occasion just like this.'

'We know,' Maya said, standing up and smoothing her dress. 'All the more reason to celebrate. Come, let's go inside, you must be hungry now and dinner will be ready.'

209

They ate well, tahdig and chelow with lamb kebabs and salad, and when the eating was done they remained at the table, chatting as if they'd known each other forever. Hearing stories of his parents and their friends brought them alive for him in a way photographs and diaries never really could; he felt, with a strange mixture of pleasure and regret, that he'd have enjoyed spending time with all of them. In their turn, Maya and Uri were genuinely interested in hearing all about Jen's work, and when the talk moved on to the girls and John produced photos, they clucked over them like proud grandparents. It was something John had missed.

'This one was taken just a couple of weeks ago,' he said, pointing. 'We took the girls to the local wildlife discovery park for their ninth birthday. That's them waving, from the top of a watch hut.'

'It looks like you all had a lovely time,' Maya said.

'We did. And rounded it off with make-your-own-pizza, which they loved.'

'They're beautiful girls. You must be very proud.'

'Thank you. Yes, I am. We both are. Do you have children?'

Maya shook her head. 'Alas, no. But we have many nieces and nephews, and we've enjoyed watching all of them grow up.' Maya moved to clear some plates, then looked back. 'Would you like to see some photos of us all, taken the year you were born?'

'I'd love to.'

As the evening wore on John noticed the older couple were becoming tired, so he feigned a yawn himself and declared himself ready for bed. Uri bade him goodnight and a peaceful sleep, and Maya showed him into the guest room; a room he could see would be bright and sunny in daylight, with twin beds, a built-in wardrobe, and a chest of drawers. It was beautifully decorated, with wall hangings that looked to have been made by children – probably those nieces and nephews.

'There are clean towels on the bed,' Maya gestured, 'and a nice, light dressing gown should you wish to use it.'

'It's lovely. Thank you, Maya.'

Maya looked around her, momentarily lost in the past. 'Karen liked this room too,' she said at length, smiling a little sadly at him. 'She lived here with us for a while before she returned home. On her own she couldn't pay the rent on the villa they'd all shared, and she was in no fit state to take care of herself at that time, let alone you too.'

'I had no idea she'd stayed here,' John said. 'It seems I owe you thanks once again, for taking care of her... and of me.'

'She was our dear friend,' Maya said. 'Recovering from a major operation, with a young baby to take care of, and grieving the loss of her husband.'

'Of course.'

'Karen was not the same girl she was, and we did our best to help. Uri made all the arrangements for the repatriation of your father's body, it was the very least we could do.' Maya put her hand on his arm. 'We were devastated to hear of her death, John. So very, very sorry.' John managed a nod. 'We did try to stay in touch,' she went on, 'but May stopped writing after a while.'

211

'We moved after Mum died,' John said. 'She must have lost your address.'

'That would explain it.' Maya smiled, dispelling the melancholy that had fallen on them. 'Please, make yourself at home, and if you need anything you only have to ask.'

John felt a wave of emotion he couldn't explain, and an overwhelming need to be close to this woman; this strong, beautiful lady who was no longer a stranger. He drew her close and dropped a kiss on her cheek. 'Thank you.'

She lifted a hand to the spot, and smiled. 'Goodnight, dear John. Sleep well.'

He unpacked his case and put his belongings away, then stood at the window and drank in the view. The same view his mother had looked on, all those years ago. There was a sense of time peeling back, for a moment, and hearing Uri and Maya moving about in their own room, their voices muffled, he felt oddly at home. And tomorrow there would be the answers he so desperately needed. He was about to call Jen, and then Todd, when the light from the Maliks' room clicked off, and he realised he would disturb them if he made phone calls now. So he sent messages instead, had a quick wash, and fell into bed.

And he dreamed.

Chapter Twelve
Revelations

John realised he was already halfway up the mountain. A vast improvement on previous trips. He heard that voice again, calling for David, and he looked around but he couldn't see anything. Frustration started to build, but he remembered what the twins had told him, and made himself sit down and relax. He looked in the direction of the voice, to the mountain's summit, and saw him: a tall, dark-haired man, beckoning. Even as John stood he was there at the summit too, face to face with his mirror image; only the long hair was different.

'Who are you?' he managed.

'Your brother. Doron. I've been waiting for you, David.'

John shook his head. 'My… brother? I don't—'

'We are twins. Separated at birth.'

Trying to get his mind to accept these words, John seized on a lesser point. 'My name is John, why do you keep calling me David?'

'It's your birth name. On the mountain we use birth names.' Doron held out a hand, gesturing for John to sit, which he did gratefully. Doron sat beside him, his hands looped comfortably over his raised knees, and gave John a smile that was almost shy. 'It's so good to see you at last,' he said quietly.

John's emotions were still tangled. 'Twins,' he said. 'I have a twin.' He let the words roll down the mountain, then turned back to Doron, ready for some answers now. 'What happened to separate us? Why would our mother let one of us go?'

'To keep us safe.' Doron looked directly at him, and John could see he was willing him to understand. To forgive. 'It was the hardest thing she ever had to do, and I know it broke her heart. She has grieved for you all these years, though she's comforted knowing you are alive and well.'

John frowned; instead of becoming clearer this was growing more confusing than ever. 'All these years? Wait, she *is* comforted? How can that be, when our mother is dead?'

'No,' Doron said gently, 'she's not.' He took a deep breath. 'Our mother is Rena, Uri's sister.' He paused, presumably to let John absorb this life-changing information, but John merely looked at him, his mind spinning, so he went on, 'We were born during the annular eclipse, at the time we were supposed to be. To fulfil the prophecy. As we came into the world, Karen and George's baby died from lack of oxygen.'

'Oh, god…'

'George was wrapped up in grief, and after Uri spoke to him he agreed to take one of us to raise as his own.'

'But did my moth… did Karen know? About the switch?'

'No.' Doron touched his arm briefly. 'And you don't have to correct yourself; Karen might not have given birth

214

to you, but she *was* your mother. She truly loved you, as a mother loves her son.'

The next question came naturally. 'Who was… is… our father?'

'A man named Shimon Shadid. They were engaged to be married, and she swore on all that's holy that he was the only man she'd lain with, and that he'd come to her on the night of their engagement. But when they discovered she was pregnant he denied everything and abandoned her.'

'Then if he was speaking the truth, how can her story also be true?'

'Because, brother, we are Nephilim. So are the children you see below you here. Our conception was by intervention and theirs was not, but we are all Nephilim nonetheless.'

John turned his gaze on the children and noticed they were smiling and waving. Mechanically he raised his hand to wave back and saw Doron was doing the same, but all he could say was, 'Oh.' He wondered vaguely why there was no sense of betrayal or anger at these revelations. There should be, shouldn't there? His entire life was being picked apart and labelled a lie, but all he felt was acceptance. Understanding. He felt… not numb exactly, but… okay. Yes, okay. At peace with it all, and able to see how it was finally beginning to make sense.

Doron was watching him closely, and with a knowing look. 'You're wondering why you don't feel as you think you should, aren't you?' John nodded, and Doron smiled. 'Up here, you think and feel with your spirit. When you wake up you might feel differently. But try, if you can, to remember this. How you feel *now*.'

There was a silence, and at last John asked the biggest question of all. 'What happens now?'

'Now we make plans to gather the children, for they are the precious ones. We will talk again soon, I promise.'

John started awake, upright and cross-legged in the centre of his bed. It was a little after four a.m., and it took a moment for him to remember where he was, but he sat still, letting the memory of the dream creep through the fuzziness of his thoughts, concentrating hard for fear of forgetting something important. The story might sound incredible, almost unbelievable to the waking and sceptical mind, yet the details fit with the conversation he'd had with Jen, Todd and Sinead, the night Todd had brought his father's paperwork around. He moved, wincing at the pins and needles, so he was sitting on the edge of the bed, and began again.

He had a brother. Their mother was Uri's sister, so Uri was his uncle…he'd lost an Aunt May and gained an Aunt Maya; he had a whole family out there that he'd known nothing about. A mess of new and complicated emotions rose, making him feel queasy and unsettled, and he remembered Doron urging him to remember how he'd felt up there. On the mountain. That had been the spirit part of him, so what was this… his human side? The Nephilim were part spirit, part human… you could drive yourself mad trying to make sense of it all.

He turned his thoughts in a different direction, just to give himself time to take it all in. As he thought of the woman he'd considered his mother he realised that the shame and anger he'd felt, believing she'd been unfaithful to her husband, had gone. But there was something else: whatever it was that had been missing from his life – he'd always assumed it had been the loss of his parents – that was gone, too. Because what had been missing was his brother. His other half. It was frightening, in a way, how everything was beginning to slide into place at last, how he was teetering on the very edge of understanding everything.

'I can't tell you how happy we are that you and Doron have found one another at last.' Maya put the coffee pot in front of John, and the aroma, rich and deep, drifted across the table.

'I'm only sorry we couldn't tell you of him before,' Uri added.

'Why couldn't you?'

'For a prophecy to be fulfilled there can be no interference or manipulation.' Uri poured coffee into three cups. 'It must happen in the natural course of things.'

'We thought about you every single day,' Maya put in, sounding almost pleading. 'We have looked forward to meeting you for so long.'

John realised they were waiting for his word that he accepted them, and he smiled. 'So, you are my aunt and uncle. It's… well, it's weird, and it'll take some getting used to, but I'm glad. Honestly glad,' he repeated, seeing the look of relief that passed between them. 'When can I see my brother for real?' He was surprised at his own eagerness, given the newness of all this, but he couldn't deny it.

'Doron lives in America,' Uri said. 'He has done since he was very young. Rena married a kind man named Alex Farmer, a state senator no less. And a member of Eagle. He took Rena and Doron to live with him in Chicago. They're very happy.' Seeing John's disappointment, he broke into a wide smile. 'Doron's flying in to see you tomorrow.'

John's heart skipped a little, part nervous, part excited. 'I look forward to that.'

'I heard you on the phone earlier,' Maya said. 'Is everything alright with Jen and the girls? What did she say when you told them about your own twin?'

'They're fine.' John smiled. 'No surprise on that score I'm afraid, Jen already knew. The girls saw us talking last night, and told her all about it. Jen sends her regards, by the way.'

'So kind. I should love to meet them all.'

'I rang Todd too, to keep him up to date with everything.'

'It's a wonderful gift you all have,' Maya said, a little melancholy now. 'I so wish the others were here to hear all about this too. We had no way of knowing the miracle that was to come.'

'But why *has* it come?' John pushed his cup away, besieged by questions again. 'Why me? Why us? Why now, and what does it all mean?' He shook his head. 'And what are we supposed to do with it all?'

Uri nodded his understanding. 'I will tell you all I know. From the beginning. I understand you've done extensive research yourself?'

'Some.'

'Then please speak up if you have any questions or theories of your own.'

Uri did start at the beginning, telling of how the friendship began with Mark and Denise, and their discovery of the tablet. Then later coming to know and admire *their* friends, Karen and George. He told of the days and nights working on the transcript, and of the burglary; of Veritas and Eagle, and the Shiloh base. Through it all, John remained silent despite Uri's invitation, letting it all sink in, and forming his questions carefully. He waited until Uri had finished.

'How did Mum manage to get the films back to England?'

Uri shrugged. 'Back then there was no really high-tech x-ray equipment at the airports, so we simply stitched them into the lining of a suitcase and hoped for the best.'

'Was she supposed to have had them developed?'

'That was her choice,' Uri said. 'We all had films, backups, if you like. Just in case we lost the work we'd done. Because of everything that happened to Karen before she went back, I imagine she kept them as a guarantee of safety for you, should she ever need it. Later she might have forgotten she even had them.'

John took a deep breath, seeing the sorrowful look on Uri's face. 'What was wrong with her, Uri?'

'I suspected a brain tumour. Classic symptoms. I wrote to her and asked her to go and get checked out, but as her

219

symptoms worsened she grew more and more confused. The headaches intensified, and a successful surgery couldn't be guaranteed. She knew that.' He gave John a sad smile. 'Knowing her as I did, I would say she'd have decided to spend what time she did have, with you.'

John swallowed a painful lump in his throat, tears stinging his eyes. Maya had no such self-control, and she pushed back her chair and hurried from the room, the back of her hand pressed to her mouth. John could hear choking sobs coming from the next room.

He waited a moment, until he felt sure his voice would be steady, then cleared his throat. 'So you convinced my… George, to adopt me. I understand he was none too keen on this prophecy theory though?'

'You're right, he wasn't. But he loved Karen, and that outweighed any of his own beliefs. He and Rena secretly buried his own baby son, and held a private service for him. A terrible time for him, grieving in secret. Rena wrote a letter to you, to explain why she'd given you up. And with it a declaration of her permission for Karen and George to bring you up as their adopted son.'

'But I've never seen that letter…' John tailed off as he remember the few sealed envelopes he'd found in the tin with his mother's papers, and how easily they had been pushed out of his mind by other things. How different might his life have been? 'You put your career on the line for us all, Uri,' he said. 'That couldn't have been easy.'

'I had help,' Uri said. 'I swapped the babies' hospital bands, and Rena held Karen's and George's poor child for a while before it was taken away. To mourn it, you know?'

'That must have been so hard for her,' John murmured.

Uri nodded. 'I falsified documents, and the surgeon was sworn to secrecy. Maya attended your births, so no-one was any the wiser. It was a strain on us both, but it is our fate to be involved in this, and it is a fate we accepted long ago.'

The door opened and Maya came back in, her eyes reddened, but her face composed once more. She took the coffee pot to the kitchen to make fresh, while John told Uri his own side of things: what the past year had brought, and what they had discovered themselves; the dreams; the girls' trip to Brighton and all they had learned there; and finally about the documents Todd had found, belonging to his father.

At this, Uri's face changed, sliding from interest, and almost excitement, into something cold and closed. He rose from the table, looking suddenly like a stranger again. From the kitchen all sounds had ceased and John felt the chill drop over the room.

'So what are you telling me, John? That your best friend, who we have invited into our home, is the son of Richard Hampton?' The name fell from his lips like poison. 'That murdering scum… How could you do this?' His fist came down onto the table, making John jump and the cups rattle. 'How could you bring *him* into our lives?'

Stunned, John could only stare. Murder? Todd's father was no saint; he'd even go so far as to say he was a dreadful human being, but a *murderer*? Before he could speak Maya came in, carrying a tray of coffee, and she

221

crossed quickly to put it down before laying a hand on her husband's arm. John could see the hand shaking.

'Uri, please… let John speak.' She turned to John, her expression sorrowful and betrayed. 'Tell us what you mean? How can you be close to such a man?'

'Uri, Maya,' he looked from one to the other, 'Todd is *not* like his father. He hates him in fact, and has not had a happy home life. Hampton was always away on business and Todd hardly ever saw him, but what he did see was an appalling father and husband.'

He watched as Uri and Maya looked to one another, and knew they wanted to believe him, so he pushed on, 'Todd and I have been best friends for over twenty years, and I would trust him with my life. And with Jen's and the girls'. If it wasn't for him we wouldn't have discovered the list of twins, or even have come this far. We know his father instigated our friendship, just to keep an eye on me, and we're not unaware of his involvement with Veritas—'

'Involvement?' Uri's voice rose in disbelief. 'John, he's one of the top men! He's our worst enemy!' He hushed Maya's murmured plea for peace, but his voice lowered, though it was no less angry. 'He and his cronies are responsible for… for *so much* evil, I…' He struggled for the words, but in the end he just shrugged off Maya's hand and went out onto the patio. John tried to follow, but Maya stopped him, and he looked helplessly at her.

'Maya, I'm so terribly sorry for all this upset. But you have to believe me, Todd's a good man regardless of who or what his father might be. I'm afraid I don't know anything about all this.' Desperate to salvage some of the earlier ease between them he threw up his hands. 'Look, under the circumstances perhaps it's better if I book a hotel room for me and Todd. I don't want either of you to feel uncomfortable.' *Nor to put Todd through the pain of more rejection*, he added silently.

'Let's wait until Uri has had chance to calm down, then we'll speak to him again. It was a shock to us both, you know.'

There was a long silence, then John asked, 'Why did he call Richard Hampton a murderer?'

Maya gestured for him to sit again, and when he'd done so she poured fresh coffee. She seemed to be using the time to gather her thoughts, so he didn't press her and eventually she began to talk.

'At the time of the prophecy, when you were born, Veritas knew of the details too. There were only two other sets of twins born on that day, within the right time frame, and all four babies died.' Her face took on a look of deep sorrow. 'Their deaths were attributed to Sudden Infant Death Syndrome, but we knew differently though we had no proof. Also,' she shot him a nervous look, 'we never believed that the car crash that killed George, along with Mark and Denise, was an accident.'

John flinched in shock, and he began to see where the grim story was going. 'Not an accident.'

'We're certain it was instigated by Hampton. But again, we have no proof.'

'How can you be so sure?'

'He was in the West Bank at that time. Our friends were transporting the first two tablets to our store in Shiloh, for safety. When they were found, off road, the car had been travelling back towards Jericho and there was no sign of the tablets. Either in the car, or at the store. Uri received confidential information from the pathologist who carried out the autopsies…' she broke off, 'I'm sorry this all sounds so clinical when we're discussing good friends, and the man you thought of as your father.'

'It's better that way,' John said. 'Please, go on.'

She nodded. 'Back then we didn't wear seatbelts, you must remember that. Anyway, the pathologist reported that the injuries were consistent with a car crash, but that there was some… bruising, that indicated they had been restrained.' There were tears in her eyes again, as she recounted what she knew, and John realised how hard it was for her. 'They… they must have escaped somehow, and we believe they were chased. The pathologist also found skin tissue and blood beneath Denise's fingernails, which didn't match either of the boys. None of this was made public, it was all hushed up. There was no investigation.'

John chose his words carefully. 'Please don't take this the wrong way, but it still doesn't prove Todd's father was involved.'

'No, you're right. Except that he returned home with a large medical dressing on his neck. At some point, before our friends' escape, Denise must have attacked him.' A look of admiration crept over her face. 'It would have been just like her. Anyway, without proof, Hampton got away with everything.' She glanced towards the patio and lowered her voice. 'Come, let's go for a walk, and leave Uri to his thoughts for a while.'

But Uri came back in then, to add, 'Shay, the man we believe responsible for the burglary at the villa, once accidentally referred to his boss as "Mr H." It's okay, Maya,' he said quietly. 'John, I'm sorry. It was a shock, but that's no excuse for my outburst and I apologise. I will trust in your judgement of your friend.'

'Thank you,' John said, relieved. 'Are you sure?'

'Of course. It's been a strain, you understand. It's not just the work we've done, but the worry of it all too. And we're not young anymore,' he added with a sigh. 'It's not just a case of questioning the facts either; we've had to question our own faith.'

'How do you mean?'

'Well,' Maya said, moving to Uri's side and slipping her arm through his, 'If the Fathers are our creators, is everything we've been taught a lie?'

'Why does it have to be though?' John asked. 'If, as you say, the Fathers created us, who's to say the scriptures are a lie? I know there have been a lot of interpretations in religious texts, but there's no smoke without fire, right? Surely there's an element of truth running through them? There might be omissions and manipulations by past generations, to make them fit what they wanted, but that doesn't mean the core is false. None of us knows who, or what, the Fathers are, and until we find out we can't jump to conclusions.' He paused for breath after such a long speech, and Uri smiled.

'You sound a lot like George,' he said, 'but more diplomatic. Thank you for that.'

John nodded, pleased at the comparison.

'Even after everything,' Maya said, 'our work really is only just beginning. This has all happened before.'

'It has? When?'

'Amnon wrote about Moses and Maor saving their people and his Father's children. We took that to mean all the people were God's children, but we were wrong. Later, we discovered that Nour – that's Maor—led his Father's children two by two, and that there were forty-six.'

John's scalp began to prickle, and Maya went on, 'The forty-six Nephilim are also mentioned in the Dead Sea Scrolls found at Wadi Qumran. That's twenty-three sets of twins with two protectors. Just like we have now.'

'What happened to them?'

Uri took up the tale. 'They lived through many generations, and we've estimated their life span to have been around 150 years.'

'*One hundred and fifty?*'

'They never got sick, and they aged more slowly than everyone else. They lived long and healthy lives, as you and your children will, if kept safe. All were gifted, and advanced in skills for their time. They helped people, and were loved and protected by them in return.'

'We're not immortal then.'

'Certainly not!' Uri gave a small chuckle. 'You might have the Fathers' spirit in your DNA, which will keep you from ever becoming ill, but your body is human, and must eventually degenerate and die.'

'So is this what we're here for then? To help people? Given everything that's happened it doesn't seem enough somehow. Don't get me wrong, that's a noble enough task but my gut instinct says there's more to this.'

226

'We truly don't know,' Uri said with a shrug. 'I'm sorry we can't answer all your questions, but we'll talk more once Doron gets here.'

Sensing a winding down of the conversation, John lifted a hand. 'Just a couple more questions first.' It was not a request, and Uri nodded.

'Go on.'

'I keep hearing phrases like "protected," and "kept safe." I need to know this: is my family in danger? Because if so I'm on the next plane home.'

'I understand. We have our people watching all the children, as a safeguard, but we don't believe they are in imminent danger. Veritas will be concentrating on keeping you and Doron apart.'

'Why does all this frighten Veritas so much?'

'Because the original forty-six brought new ideas with them,' Maya said. 'New ways. Their teachings are lost, unfortunately, but we do know they advocated for peace, for a united people. People don't like change, John, we know this, but if these children are to follow in their ancestors' footsteps, and can convince everyone to be more tolerant of one another, Veritas would become redundant. The children cannot do this on their own, they need you and your brother.'

John nodded slowly. So many questions were fighting one another in his mind, but he needed time to think, to order them.

The following day Maya took him out sight-seeing for the afternoon, while Uri waited at home in case Doron called, though he wasn't due to arrive until late afternoon.

They stopped at the historical site of old Jericho, and then Maya took him up to Al Nahkeel street, to see the villa his parents had shared with their friends during their stay. John looked at it, trying to imagine the youthful, zealous foursome, excited and fun-loving, their individual bitter fates blessedly unknown. Maya eventually drew him gently away, and as he climbed into the passenger seat of her car his phone rang.

'Todd, hi. How's it going? Maya's showing me around Jericho, it's amazing.'

'Great! Can you get her to show you a place called Hisham's Palace, if it's not out of your way?'

John relayed the request to Maya, who nodded. 'It's between here and home.'

'Yep,' John said to Todd. 'No problem. Why there?'

'I'm at the Rockefeller Museum, and I've found something interesting displayed here. A frieze. Can you get the measurements of the place it came from?'

'Damn, the very day I leave my tape measure in another country,' John said dryly. 'Okay, I'll try, but they'll only be approximate.'

Todd snorted. 'Funny guy. Yeah, approximate will do. Cheers! Speak later.'

John ended the call and told Maya what Todd had said, and she nodded. 'That's interesting. There *are* gaps in the décor, and I know where the frieze was. I'll show you.'

Maya parked the car at Hisham's Palace, and John climbed out, staring around him with deep appreciation. 'It's beautiful.'

'It's one of my favourite places to visit,' Maya said. 'There's the palace, a mosque, and a bathhouse. I think you'll enjoy it, too.' She pointed to a stone wheel as they approached the entrance. 'Look, parts of that are very like the emblem of Eagle: an eagle's wing, dissecting a circle. The actual palace was never completed, but the power and beauty of the architecture and décor must be seen to be believed.'

'Why is it one of your favourite places?'

'Because of the mosaics, my favourite art form.' She smiled. 'Wait until you see the ones in the baths.'

For a while the worries of the past few days were pushed to the back of John's mind, which was likely the intention of the trip, he realised, feeling his admiration for Maya grow. But despite her reasons, her enthusiasm for this place was undeniable, and he watched it rise as they drew closer to the bathhouse. He counted 16 massive pillars, which he guessed would have supported the roof, and as they drew closer he realised the floor was completely paved with tiles, laid out in various patterns and with a huge circular piece in its centre.

'Seven million tiles,' Maya said. 'Isn't that incredible?'

He nodded. 'Certainly is.'

'Now come and see the Tree of Life.'

They wandered among the carvings and mosaics, and Maya proved an engaging and knowledgeable guide. The last place she took him was to the palace itself, or what was left of it.

'It would have looked very different,' she said. 'A large, square construction, with round towers at each corner.

229

And a second storey too, but most of it was destroyed in the eighth century, in an earthquake.' She showed him a large, framed area on one of the walls. 'This is what Todd's interested in; the frieze was displayed here. Most of the carvings in here, and in the bathhouse, were removed for safe keeping.'

'What were they like?' John ran a hand over the wall, trying to imagine how it would have looked.

'Extravagantly and intricately carved stucco, some animal figures, some human. They were considered quite fanciful for their time.'

John took out his phone and sent a text to Todd: *We're here. Would guess approx 12' x 3'.*

They returned to the bathhouse and sat down for a drink of water, in the shade of one of the pillars. John had just uncapped his bottle when his phone went again.

'Hi, Uri. Is everything okay?'

'Yes, fine. Doron has landed safely, please let Maya know too. It will take him a few hours to get to the other side of the bridge, and he'll ring again when he gets there.'

After John had passed on the message he squinted up at the pillar beneath which they sat, and was about to ask Maya more about the site when once more his phone buzzed. He sent Maya an apologetic look, and a shrug, but she simply smiled and gestured for him to answer.

'Todd. Did you get my—'

'It all fits!' Todd's voice was laced with excitement. 'I was looking around the museum, and saw part of a frieze that said it was from Hisham's Palace, right? The carvings were two rows of people's heads. There were eleven in each row, but when I looked closer I could see that the top row was duplicated in the lower one.'

'What's so important—'

'The heads aren't in great shape, there are bits missing here and there, but the neck adornments were fine. I measured them, and if the measurements you gave me are right, or even close, the frieze would have originally shown twenty-three heads in each row! Two rows of heads with identical neck adornments.'

John frowned. 'I still don't see… wait!' He sat upright. 'Twenty-three pairs. Twins!' He looked at Maya as he spoke, and even hearing only his side she had clearly understood the subject of their discussion. She smiled again, and nodded, and John returned to Todd. 'But Maya's just told me this is early Islamic art.'

'Exactly.'

'Today Uri and Maya told me that what's happening now has happened before. So, even in the eighth century the Nephilim were still being honoured?'

'Yep.'

'That's… that's *huge!*'

'Yep!'

'Well done! Right, bugger off, I'm going to talk to Maya about this now, okay? See you soon!' He put his phone away and told Maya what Todd had said. She looked impressed.

'Very few people have worked out what the carvings here signify. Don't you think it's wonderful that the Nephilim were honoured by Jews, Christians *and* Muslims?'

231

John pondered that thought a moment. 'Do you think we're here to unite the religions?'

'Maybe. But beliefs are so strongly ingrained in our culture that I don't see how it would be possible. At least not straight away. There would be anger, suspicion, disbelief... it's not a task I would envy.'

'You're looking tired,' John said gently. 'Would you like to go back now?'

'I am, a bit.' She put her arm through his, just as she'd done to Uri earlier, and it made him smile. 'We should go home and wait for Doron.'

John felt his insides do a quick flip. His brother. At last.

***

The flight from Chicago's O'Hare to Amman had been a gruelling eight hours. Added to that, the circus that was airport security, and then immigration at the bridge, and Doron Malik was exhausted. He walked out into early Monday evening in the West Bank, and, as promised, called Uri to let him know he was on his way before looking around for a taxi. A big yellow sherut pulled up alongside him, and the driver leapt out and welcomed him, taking his suitcase.

There was only one other passenger inside, and Doron stifled a sigh; that meant he'd have to wait until the ten-seater was full before the driver would leave, and who knew how long that would take? But to his surprise the driver shut the door, and started the engine. Doron gave his destination, and sat back to enjoy the air conditioning after the stifling heat of the bridge. Neither the driver nor his fellow passenger seemed interested in conversation, which suited Doron, and he looked out at the passing landscape on the road to Jericho, wondering how it would feel to finally meet David—John, he corrected himself— in person.

He jerked awake, not even realising he'd nodded off, and looked out of the window, disorientated. The driver would have told him if they'd neared their destination, but Doron had heard nothing from him. He didn't recognise the road.

'You must have missed the turning,' he said, 'we're supposed to be going to Nu'eima. Hey!' He leaned over and tapped the driver, who jumped but said nothing.

'Sit down and be quiet,' the other passenger said, and Doron turned back to him.

'Who are you? What's going on, and where are we going?'

'Who we are is of no concern to you. We are going to Ramallah.'

'Ramallah? Why?' But even before the man replied, he knew, and his heart slithered in his chest.

'Our boss wants to meet with you.'

So he'd been kidnapped. And there was no question this was Veritas, trying to stop him reaching his brother. Doron reached over to the door handle, but it was locked, and, sinking back into his seat he slid out his phone to call Uri. He'd got no further than opening his contacts list before the phone was plucked from his hand.

'I'll take that, Mr Malik. Thank you.' The passenger opened the back and removed the battery, before throwing the phone back to him. Doron fumbled to catch it, his attention snagged by the gun resting in the man's lap. His stomach turned over, and fear made his skin clammy. There would be no chance of escape until they stopped, but perhaps in the distraction of disembarking… he turned his mind towards thinking through every possible scenario that might occur, and how he might take advantage.

Somewhere on the outskirts of Mukhamas the taxi pulled to the side of the road. The land was barren as far as the eye could see, and only a blue Ford broke the emptiness. Any attempt to run here would get him a bullet in the back before he'd got more than ten yards.

'Get out,' the passenger ordered, and within minutes he was being pushed towards the other car.

'A fucking Ford Escort!' the driver muttered, in deep disgust.

'We were told not to draw any attention, weren't we?' the passenger said. 'Get in, Malik.' He pushed Doron onto the back seat, and slid in next to him, gun in hand. There was no central locking on this old car, but still no chance of escape, and Doron sat in silence, wondering how far these people would go to keep him from meeting John.

As the Escort rattled around the streets of Ramallah, he stared out of the window trying to memorise the road names. Just in case. Ramallah Street; Ein Misbah Street… but the buildings were all so similar it was impossible to memorise the route. They entered an underground parking garage, beneath a four-storey building, and left the Escort there. Doron felt the push of the gun barrel in his lower back as he went ahead of them through the door and started up the stone steps, and with every footstep his unease grew. They had just rounded the corner and begun to climb the second flight when he realised there would never be a better opportunity, slim as this one was.

Without really thinking too hard, he let instinct take over, and he bent and twisted in one movement, driving his leg out and sending the gunman stumbling back against his accomplice. The two went down as one, cries of pain as flesh scraped stone steps, and by the time they reached the bottom they lay still. Heart thudding, Doron dismissed any idea of an escape further up the stairs, and turning, he took the lower flight three at a time, jumping over the slumped forms of his kidnappers towards the door, and freedom.

Even as his feet left the ground he heard rustling movement, and a grunt, and felt an iron grip around his ankle. A savage yank on his leg sent him crashing into the wall, and after the hideously bright flare as his head smashed into plaster, everything dissolved into darkness.

Chapter Thirteen
Brothers

The Meridian Research Centre, Cambridge, England

'Good morning, Peter,' Otto greeted the night desk guard in his barely noticeable German accent. 'Almost time to go home, eh?'

'It's six a.m,' Peter said, 'couldn't sleep?'

'Got a bit excited about some new ideas,' Otto confessed. 'You know what I'm like.'

'Certainly do,' Peter grinned. 'Make sure you leave early mind, and don't work too hard.'

'I won't.' They both knew that was a lie. Otto Fischer was a loyal, long-serving member of Meridian, and had made no secret of his delight at the new project Hampton had brought him; the blood samples had revealed mind-blowing properties, and Otto had already begun work on a synthetic gene to replicate the immunities. He even dreamed of his name on a Nobel Prize, and that wasn't such a foolish daydream after all. Not now.

Then there had been the visit that had changed everything. He'd learned where the blood had come from; from children whose parents had no more given their consent than the children themselves had, and that hadn't even been the worst of it. His boss's other activities had brought a chill to Otto's soul that the frigid air in the lab could not account for.

Now he walked through the corridors and offices until he came to that lab. He crossed the spotless floor, pausing to lay a sorrowful hand on his beloved centrifuge. It felt strange to be in here without his protective coveralls, and his mask, and he flexed his gloveless fingers for a moment, missing the extra layers, feeling oddly naked. Aware of the passage of time he did not have, he shook the feeling off and went to the fridge. He took the blood samples from the icy interior and emptied them down the sink. Then he gathered together all his paperwork and put it in his briefcase.

The computer's hard drive took a little more time to remove, but soon that too went into his case along with everything else. He paused at the door and took one last look around the place that had been his second home for so many years, then pulled the door closed. He hoped the promises had not been empty, that he would indeed be permitted to continue his work elsewhere, safely away from any investigations.

At the front desk again he handed the bemused Peter an envelope, his car keys, and said, 'Early Christmas present.' He walked home, collected his suitcase, and locked up his flat for the last time before hailing a cab.

'Heathrow, please.'

***

Nu'eima, Palestinian Territories
John watched Uri pacing, and realised the man's tension was transmitting itself to his own tightly-wound insides. He wished he'd sit down.

237

'He should have been here an hour ago.' Uri paused to check his watch. 'Something's wrong.'

Maya covered the cold dinner with a net and began carrying it to the fridge. 'I'm worried too, but what can we do? Only wait.'

'Shouldn't we call the police?' John ventured.

'It's too soon to consider him missing. Perhaps if he were a child, but he's a grown man. I've tried his phone several times, but it's just dead now.' Uri snatched up his car keys. 'I'm going to drive the route to the bridge, see if there's any sign. I knew I should have picked him up myself.' He kissed Maya, who let him go without question – it was clear he felt he had to be doing something.

'I'm going to get an early night,' John said when Uri had gone, and seeing Maya's look of surprise he explained, 'Maybe I can contact Doron like I did before. Wake me when Uri comes back?'

But with the worry, and too much information still churning in his brain, it took a long while for him to get to sleep. If he hadn't reached the mountain he'd have sworn he hadn't slept at all, but he was roused by Maya's soft voice.

'Uri's back, but he didn't see any sign of Doron. How about you, did you have any more luck?'

John pulled himself upright and ran his hands through his hair. 'He's alive, which is some comfort. I only saw him for a second or two. It was as if he was having trouble staying around.' He swung his legs off the bed. 'I'll try again later.'

It was the early hours before he felt tired enough to try again, and he put a pad and pen beside the bed. This time he had no trouble slipping into sleep, and before he knew it he was almost at the mountain cave. Some of the children waved, and a heartbeat later they stood next to him.

He smiled at them. 'Hi, kids. You're getting better at this, aren't you? Have you seen my brother?'

'Yes,' one of them said, 'but he only stayed a little while. He left a message in case we saw you, so we passed it on to everyone we saw, and told them to do the same.'

'That was clever, well done.' He managed to hide his anxiety behind another smile. 'What did he say?'

The children all chipped in with their various additions to the message. 'He's been kidnapped, by two men!'

'And they've got guns…'

His heart shrivelled.

'He's in the street of the lamp, off the road to God's Hill.'

'Oh, he said the building is opposite Kadin's Café.'

'In the top apartment.'

'Is he going to be okay?'

'Of course he is.' John reassured them as convincingly as he could. 'As soon as I wake up I'll make sure someone finds him and brings him home safely. Thank you all, that's great work. You might have saved his life.'

John fought his way back to full wakefulness by an effort of will, and frantically jotted down everything he'd been told. Then he grabbed his dressing gown and hurried into the living room, to find Uri and Maya already up and staring at him with a mixture of hope and dread.

'He's been kidnapped,' John blurted, and Maya gasped and covered her mouth. 'I think he's okay,' he went on, 'I have details of where he's being held.'

Uri put his hands on Maya's shoulders. 'It'll be alright,' he murmured, then went to the sideboard for a road map. He took the piece of paper John tore from his pad, and spread the map out on the table.

'God's Hill, you said? We know that's Ramallah. He must have travelled along Ramallah Road. But what does he mean by, "street of the lamp"?'

'The street names are in Arabic and Hebrew,' Maya muttered. 'It could be either Menorah or Misbah.'

Uri slipped his glasses on and peered more closely at the map. He traced Ramallah road, and squinted at all the roads that branched off it. 'Got it!' He looked up, almost beaming. 'He's in Ein Misbah. Good work, John.' He clapped John on the back.

'So now do we call the police?'

'No, lad. How would we explain how we know where my nephew is being held captive? Or even that we know he is? They wouldn't believe us. Eagle has its own security force in Jerusalem, they'll get him out.'

'Doesn't that mean they're Israeli?'

'Yes,' Maya smiled. 'I'm sorry John; I thought we told you that Eagle membership is for anyone who wants peace and truth. Most people here want that, no matter what their beliefs, or their political status.'

John nodded, then bent over the map. 'Look, Todd's hotel is only a short distance from Ramallah Road. It's the

Royal Court, in Jaffa Street. Can your people take him there?'

'I want him brought here,' Maya protested.

'I know you're worried,' John said gently, 'and I'm eager as hell to see him myself. But the poor guy will be exhausted from travelling, and probably traumatised as well from his abduction. Uri will question him, and you'll fuss over him, but if he stays with Todd he can rest up in peace and quiet, and Todd can bring him here tomorrow.'

'Call Todd,' Uri said quickly, 'I'll make the other arrangements.'

Then came a time of waiting, and hoping that Uri was correct; that Eagle would be able to find the place and free Doron before it was too late. The hours drew on, and John sat in silence, every muscle taut with nervous energy, and when Uri's phone rang they all jumped.

Uri snatched the phone up and began pacing again. 'Shit! No, it can't be helped... Okay, I understand. Thanks for letting me know, keep me informed.'

John saw Maya wince as Uri slammed the phone back down on the sideboard, but she was as eager as he was for the explanation. They weren't kept waiting long, and Uri's face and voice were grim.

'There's been an attack on the offices of the Diplomatic Quartet, in Jerusalem.'

'What?' Maya whispered. 'But... why?'

'Who are they?' John wanted to know.

'They're the mediators for the Israeli-Palestinian peace process,' Maya said. 'But who would want to —'

241

'Because of this,' Uri went on, holding up a hand to stay the questions, 'the Eagle security force can't get through the border. They're stuck there.'

Maya let out a wordless cry of dismay. 'What are we going to do?'

John stood up. 'I'm going to get him. I'll get Todd to meet me there, we'll do it ourselves. Uri, I'll need the car.' He held out his hand to Uri for the keys, but Uri shook his head.

'No, no you don't, lad. It's far too dangerous.'

'We can't risk losing you both,' Maya begged, and John saw tears of terror standing in her eyes.

'This is my brother we're talking about,' he said, more gently. 'I'm not losing him now I've found him. Without Doron everything falls apart. Veritas win.' He turned back to Uri. 'We can't wait any longer, we have no idea what his abductors' plans are.' He held out his hand again. 'I'm going.'

'Very well,' Uri conceded. 'But I'm going with you.'

'No.' Now the steel was back in John's voice. 'Maya needs you here, and I need you to keep trying your contacts. Hopefully someone will still be able to help us.'

Uri was clearly battling with the sense of this, but eventually he nodded. 'Okay. But you're not driving, you don't know the roads here. If you get lost you're no help to anyone.' He picked up his phone again. 'I'll organise a ride.'

Moments later it was done. 'Cal, a trusted friend, is going to take you, and he'll wait and bring you both home.'

'An extra pair of hands will be good.'

'Sorry,' Uri said. 'He can't help with the rescue, much as he'd like to. He has trouble walking, but he's the best driver I know.'

John nodded. 'Thanks. Oh, another thing, do you have a white, short-sleeved formal shirt I can borrow?'

Uri blinked. 'Uh, yes. But why?'

'I have a plan.'

Cal parked his yellow taxi at the rear of Kadin's Café in Ein Misbah Street. John looked out of the window and took a deep breath; this was it.

'Wait,' Cal said, as John put his hand on the door handle. 'You might need this.' He leaned into the back seat and picked up a holdall. From it he withdrew a pistol. 'It's a Jericho 941 semi-automatic,' he explained. As if that meant anything to John, who stared at it, his mouth suddenly dry.

'Easy to use,' Cal added, 'and fully loaded.'

That word broke the spell. 'Whoah! Loaded?' John raised his hands. 'I don't think so, thanks all the same.'

'Those thugs will have guns,' Cal pointed out. 'How do you intend to disarm them? To protect yourselves?'

John couldn't answer, and Cal nodded. 'There you go, then.'

'But neither of us has any idea how to use a gun.'

'It's pretty basic.' Cal pointed to a lever on the side of the weapon's frame. 'This is the safety catch. If it's up you can't pull the trigger. So keep it that way until you get where you're going, then slide it down. You'll see a red dot. All you have to do then is point and shoot… if necessary.' He put the gun back in the bag and handed it

243

to John. 'Uri will do his best to get help to you, and in the meantime I'll be waiting.' He clapped John on the shoulder. 'Good luck to you both.'

'Thanks. We're going to need it.'

Todd was already in the café, sitting at a small corner table with two cups of coffee in front of him. No steam rose from them; they'd been there a while. Todd looked up and saw him, and waved him over, and John felt trembling relief at the sight of a familiar and trusted face, and one which betrayed no sign of the nervousness he himself was feeling. He wondered if it were all a façade, and whether he imagined the air of false confidence as Todd spoke.

'Look at you, all dressed up for the occasion. Nice shirt.'

John put the bag under his seat and folded his arms on the table, the movement making him lean a little closer without seeming too obvious. Todd followed suit.

'It's part of the plan,' John said in a low voice. 'When I saw Doron in my dream he was wearing a shirt a bit like this, with jeans. I didn't tell Uri or Maya, but he's hurt. He had blood on his forehead.' He glanced around them, but no-one was seated nearby, or appeared to be watching. Still, he lowered his voice further. 'I figured if I dressed the same way, his abductors might mistake me for him when we knock on their door. It'll give us an element of surprise.'

Todd didn't react with the admiration he'd expected. 'We're just going to knock on the door, are we? Then what, they just let us in? Oh, come in the kettle's just—'

'Well what would you suggest?' John snapped. 'Kick down the front door? Knock them out with our amazing martial arts skills?'

Todd looked chastened. 'Well, put like that, no. Of course not, but—'

'Right.' John took a deep breath. 'You're going to pretend to be a member of Veritas, who's just found their captive escaped and outside the building. Okay?'

'Okay.'

'I'll keep my hands behind my back as if they're tied. It should throw them into confusion long enough to give us the edge when we get inside.' He nudged the bag further under the table, until it bumped Todd's foot. 'Cals's given us some leverage.'

He waited, while Todd leaned down and unzipped the bag a little way, and when his friend rose again his face was white.

'Well,' he managed, wiping the back of his hand across his mouth, 'I know I said we were in need of some adventure, mate, but this is… not what I had in mind.'

'It's the only way.' John studied him for a moment. 'And there's another thing. Todd, I'm sorry to say, but it seems your father's involved in all this.'

There was a silence, and he watched the emotions flicker across Todd's face, then Todd visibly put the questions aside.

'I'm not surprised,' was all he said.

'Well then,' John said, finding a brisk tone. 'I suppose we'd better get going.'

'The bold knights of Haverhill on a real mission,' Todd said, with a ghost of his old grin.

John smiled as he pushed his chair back. 'We've come a long way since our childhood battles, haven't we?'

'Hang on a sec.' Todd picked up the red plastic ketchup bottle and squirted some into the palm of his hand. A strong smell of vinegar filled the air between them, and John wrinkled his nose.

'What are you doing?'

Todd leaned over and, to John mingled disgust and astonishment, smeared the sauce onto his forehead. 'If you're going to pass as your brother, you're going to need a bloody head.'

Todd banged on the door of the top apartment, and John, standing in front of him, hoped Doron's description was accurate and that they were in the right building. The gun was tucked into the back of his jeans; he could feel it as he put his hands behind his back in preparation for playing his role. Todd would be able to reach it just as easily, if it were needed.

He sensed Todd about to hammer on the door again, but the cover of the spyhole slid back and they saw someone peering through the distorted lens. There was an exclamation, some loud muttering, and then the sound of the chain sliding off.

The door clicked open, and without hesitation Todd pushed John into the apartment. It was hard for John not to put his hands out to steady himself as he stumbled, but he gripped his own fingers tightly and managed to keep his balance. He looked around him, taking it all in with the frantic haste of fear. The door had opened directly into a lounge, with a hallway and kitchenette to the right, and the air was thick and heavy with the smell of old grease, sweat, and cigarette smoke.

The man who'd opened the door was tall, heavy-set, and scowling. More tellingly he had a gun in his hand, levelled at them as Todd kicked the door shut behind him. Todd pushed John up against the wall, neatly concealing the lack of bindings at his wrists, and John, filled with admiration, could hear echoes of Richard Hampton as his friend summoned all the bluster he could find and marched up to the gunman, until they stood face to face.

'Put those damned things away! Now! Don't you *dare* point them at me! Don't you know who I am?'

The gunman backed away a little but the room's other occupant didn't move. He was of slighter build, though also armed, and he was watching the scene through narrowed eyes. John hoped he wasn't as clever as he looked.

Todd was in full voice again. 'How the hell can you botch up a basic babysitting job? Huh? I found this one outside trying to hitch a *ride*, for Christ's sake! If I hadn't happened to be coming here to check on you he'd be long gone by now.' He glared first at one man, then the other, then spoke in very deliberate tones. 'My father is going to be furious over this cockup. I don't want to be in your shoes when he finds out.' He leaned a little on the word *when*, and the two men looked at one another.

'Look,' the larger of the two men said at length, 'I've got no idea how he escaped, we had him handcuffed to the bed. It's just not possible.'

The smaller man moved closer. 'Your father?' he demanded. 'Who's that?'

Todd gave him a pitying look. 'Well, I'm English, and my name's Todd Hampton. Does that give you imbeciles a clue?'

It clearly did; the two men's eyes widened slightly, and they lowered their guns. Todd held up both his hands.

'As you can see, I'm unarmed. We're all on the same side here, so put those damned guns down. Now!'

They did so, and the metallic scraping and thumping of the surrendered weapons on the Formica worktop seemed to release a tension switch in John, as relief swept through him.

'Now get away from them,' Todd ordered, and the two men obediently began moving away from the kitchen counter. Todd glanced back at John, but before either of them could say anything the smaller man stopped and peered more closely at John.

'Hang on. Didn't he have longer hair when we got him?'

In the split second that followed, he whirled to seize his gun again, and John reached back and dragged the revolver from the back of his jeans, fumbling the safety catch off in the same movement. His heart was skipping madly in his chest.

'Don't even think about it!' He heard the words burst from his lips, and a wave of unreality washed over him. He was a *teacher*, for crying out loud… But he was so much more than that now. 'Step away, and move to the back of the room! Todd, grab the guns.'

Todd picked up the weapons and moved to stand next to him. 'I'll cover them, you find Doron.'

John left him with the two men, and walked into the hallway beyond the lounge. The first door he opened was a bathroom, small and dingy, with avocado fittings and an air of grime thick enough to taste. The next door opened onto a single bedroom, and a man sitting on the bed, one wrist handcuffed to the metal frame.

'You took your time, brother,' Doron croaked.

His voice brushed away the stunned hesitation, and John managed a grin. 'Yeah, well I'm a bit rusty at this sort of thing. Haven't done it in a while.' He lowered his voice. 'You okay?'

Doron nodded. 'Apart from a banging headache, I'm fine.' He squinted at John's head. 'Tell me that's ketchup.'

'It is.'

'Good.' Doron looked down at the handcuff, and rattled the chain. 'The fat guy has the key in his back pocket,' he said helpfully.

John yelled through to Todd, who, after a minute or two produced the key and tossed it down the hallway to John. A moment later Doron was freed, and he stood up, rubbing his wrist. The two brothers looked at one another, then Doron drew John into a firm embrace and they remained locked together for a time. It was a strange feeling, at once familiar and alien, to know this man was such an integral part of his life, and when John drew back he felt his throat tighten

Doron nodded, as if he understood, and clasped John's shoulders. They gave each other a tentative grin. 'Let's get out of here.'

With Doron behind him, John stepped into the hallway again and his heart froze. Todd stood rigid in the lounge,

249

a gun pressed to his temple by the smaller, wilier looking of the two men. At the same moment the bigger man swung his own gun around until it was aimed at John's chest.

'I'm sorry,' Todd said, and he sounded desperately angry and frustrated. 'Their guns had the safeties on... I didn't know.'

'Get over there with your friends.' The two men jerked Todd towards the hallway, and at the sight of his friend stumbling and being dragged upright again, something strange and calming dropped over John. A veil he couldn't see, but that he could feel like a weight; a muffling shroud that blocked out everything around him. His head swam, and as he stared at the two men, and at his frightened and helpless best friend, the air shimmered in front of him.

He let his mind go where it would, and was vaguely aware of movement all around, ahead as well as behind him. Then he saw Todd stepping away from his captors, who looked blankly at him and surrendered their weapons without demur. He swam back until the room came into focus once more, and Todd was ushering the two men towards the bedroom at gunpoint.

'In!' Todd said, jabbing at them with a gun in either hand. He flashed a slightly troubled smile at John as they passed. 'Don't worry, safeties are off this time.'

John and Doron followed, and while Todd remained in the doorway with the guns trained on the two men, John threaded the handcuff chain through the bed frame, and Doron slipped a cuff around the wrist of each man.

It wasn't until they were leaving that Todd voiced the question that was on all their minds. 'Well, that was weird. What happened there?'

John and Doron looked at one another and shrugged. 'Beats me,' John said, as Doron went to the kitchenette and retrieved his passport and phone. 'What about your luggage?' he asked.

'It's in a sherut somewhere, I never got it back.'

'Damn.' John turned to Todd. 'You were awesome just now. Sounded just like your dad.'

'Yeah, scary eh? I was shitting myself.'

'Me too.'

'Look sharp,' Doron cautioned, 'I heard them talking and their boss is on his way.'

They were clattering down the stairs, revelling in the sudden release of tension and fear, when they saw two burly, armed men heading up the stairwell towards them. Mindful of Doron's warning, John tightened up again and was disturbed by the sudden instinct that made him reach for Cal's gun, but he relaxed as they nodded, clearly unsurprised to see them.

'Good job, lads.' They looked from Doron to John and back again, and grinned. 'Peas in a pod.'

'The guys are cuffed to the bed,' Doron said. 'Keys are in the kitchen. Sounded as if their boss is due at any moment.'

'Okay,' the first man said. 'We'll handle it from here. You get gone.'

As good as his word, Cal was waiting with his engine idling, and the moment all three were in their seats he

251

took off. John rang Uri with the good news, while Todd gave Cal directions to his hotel, and he dropped them off with the promise that he would return tomorrow, to take them to Uri and Maya's home.

Doron showered, and changed into some spare clothes of Todd's, and then went to call Rena to let her know he was safe. The moment he had stepped out onto the balcony for privacy, Todd leaned in close to John and lowered his voice.

'It's weird,' he said, 'I keep staring at the poor bloke. He's a good looking fella, this brother of yours.'

'What do you mean *he's* good looking? He's my twin! You never told me I was good looking.'

Todd laughed. 'Never underestimate the effects of a bit of style, my man.'

Doron finished his call and walked back into the room, and John watched as he came closer. It hadn't been so evident in the dreams, but in the flesh he could see exactly what Todd had meant about his brother; he was dressed casually in Todd's shirt and jeans, but there was something almost mesmerising about him. Charisma? Presence? John didn't know what it was, only that he himself didn't possess it.

'So, Doron, are you hungry?'

'Brother, I could eat a horse. And call me Ron, most people do.' He smiled. 'Doron and David on the mountain, John and Ron down here.'

Todd snorted. 'John and Ron? You sound like a couple of gangsters!'

Doron put an arm around Todd's shoulder. 'This man is a good friend. You are a lucky man, John.'

252

John nodded. 'Todd's been like a brother to me all these years, and now I have another. It's so good to have you here, Ron.' He tried the name out and although it felt strange, he knew he'd have all the time in the world to get used to it. 'We have a lot of catching up to do.'

Chapter Fourteen
The Tape

'They're here!'

John saw Maya gesture excitedly to Uri, and the two of them rushed down the steps to greet him and Doron, who had both emerged from the taxi. Maya kissed them both, through tears of relief, and they hugged each other tight, hardly able to believe they were here, and safe.

After a moment Todd also climbed out of the taxi, but he hung back to give them time, and presently Uri broke away, and went back to greet him too.

'Thank you,' he said, shaking Todd's hand. 'Thank you for helping with our nephews. You have our gratitude.'

'It was no problem at all, Dr Malik.'

'Please, you must call me Uri. Go on up with the others, our home is open to you.'

Cal beckoned Uri over to his side of the taxi, and from his vantage point on the steps John saw him slip across a small package, which Uri tucked under his arm.

'Thank you for bringing the boys back safely, Cal.'

The driver nodded. 'My honour, sir.'

Inside, Uri placed the package on the sideboard and turned to Doron. 'So, are you okay, lad?'

Doron nodded. 'Fine thanks, Uncle. Apart from a mild concussion from a bump to my head. Just a bit tired.'

'Any problems with the rescue?'

'None at all. These two were amazing! Security turned up just as we were leaving, and it was over so quickly I hardly realised what was happening. They were taken completely by surprise, I was very impressed. With my brother and his friend.'

'Let's just sit down and talk,' Uri suggested. 'Maya's gone to make some lunch, but no doubt she'll be listening in from the kitchen…' he winked, and tilted his head, and sure enough the response came back,

'No, I won't!'

'So,' Uri said, when the chuckles had died down, 'did you learn anything from those who kidnapped you?'

'They didn't say much, but did mention that their boss was to meet with them soon. He wanted to meet me, for some reason.'

'And you told this to security?'

'Of course. The two kidnappers will be questioned to find out who their boss is. They've also got security on alert all day, ready for when whoever it is shows up.'

'Good.' Uri sat back, satisfied, and looking more relaxed. 'I'm so pleased you're here, and safe.' He stood up to fetch a pitcher of water as Maya came in carrying a bowl of steaming shakshuka, and a basket of freshly-baked challah, and then brought plates to the table.

John watched carefully, not sure how to eat this sharing meal, and saw Todd doing the same, but when everyone broke a piece of bread, and dipped it into the bowl, they were quick, and eager, to follow suit.

Doron gave Maya an appreciative smile. 'This is delicious, thank you.'

'You weren't exaggerating about Maya's cooking prowess,' John added to Uri, and felt the warmth of Maya's smile on him.

As they ate, conversation turned naturally to the two lives that had taken such divergent paths; Doron had followed in his Uncle Uri's footsteps and become a well-respected doctor, and though he was still single he was pleased to hear about John's family.

'I do hope to have a family of my own someday,' he said. 'I hope I'm not leaving it too late. He reached into his back pocket, retrieved his wallet, and pulled out a couple of worn photos which he passed to John.

'Some pictures of me as a child, with our mother and Alex. I had brought more, but I'm afraid they're in my lost luggage.

John held the photos carefully, suddenly all fingers and thumbs. 'Mum couldn't travel with me,' Doron added, 'but she sends her love and hopes to see you soon.'

John found the photos he'd been showing Maya and Uri, and for a few minutes they each sat in silence, lost in what might have been as they studied each other's separate families… families which should have been one.

Around them, Maya and Uri cleared the table, and John glanced up to see Uri taking the package off the sideboard and frowning at it. 'What's that?'

Uri didn't answer, but opened the envelope and slid out a video tape. His face visibly tightened, and although there was no note, or label, it was clear it was no mystery to him. 'Okay, everyone,' he said, holding up the tape, 'we've been sent a message. Let's watch it.'

He slid the tape into the VCR and turned on the TV. 'Maya? Are you coming in?'

As soon as she joined them he pressed 'play,' and they all sat forward at the same moment, taut with curiosity. The screen remained blank, but an American-accented voice spoke.

'Hello, Uri and Maya. We trust you are well. We also trust Doron and John are both safely with you to hear this message.' A pause, and the twins looked at one another; John couldn't speak for Doron but it still felt strange to him, to be known by these people he'd never dreamed even existed, such a short time ago.

'What follows is a recording of a recent meeting between Richard Hampton and Charles Whyte.'

John looked over at Todd, and saw his friend's face pale, but remain fixed on the empty TV screen. His heart shrank a little at what must be going through Todd's mind right now, and he wished he could say something to take away that look of dread.

The voice went on, 'Louise Miller, Whyte's PA, agreed to help us and it is thanks to her that we now have the proof we need to bring Hampton to justice. With this information we can start to weed out the rest of Veritas's top members. When this goes public there are going to be a lot of politicians worrying they'll also be incriminated, and Hampton will be arrested and tried for war crimes and murder... We sincerely hope he doesn't go down alone.'

John reached out to grip Todd's shoulder. 'Todd, I'm—'

257

'Please,' Uri said, although he too sounded sorrowful. 'We will discuss this after we have heard all of it.'

'Friends,' the American was saying, 'this is big, and some of you in the not too distant future will be required to act as witnesses. For this reason, we have made arrangements for you and your families to relocate to a place of safety. Louise Miller, and Otto Fischer, Hampton's geneticist, are already en route, and you will be informed of the details soon. The Nephilim and their families will also be relocated. There will be a lot of interest in the children once the tape is made public, and I'm sure you understand we do not want them exploited.'

The voice took on a slightly less mechanical note. 'On a separate issue, you may or may not be aware that the next date that Mount Sinai falls under the shadow of a total solar eclipse is November third this year, and the central eclipse time in Mecca will be 12.38. It will be quite special as this is a hybrid eclipse, being both a total and an annular. We believe this is significant.'

Uri paused the tape, and John put a hand on Todd's back, feeling the tension there. 'Are you okay?'

'No.' Todd shook him off and stood, running his hands through his hair. 'Actually I'm not. Didn't you hear what he said? *War crimes and murder.* Christ.'

'I'm sorry,' John said in a low voice. 'I only found out myself yesterday, that he was in the frame for these things. What with the kidnap and everything I haven't had a chance to talk to you about it.'

Todd looked at him, his face impassive now, and John wondered how much fury lurked beneath that calm façade. 'I'm assuming the evidence for these accusations is on the tape too?'

'I believe so,' Uri said. 'I'm sorry, Todd, but we have to watch it. We will all understand if you don't want to, or can't.'

'Thank you, but I need to know.' Todd sat back down, and John saw him rub the palms of his hands onto his jeans, leaving a trace of sweat on the denim. 'And once it's finished there are more important issues here we'll need to discuss.'

Uri resumed the playback, and now the picture flickered into life. Todd's father, and a man John assumed to be Whyte, sitting at one end of a long conference table with coffee cups and paperwork spread out on its polished surface.

Whyte was already speaking as the recording had begun. '...conflict, which has intensified in the Congo, and the Second Intifada between Israel and Palestine, although we believe that will soon come to an end. Heads of State will no doubt be discussing treaty terms. That's to name just a few.'

'You've certainly done well, Charles,' Hampton said in his smooth tones. A glance at Todd showed a muscle jumping in his cheek, and John looked away again, feeling helpless.

'We both have, my friend,' Whyte said. 'The most obvious and highest profits are in arms and technology, which is where the people's attention is drawn. Our professions obviously get a boost in income during war times, but nowhere near the big bucks we've all made in instigating and maintaining the conflicts for certain governments.' So there it was. Baldly stated, absolutely unequivocal.

'So,' Todd's father said, 'have you brought me all this way to discuss company business, or is there something else on your mind?'

Whyte sat back; hands folded, and studied his visitor for a moment. 'I'd like to talk about Israel,' he said at last.

'Alright.'

'The conflict there has been profitable for us all, but, as we know, wars eventually come to an end.' He actually sounded regretful, and John's instant hatred of him intensified.

'It was a brilliant idea,' Whyte went on, 'considering entering into discussions with Saudi after the discovery of those tablets at Jericho. But that was, what, 30 years ago? My, how time flies.' The dry humour in his voice was belied by his words as he sat forward again.

'The Saudi economy is boosted by around ten billion dollars a year from the Hajj alone. If we only could've *proven* that Hira was Sinai, the additional billions that could have been made by opening up just Mount Hira to all religions for pilgrimages would have been substantial.'

'Agreed, and that was the general idea.' Hampton sounded irritated at being told what he already knew. 'Although some peace negotiations would have had to have been entered into,' he added, 'and that's not really our forte is it?' He sighed. 'It still rankles that the plan had to be shelved when we couldn't find the proof we needed. It's been a thorn in my side all these years that we got so close.'

'And that brings me on to why you're here. You allowed the whole thing to become personal, Richard. The discovery was world-changing, but you never recovered enough from those archaeologists. And the other most important tablets were never found, were they?'

'Hardly my fault! I'm constantly having to deal with morons!'

Whyte's voice remained calm. 'And I sympathise, of course. But your anger and sour temper over the years have been the cause of serious problems within Veritas.' He shook his head. 'Plus, Eagle has outwitted you on more than one occasion, you can't deny that.

On the screen, Hampton's mouth dropped open ready to speak up in his own defence, but Whyte went on, 'The instigation of the car accident to clear the witnesses to your illegal operation was acceptable, but the mess you left behind was not.' He scowled. 'It took a lot of our resources to keep you clean; falsifying records, and bribing the forensic expert, and so on. However,' he shrugged, 'Veritas *was* impressed with the efficiency of how you dealt with the new-born twin's disposals. Until it was discovered that the twins mentioned in the prophecy were alive and well.' His voice dropped into an angry growl, 'You had the *wrong babies killed,* Richard!'

'Firstly,' Hampton bit back, sitting up straight now, 'the incident at the Shiloh base should have been a simple theft, until the archaeologists I hired showed up with two of the tablets. They stole them from me in the first place, they had no right! I had two muscled apcs with me and *still* they managed to let them get free.'

'You managed to let a pint-sized female escape, and received a substantial wound from her in the struggle. That was careless of you, my friend. Very careless.'

Hamptons face betrayed his fury; reddened and working, and even on the tape it was possible to see a vein throbbing in his forehead. Presumably from both the memory of that encounter with Denise, and with Whyte's condescending tone.

'Luckily you had the foresight to have the Maliks, and the Milburn boy, watched,' Whyte said. 'Eagle did a good job of hiding their birth, I must say. If it hadn't been for a visit from this Doron, and you noticing the likeness to your son's friend, we would've been none the wiser.' He waved a hand dismissively. 'The discovery of the tablets is now of no consequence; they've served their purpose, alerting us to the prophecies. By the way, I understand both boys are in Israel as we speak. Isn't that rather odd?'

'Not really, they're on holiday. Todd is there on theology grounds, and Milburn is visiting his place of birth.'

'And he has no inkling as to his parentage?'

'I don't see how he could.' Hampton looked to be on firmer ground now. 'When his mother returned from Israel I promised her that if she mentioned any of the artefacts to anyone, her son would go the same way as her husband.' He shrugged. 'She was dying anyway, so I didn't have to watch her for long. I kept an eye on the boy purely as a precautionary measure.'

It was John's turn to clench his fists, and he felt, rather than saw, Todd's eyes on him in mute anguish.

'Then why have you tried to stop Milburn going to Israel?' Whyte demanded.

'Again, just a precaution. He'll no doubt be visiting the Maliks, but I wouldn't have thought they'd discuss anything, not after all this time. And would they be believed anyway? It's a crazy story, and Milburn's an academic. He'd want proof they simply don't have.' He frowned slightly. 'My only concern is whether Milburn will get to meet his brother. That *cannot* happen. According to the prophecy they have to meet as foreigners, in order to get this whole ball rolling.'

Whyte nodded. 'I assume then, that you have a detail attached to them, ready to carry out the necessary action should that happen?'

'Of course.'

'Good. We can't have the prophecy being fulfilled, Richard. If this gets out, I hardly need remind you of the level of potential threat to Veritas. Where would the organisation be, if these mutant children manage to convince everyone their religions are all hogwash?'

'I understand.'

'Mind you,' Whyte mused, 'it might be no concern of ours in the near future.'

'So I ask again,' Hampton said impatiently, 'why are we meeting privately? I mean, what we're discussing might have a personal element, but it's nothing Veritas don't know about...' He only seemed to take in then, what Whyte had said. 'And why might it not be our concern?'

'There's a rumour that Veritas want to retire us.' Hampton stared open-mouthed, and Whyte went on, 'They want new blood at the top. The board are not happy with your results, Richard, and,' he flushed a little as he admitted, 'they're no better pleased with a few of my… shall we just say *indiscretions*. I've been told that preparations are under way to move HQ to Hamburg, to be hosted by Frank Braun.'

Hampton gave a derisive snort, and Whyte flashed him a half-smile. 'We're actually alike, you and me.' He seemed to come to a final decision there and then. 'Look, the reason I called you for a private meeting, is that I have a partnership proposal for you. Just in case.' His eyes narrowed. 'Does anyone at Veritas know about your experiments?'

'No, they don't! After the time it's taken to get the research this far—'

'Why is that, exactly?'

'Do you have the faintest idea how hard it has been to find this immunity gene that they have?' Hampton lowered his voice, losing its defensive edge. 'Okay, listen. Our body cells contain 46 chromosomes, right? 23 from each parent. Within those chromosomes we have over 20,000 genes, and we've had to search them all. We thought we'd find it in the sex chromosomes, which is where most immunities are, but no, so we had to *research them all*.' He shook his head. 'With a limited amount of blood to use for our experiments, it's taken years to find it.'

'And how did you get hold of the blood in the first place?'

Now Hampton sounded pleased, almost smug. 'It took a long time to find the names of all the children, but I now have a list of all the twins born with the Nephilim genes. Each time any of them made a visit to a doctor or hospital, I acquired blood samples.' He smiled. 'I have good contacts in the health profession, most of whom owe me favours.'

'I see,' Whyte said, and nodded for him to continue.

'We finally found it in C2...' he pulled a face at Whyte's blank look. 'That's an abbreviation for Chromosome 2,' he said, with exaggerated patience, as if imparting a lesson to a small child. 'The gene is a mutation. It has encoded a protein we've named Uncategorized Encoded Protein 1, or UEP1 for short. So. The Malik twins have two identical ones, an inherited gene from their mother and a pure one from the Fathers. *Capital F,*' he clarified, with a faintly superior air the other man clearly resented.

'The younger twins also have two identical ones,' he went on, 'which means both their parents must have carried UEP1 in that gene in their DNA. From random blood samples taken from the population, we have discovered that some people carry UEP1 whilst the majority have no signs of it at all.'

Whyte sat forward, looking interested now. 'So why isn't the world full of people with this immunity?'

'If only one parent donates C2, containing the gene with UEP1, there is a one in four chance of their offspring inheriting it. Okay? If *both* parents donate, there's a fifty per cent chance.' In his element now, Hampton spoke quickly, and John had to strain to catch all he said, and to understand it.

'Normally a gene such as this could easily die out, or, if we're lucky, produce a person with two. The unusual thing

265

here, is that we have not found a single person carrying two of these mutated genes, apart from the twins in question. Which makes no sense at all, genetically speaking. The key seems to be in the multiple birth factor and it's almost like the gene has been… *controlled* somehow.'

'Controlled how?'

'We don't know. After testing rats with all known pathogenic micro-organisms on UEP1 taken from the twins, we've found they have immunity to everything. Nothing can harm them, biologically. Rats were also tested using blood from the general population that carry only the one UEP1, and these rats got sick following some tests, but recovered. Those people therefore have some degree of resistance, but not the full immunity.'

'Well, the science of it's a bit lost on me, I'm afraid,' Whyte said, and John caught the fleeting expression on Hampton's face: *no shit*? 'But,' Whyte went on, 'I'm assuming then, that this part of the donation is from the Fathers. *Capital F.*' He said this last with a heavy emphasis, which Hampton ignored.

'We believe so, yes. Along with the part they call the "spirit." All the twins have a slightly different DNA structure to the rest of us, in addition to this mutant gene. At Meridian, I've had Otto, my top geneticist, working secretly to try and duplicate the gene artificially. But we need more samples to work with.'

Whyte pursed his lips. 'Well, I must say this is wonderful news, Rich. In the event we are retired, I'd like to offer to help with the funding of your work. Veritas need not be aware of it; we'll work on it ourselves. I'm sure we can think of some way of obtaining more samples for you.' He grinned. 'The value of providing universal immunity to the population would be worth a lot of money. We could retire very rich men indeed.'

'You're missing the bigger picture, Charles.' Hampton's own smile was tight. 'We wouldn't have to provide the immunity to anyone. Have you thought about the implications to the pharmaceutical companies, if this became available to the public? They would go out of business! Worldwide pharmaceutical revenue is around one trillion dollars a year… No, *my friend*, they will pay us to keep it quiet.'

The tables turned, the men continued talking a while longer, the conversation turning back to the other members of Veritas, and who might be in line to take over their positions. Names were bandied back and forth, and finally the two men shook hands and Hampton left. A moment later the tape went black.

For a moment everyone simply looked at one another, desperate to discuss what they'd heard, but all too aware of Todd's conflict.

Eventually Todd himself broke the silence. 'He deserves everything he's got coming to him.' He cleared his throat and looked up, his eyes locked on John's. 'I'm disgusted. Embarrassed and ashamed to share my genes with that monster.'

John read more than he was saying, in that look. 'It's not your fault, Todd.'

'Then why do I feel so guilty for not knowing?' Todd shook his head, his hands balled into fists on his knees;

John had never seen his laid back, fun-loving friend so agitated. '*How* didn't I know?'

A moment later he had gone, the door slamming shut behind him, leaving the four of them who were left staring at one another in dismay.

Chapter Fifteen

Exodus

Haverhill, Surrey

The last leg of the journey had been the longest of all. It had been late afternoon when the taxi had dropped Todd off at the Rose and Crown, and John looked up to see the curtain fall back into place, hiding Sinead's anxious face. A moment later, just as the taxi driver had finished tugging Todd's suitcase out of the boot, she had appeared in the doorway, hands on hips, and, through the car's open window John heard her say, 'Well, you took your time coming back from all yer gallivanting, my lad.'

Todd had turned and grinned at John, and Sinead had waved, and John had braced himself for a long conversation he didn't want right now, but the two of them were now locked in an embrace and it was as if they were the only people there. John had felt a flicker of envy for them as they vanished indoors and the taxi pulled away, but now it was his turn.

The rattle of the diesel engine brought his own net curtains to life, and he smiled to see two eager faces that looked at one another with delight and then disappeared. As he paid the driver the front door opened, and the twins shot out to meet him on the path.

'Daddy!'

John crouched to receive their exuberant welcome, his arms open wide, but in their excitement they forgot to slow down, and the three of them tumbled to the ground in a laughing, spluttering heap. After everything that had happened it was a moment so unbelievably precious that, through the laughter, John felt his throat close up with gratitude and relief to be home. Then the news he brought with him re-surfaced, and he had to fight not to show his sudden lurch of trepidation; the sight of Jen smiling at him from the doorway only added to his churned up emotions, and he kissed the twins' heads, wondering how he was going to tell them all what must happen now.

'I've missed you two scallywags.'

'We've missed you too, Dad.' They rose, allowing him to roll onto his knees. 'You're ever so brown,' Holly observed.

'That's my cool suntan.' John climbed to his feet, feeling exhaustion setting in all over again. 'It's very hot there.' He caught Jen's eye, and with a wink at the girls, he dropped his voice. 'I'd better go and say hello to your mum before she starts sulking.'

The girls insisted on dragging the suitcase up the path between them, and when they all reached the door John pulled Jen close and folded her into his arms. 'Hi, sweetheart. Miss me?'

She drew back and smiled up at him. 'As much as you missed me.'

'Good, because that was a lot.' He bent to kiss her, and then let out a sigh against her hair. 'I'm so glad to be home, I can't tell you.'

'After everything you've been through I'm just glad you're home safe. Let's get you inside. I'll put the kettle on.'

John nodded, then squinted at the girls. 'Jen, can I just ask you one thing?'

'What?'

'Why are they wearing long johns in public?'

Holly punched his arm. 'Dad! They're leggings, not long johns!'

'Leggings?'

'They're in *fashion*.'

'Good grief,' John complained. 'I've only been away two weeks, and the world's moved on without me.' He saw a secret little smile tug at Jen's lips, and he raised an eyebrow but she shook her head. *You'll see…*

John allowed himself to be led into the sitting room, and Jen volunteered to bring his suitcase from the hall. He caught her eye again and this time his silent question was answered with a brief nod. When she brought the case in, neither of the twins noticed the zip was half undone from where she had just pushed a carrier bag into it, but John sent her a look of gratitude.

'I've bought you all something from my trip,' he announced, enjoying the way their eyes lit up. 'Only from the airport, but still.' He withdrew the bag Jen had placed there, put it to one side, then pulled out a box. 'Chanel 1932,' he announced, reading the description, 'apparently it's woody and fruity, with musk.' He winked at Jen, 'you know how I like musky stuff.'

'That's fabulous, thank you!' Jen took it and tore off the cellophane. 'I love it!' She sprayed her wrists and invited the girls to smell it, but they were more interested in what was in the bag.

'Here you go,' John said, pulling out two identical smaller bags. 'I got you both some…' He waited, watching as they pulled out the contents, then laughed. 'More long johns! Flowery ones!'

'Leggings!' They kissed him and rushed off to try them on.

'Thanks for getting them,' John murmured to Jen. 'I didn't have a clue what to buy.' He sat down and pulled her down next to him. She snuggled close and he heard her breathing deeply as she nuzzled his neck. 'You're a very weird person,' he said with sleepy amusement.

'Takes one to know one,' she returned smartly, and he chuckled.

By the time he'd eaten his evening meal he could hardly keep his eyes open.

'Go on up,' Jen urged. 'What with all the travel and that big meal, you must be ready to hit the hay.'

He had to talk to her, it was like an insistent finger, tapping on the inside of his skull. But he needed a clear head to do it. 'Wake me in a couple of hours,' he said, and dropped a kiss on her temple. He smiled once more at the twins who, delighted with their new, highly fashionable leggings, were dancing around the sitting room, and made his way up the stairs to fall into his own, blessedly familiar bed at long last.

Jen settled the girls into bed, and peeked in at John. He looked so peaceful, spread-eagled on the bed in utter abandon, that she left him to it and instead went to find

Rena's letter, ready to give him in the morning. He'd told her a great deal about what had happened during his stay with Uri and Maya, but she knew there was more, and from the distant look that had come over his face more than once, she had a feeling she wasn't going to like it.

She found the two sealed envelopes in Karen's biscuit tin, and looked at them for a long moment. What did they hold? She laid them carefully on the table, as if they were priceless works of art, and later, all the while she was trying to watch the television, she found her thoughts straying back to them. Her fingers itched to open them, after all nothing would change by her knowing... But it wouldn't be right; they were personal, and they belonged to John.

She unpacked his suitcase and put a wash on, and when she eventually felt tired enough to go to bed she was relieved to see John had moved over to his own side and now lay curled up, still asleep. She slipped quietly in beside him, and rolled over until she lay against him, skin to skin, breathing in unison. For her own peace she pushed the questions to the back of her mind; whatever he hadn't told her, he would tell her tomorrow... and tomorrow could take care of itself. He was home.

As she returned from the school run the next morning she heard the bedroom door open and close, and presently the sound of the shower running told her John was up for the day. She abandoned the need for quiet, and got busy frying the bacon and sausages she'd just bought.

'God, that smells wonderful.'

She turned to see him looking much more awake than he had yesterday, and smiled. 'You slept well.'

'A sleep and a half,' he agreed. 'You didn't wake me.'

'No, I thought I should leave you to it, you obviously needed it.' She crossed the kitchen to stand in front of him, and ran her hands through his wet hair. 'You were out for the count.'

They looked at one another in silence for a moment, and Jen could feel the stirring between them; John's eyes were hooded, though not from tiredness now, and Jen's breathing quickened as he reached out to touch her face…

The toast popped up. John and Jen looked at one another, eyes widening at the symbolic timing, and then broke apart, laughing. Jen couldn't shake the feeling that they should seize every moment of levity that came their way from now on; it looked as if it might soon be in short supply.

After breakfast they took their coffee into the lounge, and as they passed the dining table John picked up the envelopes Jen had left there. 'The ones we missed?'

Jen nodded. 'I got them out ready for you.' No point in telling him of her struggle to leave them unopened; her curiosity would soon be satisfied.

She sat close to him on the sofa so they could read the contents together. The first envelope held the results of the scan confirming Karen's tumour.

'Well, Uri was right on that score,' John said quietly, as they sat looking at the death sentence in stark black and white.

'She was such a brave woman,' Jen said. She laid a hand on John's knee, fighting tears at the thought of everything Karen, and Rena too, had sacrificed for their child. John picked up the second envelope and opened it.

'To my beautiful boy, David,' he read aloud. *'Now you are a man, Karen and George will have told you the circumstances of your birth. I write this to let you know that I did not give you up easily, and indeed almost lost the courage to do so. It is a comfort to know that you will be loved and cared for, by two people my brother holds in high esteem, and that one day you and your own brother Doron will meet again. I pray that I will live long enough to see you too, so that I can let you know that, although I only held you for a moment, I will have loved you all of your life.'*

John's voice cracked on the last words, and Jen's own tears spilled over. Through the blur she saw that the final part of the letter was Rena giving her permission for the informal adoption to go ahead, and John re-read it silently before putting it down.

'Thanks for unpacking my case. Where did you put the paperwork?'

'In the office.'

He went to fetch it. 'Here are some photos of Rena, with her husband and Doron. Ron, I mean.'

Jen went through them; it was an uncanny feeling. 'It's like looking at pictures of you, but in another life.'

'Todd reckons he's good looking, but I'm not.'

'Todd's talking out of his arse,' she said, holding up a photo of Ron next to John's face. 'You've got everything Ron's got, don't listen to him!' She smiled as he flushed. 'Rena looks lovely too, and most importantly they all look happy. I'm so glad you've found them. From what you've told me Ron sounds great.'

'Yeah, he is.' John took the photos back and flicked through them again. 'We got to know each other really well in the last few days of our stay. Once Todd was able to move past his anger at his father, and slept off his bender, we all got together to work out what to do next.'

'Poor Todd. What happened with his father, once Uri handed the tape over to the authorities?'

'He was arrested at Tel Aviv airport, on his way to meet Shay.'

'This was the burglar? And the snitch?'

'Yeah, that's him.'

Jen frowned. 'So what happens now? Will he be extradited back here for a trial?'

John shrugged. 'There's a treaty between us and Israel, so if their government and our ministry of justice agree, then yes, a prisoner *could* be returned.'

'But you don't think so?'

'I'm pretty sure Israel won't agree to it.' John's voice turned hard. 'They'll want him hanged, drawn and quartered for what he's done. Even without the war crimes accusations, he'll be held to account for the killing of Israeli babies. His life will be hell inside.'

Jen nodded. She'd spare no sympathy for him, that was for sure. 'What about Shay then?'

'He turned up at the flat where they'd held Ron when they took him, and was nabbed by Eagle security and turned over to the authorities. Todd says he was one of his father's cronies from way back, and he reckons he knew everything that'd been going on. He'll squeal, too.'

'I can't imagine what Todd must be going through. I mean, apart from everything else, to learn his father had been experimenting with blood from some of the twins.'

'Well,' John mused, 'as bad as that was, the results were a great help to us. Ron had already worked out we had a rare immune system, and had been doing tests on his own blood.'

'Oh?' Jen sat up, less revolted than interested now.

'He hadn't found the gene that contained it though,' John said. 'It was Hampton's geneticist, Otto someone-or-other, that discovered the UEP1 in Chromosome 2, or C2 as he called it. Eagle have whisked him away to a secure location to continue—'

'Hang on.' Jen held up a hand. 'C2?' She searched the niggling memory, and found it. 'Another mystery solved! Do you remember we couldn't work out what that meant?' When he gave her a blank look, she went on, 'It was written on the paperwork that Todd brought over from his father's desk. The night we first saw the list of the childrens' names.'

John's eyes widened. 'I'd forgotten all about that. You little genius.' He leaned in quickly and kissed her. 'Speaking of Todd, what time are he and Sinead due over?'

'About half one. Todd's going to see his mother first. That'll give us an hour easy, before the school run.'

'Good, we have a lot to discuss.'

Jen chewed her lip worriedly. 'That tape will have to be played at Hampton's public trial, won't it? You know what the press are like, they'll latch onto that awful thing about the children, and Todd and his mother will take all the flak. I've read some horrible stories about what happens to families once the media gets its grip on a story.'

'Don't worry,' John said, putting an arm about her shoulder. 'Eagle have that sorted. They've put an agreement in place with the authorities concerned, that states only the relevant parts of the recording will be played at the trial. The legal teams on both sides will need to see the whole thing, but that'll happen *in camera*.'

'That puts my mind at rest. Though I'm surprised it was agreed to.'

'It's basically a compromise. The press will be kept in the dark about the children until just before the third of November. Eagle will give them a story, and details of what might happen on that date, and whatever does will be covered by reporters and film crews. That's when they go public with it all, including the handing over of Amnon's tablets and any other evidence.'

'Third of November?' Jen felt a tremor of apprehension. Somehow putting a date on it made it all seem real. 'What happens then?'

'There's going to be an unusual eclipse on that date. Mount Hira is going to fall in its shadow – we think it's the same circumstances in which Moses and Maor communicated with the Fathers.'

Jen caught her breath. 'Do you… do you think you and the children will experience the same thing, then?'

'I do.' John took a deep breath, and Jen sensed that he was finally building up to telling her what had been on his mind since his return from Israel. 'For that reason,' he said slowly, 'the children, all of them, must be together.

Partly for their safety, and partly so they're all in the same time zone. So we can all synchronise our dreaming.'

'But how on earth do we accomplish that?'

'The day after we heard the tape, Ron received a phone call from his stepfather, Alex. He's a Senator. An associate of his, Paul Morgan, is the Senator for Colorado. They met with the US vice-president, and have agreed that Colorado will donate a large piece of land for our use.'

'Our use for what?'

'Hang on.' He seemed to be struggling for the right words, and Jen's blood ran a little cooler in her veins. Something big was happening, and not just in the world of dreams and mountains.

'John, what—'

'Eagle have pulled all their resources together,' John said. 'They've set up a central pot, to fund a... a compound, if you like, of modular homes for all of us. They should be finished by mid-October.'

Jen studied his face, and although she could see the answer there, she had to ask anyway. 'Are we talking temporary here, or permanent?'

He looked at her helplessly. 'It's got to be permanent, sweetheart. I'm so sorry. It's the only way to keep the children... *our* children, safe.' He rushed on, 'I realise this is a horrible shock, and everything's happening so fast. It'll be a massive upheaval for us all, the kids and their schools, my job, your research... and it'll be hard work given the time scale. But—'

'What are modular homes? Like a trailer park?'

He blinked, as if he'd expected anything but this rational question. 'Uh, no. They're more like pre-fab.

279

Permanent. I've seen the drawings and they're actually rather lovely.'

Jen nodded. The answer wouldn't have mattered, but asking the question had given her a moment to process the direction their lives must take. 'Sold,' she said, hiding the leap of fear that threw her heart into a faster beat.

'What?'

'Of course it's a shock. But if we're discussing the safety of our children there's really no decision to make, is there? I'd live in a tent in the Sahara if I had to.'

John reached out and took her hand, and let out a long, shaky breath. 'There are provisos.'

'Go on.'

'Any money we make from selling this place has to go into the central pot.'

'Makes sense. Some of the families might have nothing, we're luckier. I don't mind sharing. Anything else?'

'Just one. We – the Nephilim that is – have to give occasional blood samples, for research into developing a synthetic gene that can be used to develop vaccines.'

'That's it?'

'That's it.'

'Okay.'

He stared at her a moment, then his face broke into a smile, wider than any she'd seen from him in far too long. He looked like his carefree younger self, and she realised all over again what kind of burden he'd been carrying.

'You're amazing,' he said quietly. 'I thought you'd be so upset, that I'd have to work harder to persuade you.'

'I'm under no illusion that this will be like a holiday camp,' Jen said. 'But we'll all be together, and safe, with a roof over our heads and a new life to look forward to. It'll be bloody hard work, but no, John. I'm not upset. I'm a bit scared, I won't lie, but how could I be upset?'

He pulled her close and she rested her head on his chest, glad he couldn't see the fear that must be showing in her eyes. After a moment her thoughts straightened out and she sat up again. 'What about Mum and Dad? And Todd and Sinead? Everyone else?'

'For now it can only be the children, siblings and parents; it's going to be difficult enough to get everything ready for just us before November. But as more homes are built they're going to allow close family members of anyone attached to Eagle.'

Jen nodded. 'How on earth do you convince *everyone* to move?'

'The day before we flew back, Ron and I – with Uri and Maya's help – managed to make contact with all those who live in Israel, and were able to hire a lecture theatre in the An-Najah University. When we told them our stories we could tell they thought it was some strange cult recruitment, but once their own children got involved, and they heard them all talking in Hally, they started comparing notes on their dreams. Fair to say they were pretty gobsmacked.'

'I'm not surprised.'

'They were very taken with Ron, too. He's so charismatic and has a real way with people. It also helped when they realised we both spoke the same language as their children.'

'You both what?' Jen stared.

'Yeah, weird, isn't it?' John smiled. 'We only realised ourselves once we met with the Israeli children. Before, it had only been something that happened on the mountain, but we reckon that because we've met in real life, the subconscious has become the conscious.'

'So… did they *all* agree then?'

'Some were desperate to. They'd been so confused, worried… convinced they were alone. Others are still a bit sceptical, but I think they can be won over.'

'What about all the rest then?'

'Ron's going to focus on those in the States, which will leave two lots in France, one in Germany, and one in Spain. I've got their contact details and that'll be our job. Can you get hold of Alima and Ruhi's mum again, and explain what's happening?'

'Farrah. Yes, of course. We'll need to get a message to those others in Europe to meet in a central location. Say, Paris? We can do a group talk like you and Ron did, and we'll take the girls. I'll get onto it all first thing tomorrow.'

'Arrange it for the weekend,' John said, grimacing, 'I'm back to work tomorrow.'

'God, it hardly seems possible that all this mundane stuff is still going on.'

She spoke lightly, but John's face was grave. 'Make the most of it,' he said, drawing her close again. 'I have a feeling we're going to be wishing for the mundane again before too long.'

Todd and Sinead arrived early, and Sinead waved a paper bag. 'Jam doughnuts! Or I suppose we're going to have to get used to calling them jelly doughnuts soon.'

'We?' Jen saw a secretive little smile on Sinead's face, and raised an eyebrow.

The smile widened until it was a beam. 'Todd asked me to come to Colorado too, with him and his mum, when there's a place for us. I said yes, of course.'

It was the closest thing to a marriage proposal as it was possible to get, and Jen hugged her. 'Brilliant news!' She turned to Todd. 'That's probably one of the best decisions you've ever made, you know.'

'I do know,' Todd said, his smile matching Sinead's.

'So,' John rescued the doughnuts and gave them an appreciative sniff, 'how did it go with your mum?'

'Better than I expected, to be honest.' Todd snatched the bag back. 'She took it all in, went quiet for a minute, then summed it up with, "Sod him." He glanced around quickly to make sure there were no nine year-old girls listening.

'They're at school,' Jen reminded him.

'Excellent. Anyway, she's got no problems with the proceeds of the house and the research centre going into the pot, said she never really needed lots of things anyway, and good riddance.' He sobered. 'The rest of it was harder of course. She knew nothing about any of this, so I had to start at the beginning and it's hard not to make it sound like the ravings of a lunatic. But, in the end, it was fine.'

'That's great news, mate,' John said.

'She did ask how we would be able to go though, seeing as we're not family of any of the twins. And she wanted to know how we would support ourselves.'

'Well you can reassure her that we might not have the same blood, but we *are* family.'

'I never thought about all that,' Jen confessed. 'How *will* we support ourselves?'

'We're all to be given a small basic allowance to live on, until we become self-sufficient. We've all got good skills, I'm sure it won't be long.'

'I have a question,' Sinead put in. 'It's been bugging me a bit: why did the senator of Colorado agree to help us? And then swing it with the vice-president to boot?'

'The most basic reason of all,' John said. 'Do you remember on that list of children's names, there was a set of twins named Morgan? They're his children.'

'Blimey. Talk about handy! Still, it's going to be a tough time for everyone, uprooting and starting over somewhere new'

'Yeah,' Jen said. She was starting to feel a low tingling as a kind of realisation crept through her; a sense of being swept along with events totally out of their control, but inevitable nevertheless. 'I think I can appreciate how those poor people must have felt, leaving their homes to follow Moses and Maor to a land they'd never seen before. We're luckier; they had to walk, and there were no homes waiting for them when they arrived, but... I suppose Colorado is going to be *our* Promised Land.'

Part Five
Colorado 2013

You will not:

- *Bow down to, or worship, any Gods or idols*
- *Forget your inception nor your history*
- *Deliberately cause suffering to any living creature, save in self-defence*
- *Deliberately kill any living creature, save in self-preservation*
- *Commit adultery*
- *Steal*
- *Lie without good cause*
- *Incite others to perform any of the above*

You will:

- *Protect nature*
- *Respect all differences*
- *Take full responsibility for your own actions*

Chapter Sixteen
The Reveal

Eagle County, Colorado

After an hour's drive from the airport, John turned the hired jeep off the road and onto a dirt track. Below them the Roaring Fork Valley spread out, with stunning views of Capital Peak, Mount Sopris and the snow-capped Elk Ridge. Lakes, meadows, and forests lay bathed in the mid-October sun, waiting for the heavier covering of winter snows that would bring so many tourists and ski enthusiasts. For now, there was just this wooden arched entrance, and beyond it something that looked like a return to the Old West.

The village was laid out in a more modern style though, with two straight rows of about ten houses each, dirt tracks leading to the front steps, but the houses themselves a very pleasant surprise. Built to look like log cabins, each had a solar panelled roof, and a porch that ran the entire length of the house… Eagle had done them proud. The furniture was basic but well made, and until their belongings arrived they would manage well with what they had.

John left the girls to unpack their things and make the stark house look a little more homely, while he went to look around. Several families had already settled, and, recognising John as Doron's twin, they were keen to introduce themselves; much time was taken up with firm handshakes, and hurried stories... John recognised in each one of the people he met, the same relief to be with others, underpinned by a current of fear that ran through everything. It had the same air as he imagined an army encampment must feel on the eve of battle.

At the end of the dirt track he found a square-built, plain building that had probably been the base of operations when the village had been planned. It was empty now, but had electricity and decent plumbing; it could be used as a school room, and double as a meeting room in the evenings. Two smaller buildings, close by, could be adapted for use as a medical station and maybe a convenience store.

It occurred to John that he had no idea who was in charge here, who to ask about supplies, deliveries, communal fiscal matters... and these people were looking at him as if he had all the answers right here at his fingertips. It was a lonely feeling, and he suddenly had the urge to get back to his new home, and to those who knew him best.

On his way back he was greeted by a short man with an animated manner, and an earnest way of fixing his pale eyes on his subject. 'Excuse me, I thought for a moment you were Doron Farmer.'

'Farmer?' John frowned slightly. 'Oh, that's his stepfather's name; he goes by his birth name, Malik. But close,' John gave him a polite, but distant smile. 'I'm his brother John, John Milburn'

'Otto,' the man said, pumping John's hand. 'Otto Fischer.'

'It's good to meet you Herr Fischer,' John said, extricating his hand with difficulty. 'I understand you've been given premises to continue your experiments.' *Only this time with consenting subjects*, remained unspoken between them. Fischer's face reflected his remorse, and John didn't see any sense in bringing up the past. Not now. Fischer hadn't been a knowing part of it, after all.

'Yes,' Fischer said. 'At Colorado Mountain College, in Glenwood Springs.'

'Well, I wish you luck with it.' John moved on down the path towards his plot. But Otto wasn't ready to let him go just yet, and accompanied him, chattering all the while. John paused at the bottom of the wooden steps, and when Otto didn't leave, he bit down on a sigh.

'Would you like to come in and meet my family?'

'I should be delighted, Mr Milburn,' Otto beamed.

'Call me John. Come on in.'

In the event, John was glad Otto had been so persistent; the girls loved the enthusiastic scientist, and listened avidly while he explained about the area they'd moved to. It helped ease their first evening to play host to someone who'd been here right from the start, and John didn't object when Jen invited him to stay for a thrown-together dinner; looking at the kindly little man's gratitude it was hard to find any reason to. By the time Otto Fischer left, he and John were firm friends.

Two days later Doron arrived with his family, causing an equal stir in the settlement as another piece of everyone's puzzle slotted into place; the adult twins were the core of the community, the sun around which each set of child twins orbited, and now they were here, together. A buzz seemed to gather from the moment of the Farmer family's arrival.

But in the Milburn household there lived a different kind of pleasure, a more basic, but infinitely more fierce joy; John's heart swelled as he watched his elegant, poised, and, until this moment, unknown mother climb the steps to his home. Always aware of Doron's charisma and charm, he'd planned to open the door himself, to present the image of calm warmth and welcome, but the girls beat him to it, and with shrieks of excitement they pulled the laughing woman into the heart of their home.

'Girls,' Jen said quietly, and held out both her hands to draw them away. 'Let Daddy say hello.'

John and Rena looked at one another for a long moment, and although John felt he should have been the one to embrace his mother, when she opened her arms to him he went into them like a child. There was no awkwardness, no sudden shyness as there had been with Doron, this felt like the most natural thing in the world. He'd worried, privately, that he'd feel some sense of betrayal to Aunt May's memory, but he needn't have. He could almost see her face behind his tightly-closed eyelids, smiling and nodding. Rena held him close and stroked the back of his head, as if making up for all the years of boyhood they'd missed, and it instilled such a sense of comfort that when John moved away again he missed the contact immediately.

But the silent emotion of the moment was soon broken, and replaced by Holly and Hannah's energetic enthusiasm for anything new. Having already met their

Uncle Doron on the mountain, and after a polite greeting to Alex, all their attention was on their grandmother. In her turn Rena was delighted with their intelligence, and even enchanted by their occasional lapses into typical nine-year-old, questionable behaviour. She was also charmed by Jen, who amused John by watching her as if she were some visiting dignitary. All in all, the reunion could not have gone better, and cocooned in the warmth of his family John began to relax, and to believe that, just maybe, things would be alright after all.

On the day the last family arrived, John and Doron went around to each home, introducing themselves properly, and inviting everyone to a meeting that night, in the building on the edge of the compound. The first time they came up against the language barrier they looked at one another, almost laughing with the realisation that they hadn't considered the potential problem, but perplexed as to how to get around it. Then John spotted the children of the house lurking nervously indoors, and gestured them forward. He spoke to them in Hally, and the now smiling children relayed the message to their parents, who nodded their acceptance.

'Genius,' Doron murmured as they left, and John grinned, pleased to have found such a simple solution. They headed down to check out the meeting room.

'How many of us do you reckon there are?' John looked around the empty room, trying to calculate.

'Forty-six twins, plus their parents – those who still have both – plus siblings… I guess, maybe a hundred, hundred and twenty?'

'Will we fit?'

'Sure, we'll all be standing.'

'Ah, not necessarily,' John said. 'That truck that arrived as we were coming here, was from Clare Hampton. Todd told me she's sending furniture, teaching equipment, and medical supplies.'

'Awesome,' Doron smiled. 'She must be some lady.'

'We won't have enough chairs for all, even so,' John mused. 'But we can push a couple of tables together at the front here, and sit on them so we're set apart from the crowd tonight. It'll make it a bit more orderly at least.'

There was a general feeling of optimism as the new community began gathering at the meeting hall. John and Doron greeted everyone as they came through the doors, and they allowed a little time to let everyone mingle and begin getting to know one another, before John closed the door and an expectant hush fell across the crowd.

By unspoken consent, the two of them had become leaders, and so, as uncomfortable as that made him, John followed Doron's confident example. They took turns to speak, and to throw votes open for key positions within the community. Doron himself was unanimously selected as head of the medical facility; Jen offered to hold classes to teach those who didn't yet know how to speak and understand Hally; Farrah Naoir offered to take in mending and dressmaking, along with a friend of hers; Diego Garcia and his wife Ana, who'd run a chain of stores in their former life, agreed to take on the opening and stocking of a general store for household essentials. Those who had skills best suited to the outside world, seemed eager to turn their hands to something practical, and between them all they felt progress was being made already.

When Todd arrived, he and John would take on the bulk of the academic tutoring, but in the meantime John's own Hally skills meant he could start teaching right away; it was important to give the children some sense of normality, as new and frightening as their situation was.

Then talk turned to more sobering matters. The third of November loomed over them now, and as the noise of the crowd swelled, with emotions closer to the surface than ever, both John and Doron found it hard to make themselves heard.

'Let them go, for a bit,' Doron advised. 'We've had longer to come to terms with this than they have; it's the first time most of them have had the chance to talk about it.'

John nodded, but it gave him an uneasy feeling; the initial camaraderie was being overshadowed now, even within their own ranks, by tension and speculation... how would it be once the outside world got wind of what was going on? Eventually the noise died down again, and Doron once more took the lead; John noted how everyone stared at him, and it wasn't all with hope or interest – some of those looks were laced with a kind of defiant challenge.

'We think everyone concerned, so that means *all* the sets of twins, and myself and my brother, should be in bed by midnight at the latest.'

'The eclipse is due to happen at 12:38 in Mecca, which means 3:38 our time,' John added. 'You have to agree, as one, not to disturb the sleeping Nephilim. No matter what.'

'None of us knows what's going to happen,' Doron said, more quietly now into the hush that had fallen. 'We don't *know* if anything will, for sure, but we believe...' he glanced at John, who nodded, '... we believe something of great importance will happen that night.'

Immediately more talk broke out, ideas and shared experiences being thrown back and forth, and once again John and Doron let it run its course; the hour was growing late, but it was important to let everyone have their say. When they sensed the energy and impetus running down, Doron held up his hands and the room gradually fell silent once more.

'Before the final business of the day, some of you may wonder why, over the next few months, my brother and I will be making regular trips to our surgery, such as it is. We're donating our blood to be used in experiments in the hope that a universal immunity can be created. The geneticist in charge of these procedures is Otto Fischer. Otto please make yourself known.'

Otto held up a hand, looking very self-conscious, but beamed broadly when he received a round of applause, and nodded to everyone shyly.

'Otto, please wait for me and John at the end of the meeting, we need to discuss security measures for the surgery. We can walk home together while we do so.'

Otto nodded, and everyone's attention turned once again to the front of the room.

'OK, final business of the day. We need a name for this place.'

'New Town!'

But the verdict came swiftly back on that one: *boring!*

'Eagle Town.' The response: *we're already in Eagle County…*

'Twinsville!' someone near the back shouted, and the crowd chuckled.

'Hope.' This voice was quieter, and the laughter died down. John recognised Louise, Charles Whyte's erstwhile PA, as the one who'd spoken. People were nodding.

'I love it,' Doron said, 'but there are a lot of places here in the States called Hope. How about… Hope Ridge?'

'Hope Meadows?' This was from Jen, and John met her surprised eyes as the crowd clapped its approval, and he nodded.

And so Hope Meadows, Colorado, was born.

***

Friday 1st November. Washington DC. Press conference

A legal representative for Eagle read out a prepared statement to the assembled press, while the council members themselves watched from various offices, and those in Hope Meadows who didn't yet have TVs hooked up, gathered in neighbours' houses to watch. It was a strange-sounding tale, even to those who were living it; such ancient evidence, and the thought that there were special children born with life-saving immunities. There were so many questions being fired at the representative that many of them were lost before they were answered, and even those people most closely involved hissed in frustration.

The following day the story appeared in every major newspaper worldwide. It didn't matter that so many of the reports were dense with scathing dismissal, or cries of *cult*! It didn't matter that only a few seemed genuinely hopeful of some kind of a miracle... the story was broken, and the speculation had begun. And after all, even if the events at Mount Hira on Sunday turned out to be less than fantastic, the reports needn't reflect that.

***

Saturday 2nd November. Hope Meadows
'Why are they looking at us? Don't they like us?'

John followed his daughters' gazes to the perimeter fence, where a disturbingly large number of people from nearby towns were gathering. Not one of them ventured beyond the fence, it was as if the inhabitants of Hope Meadows were in some kind of zoo, and no-one knew what to expect from them.

'They're curious, that's all.'

'But why don't they talk to us? Ask us?'

'Maybe they've heard you talking Hally, and think that's all you can speak,' Jen ventured. 'Why don't the two of you go and find Alima and Ruhi. I want to talk to Daddy a minute.'

When the girls had gone, she turned worried eyes on John. 'Can we do something? Set up some kind of security detail? Just to be safe.'

'Eagle have promised a team later today,' John said, 'but looking at that lot, I think it couldn't hurt for us to take matters into our own hands. I'll see if I can arrange some kind of rota, to keep watch.'

'I don't like it.'

'Nor do I.' Earlier that day a helicopter had hovered overhead, and sent most of the children running for their homes. It had even spooked many of the adults; it had been so low that the downdraught had sent dust swirling, and the propellers had cut the air with heavy chopping sounds that drowned everything else out. Luckily it hadn't stayed long since there was nothing to see, but John doubted it would be the last.

'Have you seen the headlines in today's papers?' Jen went on.

He nodded. 'Some of the reports are accurate enough, but some of them—'

'Sinai Spawn? Alien Angels? Where the hell do they *get* this stuff? Don't they realise the harm they can do?'

'Makes my blood boil,' he said, remembering. 'But it's all about sensationalism. Making a buck. Headlines like that sell papers, always will do.'

'If that's what they're like now, what on earth are they going to report once they've witnessed whatever tonight's events turn out to be? I'm only surprised they haven't started talking about witchcraft!'

'Give them time!' John smiled, but Jen remained troubled.

'I'm worried, John.'

He took her in his arms. 'Everything will be fine.' It sounded like an empty platitude, but it didn't feel like one. The strength in their little community was growing by the day, and they were doing everything in their power to prepare. 'We have guards around the perimeter, and most of the locals will be asleep, and won't catch up with the news until the morning.'

'Some of those out there have sleeping bags,' Jen pointed out. But she wrapped her arms around him and held him tight. 'They won't see anything though, not here.'

'The girls are getting skittish,' John said. 'I don't blame them, but we don't want them unable to sleep. We should do something to take their minds off everything.'

'Something to tire them out physically would be good,' Jen agreed.

'I'm sure the other parents feel the same. Why don't we organise some kind of sports event this afternoon? Some of it can take place in the hall, but we can have running races out here.'

'I'll get the girls to pass the word around.' Jen had perked up almost immediately and, kissing John's cheek she left in search of the twins. He watched her go, feeling the return of that gut-tightening mixture of love and fear. Yes, as a community they were strong… but there was an awful lot of unrest out there in the world, and it was marching to their door.

By ten o'clock that night the girls, worn out by the afternoon's activities, were fast asleep in their parents' bed. John and Doron would both sleep in the girls' room, and Jen offered to spend the night on the settee.

'Not that I'll sleep,' she sighed.

'I'll stay too then,' Rena said, 'and keep you company.'

They bade John and Doron goodnight an hour later, and tried to settle to watch the television, but as the time of the eclipse drew closer they were both too nervous to concentrate, or even to talk. At 3:40, Jen looked in on her sleeping family, and sucked in a breath… she wasn't sure whether she'd thought, or hoped, that it would all turn out to be a flash of nothing, but sure enough all four lay flat, eyes wide, and white. It had started.

She pulled the door of her room closed as quietly as she could, fighting the urge to go in and wake her daughters; she would never get used to seeing them like that. And how vulnerable were they, spiritually if not physically? Who could ever know what kind of damage this was doing? She went back to the sitting room, and nodded briefly in answer to Rena's questioning look.

'Your girls, and my boys,' Rena said, and took Jen's hand. 'My dear girl, I understand that look in your eyes. I don't know if any of them truly realise how it feels to be on the outside, watching and helpless.'

***

Mount Hira, Mecca. News Report
'You join us here live at the foot of Mount Hira. It's twelve-thirty-six on the morning of the third of November. As you can see, the atmosphere is… special. It's very special. There are press helicopters here from non-Muslim publications and TV stations, of course they're not permitted to report from the ground, and the public is gathering in… simply *huge* numbers. There hasn't been anything like this as far back as I can remember. The

eclipse has begun, and even as I speak, this majestic mountain is falling under its shadow… it's almost time…

Twelve-thirty-eight. The cameras are trained on the summit, zoomed in, we hope to see… Look! Oh, my word, just *look*! Shapes. Figures… are they real? I'm counting…ten, twenty, forty, forty four… forty six. And two others, much larger. Are those the children then, and two adults?

Now I envy those in the helicopters, they must have such a clear view, but I can only report what I see, which is…they're going into the cave! All of them, yet that cave can only, possibly, hold one or two people, three at most. But there they have gone, and there they have disappeared. Now we must wait, viewers, and wonder.'

'Welcome back, it has been perhaps ten minutes, and as you can see from our pictures the smaller figures have emerged from the cave. It's hard to count them, as they are walking around… but we believe all forty-six are back. We have not yet seen the adult forms but keep watching! Wait! Look at this, the figures are gone now. All of them. Just… gone! Keep rolling, camera, we must wait for the adults.'

'And now, finally, there they are, they look either exhausted or sick, see how they stumble. They're walking very slowly, are they alright? Should someone go to them? Someone help – now they too have gone! Did you see that? They both fell to their knees, and just… disappeared.'

***

299

'We're in Hope Meadows,' Doron said, sounding confused.

'We can't be.' John peered around him, but Doron was right, at least to an extent: this place was Hope Meadows, but it was summer time, mid-day… and deserted. By unspoken agreement they began to walk down the dirt track that led through the centre of town, looking to left and right but seeing no-one, not even a movement behind windows.

'Hear that?'

John did. 'Laughing. Kids.'

'Come on.'

They walked faster, and as they neared the field at the end of the track, where only the previous afternoon his own children had run races until they were fit to drop, they saw them. All the twins of the town, plus some they'd never seen before. But still twins. John strained for sight of Holly and Hannah but there were simply too many to sift through. Those who saw them appeared unfazed by their appearance, and waved.

The adults looked at one another and raised their hands to wave back, bemused.

'Hello Doron, David.' The voice, coming from so close behind them, made them jump and turn. John's heart was thudding hard and he'd bet Doron's was, too. The stranger, a person of indeterminate gender, and of around their own age, smiled. He or she was dressed in a modern, casual style, and wore their dark hair short, yet gave off an air of someone as far from modern as it was possible to get.

'H…hello,' John stammered. 'Who are you?'

'We are the Fathers.'

'No, sorry,' John clarified, 'I meant who are *you*?'

'What you see before you has no name. As the children you see playing in the field, with your own, have no names. We did, once, when we were individual beings, but now we are one.' The Fathers shrugged. 'But if it is easier for you to think of us as separate entities for the purpose of our meeting, then please do.'

John stared, baffled, and tried again. '*What* are you?'

'We are what we are. The Fathers. It has a male meaning for you, but we are neither exclusively male or female. We are an equal amount of both.'

'I don't understand.' John looked at Doron, who shook his head, still confused.

The newcomer smiled again. 'This,' he indicated his own body, '…organism, carries genetic material, as does your own. Our fundamental existence is based on 23 pairs of constituents; those constituents are at present exchanging pleasure and information with your children. Like us, your existence is based on 23 pairs of constituents, you call them chromosomes and together they make you one—'

'Wait a moment,' Doron broke in. 'Put simply, are you telling us that *your* chromosomes, or your equivalent, are… those children?'

The creature inclined its head. 'Correct. Well put, Doron. What you see standing before you here, is a projection of us all. What you see *around* you, is a projection of where you want to be.' The Fathers turned

301

back down the path. 'Come, let's walk. We have things to discuss. You must be wondering why you are here.'

'Yes, we are,' Doron said.

'You are here to receive a message, and to protect the next generation of Fathers. Your children. The Fathers watch over our world, we have always done so.'

'*Your* world?' Doron queried.

'Our world,' The Fathers repeated, and gestured gracefully to the three of them.'

'Are you our creators?' John wanted to know. He couldn't have said why, but the notion gave him a surprisingly settled feeling.

'In a manner of speaking, David, yes. You will understand that very soon. There are few occasions where we can speak with our children, and although time passes slower here, we do not have a lot of time to be with you. This is the only time we will be able to meet within your lifetime and it is very precious to us.'

Doron frowned. 'Are you… a god, then?'

'No. When we spoke with your ancestors, their understanding of the experience was that they *had* met a god. These were a simple people though, who misunderstood our meaning. You must remember that, in their time, there were many deities created to explain things they could not understand.' The Fathers sighed. 'Our words were misinterpreted by their descendants and manipulated by those who wanted power and control.'

'And there are enough of those,' John said quietly.

'Indeed.' The Fathers nodded. 'We were most surprised at the amount of religions that have been created under that delusion; all of them claiming divine favour. We had hoped that, as you advanced as a species, you would come to see the objectivity regarding conflicting claims of religious superiority, but it was not to be. We did not want to be… *worshipped,* we merely wanted to be loved, as we love you. And for our laws to be obeyed.'

'Laws?' John asked. 'Do you mean the Commandments?'

'You have chosen to call them that,' The Fathers said. 'But they were just a guide, given for you all to live peacefully. To rise above your baser instincts. We have no control over your actions, nor can we command. We can only guide. We did not force our laws on you, nor did we threaten those who disobeyed. That is your interpretation.' The Fathers looked away, up at the mountains and then down over the glorious spread of land beneath their peak. 'We are saddened greatly by the wars we have witnessed. Begun in the name of a god who appears to wish His children dead. What loving parent would want that? Why create something, only to watch it destroy itself?'

'So you're not vengeful then?' Doron asked.

'Vengeful?' The Fathers gave him a sad little smile. 'No, it's not possible for us to be vengeful, nor for us to harm any living creature. We do have emotions, however, and we are most disappointed that our children have become so greedy, wasteful and cruel. They take what they don't need, destroy what isn't theirs, and condemn everything that is different. So much pain and suffering. We feel it all.'

John and Doron exchanged looks of deep remorse; it was all true. Every word.

But the Fathers stopped in the road, and reached out to them both. 'Do not feel shame for what you yourselves have not done, my sons. *You* are good men, and there are many more good men and women in our world. There is such beauty and kindness, love and happiness.'

Its hands dropped away, and the three of them resumed walking. 'It is only spoiled by the evil that comes from others. They blame their gods and their demons for their acts, when in truth they are created only as an excuse. They quote scriptures as the guide for their atrocities, yet within those same scriptures are acts that blatantly disobey their own commandments.'

There was a subdued silence, then John said, 'You said you had a message for us?'

'We do,' The Fathers said. 'But first we need to show you something. As adults and pure-born you will now be able to see a glimpse of your past, and a warning for your future.'

Turning to face the field, the Fathers made a small, barely noticeable gesture to the children. 'The new ones will return now. They are too young, and not strong enough to witness this. But they will learn in time, and under your guidance.'

The unknown children peeled away from the familiar, and began walking towards them. As they approached they seemed to age a little more with each step, and each of them melted into the form of the Fathers until once more it became a solitary figure. Now John could clearly see Holly and Hannah in those who were left, and they waved. He waved back, feeling a pang as they faded and disappeared before his eyes.

The Fathers beckoned the two brothers closer, and placed strong arms around their shoulders. 'Watch.'

John felt his head growing light, and he staggered a little, but the arms held him firm. Doron on one side, the Fathers on the other… he was safe, but oh, what he saw…

The Fathers' smooth, calm voice explained the visions. 'First this, a species of ape living in Africa.' John's vision doubled, and to his fascination he was able to see inside the bodies of the apes. 'Do you see?' The Fathers murmured. 'These apes had two more chromosomes than mankind, but, by fusing them together, they *evolved into* man.'

The Fathers created a new species, in their own image. 'Now listen.'

Early man started to communicate amongst themselves, but it wasn't with the grunts and guttural sounds modern man had been led to believe, it was a fully formed language. The Fathers' own language, that had become known as Hally. But as man grew curious, and learned to adapt to new environments, he spread out to explore the rest of his world and developed different languages. Soon Hally was forgotten.

What followed would haunt John for the rest of his life, so much pain and suffering, only made bearable by the glimpses of love, joy and selflessness that struggled to balance it. The caring for all living things.

'Mankind has taken so much from this world,' The Fathers said. 'From our world. There have been times throughout your history when nature has grown tired of weeping, and fought back. Restored that balance. She will do so again.'

John's eyes were still squeezed tightly shut, but the final vision was so shocking that they flew open… still he saw it. He saw Doron's face reflecting the same horror, and it was a long, terrifying moment before the vision faded, and the Fathers released the brothers to stagger back, clutching at one another in despair.

'Can't you stop this?' Doron gasped, white-faced.

'We cannot interfere, not in the way you would like.'

'Why not?' John turned on the being, knowing his anger was unjustified, but unable to contain it. 'You interfered in our evolution!'

'That was for mutual preservation, and no harm was done.' The Fathers spoke firmly, though its face showed understanding and regret.

'What about those apes?'

'We needed to survive, and that particular species was doomed to imminent extinction. David, listen, we knew this would happen one day, which is why we tried to give you all a safeguard against it—'

'The gene thing.'

The Fathers nodded. 'Unfortunately the adapted chromosome did not pass on to you all. We tried to give immunity to as many as we could, but it was difficult to compete with your own genetics, and we only had a small window of time.' The eyes found John's, and then Doron's, and the voice was gentle. 'We have done what we can, now it is up to you.'

Jen hadn't realised she'd nodded off until the sitting room door opened and she jerked awake again. Holly and Hannah came in, and Jen stumbled over to them, pulling them into her arms.

'Are you alright?'

Holly nodded. 'A bit tired, but we're fine.'

'What happened?'

'It's a bit difficult to explain, but it was lovely.'

'Is your dad okay?'

They both nodded, and Jen slumped with relief. 'Thank God.'

'We met other twins too,' Hannah put in. 'The same number as there are here, but they were a bit different, and they had to stay behind.'

'We played games,' Holly said, 'and talked about ourselves.'

'Yeah, and guess what?' Hannah added, plonking herself on the settee, 'They lived down here! Thousands of years ago!'

'They lived in Egypt,' Holly said, and perched on the arm of Rena's chair. 'You know, with the Pharaohs. They had to walk for months to go to a new home, it was very hard for them.'

Hannah took up the tale again. 'They knew Moses, Mum, and he had a twin brother! Our teacher never told us that, did she, Hol?'

'Nope.' Holly's tone said, *silly teachers*.

Jen smiled, and kept her voice deliberately light. 'That'... well, amazing. Where did you meet the other twins?'

'We went through the cave on the mountain,' Holly said, 'and ended up back here.'

'Here? What actually *here*, Hope Meadows?'

Hannah pondered. 'We thought it was a weird shortcut. But actually I don't think it was the real here.'

'Did they say what this is all about, those other twins?'

'Well.' Holly's voice turned very matter-of-fact. 'It's sort of like I'm two people, but I'm not really. I'm like this when I'm here, but the other part of me is… something else.'

'And me!' Hannah put in.

'It's the same for all of us,' Holly explained.

'When we're old, and we die… don't look sad, Mum! The other part of us will go and join the twins we met tonight.'

'What, like going to Heaven?'

'No, it's not Heaven,' Hannah said thoughtfully. 'It's just a different place to here.'

'They're called the Fathers,' Holly added.

'Oh I nearly forgot that bit. There are forty-six of them just like us, but they're actually just one person and they call themselves the Fathers. It's a bit confusing, but that's it really.'

Jen blinked and looked over at Rena. The account was garbled, but at least they were able to give it, and didn't seem to have suffered any ill effects from their sleep-fuelled adventures. They had probably told her everything they could, in the best way they could, and could more than likely do without the third degree.

Rena cleared her throat, looking equally confused, but she kept her voice light. 'So, you had a good time then?'

'Brilliant!' they said in unison, and Rena smiled.

'The only sad bit was saying goodbye,' Holly said.

Hannah nodded. 'We won't see them again until we die, and that's a long way off.'

'Glad to hear it,' Rena said, winking at Jen. 'Well we're all very tired, so give us a kiss and then back off to bed with you both. I think you've had enough excitement for one night, don't you?'

'You said Daddy was okay?' Jen prompted.

'He and Uncle Ron are still there,' Holly told her, 'with the Fathers. We had to come home, but they stayed behind to talk grown-up stuff.'

Hannah levered herself reluctantly off the settee. 'We thought you'd be worried, we were there ages!'

Jen looked at the clock, not sure how long she'd actually slept for. 'No, you've only been gone a little while.'

Holly and Hannah looked at one another, as if they thought she was joking, but put up no argument and went back to bed. Jen settled them down, and on her way back to Rena she opened the door to the girls' bedroom where John and his brother were sleeping. She was braced for the usual sense of unease, but to her horror both men's bodies were rigid and wracked with tremors. Their eyes stared blindly upwards, and Jen put a hand to her mouth to stifle a cry of dismay. Rena appeared at her shoulder, and Jen stepped back to let her see. Her face was pale, but she drew Jen back into the sitting room and closed the door.

'What's happening?' Jen pleaded. 'That can't be right! What do we do?'

'Nothing.' Rena sounded calm and authoritative, but her eyes were worried. 'We have strict instructions not to disturb them, remember? Whatever happens.'

'What if they're in danger, or they need help?'

'Whatever happens,' Rena repeated gently. 'From what the girls said though, the Fathers are not there to harm them, and if we interfere, it's possible we could harm them ourselves.'

'You're right, I know you're right.' Jen's hands twisted together as she fought the urge to return to the bedroom.

'I'll make tea,' Rena said. 'Sit down a minute.'

Jen lowered herself to the settee, but jumped back up as the sound of raised voices and rattling fences came from outside. She pulled aside the curtain, and Rena joined her, but it was hard to see, with the reflected light from the sitting room, so she opened the front door instead.

Crowds were pressed up against the gate and the wire fence, shaking them and shouting, drowning out the Eagle and Hope Meadows security details, who were ordering them to back off.

'Go back home!'

'Go back to where you came from!'

'Blasphemy on the Sabbath!'

'You're not wanted here!'

Jen turned to Rena, her mouth open in dismay, but at that moment there was a crash as the gate gave way beneath the surging crowd, and the impetus spilled people to the ground. Those who came behind didn't seem to care who they trampled on, and there were screams now

310

mingled with the roars of outrage and the bellows of the security men.

It was the Milburn home they were heading for, and Jen pushed Rena back and turned to follow her indoors, but they were both knocked aside by Holly and Hannah, who strode with a purpose far beyond their years, out into the cold November night.

'Get back in!' Jen cried, her heart crashing against her ribs. 'Girls!' She ran down the steps, her socks sliding in the wet grass, but the twins kept going. And then she saw others, the town's children all walking towards this house with determined strides, ignoring the shouts of their own parents.

In moments they had formed a ring around the Milburn plot, and stood watching the suddenly hesitant crowd as it came closer. Albeit more slowly now.

'Girls?' Jen breathed, and Holly turned and flashed her a tight smile. 'It's okay, Mum. You and Grandma go back to the porch.'

'Come on, Jen,' Rena urged. 'I think they have it.' She caught Jen's shoulders and pulled her back, and Jen went, stumbling backwards but ready to run forward again at the first hint her children needed her.

The crowd stopped a short way from the ring of twins. 'Where's your leader?' The voice had an edge of bravado, but Jen sensed that's all it was. There was less anger here now, than fear, but that was more worrying than ever. You could reason with anger, but fear could make people do deadly things.

'I don't know who you mean,' Holly shouted back. 'We haven't got a leader.'

311

'Who's in that house, then?'

'My dad. He's sleeping.'

'Get him.'

'No-one's supposed to wake him, please… go away!'

'What's he doing in his sleep then, talking to the Mother Ship?'

'What do you—'

'OW!' Hannah clutched at her shoulder, and Jen saw another rock come flying out of the crowd, this time thudding harmlessly to the ground. She was about to go to Hannah, when the girl gulped into silence, and all the children, moving as one, turned to face the crowd. In the light from the nearby houses it was possible to see every twins' eyes turning pure white, and as the stunned crowd looked on in horror, a wraith appeared in front of each child, matching the twins' stares with fixed, expressionless gazes of their own.

The crowd fidgeted, and as the twins and their ghostly companions kept very still, watching them, they fell to muttering among themselves, and Jen saw the stragglers at the back drifting away first. Soon others followed suit, and when those at the front, who'd been most vocal, most determined, realised they were now alone, they too turned and hurried away.

As soon as the last intruder had gone, the spirits faded, and the children's eyes returned to normal, blinking and a little disorientated. Their parents took them gently back to their own homes, throwing curious looks at the Milburns and Rena as they went; clearly dying to find out what had happened but wisely saving their questions for another time.

'What the hell just happened?' Jen said to Rena, in a low voice.

'I don't know, but as Doron would say, it was pretty awesome.'

Holly and Hannah came up the steps, and Jen kissed Hannah's head. 'Are you alright, love?'

Hannah nodded. 'We're sorry, but we had to stop them from waking Dad and Uncle Ron.'

'I thought you could only do that on the mountain,' Jen said, rubbing the sore spot on her daughter's shoulder.

'So did we,' Hannah said, glancing at Holly. 'But I suppose we're stronger now we're all together.' She smiled suddenly. 'But we scared them, didn't we?'

Jen couldn't help smiling back. 'You certainly did! But listen, don't try that again. What would you have done if they'd attacked you? What would we all have done? And by the way,' she frowned, 'what *did* you do?'

'We just put a thought in their heads,' Holly said, with no small amount of pride. 'We suggested it would be nicer to be at home, and off they went.' She shrugged. 'We're not allowed to hurt anyone, so I suppose we just do the convincing and staring thing.'

'Convincing and staring thing,' Jen muttered, a sense of unreality wrapping itself around her. 'Okay, well I can't argue with that. Come inside and we'll look at your shoulder, Hannah.'

'I'll see to it,' Rena offered when they went indoors. 'You check on the boys.'

With a sweating hand, Jen pushed open the bedroom door, dreading what she might see. But even as the light fell across the beds she saw John's eyes flutter, and

Doron's did the same. They both blinked, and it looked as if their eyes had been watering from staying open so long… or had they been crying? As she had with the girls, a lifetime ago, she knelt between the two beds and took one of their hands in each of hers.

'Are you okay?' she asked softly.

John managed to speak first, and his voice was hoarse and weak. 'Yeah, we are. The girls?'

'They're fine.' There'd be time enough later to tell them what had happened.

Doron struggled to a sitting position. 'We know why we're here now, Jen. And part of it's not good.'

Jen's insides twisted. *You mean this isn't over?* 'Not good how?'

'There's a virus coming.'

John sat up too, and the hand he laid on Jen's cheek was trembling. 'And it's going to wipe out everyone who doesn't have this immunity gene.'

Chapter Seventeen
Betrayal

Jen heard the sound on the television creep up, as she headed for the living room, and the usual, overly-hearty voiceover blared.

'Good evening, and welcome to Denver Newsnight. You will be familiar with these gentlemen by now, please welcome our guests *live* tonight, with your host, Bryan King... John Milburn and Doron Malik, better known as... The Malik Twins!'

'Mummy! Grandma! Grandad!' Holly beckoned them all into the room excitedly. 'Daddy and Uncle Ron are coming on!'

'Hurry or you'll miss it!' Hannah added, already turning back to the TV.

On the screen John and Doron walked onto the set, smiling at the studio audience. They shook hands with the show's host and sat down, loosening jacket buttons and appearing perfectly at ease, but Jen knew that John, at least, would be churning inside; a lot rode on this. Perhaps everything.

'Welcome, gentlemen,' Bryan King purred. 'Good to have you on the show.'

'Good evening to you, Mr King.'

Rena leaned over and whispered to Jen, 'My, don't they look handsome?'

'Yes,' Jen smiled, seeing her own pride reflected in the older woman's face. 'They do, don't they?' She turned her attention back to the screen, her nerves returning, and only vaguely aware she was crossing her fingers.

In the studio Bryan King had begun, without further pleasantries, and John focused his attention on the man's manner as well as his words; the tone was friendly enough, but there was iron behind those eyes, and John readied himself for a rough ride.

'There has been a lot of controversy, over recent events that you have both been involved with.' King eyed them both in turn, a little like a stern headteacher. 'I understand your story has only come to light following the incarceration of your friend's father, Richard Hampton.'

'Yes, that's right.' John nodded. 'Through the organisation he belonged to, he murdered my adopted father and his friends…' he cleared his throat, seized by a sudden, strong emotion. '… to keep important historical finds from being made public. He also orchestrated the murder of twin babies in Israel, to try to make sure we didn't survive.'

Although this was well known by now, a rising murmur from the studio audience had the floor manager making frantically hushing gestures. John exchanged a quick glance with Doron; the emotive subject had quickly found them some supporters.

King had also noted this, and his voice took on a harder, more cynical edge. 'And all because of the so-called *prophecies*, surrounding your birth, and indeed the births of the other twins.' He checked his notes. 'You have declared yourselves as Nephilim.'

Doron visibly bristled. 'These *so-called prophecies*, as you put it, have been date-tested for authenticity, and all other evidence has proven to be genuine. The information gathered has amazed historians, and has helped to answer previously unanswered questions about Biblical events.'

'But Nephilim?' King raised an eyebrow. 'Really?'

'Why is that so hard to believe?' John managed to inject a note of mild amusement into his voice. 'You believe in your scriptures, don't you?'

'Of course!' King fired back, as John had expected. 'I'm a God-fearing man, Mr Milburn.'

'Then why do you believe what was written thousands of years ago, and not what's in front of you right now?' John shrugged. 'Maybe in another thousand years, our experiences will be believed too.'

King shifted in his seat, and John saw him shoot a glance over at the producer, who made a subtle gesture of encouragement with her hand. 'Anyone can claim contact with God,' he said, directing the question to both guests, 'but how do you prove it?'

Doron smiled, a little tightly. 'But I thought that was the very foundation of faith? To believe in something, or someone, without absolute proof of its existence? But then, we're not claiming contact with God.'

'Ah, that's right.' King shuffled his notes again, and John almost felt sorry for him, but that soon passed. 'And that's the reason you have the whole world up in arms, isn't it? We have all seen the footage of your... *spiritual* trip into Mount Hira, and have heard your version of our

317

creation by these Fathers.' He shot a conspiratorial grin out towards the audience and camera crew. 'I think you all may have been on a different kind of trip!'

John's skin tightened, but he kept his voice level. 'Mr King, are you saying that *all* the reporters, newscasters and spectators that witnessed that event were on drugs? I think that's tantamount to slander.'

Doron nodded. 'We've reported what we experienced, but we're not forcing anyone to believe us. We feel we have a duty to inform you because it's the truth; we were given prophecies, which,' he pointed out, 'have all come true so far. We have also been given the commandments as they should have been recorded originally, and a warning for us all.'

'Yes, I read them before you arrived,' King said. 'They're very similar to those quoted in Exodus, although I was surprised to find your gods want us all to become vegan.'

'Not vegan, sir,' John said politely. 'Vegetarian. We are to treat all living creatures with respect; animals and humans alike. No more suffering and no more killing. Surely that's something worth aiming for, whatever your beliefs?'

'And the Fathers are not gods,' Doron added. 'They live in our world, as we do. Just in a different way.'

King glanced at his producer again, who glared back, her expression hard. He was visibly perspiring now. 'So… what's this warning that you have for the world? *Armageddon*?' A low chuckle from the camera crew seemed to help restore his confidence, and he fixed the twins with a faintly belligerent, challenging stare. But if he was hoping for either of them to back down he was doomed to disappointment.

'It certainly will be of apocalyptic proportions,' Doron said, his face grim. 'We've been warned that a super virus is coming, but, unlike your Armageddon, it will not separate believers from non-believers. Instead it will separate those with immunity from those without it.'

A brief silence was broken by another rustle of notes. Then King gave a rather theatrical sigh. 'It does seem to me that all this drama is a form of… attention-seeking.'

John's lips tightened. 'To what end? We've been ridiculed - just as we are being ridiculed now,' he added, 'we've been ostracised, and persecuted, and our children have been bullied. Who would actively seek that kind of attention?'

'Don't you feel to blame then, for your children's distress?' King produced the question with an air of triumph, and John looked over to see the producer nodding emphatically.

'We mean no offence to anyone,' Doron said. 'We have just told the facts as they are. The facts as recorded by Amnon and other scribes.'

On a roll now, the show host sat back and folded his arms. 'Facts, gentlemen? All the facts we need are in the Good Book! Why should we believe the writings of some scribes from over 1,000 years ago?'

Own goal! John almost laughed aloud, and Doron gave King a sharklike grin. 'We rest our case, sir.'

'Cut!'

***

319

'You got him, boys!' Alex pumped his fist in the air, making Jen laugh. 'I told you you would,' he went on, talking to the men on the screen as if they could hear him. 'Keep it calm, polite, wait for the idiot to walk right into it. That's what I told them, didn't I, Rena?'

'You sure did, sweetheart.' Rena hugged his arm. 'I also think your advice in insisting on a live interview was good.'

'Better than giving them a chance to cut anything they didn't like. The boys got their point across for the world to see, and made everyone see what an idiot Bryan King is.'

'But the whole point of that interview was to warn everyone about the virus, and King didn't even pick up on it.'

'We'll try again,' Alex said. 'Ron mentioned it, that's a start. People will want to find out more, it's only natural.'

'They're superstars!' Holly whooped.

'Yeah!' Hannah agreed. 'What was that bit about a virus, mum?'

Jen's relief faded a little. 'You know a virus is what gives you the flu, or measles, don't you? Well, the Fathers know that a bad virus is going to come, and a lot of people are going to get sick.'

'Will they die?' Hannah asked in a small voice.

Jen took a deep breath, and decided it was too late for anything except truth now. 'Yes,' she said, 'I'm afraid they will.' Seeing her girls' faces grow pale, she hurried on, 'But our friend Otto is busy trying to make something that will stop the virus, and save people.'

'But how?'

'It's in our blood Hannah, Holly interjected. 'Isn't it, Mum? It's that Whoopy One thing that stops us getting sick. That's why Daddy and Uncle Ron keep giving blood to him for his work, isn't it?'

Jen blinked. 'Whoopy One?'

'I think she means UEP1, Jen,' Rena said, smiling.

'Oh!' Jen felt yet another rush of pride, this time for her fiercely intelligent daughters. 'Yes, Holly, you're absolutely right.'

'So why can't we all give our blood to save everyone?' Hannah wanted to know.

'It's not that easy, girls,' Jen said. 'The blood is being used for tests, to try and make something that works the same way that your blood does. We can't just use what *you* have, there's not enough to go around the whole world. And if we take too much, you'll all look like prunes!'

Hannah's lips turned down in a pout. 'But if we helped everyone get better, maybe they'd like us more.'

'Oh, sweetheart.' Jen pulled her close. 'I know it's not easy, but it's not that people don't like you. Who couldn't like *you two*? They're just... scared, because you're different. They just don't understand how wonderful you are.'

Hannah pulled back. 'But they don't even try. Alima and Ruhi went into Eagle town with Farrah the other day, and no one would sell them anything. I don't understand! We haven't done anything bad to them.'

'And someone spat right in Farrah's face,' Holly added. 'That's disgusting.'

321

'I didn't know that,' Jen said. 'I'm sorry to hear it. Look, it might be better if we stay in Hope Meadows for a while, we can order in supplies. I'll go and see Farrah tomorrow.'

The twins went off to ready themselves for bed, and Alex smiled after them. 'They're very bright girls, Jen.'

'I know.' She shook off the brief melancholy and turned to practicalities. 'Speaking of which, we need to organise separate classes for the children. The curriculum we have for the twins' age group isn't advanced enough for all of them. The current curriculum is working fine for the other children but I'm guessing the twins are GCSE level, and possibly ready to surpass even that.'

Alex nodded. 'We'll organise that at the next meeting, I'm keeping notes for the next agenda. By the way, Otto has been moved to the Horizons Clinical Research Centre in Denver, he's being joined by other geneticists to work on the synthetic gene experiments.'

'I'll bet he loves that.'

'He's over the moon, but it's too far for him to travel each day, so he only comes home on Saturday afternoons.'

'Then we'll arrange the meeting for this Saturday.'

By the following day the papers were full of the mysterious virus. Bryan King's show was rumoured to have been relegated to the small hours, and King himself was said to have been lucky to keep his job, after his network head had learned he hadn't pressed for more information about the approaching danger, once it had been mentioned. Some newspapers came right out with

322

public speculation that someone, somewhere, knew its origins, and that the twins had simply heard about it.

Who is behind this threat? They demanded. *Which government is to blame for these experiments? Who is their target?*

Eagle's council had been in touch with John and Doron, urging them to maintain their silence on the matter, but they had both been in firm agreement; their own beliefs didn't factor at all, the people had the right to know. How could they live with themselves in the knowledge they hadn't done the right thing? And with Otto working hard every spare moment a vaccine must surely be forthcoming soon, and they would ensure as many people received it as possible.

The town meeting began well; John and Doron received a standing ovation for the way they'd handled the TV interview, and the mood was generally positive. Alex, self-appointed secretary, sat with the brothers and kept notes, scribbling furiously to keep up with the free flow of ideas and suggestions.

The first item was the school curriculum; a new timetable of classes needed to be organised, once they had the most appropriate work in place for the twins. The production of food was next; an area of land had been set aside for planting vegetables, and many of the parents had worked together to get seeds in, for those that could be winter-planted. They had worked out a rota for the next batch, to be planted in spring. Chickens and cows were on their way, along with more fencing. A coop was being constructed ready for the chickens, and was almost finished.

They were about ready to wrap.

'Any other business?' John asked, gathering his notes together ready, his mind on his warm home and a good supper.

'What about Christmas?' someone called out. John and Doron exchanged a surprised glance, and Doron nodded.

'There's actually a lot to discuss,' he conceded, 'now so much question has been raised over what we thought we knew, or believed at least.'

'Right, question open to the floor,' John said. 'Raise your hands, please! I know we've all got our own different ideas, so let's keep it orderly.'

Despite his appeal for order, people soon began speaking over each other, and voices had to raise to be heard, becoming shouts.

'Wait, everyone! Wait!' Doron's own voice became a roar, and gradually the noise from the floor died down. 'Right. We're agreed on the date, at least, yes? Winter Solstice, December 21st?' Murmurs indicated that much. 'Good. I propose this, then. That on that date we honour the Fathers and *all* prophets, for their contributions to mankind as it stands today. They might have been Nephilim themselves after all. And it incorporates Yule, which begins on that date. Now, a name for this new festival?'

There was a brief silence while everyone's creative minds got to work, but before anyone else spoke, Farrah called out, 'Bada Din?'

'Bada Bing? What's this, the Sopranos?' There was a ripple of good-natured laughter, and even Farrah smiled.

'Bada *Din*! It means big day, in Hindi,' she clarified, and an appreciative clap started somewhere near the back, and was quickly picked up.

Date and name sorted, it felt as if something momentous had been achieved in here tonight, and John felt a further lift in the spirits of the new townspeople. He could see Doron felt the same, as he stood up, smiling.

'Right, that's all the discussion done. Just to reassure you we do have more cabins on order, twenty in total. So those of you who are waiting for family, and that includes us, our wait shouldn't be much longer.' Uri and Maya, and their families, and also Jen's parents, would be arriving soon. Todd, Sinead and Clare wouldn't be far behind.

'Hold on,' Brad Turnbull called out. The engineer stood up, wiping his hands on his jeans and looking nervous at speaking publicly, but his voice gained confidence as he began. 'Twenty more cabins, yes? We've got off-grid power, sure, and our own well, but how far will those resources stretch?'

'Good point,' put in Diego Garcia, who ran the store with his wife. 'I can see how many people we have here better than most of you, so how many people can we sustain with the little we have?'

'We're looking into this,' Doron promised. 'We've got—'

'It's gone!' The crashing open of the door almost drowned out the shout.

'Ravi?' Farrah hurried over to her husband, who stood in the doorway breathing hard. 'What's happened?'

'It's all gone. The money in the pot!' He took a deep breath and began again. 'I rang the company that manufactures our cabins, to find out when the next lot were coming, and they told me they'd received no new order.'

People began talking over one another again, and Ravi raised his voice to a shout. 'Nothing is being produced for us! I then went to the bank to withdraw our living allowances, and… there's *nothing there*!'

Chairs scraped as worried townspeople rose to their feet, directing their angry questions at each other as much as at Ravi, and it was a minute or two before Doron was able to quiet them. He finally gave a piercing whistle between his fingers, and John winced, but it did the trick.

'I would have said the new homes issue would be a paperwork error,' Doron said, when everyone had settled back into their seats. 'But the living pot being empty does throw a different light on things.'

John didn't like the way the people were looking at them, it reminded him of the way Bryan King had only been waiting for his chance to put the boot in. 'You could call the council,' he suggested. 'They should be able to explain it.'

Doron nodded, and picked up his phone, but presently his expression told everyone there was no reply. 'I'll try again later. Meantime I'll call our Uncle Uri, and we'll get it sorted.'

'What if it's not?' Turnbull demanded.

'If there are no new houses, where do we put everyone?'

The questions were coming thick and fast again, but they were all variants on the same theme and John held up a hand. 'I'm sure we'll find it's a clerical or computing error. But listen, worst case scenario, we'll all open our homes – they're family after all, even if not all our own. Besides, we have materials to start building, and we definitely have the expertise.'

'We were better off where we were,' came a voice from the middle, and it was followed by the slap of a hand on flesh, and a low growl from the man's wife. A few laughs eased the tension, and Doron spoke again, his voice calm and quiet.

'We all miss our homes,' he said, 'and our families and friends. And… well, it is hard work at the moment. For all of us. But we'll survive here, and we'll be safe.'

'Actually,' John peered around the room. 'Isn't Otto supposed to be here tonight, to update us on his work?'

Everyone looked around, as if they half expected the scientist to be sitting next to them, but soon turned back to face the front, expectantly. John frowned, but gathered up his notes again. 'Well, if there's no further business, that's it until next week. Thank you, everyone.'

People began filing out, but as John turned to Doron to broach the subject of building, he noted a commotion by the door, and several people fell back to allow a flustered-looking and breathless Otto to push through. When he came up to the front John could see he was sweating profusely.

'Sit down,' he said, his own heart beating uncomfortably fast; it was unusual, not to mention worrying, to see the German scientist so agitated. 'Just take a breath, then speak.'

'It's started,' Otto managed, his voice hardly more than a croak. He sank into the seat to which John had guided him. 'It began a week ago in Ghana, but everyone thought it was just the flu.'

'Christ…'

'It's already in Niger, and spreading fast. My team heard about it from their foreign colleagues, it hasn't hit the international news yet.'

The hall was now filled again, with people straining to hear what the scientist was saying.

'Tell us all, in simple terms,' Doron said. 'Speak up, if you can.'

'The outbreak is a variant strain of Ebola.'

The murmurs grew; many had heard of it, but few knew what it meant.

'It's a viral haemorrhagic fever,' Otto explained. 'It's normally passed via bodily fluids, which would make quarantines easier to handle, but this is moving too fast.' He shook his head, his expression hopeless. 'This virus is copying itself, and each time it mutates it changes.'

'And now?'

'They think it's mutated into an airborne infection, mimicking pneumonic plague.'

'The *plague*?' Farrah cried out, in horror, and other voices joined her.

'That same one that wiped out fifty million people?'

'But that was centuries ago!'

'We think it's been around a lot longer than that,' Otto said. 'And believe me, I wish it was the plague, we can give antibiotics for that, nowadays. But for Ebola there's no known vaccine or cure… and it's a dreadful way to die.'

'But if it's known, how isn't it contained?' John wanted to know. He felt sick, and it was all he could do to remain in the hall and not run back to his family and whisk them away somewhere. But nowhere would be safe.

'No-one thought the virus would ever mutate this way,' Otto explained dully. 'It was more efficient for it to travel through fluids, rather than the air. No other virus that we know of has ever changed its mode of transport among humans. This is a clever one.'

'What can we do?' Doron wanted to know. 'Is there any chance of your universal vaccine being produced in time to halt it?'

'Unfortunately no. All attempts to duplicate the immunity you twins have, has been unsuccessful. We were doing so well, and had high hopes, and given time we might have done it. The only success we've had, has been with the single UEP1, but ….' His voice trailed off, and John and Doron looked at one another, their faces grim.

'But what?' Doron prompted.

'Everything we've been working on, our formulae, our notes, samples… they've all gone.'

A brief, stunned silence was broken by cries of disbelief that quickly rose to a roar, and this time it took much longer for John and Doron to subdue it.

'Let him speak!' Doron yelled at last, and although there was still a lot of whispering, it was quiet enough for Otto to continue.

'Everything was in place yesterday,' he said, 'but when we went to add more to the stock, both the fridge and the freezer were empty. Access was by code only, and the only ones who had it were myself and my team. I'm certain it was none of my team.'

'So,' Doron said, 'the blood *and* our allowances have been stolen.'

'What?' Otto half-rose in surprise, but John pushed him gently back down.

'I hate to say it,' Doron went on, 'but it seems increasingly likely that someone on the council has betrayed us. I don't know how they got the access codes to the lab but they're the only ones with complete access to the bank account.'

'But they've always helped us,' John protested, though he had to admit Doron's point made sense. He shook his head. 'We don't have time to go looking for those responsible,' he said. 'For now we have to concentrate on what we can do here. Otto, what are our options?'

'Well the synthetic gene option is out, and, given the rate the virus has spread, I don't think we have time to develop an active immunisation.'

'What's that?'

'It's when a vaccine is made in bulk from a pathogen, or from a person who has recovered from the illness caused by said pathogen. That's not going to happen, I'm afraid, it would take too long to develop and we don't know what we're up against. There's only one option left.'

'Which is?' John was growing impatient now.

'Passive immunisation.' In answer to the buzzing questions, he went on, 'Antibodies are passed through the blood plasma of a person known to be immune, and are given to another person to provide immunity. The advantage is that it's very quick to work, but the downside is that it has to be administered intravenously. It's time consuming, and we might need a few boosters to keep the immunity going. There's no time to test the whole world population to see who carries the single UEP1, or to harvest and categorise enough blood.'

'What are we going to do?'

'What about our families?'

'Okay,' Doron said. 'Listen up, everyone! We can't save the world, but we can help. First, I want you all to go away and contact your families. If we get them here now, we can save them. If the virus is going to spread as fast as Otto says, then all modes of transport will soon be stopped; there'll be no planes, no trains and there *will* be roadblocks. We'll worry about where to put everyone later, just get them here.'

'Alex,' John said, 'make two lists: One of the Nephilim and their parents, they'll all have UEP1. The other with everyone else, including those who haven't got here yet, they'll need to be tested for immunity. Everyone with UEP1 is to donate blood to Otto, including the children.'

'I have blood storage facilities in my car,' Otto added. 'It can be taken to the lab and the plasma prepared for administration. Alex, put an extra column on each list to record everyone's blood group.'

Doron picked up his jacket. 'John, Otto and I will head off to Denver now, and get ourselves back on live TV.'

'What for?' Otto asked, puzzled. 'Surely I can be of more help here?'

'We know that UEP1 would most likely be found in the descendants of Levi, most of which would be within the Jewish and Muslim communities, we'll appeal for their help.'

Otto's expression cleared. 'Of course. And I can issue instructions to other countries, on how to test for it and use it.'

Doron appealed to the room at large. 'Anyone who wants to help but who can't help with this, please get to work chopping trees, and start building temporary cabins. And we need some volunteers to make a list of survival equipment too, for example a petrol generator, should we need extra power, candles, camping stoves etc.' He nodded his thanks at those who raised their hands, then turned to John. 'I'll ring Uri, to see if he can find out what's going on with the council, and to get him to move now.'

'I'll ring Todd and do the same.' John turned to the people as a thought occurred. 'If any of your family has sold property ready to donate to the pot, tell them *not* to transfer it there.'

'Good thinking,' Doron said.

John nodded. 'The money can go into one of our accounts so we can use it to live on, buy equipment, and help with housing.'

Paul Morgan, the former senator, caught his arm as they left. 'I might have resigned from the Senate but I still have some clout, Let me go with you, in case you need any help.'

John would later look back on that night, with its hasty farewells, its hopeful travel and its frantic negotiations, as a time of naïve optimism; by the time Otto had burst through the door to tell everyone what he'd learned, it had already been too late to stop it.

April 2004

In January the airports had closed, effectively cutting Hope Meadows off from the rest of the world. Those whose families had not made the journey in time—thankfully few—were inconsolable in their grief, and fights had broken out, with people threatening to leave and take their share of the antibodies with them. Eventually subdued by common sense, they eyed the luckier ones with bitter envy, and remained an unpredictable source of tension. But most heartbreaking for the Milburns was the news that Alima and Ruhi's older brother, Sunil Nasir, had become embroiled in a demonstration outside the Parliament buildings, and detained… he had not been released in time to make the flight out. Farrah and her family had withdrawn from the community in shock and grief, and only in the past few days had they begun to move among their friends again, taking strength from them where they could.

The virus, named the Ghanian Ebolavirus, had spread rapidly and soon run out of control, and even when Otto's advice had been carried out, time had simply been against them. Whole towns succumbed, cities were ravaged, and despite the best efforts of medics everywhere, the pandemic had already claimed the lives of millions.

Hope Meadows stood undefeated, but lost. The families who'd arrived after the funds had been stolen had put all their money into helping to build cabins and shelters, and to buy trailers to house themselves and others, but while all around them the crops grew and the lambs were born, the heavy shadow of fear hung over the community. When would the sickness come to claim them, too? Would the antibodies, given to them by Doron and John and their friends, protect them?

The hall had become part plasma-storage bank, part equipment store, meaning there were no more meetings happening on the same scale as before, and the townspeople clearly felt cut off from the hub of knowledge. That had led to a cooling of the camaraderie they'd all felt when Hope Meadows had first become their home, and John often caught someone glancing at him with mistrust rather than curiosity and friendship.

Otto and his team had ensured there was enough booster plasma in the hall freezer for all residents of Hope Meadows. His team and their families were given their own supply, and he continued to take donations and sent them out to as many communities as he could, but with transport at a standstill it was not easy. When broadcasting facilities and the electric generating stations went down, they closed the lab, went home, and waited.

Diego Garcia woke, and sighed as he glanced at the clock; only a little past two… if he didn't whizz now he'd be awake for the rest of the night. Best get it over with. He padded to the bathroom in his pyjamas, and while he stood letting nature take its grateful course, he let his eyes roam around the room. As they rested on the darkness beyond the window his attention was snagged by a brief flicker of light, and to entertain himself he tried to identify the house from which it came.

Then he frowned; it wasn't a house at all, it was the hall. His heart speeded up, and as soon as he'd finished he shoved his feet into his shoes, seized a torch and his coat, and slipped out of the house and into the chilly night. Some instinct stopped him from going directly to the hall, however, and he took a quick detour to his neighbour's house and rapped gently on the bedroom window.

After a moment the curtain twitched aside, and Ravi's face appeared, mouthing, 'What?'

Diego held a finger to his lips, and gestured for his friend to come outside. He pointed to his torch, and Ravi nodded and vanished, reappearing with his own.

Together they walked to the hall, and Diego caught at Ravi's arm and nodded towards the door. It hung open by a few inches, and the wood was splintered and rough-looking; it had been jimmied open for sure. They exchanged a glance, then both sheltered their torchlight with a free hand and crept into the hall, to see two shadowy figures by the largest of the fridges. They moved their hands away from their torches and let the full strength of the beams fall on the intruders, who flinched and threw their own arms up to block the light.

But it only took them a moment to adjust and, realising their exit was blocked, they pocketed what they were carrying and charged at the men in the doorway. Diego felt the breath knocked from his body as he was flung backwards into the yard, and he shot out a hand and grabbed whatever he could find, relieved to realise he held fast to the coat of one of the intruders. The torches had fallen to the ground and shone pointlessly up the street, while all around him he heard the scuffling and grunting of desperate men as the intruders fought to escape.

With some relief he heard the familiar voice of one of the Malik twins; the American one. Doron? Ana must have roused him when Diego had gone creeping out of the house, clutching his torch like a weapon but offering no explanation. He wasn't alone, and before long the intruders were subdued and secured, and taken back into the hall.

Doron checked Diego and Ravi were unhurt, then fixed his gaze on the other two men. In the bright, indoor light he realised one was much older than the other. They kept their heads down and he didn't recognise them as Hope Meadows inhabitants. The thought that they'd been targeted gave him a helpless, crawling sensation.

'You're trespassing on private property,' he said. His voice was hard. 'We don't appreciate people coming onto our land, particularly not with stealing in mind. What were you after?'

'What do you think?' the younger man said, somewhat bitterly. 'We're all sick, in the lower valley, we've heard your blood could save us.'

'We only have enough for ourselves,' Doron protested. 'You'd save yourselves by condemning others to die, would you?' He held out his hand for the phials and bottles Diego had retrieved from the men's pockets. 'We've already sent what we can, don't you think we'd have sent more if we could?'

'It wasn't enough!' The young man's voice rose, and cracked, and he started to cough. He looked up at Doron for the first time. 'Me and my dad just came to take a little, to give to my children.'

Doron flinched as the light fell fully on the man's face, illuminating the rash and the fever flush. He looked at the older man, who looked almost as sick. His anger faded, and was replaced by deep sadness and an unbearable wash of sympathy. But what could he do? He dropped a hand on the young man's thin, shaking shoulder. 'Go home, kid,' he said softly. 'I'm so sorry. Go back to your family.'

Father and son walked back towards the perimeter fence, and Doron's torch picked out the figure of a woman, kneeling on the ground, holding two very young children to her. Behind him he was aware more people had come out of their houses and were gathered to watch, and although he'd have preferred to preserve the outsiders' dignity he said nothing to send them away. Perhaps it was better that they didn't feel cocooned in their safe little bubble to the extent that they never saw the devastation that was happening beyond the wire.

The men had reached the fence, and the woman looked up hopefully, only to drop her face into her hands and begin to sob when she learned of the failure of her husband's quest. The men helped each other to climb over the fence, and the younger man took his wife's hand and drew her to her feet. Doron thought his heart would break.

As the outsiders' began walking away, the young woman seized her children's hands and hurried back to the fence. 'Please, help my children!' As she called out in despair she began to cough.

'We're so sorry,' Farrah called, and she too sounded close to tears.

'We don't have anything spare,' added a voice Doron didn't recognise. It sounded so harsh, but it was the stark truth.

He turned as he heard hurrying feet behind him, and he saw Clare Hampton pushing her way through the group. She marched up to the fence and held out her arms, and the young woman stared at her for a moment in disbelief, and hope. Clare nodded, and the woman's expression changed to fear, grief, and finally gratitude. She lifted the first of her children over, and Clare received him with a comforting kiss on the forehead, but the moment she set him down he flung himself on the wire fence, crying for his mother. The woman passed the other child over more easily, though she held on for just a second longer before she let her go. The little girl was shivery, and probably too confused to make a fuss, but the little boy rattled the fence, his sobs tearing through the night as his distraught mother mouthed, 'thank you,' to Clare before stumbling after her dying husband.

'What do you think you're doing?'

'Are you mad, Clare?'

The questions were met with surprisingly sharp anger from the normally placid Clare, as she whipped around to face them. 'These children aren't even five years old! How could we turn them away? I know we can't save everyone but I'm sure we can help these two.'

'But we've no spare plasma!'

'There are three lots for each of us and my supply will work on anyone.' Clare's voice was grim. 'I'll risk my boosters, for them. You don't have to give any of yours.' She took the boy's hand and, still holding tightly to the little girl she walked away towards her cabin.

'They're *sick*, Clare.' This was Diego, who could clearly barely contain his fury now. 'You've brought the plague to us!'

'Their family already did that when they broke into the hall,' Todd said, as Sinead went to help Clare with the children. 'My mother isn't stupid. Besides, we couldn't have escaped it forever anyway.'

Clare looked at him gratefully. 'Please get Otto to start readying my share of the plasma,' she said, 'I know I've made the right choice, so thank you. I only hope the others see it that way and don't take it out on these poor mites.'

Sinead helped Clare undress the children, and wash them down to help cool their fever, and Clare produced some of her own pyjamas and cut the arms and legs off. 'We can get properly-fitting things for them in the morning, that'll do for now.'

'How old would you say they are?' Sinead asked, squatting by the side of the bed.

'The girl can't be more than two, and I'd guess the boy's around four.'

As if in response, the boy sat up and pressed his hands to his eyes. 'I want my mama.'

'Oh, you poor thing.' Sinead sat on the bed. 'Your mummy's not well, love, so she can't really look after you at the moment. You're sick too, wee man, so we're going to make you all better, okay? What's your name?'

'Karl,' the boy sniffed. 'And she's Emily. Emily wants Mooshy.'

'Mooshy? What's that?'

'He's her teddy. She dropped him by the fence.'

'Well no worries, Karl, I'll fetch him for her. You're a brave boy, so you are.'

Outside by the fence, with the dew-laden grass tickling her ankles, Sinead tried to remember exactly where the boy's mother had been kneeling. She played her torch across the ground, back and forth, and was about to give up when she saw a fluffy foot lying half hidden in a clump of grass. With a small exclamation of triumph she kept her torch focused on it, and bent swiftly to pick it up, her mind already seeing the frightened little girl's smile.

Her heart stopped as a strong hand fastened itself to her wrist, and as she drew a shocked breath, another clamped across her mouth and stifled her scream.

Chapter Eighteen
Kidnap and Aftermath

'Tie her legs,' the voice behind her grunted, and Sinead felt the warmth of sour breath on her cheek. 'We'll carry her through the fence. Quick! She's a wriggler.' The hand across Sinead's mouth tasted of sweat and dirt, and she gagged and wriggled harder as she tried once more to scream.

'You just keep her quiet,' the other voice whispered, harsh and furious. 'We'll have the whole goddamn town out on us.'

Through the shadows Sinead could only see the dark outline of a man, and as he knelt in front of her she heard him uncoiling a rope and kicked out as hard as she could, blindly, and with little hope. But her foot connected, catching him under the chin and his head snapped back as he fell sideways, knocking her dropped torch so that it spun around, cutting through the dark. With the leap of hope that perhaps someone would see the light and come running, Sinead summoned the last of her strength to fight back. If she could only make some sound…

She reached up behind her, her fingers hooked into claws, and raked the face of her captor as hard as she could. He yelled out and his grip slackened. Frantic, she pulled away, her heart jumping in relief as she got free, only to be brought down again as she stumbled away.

Between them the two men dragged her to her feet and began tying her, and Sinead drew a deep breath and screamed as loudly as she could. A second later her breath halted as one of her assailants drove his fist into her diaphragm.

'Bitch!'

Winded, Sinead sagged, struggling to breathe, tears of panic spilling over her cheeks, and then she heard a ripping sound and her mouth was sealed shut with metallic tape. With the tears clogging her throat Sinead prayed they wouldn't stop her from breathing through her nose too, and her last sight before she was dragged through the hole in the fence was of the torchlight shining on Mooshy, half-buried in the grass.

Todd was thinking over his discussion with Otto as he made his way back home. The scientist had tried to argue against readying Clare's portion of the antibodies, but Todd could see it was for form's sake only; the children really were the future of mankind and they had to be—

A scream cut through his thoughts, and, heart hammering, he whirled towards the sound. By the fence, a light shone along the ground, and through its weakening beam he saw two figures stoop, with a third slung between them. The rattle of the chain link fence told Todd they had pushed through, and as he stared his stomach twisted in terror… that was Sinead they were carrying.

He let out a bellow of fury and broke into a run, his legs rubbery and uncooperative, but somehow propelling him towards the fence. Behind him he heard footsteps and he risked a glance over his shoulder to see Otto, his face white in the moonlight.

'They've got Sinead!' Todd yelled, slipping and righting himself as he shouted back to the scientist. 'Go and get John and Ron!'

With a plummeting feeling of despair he heard the men's vehicle start up, and a second later bright headlights swept the grassland beyond the fence as Todd searched for the hole through which they'd escaped. One of the men was still manhandling Sinead into the back of the pick-up, and, even as Todd saw the ragged hole in the fence and pushed his way through, the man climbed in after Sinead and banged frantically on the back window of the cab.

The pick-up's wheels spun for a second, giving Todd a fresh flare of hope, but they gained traction just as he reached the truck, and the vehicle roared off into the night. Still he kept running. The terrain was flat, and his eyes burned as they tracked the red tail lights into the distance, his heart aching for whatever Sinead had gone through... was still going through.

Only when the truck finally disappeared around a bend did he stop running, sucking in deep, painful breaths, and bracing his hands on his thighs to keep himself from collapsing. Through the roaring in his ears he heard the sound of another vehicle, this time coming from behind him, and he turned to see John's jeep, bowling towards him over the lumpy grass. It slid to a stop beside him and John leaned over and pushed open the passenger door.

'Come on!'

Doron, in the driving seat and gripping the wheel with whitened hands, barely waited until Todd was in before throwing the jeep into gear again, and they took off. They hit the road and slid, and Todd could hear dust and stones spewing out behind them as Doron floored the accelerator once again.

'There!' John pointed ahead. With the power down there were no street or house lights to confuse things, and it was easy to see the pick-up's tail lights in the distance.

'They're headed onto Highway 82,' Doron shouted over the roar of the engine. 'Good, that's a nice straight road.'

'Can we catch them?' Todd leaned through the gap in the front seats, as if he could urge them faster.

'With any luck,' Doron said. 'This time of night we can at least follow them easily. I've got my foot right down.'

John twisted in his seat. 'What happened?'

'I don't… All I saw was Sinead being carted off by two men.' Todd's voice seized briefly, as his own words sunk in. 'Why? Why would anyone do that?'

'Only one reason I can think of,' John said grimly, turning back to face the front. Todd stared at the back of his friend's head for a moment, trying to force himself to think beyond the fear.

'What… No!' He gripped John's shoulder. 'We've got to get her back!'

'We will, mate, don't you worry.'

'Why not just take what they want from the stores, like the others tried to?'

'Maybe that's where they were going when they stumbled on Sinead. Or maybe they just didn't know about it.'

'What the hell has happened to our security detail?' Todd demanded, anger rising again.

Doron eased off the accelerator as they hit an undulating section of the highway, and shrugged. 'Eagle security left long ago. I've no idea where our own look-out for that area was, but he wasn't where he should have been.'

'I'll deal with him when we get back!' Todd muttered, and gripped the back of the seats in front as Doron nodded and drove his boot down once more.

After around fifteen minutes they saw the outskirts of Glenwood Springs, and watched the pick-up take a right turn off the highway. A minute later they slowed to take the same exit.

'Where'd it go?' Doron peered through the darkness, and John and Todd both leaned forward too.

'No idea,' John muttered. 'It couldn't have disappeared that quickly. Just keep driving, we'll keep watch.'

With no car lights anywhere to be seen, and no house lights either, it gave the whole experience an eerie feeling; as if the town were already dead. Todd, still struggling with what he'd learned, strained his eyes for any sign of movement.

'Right, let's think clearly a minute. If you've kidnapped someone to take their blood, you have to be able to do it properly. With medical equipment. They've got to be headed for the hospital, right?'

'That's not far from here,' Doron said, and changed down a gear. 'It's our best bet. Hold tight.' The jeep surged forward again. 'Todd, grab that rifle under the seat, it's the only weapon we have.'

Todd fumbled beneath the seat and dragged out the gun. It felt heavy and unwieldy, and a bit greasy in his sweating grip. 'I don't know how to use this!'

'Up until recently you didn't know how to use a pistol either,' John pointed out. 'Just look as if you do. This one's not loaded.'

'Here we go again,' Todd muttered, and tightened his grip on the rifle.

The headlights picked up and reflected the hospital sign, and as the jeep swung into the entrance John leaned forward, his hands braced against the dashboard. Then he gave an exclamation and pointed. 'There! There they are!'

The pick-up had stopped at the ambulance bays, and as Todd saw a waiting group surge forward to help grasp the struggling Sinead and drag her from the back, he found himself wishing the rifle were loaded after all. Before the jeep had even stopped, he had leapt from the back, closely followed by John, and then Doron.

He levelled the rifle at the group. 'Let her go now, or I fire into the lot of you!'

There came a tight bark of laughter from the pick-up's driver. 'And risk hitting her?'

'We outnumber you three-to-one!' his companion added. 'How far do you think you'd get?'

'She's no good to you,' Doron said. 'She doesn't have the immunity.'

'You're lying, boy,' the driver said, and his voice was scratchy now he'd quietened. 'All you strangers have it, that's why the government put you there. Look at her, she ain't sick like us.'

'Not yet,' John agreed, 'but it's only a matter of time. Only we have what you really need.'

The three of them moved closer together, Todd still clutching the useless rifle, but now with the barrel lowered. They glanced at one another, and he saw the same determination in the twins' eyes as he knew was in his own; they would each give everything if they had to. He straightened, and his shoulders came up, and he faced the hostile crowd head on. 'Let her go, take us instead.'

Sinead felt like crying as she watched the men move together. Seeing Todd running after the pick-up had been heart-liftingly hopeful, but also terrifying; she'd expected a shot to ring out at any moment, and to see him fall... but no-one had fired. They didn't need to, there was no way he could have caught up with the truck on foot. He'd vanished from view, leaving her with a kind of frightened grief already taking hold; she'd never see him again.

Now he stood here with his best friends, shoulder-to-shoulder, all of them prepared to give themselves up for her. To die for her. The tears of relief and fear battled with those caused by the lingering pain from the blow she'd taken, and with the burns on her skin from the rope, but if she gave into them she'd be unable to breathe. Besides, she needed to give her rescuers a show of strength. She raised her eyes to them to show she would not stand helplessly by, while they risked everything, but

347

as she did so she saw a couple of shadows moving behind the three men. She drew a sharp breath through her nose, and tried to wrench herself free from the hold her kidnapper had on her, nodding frantically and making muffled sounds to alert her friends, but before they could turn around they were halted by the rifles pressed into the backs of their necks.

'Well, I reckon we can take you too,' the man holding Sinead said, and she heard the grin in his voice. He turned to yell at the crowd behind him. 'The more the merrier, I say!'

'Drop the rifle,' the pick-up driver said calmly. 'Put your hands where I can see them. On your heads, come on.'

Sinead watched in despair as Todd let his own rifle clatter to the ground, and he and John and Doron were pushed at gunpoint towards the rest of the crowd. Todd tried to move next to her, but she felt a tug on her bound wrists as she was yanked away, and the rope on her ankles was cut.

'In,' the driver barked, and the four of them were shoved towards the hospital door. They waited while it was manually pulled open by two of the burlier members of the waiting crowd, and once indoors their way was lit only by torchlight… the glimpses Sinead caught told her this was likely a mercy.

The floor was littered with people, some on thin mattresses, some simply lying on the bare tiles, but all either dead or close to death. The ebolavirus struck indiscriminately, they all knew that, but seeing the evidence from which they'd been sheltered, and smelling the stench of it, Sinead felt fresh tears start into her eyes. There were children here, as well as the elderly, and every age in between, some of these people might have been saints, some sinners, but here they were laid low and equal, in sticky pools of their own blood and vomit, and that of their neighbours. By the double doors leading out of reception and into the main hospital, what looked like a pile of discarded bedding showed itself to be a mound of bodies and their contaminated blankets.

As Sinead passed a smaller crumpled heap, the woman shifted her head to watch, beseechingly, and managed to raise her hand a few inches off the floor before letting it fall back, exhausted and hopeless. One of the torches swung towards the sound of the woman's low moan, and Sinead saw blood pooling in the corners of her eyes, dribbling from her nose, and crusted in her ears.

She tried to stifle a sob, but as her breath hitched she felt bile rise into the back of her throat, and a momentary panic made her swallow hard. Her nose stung, and as she tasted the sour bile her aching stomach heaved and she retched helplessly. She staggered, slamming into the wall, and fighting for breath, and somewhere in the distance she heard Todd's voice, urgent and angry.

'She's choking! Take the tape off her mouth!'

Sinead felt a hand tighten on her arm, but her momentary relief was wiped out as she was dragged upright again and shoved stumbling forward.

'Keep walking.'

'I said take the tape off. Now!'

Through the daze of terror and pain Sinead heard a scuffle and turned in time to see Todd, John and Doron pushing their way towards her. As she watched, two of the men holding rifles on them swung their weapons, cracking them against John's and Doron's heads. The twins dropped to the floor, and a second later Todd was pulling the tape from Sinead's mouth. It hurt, but oh, God, the relief… she dragged in breath after breath, spitting and retching while she fought to get her heart beat under control. She felt Todd's arms around her and sagged against him, unable to really believe he was there.

He began blindly tugging at her bindings, but abruptly his low, soothing murmur halted, and she felt him twist to look at something. She pulled back and followed his gaze; he'd been checking to ensure John and Doron weren't badly hurt, but as they both watched, the twins slowly raised their heads and rolled onto their knees. A hush fell over the death-ridden room, and even the weak coughs and the groans seemed to fall into an awed silence.

John's and Doron's eyes were wide open, and pure white, and as they stood up the air shimmered in front of them; within seconds each twin had his ghostly replica standing before him, their hands rising with perfect precision until they were stretched out before them. They hardly seemed to move, but a slight pushing motion had the effect of a shot fired from a cannon, as the two riflemen jerked and flew backwards. They fell spreadeagled on the pile of corpses by the doors, and didn't move.

The twins turned to face the others in the crowd, who were staring at them in utter terror, and the spirits turned with them. The hands pushed at the air again, and every member of the crowd was slammed backwards, crashing through the doors and into the corridor beyond. Again, no further movement was visible, not from anyone, and Sinead felt her head grow light, both with wonder and relief.

The four beings had once again become two, and John and Doron came to help untie the ropes at Sinead's wrists. The moment she was freed she flung her arms around Todd, and gave in to the tears she'd been holding in check. He buried his face in her neck, and she realised the depths of his own fear and whispered, 'It's going to be alright now—'

'We have to go,' John said urgently, 'we don't know who else might show up.'

Todd and Sinead climbed into the back of the jeep, and Sinead rubbed at the raw skin on her wrists while Doron started the engine.

'Is everyone okay?' John asked, pulling his door closed.

'Yeah,' Todd said. 'Thanks to you two. What the hell just happened, anyway?'

'It was like that thing the children did,' Sinead put in. 'Only with force instead of suggestion. I mean, your spirits threw everyone around like rag dolls!'

Todd tightened his hold on her. 'Did you kill them all?'

'No,' Doron said, reversing at speed away from the hospital entrance. 'They're out cold, but not dead.'

'We're not allowed to kill,' John added. 'Not unless it's our only option.'

'So, I ask again,' Todd insisted, 'what happened?'

'Truth is, I don't know, but the sensation felt familiar.' John looked at his brother. 'I think it happened before, only it was weaker. Remember when we were rescuing you, and the kidnappers just… froze?'

Doron nodded. 'Yes, you're right. I felt it too, but at the time I thought it was my concussion.'

'And I thought it was a rush of adrenalin. We certainly didn't know we could do that, did we?'

'Nope. But we do now.' Doron shifted into gear and they headed back to Highway 82 and home.

John saw Todd and Sinead back to their cabin, and they climbed slowly from the jeep, Todd's arm about Sinead while she still rubbed at her wrists. They turned to wave and under the porch light the twins could see they were not looking at all well.

'Go to bed and drink plenty of fluids,' Doron called after them.

'I'll tell your mother you're okay,' John added, and the two of them nodded their tired acknowledgement before vanishing indoors.

Doron parked the jeep outside Clare's cabin, and made his way back to his own home, while John knocked on Clare's door. To his surprise it wasn't Todd's mother who opened the door, but Otto. He looked pale and drawn, and gestured John inside with a whisper.

'Come in, come in. Clare and the children are sleeping now. They're all sick, so I offered to stay.'

'Thank you. You don't look too good yourself,' John observed, following him in. 'Can I do anything?'

'Thank you, but no. It was only a matter of time, eh?' Otto coughed, and then sighed. 'I won't be well enough by morning to give the little ones their IV treatment, I'm afraid.'

'Don't worry about that, Doron is perfectly capable of handling that himself, and we'll help. The main thing is to take care of yourself.'

He began urging Otto back indoors, but the German resisted. 'So, everyone is okay? You two, your friend? The girl? Is she—'

'We're fine,' John said gently, and Otto visibly relaxed and allowed John to guide him into the sitting room. 'Go and lie down now, see if you can get some sleep. I'll come back in the morning.' He watched Otto stumbling across to the sofa, and sinking down onto it with a groan, and as he turned to leave another, ice-cold thought struck him. Jen…

He ran up the road with, he imagined, the same deep-seated fear as Todd had felt on seeing Sinead snatched away. Otto had looked really sick, and it had been hours since he had spoken to Jen. What if her own antibodies weren't enough?

But she was waiting for him, framed in the doorway, and, suddenly bone-weary again, he trudged up the steps and into her embrace. They held each other silently for a long moment, just breathing and thinking, and grateful for one another, and John closed his eyes tightly, willing the world away just for a short while.

Eventually they released each other, and Jen took his hand. 'I heard the jeep come back. I've been so worried… are you okay? What happened to your face?' She lifted her free hand and brushed the bruise that he could feel swelling his cheekbone.

'We're all okay, sweetheart, I'll explain it all later. You look exhausted. Are you and the girls alright?'

'The girls are fast asleep.' She led him indoors. 'I tried to sleep too, but I couldn't, not until I knew you and the others were safe.'

'What happened after we left?'

'Otto found Paul Morgan unconscious behind the surgery. Whoever kidnapped Sinead must have knocked him out, and he was hit by the fever before he even woke up.' Her voice broke as she looked at him, despair in her eyes. 'Everyone's ill, John… I'm the last one standing, and I don't know how long that'll be for.'

'Don't…' he took her in his arms again and pressed his lips to her temple. Her skin was warm, too warm. He tightened his arms around her and felt her own arms wrap around his waist. 'You have to go and lie down, we'll get you well again.'

'I feel awful,' she sighed against his neck, and he swallowed his fear, and picked her up and carried her to their bed.

'Come on, we need you, Mrs Milburn. It's going to be a long few days.'

The following morning John helped Otto back to his own home and Doron brought the IV equipment to Karl and Emily, but they eyed it with mistrust and fear. They lay either side of Clare, and even her reassurances didn't help.

'Don't be scared,' Doron said gently. 'It's to help you, I promise.'

But, led by her older brother's quiet terror at the sight of the needle, Emily screamed and flailed until Doron wheeled the drip away from the bed.

'What do we do?' Clare said helplessly. 'I don't want to frighten them by forcing anything.'

'We'll have to let them watch us administer it to someone else,' Doron began, but broke off at a knock on the front door. 'Go away!' He rubbed his eyes wearily, and winced as he accidentally rubbed the bruise on the side of his face. Footsteps in the hall made him turn irritably to the door.

'I said go—'

'You might need this,' Sinead said with a little smile, tired-looking and flushed, and in her hand she held the one thing guaranteed to ease Emily's panic. 'I remembered where I'd seen him last night,' she said, handing Mooshy over to the red-eyed little girl. 'He's a bit mucky, but I don't expect you'll mind that.'

Clare's eyes widened and she flashed a look at Doron. She pulled herself up against her pillow and stroked the teddy bear's head, and made a little noise of concern. 'I'm worried, he's been out in the cold all night. I hope he's not sick like us.'

Emily clutched her bear, coughed and turned her beseeching eyes up to Doron. 'Make Mooshy better?'

Doron bit his lips together to hide the relieved smile, and nodded solemnly. 'If you'll let us try.'

Sinead took Karl's hand. 'Look at me, love, there'll be a little scratch, and then all you have to do is lie still for a while. Show your sister how brave you are, hmm?'

With the last of her strength, Clare mouthed a thank you to Sinead before closing her eyes.

Once the children were comfortable receiving their treatment, Doron sent the feverish Sinead home with strict instructions not to leave her bed again. John and Doron called all the twins together to give them their instructions. It was a noisy affair, but eventually the children understood they were to take care of their own parents; any additional family members would fall to John and Doron to care for.

'We'll check in on you regularly,' John reassured them, 'and if you need anything, or if you're scared, you know where we live. Call on either of us, at any time of day or night. Okay?'

'I feel bad all this has got to burden such young shoulders,' Doron said, as they watched the children returning to their homes.

John nodded. 'We've no choice though. I just hope the antibodies will rein in the symptoms for those worst hit.'

As the days went on it was clear that, within Hope Meadows, this epidemic was going to be no worse than a bad outbreak of flu. Two died, and they were both elderly and suffering from underlying illnesses, but it was still a sad and solemn time, and required a great deal of reassurance from the medically trained in the community.

The remaining sufferers were confined to their beds, and they mostly slept the illness away; those who could not care for themselves were treated by their loved ones, and after three days of solid, exhausting work, the people of Hope Meadows began to recover. It was a slow process, and as those hit by the virus regained their strength, those who'd been caring for them began to flag and were ordered to rest.

One of the last to recover was Jen. John sat by her side almost constantly once his other pressures began to ease, and although it was hard to keep the girls' visits to a minimum he was aware of them hovering outside the door whenever they could. He looked down at his extraordinary wife, and thought yet again about all she'd done, right from the start. She'd been dealt a marked card, marrying him, and she'd played it without complaint; she'd been strong, kind, wise, and she'd given up everything she'd known.

Now she lay, breathing softly and shallowly, the beads of sweat on her brow trickling down to darken her hair at the roots, having given her last ounce of strength to wait for him to come home. He dipped the flannel he was holding into the bowl of cool, clean water, and draped it gently over her forehead, noticing how his hand shook and so transfixed by the sight that it was a moment before he realised Jen's eyes had opened.

'John?' she breathed, and tried to move her head, only to groan and abandon the attempt.

'Lie still, sweetheart,' he whispered, not trusting himself to speak aloud. 'You're going to be a bit weak for a while.'

'How long was I out of it?'

'A couple of days. You've had a fever.' He found a grin, though he knew his glistening eyes betrayed his emotions. 'You had a snotty nose, too, and talked a load of rubbish.'

'Nothing new there, then,' she said, and returned his smile. 'How are the girls?'

'They're fine. Better than fine. They've worked like Trojans, all the children have. They're the ones who took care of you, I'm just taking the credit.'

'Oh, bless them,' Jen said, and now her eyes were flooding, too. 'They're too young to have to go through this.'

'They've taught us grown-ups a thing or two.'

'I'll say. How's everyone else?'

'We've been so lucky, Jen. Everyone's pulling through.' There was no need to tell her about the two isolated fatalities.

'Thank goodness it's over,' Jen said, and closed her eyes again. Her voice dropped to a barely audible mumble. 'Love you.'

John leaned down to kiss her forehead. 'Love you too.'

But as he straightened, and turned to his daughters in the doorway, the thought kept ringing in his head: *the illness might be over, but everything else is just beginning.*

Epilogue
May 2004, Hope Meadows

John closed his front door behind him and handed cans of beer to Doron and Uri, before joining them on the steps. It had been a long, hot day, and the clearing of bodies from the areas surrounding Hope Meadows was going to be a long job. Made longer by the fact that only those blessed with UEP1 were permitted outside the compound during the quarantine period. He and Doron had gone into the lower valley that day too, to pick up much-needed supplies, and to introduce themselves to the new settlers who were steadily making their way to the area to re-build their lives.

He popped the tab on his can, and drank the froth before it spilled down his shirt. 'I've been daydreaming about this moment all day.'

'You're doing an amazing job out there,' Uri said.

'There's a lot more to do yet.'

Uri nodded. 'Otto tells me he reckons there'll be fewer than three million survivors worldwide.'

Doron shook his head. 'With a population of seven billion, that's less than half a per cent. Horrifying loss of life, hard to really process.'

'I'm grateful every day that we're all alive and together,' Uri said. He raised his can in a toast. 'We'll just take each day as it comes, and thank the Fathers for their help.'

'Talking of the Fathers,' John said, after another long gulp at his beer, 'they told us once that when our Nephilim children die, their spirit forms will join together to become the new generation of Fathers. They also told us that they, and we,' he gestured at himself and Doron, 'would live long lives.'

'Right,' Doron agreed. 'You look puzzled.'

'Because… if we're also Nephilim, what happens to *our* spirits when we die? Where do they go?'

Doron looked at him blankly, then gave a short laugh. 'D'you know, I never thought of that. I have absolutely no idea, guess we'll just have to wait and see.'

'So nothing's changed there, we're in the same boat as everyone else.' John looked at Uri, remembering something else that had been bugging him. 'Any word yet on who was responsible for betraying Eagle?'

'They have a good idea. The council members are safe, and all but one accounted for. Once he's found, they'll deal with him. And,' he added quietly, 'there's news on who betrayed Hope Meadows to that council member.'

John's eyes widened, and he and Doron looked at Uri expectantly. Whoever it was, now Eagle had discovered their duplicity they would be severely punished along with their rogue council member. The question flashed between them: who hadn't they seen lately?

'It was Louise Miller,' Uri said, and for a moment John couldn't place the name. Then he remembered.

'The woman who provided the tape that convicted Todd's dad? The secretary?'

'The same.'

'But I thought she was on our side!'

'She thought so, too. Miller worked for Gleed and Whyte Architects, right? Someone from Eagle got hold of her, someone with an American accent, and persuaded her to record meetings that went on in the New York office, so she did. Luckily one of those was the conversation between Charles Whyte and Richard Hampton, which led to Hampton's arrest along with possibly other members of Veritas.'

'So she was duped.'

'She was promised safe passage for herself and her mother,' Uri explained. 'Miller went first; she was going to be a witness at Hampton's trial, so Eagle couldn't risk anything happening to her. Her mother stayed behind to wrap up her affairs, sell her house and so on.

'So what made Miller help someone risk all our lives?'

'She was contacted with the request, and told that only some of the blood would be taken, but she still refused. The traitor then threatened the life of her mother if she didn't co-operate. At that time no-one knew about the start of the virus so she didn't think it would cause an immediate problem. There was time to collect more.'

'And when we *did* find out about it?'

'Naturally Miller contacted her mother, as did everyone else with their loved ones, and told her she had to get here, but her mother's in her seventies, and not in the best of health. She lost her passport, things got delayed… you know how it was.'

John remembered those families who had effectively blamed himself and Doron when their loved ones had not reached the safety of Hope Meadows in time. 'So she was angry and upset. Felt betrayed.'

Uri nodded. 'An easy target. This man told her to get him the access code to Otto's lab.'

'And how did she find the code?'

'She already knew it. Otto told you two he always used his date of birth for everything, remember?'

John and Doron frowned at one another, then Doron's brow cleared. 'I do remember that conversation, yeah. We must've been standing outside Miller's home. He said his memory's shocking.'

'Almost as shocking as his instinct for security,' John said, and sighed. 'I remember too.'

'Well Miller overheard it. Didn't make anything of it at the time, of course. But once she had her brief she got into Otto's cabin, found his passport and sent her contact his date of birth, and bingo. Eagle's rogue council member has access to everything, and likely already had access to the banking information in order to clean out the pot.'

'And Louise Miller's mother never made it to Hope Meadows anyway.'

Uri shook his head. 'Eagle have arrested Miller, she'll stand trial once the justice system is properly up and running.'

'What she did was wrong,' John said, 'but she was forced into it. I feel sorry for her.'

Doron shifted on the step and shrugged. 'Makes no difference now, anyway. The money's gone, the virus has done its worst – we hope – and we're re-building now, not running scared.'

'He's right,' Uri agreed.

They sat in silence for a while, perhaps they were all pondering whether they'd missed any clues, John certainly was. But in his heart he knew they could never have known or prevented any of what had happened to them and their home.

'You know,' he said at length, 'it wasn't that long ago that Jen and I were going for an anniversary meal, and my Aunt May was babysitting. If she hadn't become ill, I would never have seen the contents of my mother's biscuit tin.'

Uri looked at him quizzically, waiting for him to continue, but he could only find more questions. 'What if she hadn't got ill, Uri? What if the prophecies hadn't been found? Where would we all have been then?'

'We'd be right here, where we are now, having this same conversation.' Uri smiled gently at John's frown. 'Fate, lad. Always has a way of getting what she wants.'

'I don't believe in fate,' John said. 'I can't... I *don't*, accept that I have no control over my own actions.'

'Then we'll call it destiny.' Uri patted John's knee. 'We were all destined to travel the paths we have followed, and to all be here together now, like this. Alive.' His voice trailed off, and his smile faded.

'Are you alright?' John asked.

'I'm fine, just a touch of déjà vu.' Uri ran his hand through his hair and found another smile, this time a little sad. 'I had a similar conversation many years ago, with your father George. I miss him. I miss them all.'

Doron lifted his can in another toast. 'To absent friends,' he said, with a slight break in his voice. 'And loved ones.'

'Absent friends and loved ones.' Three cans clunked together, spilling beer down three tired arms, and three men sat staring out into the gathering dark, lost in their own thoughts. The world would begin again, and become filled with new memories; it wasn't perfect, and it never would be, but there was a glimmer of hope in these three hearts that maybe it would be a better one than before.

**The story continues in
Children of Sinai II: The Sixth Fire**

Acknowledgements

This story has been bouncing around my head for many years, and putting it down on paper has been the hardest thing I've ever had to do. It was originally only going to be put in print for friends and family. I asked my dear friend, and brilliant author, **Terri Nixon**, to check through the manuscript for me. Terri was so impressed that she encouraged me to publish it, but my writing skills were not publishing worthy. Terri added her own style of writing and magic to my own and here we are with a book. Terri and I worked together so well that we have also co-authored the sequel Children of Sinai II:The Sixth Fire.

I would like to thank my husband **Kev**, for believing in me and for his unwavering support; my dad **Milburn**, for being the first storyteller I ever knew; my children, **Todd** and **Holly**, for being my first two critics; all my family and friends from whom I've stolen names and experiences included in the story and my beautiful step-granddaughter **Poppy Anning** for being the perfect model for the twins.
Shelley Clarke

Both Terri and I would like to thank beta readers **Todd Jones** and **Jane Clements**; **Nigel Welsh (Omega Print and Signs)** and artist **Kyle Elliott**, for their wonderful work on the original cover; **Chris Bloodworth Photography** for his patience, super photographic talents and work on the new cover design; **Dr Niki Cartwright** for helping to use the correct scientific terminology; **Anne Cater**, **Rachel Gilbey** and their book bloggers for their hard work in achieving hugely successful book blog tours and all our dear friends, families and fans for their support.

Thank you all.

Finally, we would like to acknowledge the following works and their authors, who were inspirational in writing this story:

And the Miller Told His Tale: Ken Miller's Cold (Chromosomal) Fusion by Casey Luskin. "Miller started off his 'prediction' by simply observing that humans have 23 pairs of chromosomes and apes have 24 pairs; therefore two ape chromosomes were fused into one human chromosome."

Perianez and Abril for their work on: *A Numerical Modelling Study on the Potential Role of Tsunamis in the Biblical Exodus.*

About The Authors

Clarke Nixon is author duo Shelley Clarke and Terri Nixon, who first met while working together in the Faculty of Arts at the University of Plymouth. They quickly became friends, and when Shelley had an idea for a story, Terri, already an established author, helped her to shape it into a novel and get it into print. Not only were they compatible colleagues, but they discovered they were a great writing team too.

Shelley Clarke was born into a naval family in Kent in 1958, and consequently moved house a lot as a child. She had ambitions to follow in her father's footsteps and join the Royal Navy, and to become a carpenter, but these were not female occupations at that time. So she learned to type... which has come in jolly handy for putting her stories first onto paper, and now onto screen.

Shelley is a keen painter, poet, and karaoke enthusiast; she loves mad family get-togethers, hates olives, ironing and gardening, and currently lives in Devon with her husband Kev, and their two Tibetan Terriers Nena and Pepi, who make them smile every day.

Shelley often forgets she is a grown-up.

Terri Nixon was born in Devon, but grew up on the edge of Bodmin Moor, Cornwall, where she discovered a love of writing that has stayed with her ever since.

She also discovered apple-scrumping, and how to jump out of a hayloft without breaking any bones, but no-one's ever offered to pay her for doing those.

Terri writes family sagas for Little, Brown, and thrillers for Hobeck Books, under R.D. Nixon. She has also written horror, as T Nixon, and contributed to several multi-author anthologies using a number of variations on her name/s. She might be forgiven for not knowing who she is on any given day.

www.terrinixon.com

Printed in Great Britain
by Amazon